Praise for
## Kristin Hannah's novels

### DISTANT SHORES

"Hannah is superb at delving into her main characters' psyches and delineating nuances of feeling."
—*The Washington Post Book World*

"An exquisite tale of a woman at the crossroads of her life . . . There are real-life lessons here told with truth, humor, and courage. You will love this story."
—ADRIANA TRIGIANI, author of *Rococo*

"Hannah . . . proves that her graduation into the big leagues . . . is well deserved."
—*New York Post*

"Certain to strike a chord . . . winning characterizations . . . and a few surprises."
—*The Seattle Times*

"[Hannah] writes of love with compassion and conviction."
—LUANNE RICE

### BETWEEN SISTERS

"Rich in the details and nuances of family relationships."
—*Library Journal*

"Kristin Hannah touches the deepest, most tender corners of our hearts."
—TAMI HOAG, author of *Dark Horse*

### THE THINGS WE DO FOR LOVE

"This wonderful book is a classic example of the enormously touching and thought-provoking stories that are Hannah's specialty. The warmth and complexities of these characters grab hold of the heartstrings."
—*Romantic Times Bookclub*

BY KRISTIN HANNAH

*A Handful of Heaven*
*The Enchantment*
*Once in Every Life*
*If You Believe*
*When Lightning Strikes*
*Waiting for the Moon*
*Home Again*
*On Mystic Lake*
*Angel Falls*
*Summer Island*
*Distant Shores*
*Between Sisters*
*The Things We Do For Love*
*Comfort & Joy*
*Magic Hour*
*Firefly Lane*
*True Colors*
*Winter Garden*
*Night Road*
*Home Front*

home again

# home again

A NOVEL

## KRISTIN HANNAH

Ballantine Books Trade Paperbacks • New York

2012 Random House Trade Paperback Edition

Copyright © 1996 by Kristin Hannah
Reading group guide copyright © 2012 by Random House, Inc.

Published in the United States by Ballantine Books Trade Paperbacks, an imprint of The Random House Publishing Group, a division of Random House, Inc., New York.

BALLANTINE BOOKS TRADE PAPERBACKS and colophon are trademarks of Random House, Inc.
RANDOM HOUSE READER'S CIRCLE & DESIGN is a registered trademark of Random House, Inc.

Originally published in hardcover in the United States by Ballantine Books, an imprint of The Random House Publishing Group, a division of Random House, Inc., in 1996.

ISBN 978-0-345-53082-0
eBook ISBN 978-0-345-490-92-6

Printed in the United States of America

www.randomhousereaderscircle.com

2 4 6 8 9 7 5 3 1

This book is about old friends,
and I dedicate it to the following people:

Benjamin and Tucker, my deepest loves,

all the friends from the old days and the old neighborhoods—Charlotte Stan,
Mary Kay Atchison, Gretchen Lauber, Kim Heltne-Newland,
Karie Dovre-Bennett, and Karen Abner. Out of touch, perhaps,
but never out of mind. . . .

And to the newest members of my family—
Debbie Edwards, Julie Gorset, and John Turner.

Thanks to you all.

# Acknowledgments

I couldn't have written this novel without the help and advice of many people. To Reverend Roger Decker, Rena O'Brien, Cathy Sanders, and Gardner Congdon of the Northwest Organ Procurement Agency; and to Lydia Carroll and Sandy Kruse at the University of Washington Medical Center, thanks so much for your time.

Many thanks to Dr. Barbara Snyder, who set aside her own incredible workload to check the accuracy of this book. I owe you a big one.

And to Andrea Cirillo, agent extraordinaire, who believed in this book from the beginning . . . and kept believing.

home again

# chapter one

Reporters had been circling the event for days now. Headlines flourished. Innuendo about drug use and illicit behavior nipped at the heels of the celebrities who'd congregated in the small Oregon town. It was a wrap party for a major motion picture, and things like this didn't take place in LaGrangeville. The Elks Hall hadn't been used for anything other than quiet meetings in years, but tonight it pulsed with loud, discordant music. Townspeople and photographers swarmed the narrow main street, seeing themselves in the mirrored windows of the limousines that prowled past, waiting for something explosive, something totally *Hollywood*, to happen.

But even so, even with all the articles and interviews and paparazzi, no one knew how close to the truth the *Enquirer's* headline sentence would be: *It was a party to die for.*

*    *    *

Angel DeMarco emerged from the temperature-controlled co-coon of the limousine. Through a blur of cigarette smoke and drizzly rain, he saw the crowd gathered across the street. Face-less bodies huddled behind a long yellow police line.

"It's him, DeMarco!"

Cameras erupted in buzzing bursts of light. The rain looked surreal, streaks of prismatic silver, puddles of impossible light on the black street.

"Angel . . . look this way! AngelAngelAngel . . ."

Their adoration swept through him in an exhilarating wave. God, how he loved his fame. He took a long drag off his ciga-rette and exhaled slowly, then flashed them *the smile,* the grin that just last week *People* magazine had labeled the "twenty-thousand-megawatter." He waved. The gray trail of his cigarette smoke snaked through the air.

He stepped sideways to allow his date—he couldn't remem-ber her name—to get out of the car.

She surfaced slowly. A high-heeled black leather shoe and long, slinky leg shot out of the darkness. Her heel clicked hard on the pavement. She leaned forward, thrust her teased pile of peroxide-yellow hair forward, followed it with a magnificent amount of cleavage, and thrust out of the car. Instinctively she turned to the crowd, adjusting her pink rubber dress as she smiled and waved.

Angel had to give her credit: the woman knew how to make an entrance.

He took her hand and pulled her toward his adoring fans. Her ridiculous heels clicked and skidded on the slick pavement, but the sound was soon drowned out by the roar of the crowd, when they realized that *he* was coming toward them.

Young girls screamed and reached out for him. A few of them, he recognized—they were the same freckle-faced small-town teenagers who had skipped school to watch the filming of his movie. They'd stood on the perimeter every day, bunched together behind the barricades, screaming and giggling and crying when he emerged from his trailer to shoot a scene.

They asked nothing of him, this crowd of admirers, nothing except his presence. He could be wild and immature and selfish, and they didn't care—they only cared that he gave his all to the screen. He gave them his biggest, sexiest smile, allowing his gaze to scan the crowd. He presented each girl a moment, a single heartbeat of time when he was looking at her alone.

"Angel, can we have your autograph? What do you think of LaGrangeville? When will the movie be out? Will you show it here first?"

The questions came as they always did, shooting from the rain like darts. Some he heard, others he didn't, but he knew it didn't matter. They didn't expect an answer, they just wanted to be around him, to see if a few drops of his Hollywood glitter would dust their ordinary lives for a second.

"Angel, could I get a picture taken with you?"

He glanced up from the autograph he was signing and looked at the young girl who'd asked the question. She was short and round, with cheeks that looked like china plates, and waves of frizzled brown hair.

He knew her in an instant—she was the girl who never got invited to the best parties, and tried desperately not to care.

He knew all about that. Even now, years later, he could remember what it felt like to be a teenaged boy on the outside looking in. How much it hurt.

He smiled at her, and her eyes widened in surprise. She stared at him as if he'd hung the moon, and that was all it took—that one look from a stranger shot through his bloodstream like a drug.

"Why, darlin', I'd be honored." He pulled away from his date and ducked under the police tape. He felt hands all over him, smoothing along his jacket, tangling in his hair. It used to bother him, that unsought intimacy, but he'd learned to live with it, even enjoy it if they didn't go too far. He slipped an arm around the girl and drew her close, huddling beneath the overhang of the old brick building. Another girl—tall and gangly— flashed a quick photo of them.

"You look awfully pretty tonight," he said. The girl was wearing a floor-length white satin dress.

"It'th Homecoming," she lisped, almost blinding him with the silver from her braces.

*Homecoming.* It was a word he hadn't heard in a long time, a lifetime, and suddenly he felt old. If he were this girl's father, he would have watched her get dressed in sparkles and beads for a school dance. He wondered what that would have felt like. . . .

He brushed the vague sense of regret aside. "Where's your date?"

A blush crept up her fleshy cheeks. "I don't have one. Me and thome . . . girlfriends thought we'd just watch. We were on the decorating committee. . . ."

For a split second he wasn't Angel DeMarco, movie star; he was Angelo DeMarco, the kid from the wrong side of the tracks. "Where's the dance?" he asked softly.

She pointed down the street. "At the high thchool . . . the gym."

Before he had time to think about it, he grabbed the girl's hand and led her down the street. The crowd hushed, then parted for them.

"Angel!"

He heard his name and paused, turning around. Val Lightner, his agent and friend, was standing alongside Rubber Dress. They were both waving at him. "Where are you going?" Val yelled, flicking his cigarette into the street. "They're waiting for you inside."

Angel grinned. That was the greatest thing about fame—they always waited. "Be right back." Still smiling, he led the awestruck girl across the street. Together they slipped into the gymnasium. The place was decorated with what must have been ten reams of toilet paper. Up onstage, the band was pounding out a horrible rendition of Madonna's "Crazy for You."

He heard people gasp as he led the girl onto the dance floor. Fingers pointed, drinks fell, giggling stopped. But he didn't look around. He looked at the girl, only the girl. "May I have this dance?"

She opened her mouth to answer, but nothing came out except a high-pitched squeak.

He took her in his arms and danced with her for the last thirty seconds of the song, and when it was over, he drew back.

Feeling surprisingly good, he strode from the auditorium. The kids were swarming their new queen.

"How very touching," drawled a voice from outside.

Angel forced a grin. "Eleven to seventeen," he said harshly. "It's my audience."

Val clapped Angel on the back and pulled him out into the rainy night. "You'll have women sobbing on *Hard Copy*, for God's sake, and teenaged girls sending you invitations to the prom."

"Yeah, yeah. I know. Now, let's get to the goddamn party. I need a drink."

They raced back across the street. Angel's date was standing exactly where he'd left her, in the rain. For a split second he wished he'd brought someone else—someone who mattered—but he couldn't think who the hell that would be.

Irritated by the thought, he grabbed the woman's hand and pulled her toward the Elks Hall. Together, ducking from the rain, they surged into the building and climbed the rickety stairs to the huge lobby. Weak overhead lighting pushed through the murky interior, creating pockets of marshy gold amidst the shadows. Upstairs, a heavy metal band rocked the floorboards. Dust filtered from the cracks. Along the far wall, a makeshift bar had been set up, and dozens of celebrities mingled with wannabes and slurped up booze.

Angel felt as if he'd come home. He drew in a deep, satisfied breath, loving everything about this moment—the raucousness of the music, the sickly sweet scent of marijuana, the humid odor of too many bodies in too small a space. Val muttered a quick good-bye—something about getting laid—and disappeared into the crowd.

"You thirsty?" his date asked prettily.

Angel started to answer, but before he could get the word out, he felt a tightening in his chest. He winced, rotated his shoulder to work out the kink.

She frowned. "You okay?"

The pain eased, and he smiled at what's-her-name. "My body's reacting to a lack of alcohol," he said easily, slipping his hand down the rubber-coated curve of her waist, settling on her hip with a familiarity he didn't have, didn't need with a woman like her.

She flashed him a bright, cap-toothed smile. "Tequila?"

He grinned. "You've been reading the *Enquirer.* Naughty girl." He pulled her close. The gardenia scent of her perfume filled his nostrils. "Have you heard what I do to naughty girls?"

She wet her lips and all but purred. "I've heard."

He stared into her eyes, heavily mascaraed, blue-shadowed, and saw his own reflection. For a second he was disappointed that she was so easy, that it was all so easy, and then the moment was gone. He was too sober, that was the trouble. He thought too much when he was sober, wanted too much. When he was drunk or high, he was *Angel DeMarco,* Academy Award–nominated actor. He was *somebody,* and he needed that feeling like air.

"Get me that drink, willya, darlin'?"

She gave him a quick peck on the cheek and wiggled away from him, oozing across the room, toward the bar. Her surgically enhanced body was perfect—all dips and swells coated in pink rubber. His heartbeat sped up, his throat went dry. He leaned against the splintered wooden wall and started to think of ways to use that delicious body of hers, thought of them tangled together, buck naked and stoned and going at it like . . .

Nausea prickled his stomach. At first he thought it was nothing—a lack of booze—then his vision blurred, his stomach lurched, and he knew what was happening.

"Oh, God . . ." He pulled away from the wooden wall, and felt it—the invisible fist squeezing his chest.

Warning bells sounded in his head, loud enough to drown out the throb of the music. He sucked greedily at the smoky air, gulping, gasping, trying to fill his lungs. Pain chewed across his chest, bled down his left arm until his fingers were tingling and hot. He clutched the slick wooden handrail, but it was as loose as an old tooth and wobbled in his grasp.

"Oh, Christ . . ." *Not now, not here . . .*

Sweat slid in a cold streak down his hairline. The rickety wooden steps that led up to the dance floor seemed to magnify before his eyes. The dark slats blurred into one another, elongated like the hallway in that movie *Poltergeist*. For a split second he saw JoBeth Williams, racing down the doorless expanse, screaming.

What had she been screaming about? He tried to concentrate on that single meaningless question. Anything to still the racket in his chest.

"Angel?"

It took a moment to recognize his own name. When he understood, he tried to look up, but he could barely move. His heart clattered and pounded, an unoiled gear slipping on and off its track. He wet his powdery lips and tried like hell to smile as he slowly lifted his head.

The woman—Judy, he remembered suddenly—stood in front of him, holding a bottle of tequila and two shot glasses. A shaker of salt lay cradled in the vee of her cleavage.

Her pretty, made-up face scrunched in a thoughtful frown. "Angel?"

"Don't . . ." The word shot out on a wheezing breath and hung there. He tried to add to it, but he couldn't think straight, couldn't see. *Christ, he couldn't breathe, it hurt so bad.* "Don't feel good. Get Val over here."

Panic darted across her face. She glanced quickly up the stairs, to the throng of partygoers, uncertainty pulling at her penciled brows.

He let go of the handrail and grabbed her slim wrist. She

made a quiet gasping sound and tried to pull away. He wouldn't let her, he held on with everything inside him. He stared at her, trying to remain calm, trying to breathe. "Get—"

It hit. Red-hot pain, exploding, crushing his chest. He couldn't do anything except stand there, swaying, gasping, his hand clamped over his heart. Hurting, oh, Jesus, hurting like he hadn't hurt in years.

"Please . . ." he wheezed, "don't let . . . me . . ."

*Die*. He wanted to say, don't let me die, but he couldn't get the word out before the world went black.

He woke to the electronic *blip-blip-blip* of the cardiac monitor. Computer-generated sound, electrical and inhuman.

And beautiful. Christ, so beautiful.

He was alive. He'd done it, beaten the son of a bitch grim reaper again.

He could sense the drugs in his bloodstream, the blurry softness of Demerol that made him feel as if he were drifting on a warm, soothing sea. He knew that soon the drugs would wear off, and the pain would be back, tightening his chest, stabbing through his lungs and heart, but right now he didn't care. He was alive.

The door whooshed open with a whining creak. Rubber-soled shoes squished across the floor—speckled white linoleum, no doubt—and paused beside the bed.

"Well, Mr. DeMarco, you're awake."

It was a deep, masculine voice. No nonsense.

*Doctor. Cardiologist.*

Angel slowly opened his eyes. A tall, undernourished man with a deeply etched face and flinty black eyes stared down at him. Untamed gray hair stood out in a dozen different directions around his face. Einstein on Slimfast.

"I'm Dr. Gerlaine. Head of cardiology at Valley Hospital here

HOME AGAIN    11

in LaGrangeville." He bent and pulled up a chair, sitting down as he flipped through Angel's charts.

Here it comes, Angel thought. The stand-up routine.

Gerlaine closed the chart—so goddamn symbolic, that quiet closing. "You're a very sick young man, Mr. DeMarco."

Angel grinned. He was still alive, still breathing, and he'd heard this doctor's shtick for years. *You're playing on borrowed time, Mr. DeMarco. You need to change your life—change your life—change your life.* The conversation lived on tape in his brain, winding, rewinding, replaying a million times in the darkness of the night, but he didn't want to change his life, didn't want to eat right or exercise or play by the rules.

He was thirty-four years old, and years ago he'd started down a dark road of rebellion for rebellion's sake. He knew it was a useless, meaningless existence—that's what he *liked* about it. No one counting on him, or needing him. He flitted from party to party like an acrobat, swinging through, swilling booze, having sex, and moving on.

"Yeah, yeah, yeah," he answered. "No shit."

Dr. Gerlaine frowned. "I've spoken with your doctor in Nevada."

"I'm sure you have."

"He told me you were a cardiologist's nightmare."

"That's why I like Kennedy. He's more honest than your average doctor."

Dr. Gerlaine slipped the chart back into its sleeve. "Kennedy says he told you six months ago that if you had another episode of heart failure, you were going to—in his words—be in deep shit. And son, it doesn't get much deeper."

Angel laughed. "Slow down, I can't keep up with the technical jargon."

"Kennedy told me you'd make jokes. But I don't think anything here is funny. You're a young man. Rich and famous if the girls at the nurses' station are correct."

Angel thought about the stir his presence must be creating and felt a jolt of adrenaline. "They're right. I'm both."

There was a pause before the doctor spoke again. "You're not taking this seriously enough, Mr. DeMarco. You've been sick for a long time. The viral infection you had as a young man weakened your heart. And *still* you drank and smoked and used drugs. The cold, hard truth is that you've been using up that heart of yours at a very rapid rate, and if we don't do something soon, we may not be able to do anything at all."

"I've heard that before. But I'm still here, Doc. You know why?"

Gerlaine eyed him. "It's certainly not because you listen to doctor's orders."

"Nope." His voice fell to a conspiratorial whisper. "Here's my secret, Doc: Only the good die young."

Gerlaine leaned back in his chair, studying Angel. Minutes clicked by on the rhythmic tide of the monitor. Finally the doctor spoke. "Do you have a wife, Mr. DeMarco?"

Angel gave him a disgusted look. "I think she'd be here if I did."

"Children?"

He grinned. "Not that I know of."

"Dr. Kennedy said in all the years he'd treated you, he'd never seen anyone visit you in the hospital except your agent and a horde of reporters."

"What is this, Doc, some macabre *This Is Your Life*? You going to bring out my high school guidance counselor to confirm that I never played well with others?"

"No. I'm asking who will grieve for you if you die."

It was a mean question, designed to hurt, and it succeeded. He thought suddenly of his brother, Francis. All at once his childhood was inside him, and the nostalgia was so sharp and sweet, he could smell the grass and the rain and the sea.

Thinking about the past made him feel . . . disconnected. He knew that his Hollywood acquaintances were just that. Not the kind of friends his brother had once been. They didn't *see* him, that group of hangers-on who drifted through the movable feast that was filmmaking.

For a split second he felt a stinging regret, a sense of loss for all he'd walked away from, the brother he'd left behind. Ruthlessly he shoved the emotion aside and stared hard at the doctor. He wanted to tell him to go to hell; but damn it, he needed the man. It was time to turn on the charm that had gotten him so far, so fast. "Hey, you're right, of course. This must be where they got that famous line 'serious as a heart attack.' Well, you can bet your ass I'm going to take my health seriously from now on. No drugs—or hardly any. And I'm going to give up booze. Just beer. Beer's okay, right?"

Gerlaine stared at him in obvious distress. "If you don't do something quickly you're going to die, Mr. DeMarco. *Soon.* And whatever dreams and hopes you have will die with you. No second chances."

Angel smiled. *Same old schtick.* "Define 'soon' for our viewers."

Gerlaine responded with the expected shrug.

Angel smiled triumphantly. That was always the way of it— that shrug was doc body language for sometime between this second and 2010. They didn't have any real answers, just advice and more advice. "I'll die someday, is what you mean. Well, pal, so will you."

"No, that's not what I mean," Gerlaine answered evenly. "If you don't do something, Mr. DeMarco, I think you'll die this year."

Angel's cocky smile faded. "This *year*? But it's almost October."

"Yes, it is."

Angel couldn't comprehend what he was being told. Something was wrong, his hearing was going. "Are you shitting me?"

Gerlaine gave him a superior look. "I don't 'shit' patients, Mr. DeMarco, I inform them."

*This year.* No one had ever said anything like that before. It was always a bunch of hemming and hawing about somedays and future times. Lectures about alcohol abuse and the accumulated effect of cigarette smoking and fat in your diet.

Angel wanted to hit something, punch his fist into a solid brick wall and feel the familiar pain radiate up his arm. "So fix me," he snapped. "Cut me open and repair the damage."

"It's not that easy, Mr. DeMarco. The damage done by this last episode is too extensive. I've spoken to Chris Allenford at St. Joe's, and he concurs that repair isn't a viable option."

*Damage. Too extensive.*

Bad words, very bad words.

"Are you telling me I'm going to die and you can't do anything to save me?"

"No. I'm telling you that standard heart surgery isn't an option. It's too late for that. You need a new heart."

"No. You don't mean . . ."

"Transplant."

For a split second Angel couldn't breathe. Ice-cold fear stabbed deep, deep in his heart. "Jesus," he said on a breath. "Jesus . . ."

*Transplant.* A new heart. Someone else's heart in his chest. A dead person's heart. Beating, beating.

He stared at Gerlaine, trying to sound normal, unafraid. He forced a weak smile. "No way. I don't even buy used *cars*."

"This is no joke, Mr. DeMarco. Your heart disease is in end stage, and that is as bad as it sounds. You're going to die unless you receive a healthy heart. We'll put you on the transplant list and hope a donor is found in time."

A *donor.* Angel thought for a second he might puke. "And give me a life as what—Frankenstein's pet project?"

"It's a surgery, Mr. DeMarco, not unlike other surgeries. There'll be guidelines, of course, restrictions on activity and diet, but with a few lifestyle changes—"

Angel was almost speechless. "Jesus Christ . . ."

"There are excellent psychiatrists who are trained to help in times like this. . . ."

"Really?" Angel shot the word back. He knew he should be charming right now, try to get what he wanted with honey instead of piss, but he couldn't manage it. He felt as if he were falling off a cliff into a deep, dark pit, and the helplessness of it made him want to scream out in anger. "How many heart transplants have you done, Mr. Head of Cardiology for LaGrangeville Hospital?"

"None, but—"

"But nothing. I'm not taking your word for anything. *Anything.* Do you understand me? Make arrangements to fly me to the best transplant center in the country." He glared at the doctor. "Now."

Gerlaine slowly pushed to his feet. "Kennedy told me you'd take this poorly."

"Take it poorly?" Angel mimicked. "Take it poorly? What is that, some kind of *joke*?"

Gerlaine pushed the chair aside and sighed deeply, shaking his head. "I'll make arrangements for a transfer. St. Joseph's Hospital in Seattle would be your best bet. Allenford's probably the top cardiovascular surgeon in the country."

"Seattle?" His heart hammered out of control, sent that idiotic monitor clicking and blipping. He was so furious, he could barely breathe. "Jesus Christ, it's a comedy of errors. You're sending me home."

Gerlaine brightened. "Really? I didn't realize you were from Seattle. Well—"

"If anyone finds out about this—*anyone*—I'll sue this goddamn hospital so fast, you'll be emptying bedpans at a nursing home, you got that, Doctor?"

"Mr. DeMarco, be reasonable. You came here from a Hollywood party. People saw you arrive."

"*Nobody* is gonna think I need a new heart. You figure out a way to hide it, Doc."

Gerlaine stared down at him, frowning. "You have strange priorities. . . ."

"Yeah, yeah, bite me. Now, get out of my room."

Gerlaine shook his head and shuffled wordlessly to the door. He turned, gave Angel a long, worried look, then left the room. The door clicked shut behind him.

Quiet descended, settled uncomfortably onto the blank walls and speckled linoleum. The monitor blipped on and on and on.

Angel stared at the closed door, feeling the blood hurtling through his body, pounding at his temples, catching and releasing on the tired old valves of his heart. His fingers were cold, so cold, and he couldn't draw a decent breath.

*A transplant.*

He wanted to laugh it all off, to tell himself that he was in some backwater, low-rent hospital getting bad advice, and part of him even believed it. But not all of him, not deep, deep inside of him where the fear had always lived, the dark spot in his soul where even the booze and drugs couldn't reach.

*Transplant.*

The word circled back on itself and returned.

Transplanttransplanttransplant.

They wanted to cut his heart out.

Drugs swirled soothingly through Angel's body. He couldn't keep his eyes open, and his body felt weighted and tingly. Consciousness came and went with the ticking of the wall clock.

*Home.* They were sending him home.

He tried not to think about it, but the memories were persistent. He didn't have the pills and the booze and the women to keep them away this time, and without his narcotic armor, he was so damned vulnerable. He closed his eyes, and slowly, slowly, the antiseptic smell of the hospital was blown away by a rain-sweet breeze. He no longer heard the monitor, but the growl of an engine. . . .

He was seventeen again . . . riding his motorcycle, the Harley-Davidson that had cost him his soul. The engine throbbed and purred beneath him. He drove and drove, not knowing where he was going until he reached the stoplight. The sign hovered above him at a cockeyed angle: *Wagonwheel Estates Trailer Park*.

He urged the bike forward, inching past one trailer, then another and another. Each mobile home huddled on a thin strip of asphalt, living rooms shored up with piles of concrete blocks, backyards a six-by-six square of gravel.

Finally he came to his boyhood home.

The trailer, once butter yellow, now grayed by time, sat in a weed-infested patch of meadow grass. Trash cans heaped with garbage lined the chain-link fence that separated the DeMarco "estate" from the Wachtels' domain next door. A dilapidated Ford Impala was parked at a suspicious angle in the driveway.

He pulled up alongside the chain-link fence and cut the engine. He sat there a second, uncertain, then very slowly he set the kickstand and got off. He walked along the fence and up the split asphalt driveway, across the necklace of aggregate gravel stepping-stones that led to the front door.

As he passed it, Angel glanced at the garbage can, saw the crushed paper bags and bent pop cans that peeked over the rim. It was his job, never Francis's, to carefully construct the rubbish facade. The real garbage—the weekly allotment of gin and vodka bottles—had to be hidden at all costs.

As if the neighbors didn't know. For years they'd heard the raucous, drunken fights that emanated from the piss-colored trailer, had heard the slamming doors and breaking glass every Saturday night.

The music of Angel's youth.

He climbed the creaking metal steps and stopped at the top, staring at the dirty door. For a second he didn't want to go in. It was crazy, he knew, to be seventeen years old and afraid to enter your own home, but it had been that way for as long as he could remember.

There was a rustle of movement from within. The trailer shifted and whined on its blocks as footsteps thudded toward the door. Suddenly the knob twisted, the door arced open.

His mother stood in the doorway, a cigarette in one hand, a glass of gin in the other. Her skin had a sick yellow-gray tinge, the mark of chain-smoking, and accordion-pleated wrinkles creased her cheeks. Black hair—a color too severe to be found in nature—lay in frizzled disarray around her pudgy face. Puffy purplish bags underscored her bloodshot brown eyes.

Eyeing him, she took a long drink of her gin, draining the glass and tossing it back onto the brown shag carpet. "Where you been?"

"What do you care?"

She burped, wiped the moisture from her mouth. "Don't you sass me, boy."

Angel sighed. Why was he here? What had he hopped for? A smile, a welcome, a come-on-in? When would he stop wanting something from his mother? "I got a problem, Ma."

One bushy gray eyebrow shot upward. "You're in trouble." She said it without a hint of emotion, just a flat statement of fact.

"Yeah."

She took a deep drag off her cigarette, then blew the smoke in his face. "Whaddaya want from me?"

He felt a stab of disappointment, and it pissed him off. "Nothing."

She flicked the still-burning cigarette onto the driveway. "Francis brung me his report card yesterday. It was the best present a mother could get."

Angel fought the immediate resentment, refused to let it get the best of him. It had always been this way with his mother, and it always would be. Francis was her golden boy, her fair-haired child. Francis the good and pure, Francis the altar boy. Her ticket to Heaven. And Angel was her shit-kicking, hell-raising mistake. How many times had she told him she "shoulda had an abortion"?

"You wanna drink?" she asked, still eyeing him.

"Sure, Ma," he said tiredly. "I'll have a drink."

"Martini?"

He knew what her martini was—eight ounces of gin and two ice cubes. "Fine."

Without another word, she turned away from him and headed for the kitchen.

Reluctantly he followed her into the murky interior. Pale light shone through a dirty beige lampshade, reflected on the shag carpet. A faded bronze velour sofa was pressed against the fake-wood-paneled wall. Pressboard end tables were littered with celebrity magazines and piled with ashtrays. There was a fine dusting of ash on the floor beside a black Naugahyde La-Z-Boy.

Angel sat down on the sagging sofa. Within seconds his mother was bustling back toward him, drinks clanking in her hands. He tried not to care that she didn't speak. She didn't want to talk with Angel, didn't want to be with him, but she always had time to drink with him.

Back when he was a kid, ten, eleven, she'd started him on the road to alcoholism with a motherly shove. She'd wanted someone to drink with, and she'd never ask pious Francis. Angel was the perfect choice—as long as he didn't talk much.

It was pathetic how much he'd valued that time with her. For a while it had felt as if she'd chosen him, *wanted* to be with him. By about seventh grade, he understood the truth. She'd share a drink with Adolf Hitler if he stopped by at "cocktail hour." Anything or anyone to prove to her soggy brain that she was a social drinker.

For the longest time, they sat there, he on the sofa, she on the La-Z-Boy, drinking silently. The rattling ice and swallowing gulps seemed inordinately loud in the quiet room. Angel wanted to tell her what he came to say—good-bye—but he couldn't face the look in her eyes when he said the word. She'd know instantly that he was running from trouble, and her triumphant smile would confirm everything she'd ever said about him.

After a while, he heard a car drive up. The engine roared, sputtered, died. Footsteps clanged up the metal steps.

Ma put down her drink and flew to the door, wrenching it open. She threw her arms wide and squealed with delight. "Frankie!"

Angel put his drink down and got to his feet. Anxiety twisted his gut into a knot. He stood there, waiting. His heart started beating hard in his chest. He wasn't ready to tell his brother good-bye, not yet. . . .

Ma moved aside and ushered her savior inside.

Francis came into the trailer and dropped his book bag on the sofa. "Heya, Angel," he said.

Ma thumped Francis on the back so hard, he stumbled forward. "You're just in time for dinner. I'll go to the kitchen and make sure I got your favorites. Franks and beans for my Frankie." With a final squeak, she hustled down the hallway and disappeared into the kitchen.

Francis looked at him. "There's a brand-new Harley-Davidson in the yard."

Angel shifted nervously. "I'm in trouble, Franco. I gotta leave town. I just . . ." To his humiliation, he felt tears burn his eyes. "I just came to say good-bye."

"Don't do it, man," Francis said softly, shaking his head. "Don't just run away. Whatever it is, we can talk about it. Figure out what to do. Don't go. Please . . ."

"I have to." He turned away from the disappointment in Francis's eyes, and ran out of the trailer. Jumping on the motorcycle, he started the engine and roared out of town. He never let himself look back. He was afraid that if he did, he'd start crying . . . and wouldn't be able to stop.

The antiseptic smell returned, sharp and bitter. The hospital lighting stabbed through his watery eyes. He'd stayed away from Seattle for seventeen long, lonely years. Now, after all this time, he was going back.

Going home.

# chapter two

Angel stared at the pockmarked ceiling.

It was too damned quiet in here; the stillness grated on his overstretched nerves. He wanted suddenly to fill the silence with noise, loud, boisterous noise that said *I'm here, I'm still alive*. He wanted to take strength from that simple sentence, pleasure from the knowledge that his lungs still pumped air. But it wasn't enough anymore, not nearly enough. Now there was a vial of liquid nitrogen inside his chest, a dark ugly splotch that could explode at any second. Any second.

Just a *blip* on the screen and it was over. Flat line.

He closed his eyes, trying to ignore the headache pulsing behind his eyes. He didn't want to think about this crap anymore. He wanted it all to just go away.

"You look like shit."

Angel heard the drawling, southern-fed voice and almost smiled. Would have smiled if he hadn't felt so damned low. He cracked his eyes open, blinked hard as the fluorescent lighting stabbed through his brain.

"Thanks." Angel inched his way to a sit. The needles in his veins pinched with every movement. By the time he was upright, he was winded and his chest hurt like hell.

Val stood in the doorway, his thin, designer-clad body angled against the doorframe, his tangled blond hair tucked self-consciously behind one ear. He pushed away from the door and glided into the room in that slow, loose-hipped walk that always drew attention from the media. He reached out, grabbed the bedside chair with long, delicate fingers, and twisted it around, slumping casually onto the hard seat. Leaning forward, he rested his chin on the chair back and dangled his arms over the mustard-colored fake leather. A slow frown pulled at his eyebrows as he studied Angel. "I mean, you *really* look like shit. Even worse than last time."

Angel didn't have the strength to smile. "Give me a cigarette, will you?"

Val reached into his pocket and pulled out a pack of Marlboros. Flicking the hard pack's top, he checked the contents and shrugged. "Empty. Sorry, I wasn't thinking." He pulled a pint of tequila from inside his coat and grinned. "But I'm not completely useless." He set the bottle down on the bedside table. "I just watched the dailies for yesterday. That death scene of yours was unbelievable—even *I* didn't know you were that good. The writer went ape-shit. When you get out of here, we're going to start the Oscar hype immediately. The publicist thinks . . ."

*Blah, blah, blah.* Val's voice droned on and on, but Angel stopped hearing, stopped listening, anyway.

He stared at the man who'd been his friend, and then agent, for sixteen years and tried to summon a smile—to act like a film performance mattered right now. But he couldn't do it; he wasn't that good an actor.

He remembered suddenly the night he'd met Val—it had been in New York, the middle of a winter's night in a seedy tavern, when they'd both been cold and hungry and lonely. Angel had been just a kid then—barely eighteen and already on his own for more than a year.

They became friends almost instantly and spent the next year moving from town to town, running and running until it wasn't fun anymore—just a series of fleabag motels in towns with no names, swilling booze, and eating from Dumpsters.

Amazingly, it had turned around in a single day . . . a day that started with old tuna. Val had gotten violently ill from a tuna sandwich he'd stolen from a hot Arizona lunch counter. At the hospital, he called his parents. Within hours, the two boys were ensconced in the Lightners' gorgeous New York penthouse apartment.

Val's mother was the most beautiful woman Angel had ever seen. Cold as ice, hard as diamonds. Val delighted in telling her where they'd been and what they'd done. She was horrified, of course, and Val made her promise to give them an apartment and put them in college.

"But you haven't even finished high school," she said in a nasal, white-bread voice.

Val only laughed. "Please, Mother. You're rich."

She'd wagged a ringed finger at him. "Life will not always go your way, Valentine."

He'd given her a disarming smile. "You can always hope, Mother."

Angel shook his head to clear the memories. Then he looked at Val. "They want to cut my heart out."

Val patted another pocket, still looking for smokes. "They'll have to find it first."

"I mean it, Val. They want to do a heart transplant."

Val's smile faded. "You mean, take your heart out and stick in a dead guy's?"

Angel felt sick. "Close enough."

"Jesus." Val slumped forward.

Angel sighed. Somehow, he'd expected more of Val, but he

didn't know what that more was. "I need a donor," he said, forcing a smile. "A really good agent would offer."

"I'd give you my brain, buddy. God knows, *I* don't use it. But my heart . . ." He shook his head. "Jesus . . ."

"Unless you're praying," Angel snapped, "try to say something more helpful. I need advice here. Hell, if I'd known a *transplant* was in my future, I'd have quit smoking and drinking years ago."

It was another lie, another in the long string of lies he'd told himself. He'd known for years that his heart was bad—and it hadn't stopped him from drinking or smoking. His only lifestyle change was to drop a heart pill before snorting a line of cocaine.

He had never wasted time thinking about the future. His life had always been a roller-coaster ride, with him strapped willingly in the front seat. The days and nights hammered forward at blinding speed, turning, dipping, plunging. Never slowing, never coming to a bump stop.

Until now, until yesterday, when the coaster had rammed into the brick wall of his own mortality.

And as if death weren't bad enough, they wanted him to go to *Seattle* for the surgery. Christ, what a mess . . .

The more he thought about it, the angrier he became. It wasn't fair. He didn't deserve this. Sure, he'd been an asshole in his life, he'd hurt people and lied to them. But he was supposed to go to hell for that. He'd been raised Catholic, he knew the rules.

Hell was *after* death.

Not hell on earth, not a heart transplant, not half a life.

"This is stupid," Angel said. "I refuse to worry about it anymore. What does some low-rent doctor in a backwater hospital in the middle of nowhere know about cutting-edge technology? He probably wouldn't know a heart transplant patient if he backed over one with his car."

"Oh, and you would." Val crushed the empty cigarette pack. "So when do you have the surgery?"

"I'm not going to."

Val frowned. "Don't be a jerk, Angel. If you need a new heart, get one. It's probably a breeze now. Hell, they separate Siamese twins and turn men into women. What's the problem?"

"I may not be Albert Schweitzer, Val, but I think a new heart would change your life just a little."

"Death might be a harder adjustment." Val tried to look casual, but Angel could see the fear in his friend's eyes. It was frightening, that look, for Val was fearless, the only person Angel knew who played as close to the edge and lived as recklessly as Angel did. A dilettante bad boy who handled the careers of some of Hollywood's most famous people.

Angel wanted to look away, but he couldn't. "Did you see that movie The Hand, with Michel Caine? The one where he was a pianist, I think, and he lost his hand. They sewed a 'donor' hand on the end of his stump. Catch was, it was a serial killer's hand. Caine went around killing everyone he saw."

"Oh, for God's sake, Angel."

"Well? It could be true, it could happen. What if I get some namby-pamby heart, and after the surgery my biggest dream is to dress like Doris Day?"

Val let out a bark of laughter. "I don't know. You've got a hell of a pair of legs. I could probably book you in some La Cage aux Folles nightclub. You could be Liza Minnelli." As soon as the words were out, Val stopped smiling. Then he leaned forward and drilled Angel with a hard look. "The point is, your heart's a goner. That's a fact."

"Easy for you to say."

"Easy?" Val echoed the word, a small frown tugging at his full lips. "You're my best friend. None of this is easy."

"What about my career? The New York Times said my acting had heart."

Val didn't look away, though Angel could tell that he wanted to. "Acting is the least of your worries. I got you more money than God for that piece-of-shit action picture."

Angel started at the empty cigarette pack in Val's hand. He wanted a cigarette, a shot of tequila. Anything that would magically take this moment and transform it into something else. He wanted it to be yesterday, last month, last year.

He wanted not to be dying.

But with every breath, every aching, pain-riddled breath, he felt the truth. His heart was throwing in the towel. The realization brought a gnawing sense of loss and frustration. "I don't want to go public with this, man. I'll feel like a freak."

"I'll leak a story that you're exhausted—they'll think you had a drug overdose, but that's no big deal." Val waited a minute, obviously thinking, then he leaned toward him, looking as serious as Angel had ever seen him. "But, Angel, you've gotta get your head straight. Image is not your biggest problem."

An uncomfortable silence fell between them. Angel didn't want to say anything, didn't know what to say, but the quiet ate through his nerves until he couldn't stand it. "I want to be mad at God, you know? But if there's a God, there's a hell. And if there's a hell, my whole life has been a race into the fire."

Val winced. "Let's not get philosophical. I've got two women and a bag of coke in the limo downstairs." He smiled, but the look in his eyes was sad.

And suddenly Angel knew what Val was thinking. The two of them had done the same drugs, screwed the same women, walked the same razor's edge. If Angel was dying, Val wouldn't be far behind.

What would this do to their friendship?

Angel felt a fluttering of panic. Suddenly he understood the price of his recklessness, and for a second he wished he could take it all back, change the way he'd lived. Anything so that he had friends right now, real, honest-to-God friends who cared about him. . . .

"Sorry, pal," Val said in a quiet voice. "But it's *over*. The booze, the drugs, the parties—they're gone. I don't care if you have the operation or not, those days are gone. I'm sure as hell not going to party with you again. Christ, you could snort a line and drop dead on the coffee table." He shivered at the thought, then moved closer to the bed. "I know you're scared, and when you're scared you get belligerent and pissed off, but you need a clear head about this, Angel. We're talking about your life."

"Some life. And you haven't heard the best part—they're sending me to Seattle for the 'procedure.' *Seattle*."

"Good."

Angel frowned. "What the hell is good about it?"

"You'll have your brother. I was afraid you'd be alone. I have to go to the film festival, and I have the Aspen house booked for two weeks."

"By all means, don't let my death screw up your vacation plans."

Val flashed a guilty look. "I could cancel. . . ."

Angel had never felt so alone. He was world-famous and it didn't mean shit. His life was like his star on Hollywood Boulevard. A beautiful, glittering thing to behold, but frozen in the pavement and cold to the touch. "No, don't bother. I'll be fine."

Finally Val said, "You're stronger than you think you are, Angel. You always have been. You're gonna make it."

"I know."

After that, there was nothing left to say.

Dr. Madelaine Hillyard entered the ICU in a breathless rush, her name still crackling over the paging system.

The room was bright and impersonal. A single bed cut through the center of the small, private room. Beside it stood a table, its surface heaped with pitchers and cups.

Her patient, Tom Grant, lay in the narrow bed, a pale, motionless body, eyes closed, throat invaded by tubing that connected him to the life-sustaining ventilator. Intravenous lines flowed from his veins. Two huge chest tubes stuck out from the skin beneath his ribs, suctioning blood from his surgical wounds to a bubbling, hissing cylinder.

Susan Grant sat huddled against the bed, her arms uncomfortably looped over the silver metal bed rails, her hand curled tightly around her husband's limp, unresponsive fingers. At Madelaine's entrance, she looked up. "Hello, Dr. Hillyard."

Madelaine gave the woman a gentle smile and moved toward the bed. Wordlessly she checked the tubing, made a note on his chart that the canister needed to be emptied more often, and checked his medications. Pressors, immunosuppressants, and antibiotics—they were all working overtime to keep Tom's battered, cut-up body from rejecting the new heart.

"Everything looks good, Susan. He should come to any time."

Tears squeezed past the woman's lashes and streaked down her cheeks. "The children have been asking about him. I . . . I don't know what to say."

Madelaine wanted to tell her that everything would be all right—would be better than all right—that Tom would wake up and smile at his wife and hold his children, and life would be good.

But Tom was a very special patient. This was his second heart transplant. In the twelve years since his first operation, he had proven that transplant could truly give a patient a new lease on life—he'd fathered two more children, become a marathon runner, and been active in spreading the word nationwide that transplantation was an ever-increasing success. Still, the heart had finally given out, and now he was a pioneer again. One of the few patients ever to get a third chance.

"I don't know how to thank you," Susan said softly.

Madelaine didn't answer; it wasn't necessary. Instead, she pulled up a chair and sat down. She knew that her presence would comfort Susan, give the woman an anchor in the silent, terrifying world of post-op recovery. Her gaze shot to the wall clock, and she made a mental note of the time. She had forty-five minutes before her next appointment. She would be able to stay with Tom for a while.

On the bed, Tom coughed weakly. His eyelids fluttered.

Susan lurched forward. "Tommy? Tom?"

Madelaine hit the nurses' button and got to her feet, leaning over the bed. "Tom? Can you hear me?"

He opened his eyes and tried to smile around the endotracheal tube. Reaching up, he pressed his hand to his wife's face.

Then he looked at Madelaine and gave her a thumbs-up.

It was the kind of moment Madelaine lived for. No matter how many times she stood at a bed like this, she never got used to the adrenaline-pumping thrill of success. "Welcome back."

"Oh, Tommy." Susan was crying in earnest now. Tears dripped down her face and plopped on the pale blue blanket.

Madelaine performed a few quick tests on him before easing out of the room to give the couple their privacy. In the hallway she stopped the head transplant nurse and quietly gave her an update, then grabbed her coat from her office and raced from the building.

She drove out of the parking lot and sped down Madison Street toward the freeway. For the first few moments she was flying high, exhilarated by Tom's progress. Soon he would be getting out of bed, kissing his children, holding them on his lap, twirling them in the air on a bright spring day.

She, the other members of the transplant team, and the donor's family had all done their part to make that miracle. No matter how often it happened, she never failed to feel an incredible, humbling sense of awe. When a patient woke up after surgery, she felt on top of the world. Oh, she knew that it could end tomorrow, knew that his body could reject the heart and turn on itself like a rabid dog. But she always believed in the best, prayed for it, worked for it.

She glanced up, saw her exit sign, and the good mood fled as quickly as it had come.

She was on her way to a meeting with her daughter's high school guidance counselor. She did not expect it to go well.

Madelaine sighed, feeling the first telltale pulsings of a migraine headache. Yes, the Tom Grants of the world were the reason she did what she did, why she'd spent years in college, years without sleep or a social life, working herself like a demon to become a cardiologist. But there had been a price. As she got older, it was the truth she'd come to understand. There was always a price.

She was losing her daughter, watching Lina drift farther and farther away. Madelaine tried to be the perfect mother, just as she tried to be the perfect physician. But being a doctor was a snap compared to being a single parent. No matter how hard she tried, she failed with Lina, and it had gone from bad to worse. Lately their relationship had been hanging by a thread.

Madelaine wanted so badly to do the right thing, *be* the right thing, but what did she know of motherhood? She'd gotten pregnant as a teenager—much too young. She'd known she had to take care of her daughter, give Lina a good, stable life. Medical school had been a pie-in-the-sky goal at first. Madelaine had never believed she'd actually make it, but she'd kept plugging away, spending the trust fund that was her mother's legacy. She'd worked her ass off to become the best and brightest of the graduating class, and she'd finished early.

But somewhere along the way, she'd gone wrong. At first it was little things—a missed birthday party, an emergency call on family night, a field trip she couldn't make. Madelaine had been so consumed by her own ambition, she'd never noticed when her daughter stopped inviting her places, stopped counting on her to be somewhere or do something.

Now she was paying the price.

She pulled into the school parking lot, got out of the car, and strode through the school to the counselor's office. At the closed door, she knocked sharply.

A muffled "come in" answered her.

Exhaling steadily, Madelaine collected herself, then went inside.

The counselor, a pert brunette named Vicki Owen, smiled broadly and extended her hand. "Hello, Dr. Hillyard. Come in. Sit down."

Madelaine shook the woman's hand. "Call me Madelaine, please."

Vicki took a seat behind her desk and pulled out a stack of papers. "I asked for this meeting because Lina is exhibiting some serious behavioral problems. She's skipping classes, forgetting to turn in homework, mouthing off. Frankly, her teachers are at a loss. She used to be such a wonderful student."

Madelaine felt every word like a blow. She knew it was true, knew her daughter was in trouble, but she didn't know what to do about it.

Vicki's face softened in understanding. "Don't worry, Madelaine, it's not just you. Every mother of a sixteen-year-old daughter feels the same way."

Madelaine wanted to believe the counselor's words, but she couldn't allow herself such an easy way out. "Thank you," she mumbled.

"Would you like to talk about it?"

Madelaine gazed steadily into the counselor's dark eyes. She wanted to share her burden with this young woman, to lay her cards on the table and say *Help me, I'm lost*, but she didn't know how to be so open. She'd been taught from earliest memory to buck up and be strong. Showing weakness was incomprehensible to her. "I don't think talking will solve my problem," she said evenly.

Vicki paused for a moment longer, waiting, then she went on, "Lina's teachers tell me that she responds well to discipline. Rules."

Madelaine flinched at the subtle reproach. "Yes, she does. I just . . . " She stared at Vicki. *I just don't know how.* "I think she needs more time with me."

"Perhaps," Vicki answered doubtfully.

"I'll talk to her."

Vicki folded her hands on the table. "You know, Madelaine, some things can't be talked out. Sometimes a teenager needs to feel the wrath of God. Perhaps her father . . ."

"No," Madelaine said quickly—too quickly. She tried to force a smile. "I'm a single parent."

"I see."

Madelaine couldn't sit there another minute, couldn't take what she saw in the counselor's eyes. Her shame and guilt were overpowering. She lurched to her feet. "I'll handle this, Vicki. You have my word on it."

Vicki nodded. "The supermom is a tough row to hoe, Madelaine. There are several outstanding support groups that can help out."

"Thank you. I appreciate your concern." With a final nod, Madelaine turned and walked from the office. When the door clicked shut behind her, she closed her eyes for a second.

*Perhaps her father . . .*

She groaned. God, she didn't want to think about Lina's father. For years she'd pushed him out of her thoughts. And if, sometimes, late at night, the memories came to her, she shoved them away with a cold shower or a run around the block.

It had worked, too. After a while she stopped thinking about him, stopped needing or wanting him. There had been a time when she'd almost forgotten what he looked like.

Then Lina had begun to change. It had been subtle at first, the transformations. A few more holes in her ears, tears in her Levi's, dark mascara smudged around her beautiful blue eyes.

As usual, Madelaine had barely noticed. Then, one day, she looked up at her daughter and saw him. She'd realized then what she should have seen since childhood. Lina was the spitting image of her father, a wild teenager who lived life at a full run, taking no prisoners, asking for nothing. Like her father, too,

Lina saw through Madelaine's brittle exterior, saw the weak woman inside. A woman who couldn't make rules, couldn't enforce even the simplest conditions. A woman who was so desperate for love that she let people walk all over her.

Lina Hillyard took a long, stinging drag off her cigarette and exhaled. The smoke collected against the windshield and hung suspended, mingling with the massive cloud that was already there. She held back a hacking cough by sheer force of will.

Shifting uncomfortably on the narrow seat, she cast a surreptitious glance at the boy beside her. Jett was driving fast, as usual, his foot slammed onto the gas pedal, his free hand curled around a bottle of Jack Daniel's he'd stolen from his parents. On the other side of her, Brittany Levin was sucking on a lime—the last stage of her tequila slammer. Everyone was laughing and talking and singing along with the radio. It was blasting a song by the Butthole Surfers.

The song ended and something softer began. Jett cursed loudly and switched the radio off, then swerved onto the side of the road and hit the brakes so hard that all of them were hurled forward. Lina's hand shot out instinctively, slammed against the windshield. Her cigarette hit the dashboard and rolled toward the vent.

The little Datsun's doors flipped open and everyone spilled out. Lina reached for her cigarette. By the time she'd retrieved it, the gang was already outside, milling beneath a huge cedar tree in the center of the clearing.

It was their Saturday night party spot. Yellowed cigarette butts already littered the ground, alongside empty liquor bottles and roach clips and crumpled smoke packs. Someone had brought a boom box, and loud music vibrated through the air.

Lina dropped her cigarette and ground it out beneath her heel, then headed toward the group. Jett was standing alongside the tree, guzzling Jack Daniel's as if it were water. The golden alcohol trickled down his stubbly chain and dripped onto his T-shirt.

She wished she knew what to say to him now—just the right thing that would make him look at her, *see* her. She'd had a crush on him for as long as she could remember; he was so cool. And they had something in common. Jett had grown up without a father around. Lina was certain it meant something—some destiny thing—that their lives were so alike. But he never seemed to notice her, none of them did. She was like a ghost, hovering on the perimeter of their friendship, trying to find the words that would admit her.

"Hey, Hillyard," Jett called out, wiping the back of his hand across his mouth. "You got any money? We need more smokes."

Lina grinned and tucked a stray lock of black hair around her ear. It wasn't much, she knew, but it meant that he wanted something from her, needed something. She always had more money than the rest of the kids. (It was the one cool thing her evil mother did.) "Yeah, I got enough for a couple of packs," she answered, digging into her jeans pocket.

Brittany gave her a stinging look. Then she flipped open her purse and pulled out the pint of tequila. "Here, Lina, have a drink."

Lina grabbed the bottle's warm neck and took a burning drink. The tequila ignited along her throat and exploded in her stomach.

Brittany ran a hand through her short-cropped hair and sidled up to Jett. Staring triumphantly at Lina, she reached up and planted a long, wet kiss on his mouth. Jett's hand slid around Brittany's waist and pulled her close. "You taste like tequila," he murmured. Then he looked around. "Who's got the pot?"

Within seconds, the night air was thick with the sweet scent of marijuana. The kids drew together in a circle, passing the joint from one another, laughing and dancing.

Lina felt the effects of the stuff in her bloodstream. The world seemed to slow down. Her body turned to heavy syrup and she sank slowly, slowly downward.

She closed her eyes and swayed. God, it felt good to be zoned out. When she was like this, there were so many things she didn't care about. Suddenly it didn't matter that her perfect mother was meeting with the school counselor today. Nothing hurt her when she was high.

Even the questions that had haunted her all day now felt as insubstantial as the smoke rising from her cigarette.

Brittany plopped down beside her. "I saw your dipshit mom going into Miss Owen's office today."

Jett laughed. "Ooh, you're in trouble now, Hillyard."

"Yeah, I saw her, too," someone cut in. "She may be a bitch, but your mom is *hot*."

"She could be a model," Brittany said, then leaned close. "You sure don't look like her. Who do you look like in your family?"

Lina flinched and reached for her smokes. Sometimes she hated Brittany more than she could stand. "My dad, I guess."

Brittany gave her a cold, assessing look. "Course, that's just a guess." She took another huge gulp of tequila, laughing as she swallowed. Then she surged to her feet. "Hey, I got an idea." She raced over to Jett and whispered something in his ear, and they both started laughing.

Jett dropped the empty bottle of Jack Daniel's and made his stumbling, lurching way to the car. He opened the trunk and rummaged through the stuff in the back, grabbed a few things, then ran back to the clearing. A big, alcohol-soaked grin exploded on his face. "Hillyard, we're going to figure out who your dad is."

Lina didn't answer. They didn't understand—none of them understood—how much they could hurt her with their careless words. "What do you mean?" she asked softly.

He squatted until he was eye level with her. "We're going to see who you look like. It'll be cool. You'll see." Before she could think of what to say, he'd slapped an old baseball cap on her head and whipped out a pair of scissors. "I'll cut around the outline of the hat—it'll be awesome." He hiccuped drunkenly and laughed.

Alarm flared in her. "Wait a second—"

"My old lady's a hairdresser. I know what I'm doing," Jett said.

Brittany stared down at her. "You aren't chicken, are you, Lina?"

The other kids closed in around them.

Lina bit down on her lower lip to keep it from trembling, but she never looked away from Brittany's face. "I'm not chicken," she said. "Besides, short hair is way cooler." She turned to Jett, giving him her biggest, bravest smile. "Go ahead."

Jett started snipping. Big clumps of jet-black hair slid down her Levi's jacket. She flinched at each *snip-snip-snip*, and felt as if pieces of her were falling away.

Brittany fished a mirror out of her purse and handed it to Lina. There was a victorious gleam in her brown eyes.

Slowly Lina picked up the mirror and stared at her own face. For a second she couldn't breathe, but after a minute, she wasn't looking at the shaggy, hacked-up haircut. She was staring at her own reflection.

The questions came flooding back, and this time the booze and pot offered no sanctuary at all. Suddenly she was thinking of her father—the mysterious father—who'd marked her face and imprinted her soul. As always, she wondered what he was doing right now. Was he coming home from work? Kissing some other child he'd fathered along the way, one he'd stayed around to raise?

*Everything would be different if I knew you*, she thought for the millionth time.

"She looks like Mr. Sears," Brittany said, laughing shrilly. "Hey, Hillyard, maybe the school janitor is your dad."

Jett picked up a joint and took a hit. Smoke poured from his mouth as he said, "I don't know why you don't just ask your old lady. My mom gave me my dad's address a few years ago. She told me to go live with him, and good riddance."

*Just ask.*

Lina shivered at the thought. Maybe she would this time. Her sixteenth birthday was coming up. . . .

The thought coalesced, took shape in her mind until her whole body was shaking. Anticipation blossomed into a living, breathing presence inside her. She knew suddenly what she wanted for her birthday. "It's time," she said to herself, feeling the beginnings of a smile.

"What do you think, Lina?" Brittany's nasal voice broke into her thoughts.

Lina's gaze jerked up. For a split second she couldn't figure out what they were all waiting for; then she remembered. The haircut. She looked first at Jett, then at Brittany—who was so clueless, she thought a frigging haircut mattered. "It's way cool. Thanks, Jett. Now, hand me the tequila."

# chapter three

Madelaine dropped the expensive shopping bags on the creaky old dock and sat down.

Salty air caressed her cheeks, tugged at the short strands that framed her face. The dark green water stared back at her, rolling gently, spanking the barnacle-studded pilings, coughing up foam. The dock groaned beneath her, shifted with each push of the tide, as if it were fighting to hold its place against the monumental force of the sea.

"Hi, Mama," she said, her voice as soft and low as the wind whispering through the decrepit boards.

The sea gazed back at her, waiting, rolling.

She ached to feel close to her mother here, the only place on earth where such a feeling was even possible, but it was difficult, manufacturing a tie that had been broken so many years before. Yet still she tried; the first Sunday of each month she returned and spoke to the woman who should have shaped her life.

She'd first come here when she was six years old. A reed-thin, plain-faced child dressed like a tiny doll, her black patent Mary Janes pressed together at the ankles, her black satin dress billowing in the wind.

She closed her eyes and let the memories flow, all that she had left. Her father, standing on the edge of this dock beside her, his Burberry coat flapping, his cheeks reddened by the cold. He'd seemed so big then, huge and indestructible, with a voice like a foghorn and eyes that never looked at her.

Her mother's ashes floating on the surface of the water . . .

*Don't cry, girl. It won't bring her back.*

Madelaine had done as he asked, as she always did, holding back the tears one breath at a time. The sea had blurred before her eyes, shimmered into a huge, endless swath of blue that once had meant nothing to her, and now held all that remained of her mother.

It had taken her years to come back to this place, and once she did, she couldn't stay away.

Behind her, the packages rustled again, reminding her of why she was here, of the reassurance she needed from her mother.

"It's Lina's birthday tomorrow," she said quietly.

The words were lost, taken and twisted and swallowed by the breeze. After a grueling workday, she'd gone shopping, agonizing over each purchase, wanting each one to be just right. The bridge that would bring her and Lina back together. A miraculous glue that would bind the fraying seam of their relationship.

She wanted tomorrow's party to be a new beginning for her and Lina, the mother and daughter who'd slid so far apart. But how?

That was the question she'd brought for her long-dead mother. How did two people who were supposed to love each other find their way back? How were wrong paths made miraculously right?

*Help me find my way, Mama.*

She lifted her head, stared out at the sparkling water. As

usual, no answer came to her, nothing but the ceaseless rhythm of the waves slapping against the dock. The wind picked up, pushing the waves harder and harder against the pilings. Overhead, a gull wheeled and cawed and dove into the sea.

"I thought I'd find you here."

Francis DeMarco's voice was a warm, welcome balm. She should have known that he would show up. Smiling, she twisted around to see him.

He stood a few feet behind her, tall and straight, his long arms dangling at his sides. He looked, as always, slightly awkward and unsure of himself in his severe priest's clothes, the jet-black cloth a stark contrast to his pale, clear skin. A lock of tangled, wheat-colored hair lay flopped across one eye. Impatiently he shoved it aside, and it fell right back.

Madelaine's heart swelled almost painfully at the sight of him. He stared at her as he always did, his eyes shining and intense, his mouth poised on the brink of a smile.

"Hey, Francis," she said.

He smiled in that boyish way of his, his whole face crinkling with the motion. He looked heartbreakingly naive for a man full grown. "I missed you in church this morning."

She grinned at the old joke. "I prayed in the OR. And at the cosmetics counter at Nordstrom's."

He moved toward her, his heels clicking on the tired old wood. His knees creaked as he sat beside her. His gaze cut to the sea. "She answer this time?"

From anyone else, the question would have stung, but not from Francis, her Francis, who knew her better than anyone else in the world. Sighing, she leaned against him and slipped her hand in his.

He'd been her anchor for so many years. Her best friend. The strength she'd never found in her own soul, she'd always found in his.

"No, no answer."

"You ready for the party tomorrow? I see you've cleaned out Nordy's and Tower Records."

She laughed, and it felt good. She didn't laugh nearly enough. "Classic single-parent-with-a-troubled-teen syndrome. Buy, buy, buy."

A companionable silence slipped between them. Madelaine stared out at the sea, listening to its rhythmic breathing, feeling its movement in the wood beneath her.

When Francis started to speak, his voice was so quiet that for a second, Madelaine didn't even notice.

". . . Old Mrs. Fiorelli. She's not doing well."

Madelaine squeezed his hand. "I'm sorry to hear that, Francis. I know how much you care about her."

"Yeah. I've got to go see her."

Madelaine turned to him, and saw with surprise that he looked sad. She reached out, grazed her knuckles along his cheek. "What is it, Francis?"

He plunged a hand through his blond hair. She waited for him to laugh, say it was nothing, but he remained uncharacteristically quiet, looking at her now with an unsettling intensity.

"Francis?"

He leaned forward. Their gazes held. The moment spilled out, lengthened in an odd way that made her heartbeat speed up.

Before she could say something, it was over. "It's nothing, Maddy-girl. Nothing at all."

She felt—crazily—as if she'd just let him down. "I'm always here for you, Francis. You know that."

"Yes," he said, giving her a sad, gentle smile. "I know you are."

Lina climbed off the hard plastic seat of her ten-speed and set the kickstand. The lightweight bike slid to the left and locked in place. She whipped the helmet off her head and shook out her boy-cut hair, plunging her fingers through the damp, sweaty mass to make it look as spiky and unkempt as possible.

Her mother had hated the haircut, of course. *Like Billy Idol, Lina. Do you really want to look like Billy Idol?*

The truth was, her mother couldn't have paid her a higher compliment and, besides, today was the perfect day to look like Billy Idol.

It was Lina's sixteenth birthday, and she was ready to make some trouble. Heck, she was itching for it.

Because there was only one present she wanted to receive— and when she asked for it, a truckload of turds was gonna hit the fan.

She reached inside her leather biker jacket and pulled out a crushed pack of Marlboro Lights. She lit one, then took a long drag. Her lungs burned and she coughed, but it was worth it.

Mom hated it when she smoked.

Smiling, she sauntered up the brick pathway, through the Martha Stewart–perfect front yard, toward the white farmhouse with the huge wraparound porch. It stood alone at the end of the street, this house that had once been in the middle of a hundred acres of farmland. Now it was the only old-fashioned home on a street of cookie-cutter tract houses. As always, every bush and tree was precisely trimmed, and the grass was a carpet of shaved green. Pots of autumn color lined the steps up to the porch.

The only thing that looked out of place in this picture postcard of suburban domesticity was Father Francis's scruffy yellow Volkswagen bug sitting in the driveway. She noticed a new dent in the rusted front fender and wondered briefly who he'd nailed this time.

On the porch she paused, running a hand through her hair again. She knew she looked especially bad today—cheap and sleazy and in trouble—exactly the way she wanted to look. Three earrings in her right ear, four in her left. Blood-black lipstick and blue mascara. Skintight black Levi's with a dozen fraying holes and a stained white men's T-shirt.

She knew it was immature to dress this way just to irritate her perfect mother, but she didn't care. It was a good enough reason. Everything she did was designed to get her mother's attention. *Doctor* Hillyard, the Virgin Mary of medicine, who looked gorgeous after a ten-hour shift at the hospital and never seemed to do anything wrong. Every time Lina looked at her mother, she felt small and stupid and inept. It used to bother her, used to make her cry herself to sleep, wondering why she wasn't more like her flawless mother.

But it had gotten so boring, all that crying and wanting and needing. This year she'd realized that she'd *never* be like her mom, and the realization had freed her. Lina stopped trying to get good grades and make good friends and do everything well. She had flourished in her rebellion, reveled in it.

After a while, though, even that wasn't enough. And finally she had begun to understand what was wrong.

*Daddy.*

It was ridiculous that she thought of him in such childish terminology, but she couldn't help herself. She remembered to the very day when she'd first started missing her father. Not in a vague I-wish-he-were-here way, but with a serious gnawing-in-the-pit-of-your-stomach sense of loss.

It had been in the sixth grade, a year before she started her period. She'd finally found the nerve to ask her mother about him, and Madelaine had looked startled at first, then she'd gotten a sad, faraway look in her eyes and said that he had left them long ago. That he wasn't *ready* to be a father. But it had nothing to do with Lina, Madelaine said fiercely. Nothing at all.

Lina could still remember how that had felt, the loneliness of it.

Now, every time she looked in the mirror, she saw a stranger's eyes, a stranger's smile. With every day, she felt lonelier and lonelier, more lost.

It was then, that cold December of her sixth-grade year, when Lina realized she was alone in wanting her daddy, alone in thinking that something was wrong with her family. That was when things started to change with her mother. Lina had taken her questions to her bedroom, huddled with them, embraced them as she'd once snuggled with her teddy bear. A cold wariness settled between her and her mother, a watchful distance that seemed designed to deflect more questions.

Lina had cried herself to sleep so many nights. It felt as if she'd wept for him forever, this mysterious father who had never come for her, never asked about her, never called on her birthday.

She'd grieved until there was no grief left inside her, and then slowly, insidiously, she'd begun to think. Maybe he didn't know about her.

Once the thought was planted, it took root. Lina fed it daily with the water of possibility, until one day she believed it. Wholly, completely. Her father didn't know about her. If he did, he'd be here, beside her, loving her, taking her places, buying her all the things Mom wouldn't allow.

*He* wouldn't demand so much of her, wouldn't shake his head and cluck his tongue in disapproval when she asked for a tattoo. He'd answer her questions and comfort her. He'd let her stay at her boyfriend's house all night.

Maybe he'd even hold her after a bad dream and let her just cry. . . .

Clamping the cigarette between her teeth, she yanked the front door open and went inside. She tossed her coat on the rack and wandered down the airy hallway, turning in to the kitchen.

It was empty.

She took another burning drag off the cigarette and looked around, uncertain suddenly of what she should do. The kitchen table was draped in color and piled with packages wrapped in bright foil paper. In their midst was a white cake in the shape of a Harley-Davidson Low Rider. Balloons filled the small kitchen, winked at her from a dozen different locations—the backs of chairs, the chrome handle on the front of the stove, the refrigerator door. Big Mylar balloons that all read *Happy Birthday*.

There were sixteen candles on the cake—those silly pink twisty candles that came thirty to a box at Safeway.

Tears stung her eyes, blurring the cake and tablecloth into a white-and-red-checked smear. Angry with herself, she wiped at the moisture with the back of her hand and spun away from the table.

What was wrong with her? Who looked at a stupid old cake and wanted to cry?

But she knew what it was. Her mother had tried to put up the right balloons, buy the right cake. Lina had no doubt that her mom had agonized over every present.

She also knew that each gift would be wrong: too young, too old, too late, too soon. It was just the way it was between her and her mom. They never got anything right.

Not like the old days, back when "You and Me Against the World," by Helen Reddy, had been her and Mom's song. When they'd sung it all the time, laughing, dancing, hugging.

Now she looked at a stupid store-bought cake and she missed it, missed the nights she used to snuggle in her mom's bed, the mornings they used to make pancakes together and sing dopey songs. Jeez, it was embarrassing how much she missed it. . . .

"Happy Birthday, honey!" Her mother's throaty voice rang through the kitchen.

Lina's head snapped up. She saw her mother, standing in the open archway that separated the kitchen from the living room. Father Francis was beside her. They were both grinning.

Lina couldn't believe she was crying. *Crying.*

She threw her shoulders back and sniffed hard, then slumped lazily against the wall. She felt herself sinking into the image she'd created, the rebel in the black leather jacket. Back to a place where no one expected anything of her expect a sharp mouth and a snotty look. A place where things like loneliness and missing your mom didn't exist. She drew on the cigarette, inhaling deeply, then smiled—just a twitch of the lips like Elvis—and mumbled, "Thanks, guys."

Madelaine stared at the cigarette. Her bright smile faded, and disappointment darkened her hazel eyes. "I've asked you not to smoke in the house."

*Then make me stop.* Lina stared at her, unblinking. Almost smiling, she strolled forward, her motorcycle boots clicking on the hardwood floor. When she was directly in front of her mother, she took another drag. "Really?"

For a heady second she thought her mother was going to actually *do* something, say something. Lina leaned forward, waiting.

Madelaine gave a helpless little shrug. "It's your birthday. . . . Let's not fight."

"Lina, put out the cigarette or I'll make you eat Communion wafers," Father Francis said.

"Jeez, have a cow about it, why don'tcha?" Twirling, she strode to the kitchen sink and doused the cigarette under running water.

When she turned back around, no one had moved. Father Francis and Mom looked like a pair from Madame Tussaud's wax museum. They were standing side by side, together, as always. Best friends.

Today Francis looked even more handsome than usual. He was tall and thin, built like a dancer, and though he always looked slightly out of place in his clerical clothing, he looked positively fine in civilian clothes. Like now, he was wearing a pair of faded blue Levi's and an oversized Gap sweatshirt, and there were sixteen-year-old girls across the country who would faint at his killer smile.

Francis shoved a hand through his thick, unruly blond hair and grinned. "So, Lina-ballerina, how does it feel to be sixteen?"

Lina shrugged. "Fine."

Mom gave her a rather sad smile. "I remember sixteen."

Francis looked at her mother, and Lina saw the same sadness reflected in his blue eyes. "Yeah," he said quietly. "It was just about this time of year."

They were doing it again, leaving her out. "Hel-*lo*," Lina interjected with a snort. "It is my birthday here, not old folks' memory day."

Mom laughed. "You're right. What do you say we open presents?"

Lina's gaze darted to the pile of packages on the table. Big, bright, beautifully wrapped boxes that didn't contain what she wanted. Couldn't contain what she wanted.

She looked back at her mom, and suddenly she was afraid of what she'd planned to do today. Her mother had worked so hard . . . always worked so hard, and this would break her heart. . . .

Mom took a step toward her, hand outstretched. "Baby, what is it?"

Lina stiffened and jerked back, away from the comforting sadness of her mother's touch. "Don't call me baby." Horrifyingly, her voice broke.

"Honey—"

"What's his name?" The question shot from her lips before she was ready, and it sounded harsh and ugly. She cringed. But it was there, hanging between them, and there was no going back.

Her mother stopped. A frown pulled her thick, winged brows together. "Whose name?"

Lina felt herself losing control. It started as a shaking in her fingers that she couldn't stop. She wished she had a cigarette, or a glass of water. Something, anything to hold on to, to stare at. Any place to look except into her mother's confused gray-green eyes.

And that damned song kept going through her mind. *You and me against the world.*

It would change everything, her next question. Take what little she and her mother had left and rip it apart.

*He doesn't know about you. He'd love you if he did.*

Lina seized the comforting thought until her fingers stopped shaking and the lump in her throat melted away. Slowly, drawing a deep breath, she closed her eyes, unable to look at her mother when she asked the question. "What's his name, Mom? That's all I want for my birthday. Just a name."

For a second, everything went quiet and still.

"Whose name?" Mom said at last, her voice soft. So soft, as if she knew, knew and was afraid.

Lina opened her eyes and met her mother's gaze. She felt a little sting of conscience, knew how much her next words would hurt her mother, but she pushed the feelings aside. "My father."

"Oh my God," Francis whispered.

Lina didn't spare him a glance, just stared at her mother, who was so motionless, it looked as if she weren't even breathing. She stood frozen in the middle of the room, her honey-brown hair curled gently away from her face, her clear, pale skin flushed. The bright red silk of her blouse was a jarring smear of color against her throat.

"Well?" Lina prompted.

Color crept up her mother's long, slim neck. She brought a shaking hand to her forehead and pushed away a nonexistent lock of hair. "Your father . . ." She stopped, threw an uncertain look at Father Francis.

Lina had a sudden, horrifying thought. "Is it him? Father Francis and the Virgin Mary of medicine?" She laughed sharply, almost hysterically, but it wasn't funny. How was it that she'd never considered this possibility? Her middle name was *Francesca*. Oh, God, it was hysterical, really it was. Who better for her perfect mother than a man of the cloth? "How many Hail Marys would they give you for *that* one?"

"No," Francis said. "I wish I were your father, Lina, but I'm not."

Lina's breath exploded in a sigh of relief. He wasn't her father, hadn't lived beside her for all these years a hidden liar, a father who wouldn't admit it. He was still her friend, the uncle she'd never had, the only extended family she'd ever known. All at once she remembered a hundred moments in her past when he had been there for her, washing a scraped knee, playing Candy Land, taking her to the father-daughter luncheons. She moved woodenly toward him, her eyes, fixed on his face. Embarrassingly, tears filled her eyes, but she couldn't will them away. "But you know who he is, don't you? You know."

Francis paled. He shot a confused look at her mother. "Mad—"

"Don't ask her." Tears spilled down Lina's face. She grabbed Francis's hand and squeezed it. "Please . . ."

"Francis won't tell you," Madelaine said in a tired voice.

Lina saw the truth in Francis's pale blue eyes. He might love Lina, but not enough to go against her mother's wishes. Never enough to cross the great and perfect Madelaine.

Lina felt a sudden, blinding rush of anger. How dare her mother keep this information from her? How *dare* she?

She spun around, surged toward her mother. "Tell me."

Her mother reached out and placed her ice-cold hand against Lina's cheek. "Let's talk about this, baby. This isn't the way to do it, not so—"

Lina slapped her hand away. "I don't want to talk about it. I want an answer." Her voice broke, tears fell. "You always talk and I'm sick of it. I'm tired of being loud and different." She stared up at her mother, blinded by tears, sick with confusion.

"I'm sorry, baby, I didn't know." Mom's voice slid into a whisper. "I should have told you years ago."

Lina grabbed her by the shoulders. Fear and panic were coursing through her, obliterating everything except the need to finally have an answer. *"Tell me."*

"Your father didn't want . . ." Mom looked at Francis, gave a watery laugh. "Oh, God, Francis, how can this still hurt so badly?"

Lina went cold all over. She could feel the answer, swirling around her. She wanted to cry, wanted it so badly, her mouth felt dry and her throat swelled. But suddenly the tears were gone. "He didn't want me."

"No, that's not it." Madelaine moved forward, her gaze fixed on Lina's face. "He . . . didn't want me, baby. Me." She gave a brittle laugh. "It was me he left."

Lina jerked back. "What did you do to him? *What?*" She

looked at Francis, then at her mother again, feeling panic rising in her blood, making her sick and dizzy and angry. "You shoved him away, didn't you? Made him sick with all your Goody Two-shoes perfection." Her voice shattered and she started to cry harder. "You made him leave us."

"Lina, listen to me. Please, I love you so much, honey. Please, let's—"

"*No!*" Lina didn't even realize she'd screamed. She backed up, her hands clamped over her ears. "I don't want to listen anymore." She turned and ran for the door, yanking it open. As she stepped through, into the bright sunlight of the day—her sixteenth birthday—she felt a strange calm descend. Her tears dried into a hard, cold knot in her stomach. Slowly she turned to her mother. "Am I like him?"

For the first time, Lina would have sworn she saw the sheen of tears in her mother's eyes. But of course, that was impossible. She'd never seen her mother cry. "Lina—"

"Am I like my father?"

Madelaine stared at her for a long moment, then turned slightly. Her gaze softened. "You're exactly like him."

At first the look in her mother's eyes confused Lina. Then realization washed through her in a chilling wave.

Her mother was remembering *him*.

Memories that ought to belong to the family, ought to be stored in Lina's heart, in that place where there was nothing but a dark hole marked *Daddy*. Lina had tried so hard to fill that void in her life, to conjure images of a man who'd walked away a long, long time ago, and never looked back. And all she had to do was ask a simple question, and her mother remembered a million things about him. How he looked, how he smiled, what his hand felt like when it held yours. Everything Lina ached to know and could never find out.

Lina looked at Madelaine, hating her more in that moment than she'd ever hated anyone. "Then I know why he left you."

# chapter four

⟋∾⟍

Francis stood frozen, unable to dredge up a coherent thought. He was breathing fast, too fast; he sounded like a marathon runner, but he hadn't taken a step. He glanced at Madelaine, who stood rooted in place, her hands fisted at her sides, her spine ramrod-stiff.

He couldn't see her face, but he didn't need to. He'd known her and loved her for almost seventeen years. He knew what she was feeling.

He moved awkwardly toward her. "Maddy?"

She didn't seem to hear him.

"Madelaine?"

Her voice, when finally she spoke, sounded thin and faraway. "Well, that was certainly a bust."

It broke his heart that she still had to pretend she was indestructible. "Don't . . ."

She sighed heavily. "I should have told her about him a long time ago, Francis."

They'd had this discussion a hundred times over the years, and he knew that now she was going to beat herself up over the choices she'd made. It was her way; she always took the blame on herself. Took responsibility for the whole world's unhappiness.

He stood beside her, holding her hand. He wanted to say something, but he felt uncertain, as he always did around her. She was so strong, so resilient, and yet so blind. She couldn't see that Lina loved her, couldn't imagine that Francis did.

It was all her father's fault. Up in that big mansion on the hill, Alexander Hillyard must have done terrible things to his little daughter who'd lost her mother, because even now Madelaine believed she was unlovable. Truly believed it.

"Lina loves you, Maddy. I've told you this a million times. She's just confused."

Madelaine shook her head—as he'd known she would. "No. I should have told her."

"Yeah, maybe you should have, but that's water under the bridge now."

"I can rectify it. I can tell her now."

He stared at her, shocked. "You can't."

"Of course I can."

Francis shivered involuntarily. If Madelaine told Lina about her real father, it would all come crashing down, the make-believe house Francis had constructed to hold the family he wanted so badly to be his. He'd always thought of Lina as *his* daughter. He was the one who had bandaged her scraped knees and held her when she cried. And he was afraid—God have mercy on him—he was afraid she wouldn't want him anymore if she found her real father. It was wrong, what he was about to say—an awful, horrible sin—but he couldn't help himself.

"Let sleeping dogs lie," he said firmly. "He'd only break her heart, anyway."

"I'm so afraid of losing her, Francis. I can't seem to do anything right." She glanced away from him, stared at the open door. "I thought . . . after my own father . . . I promised myself I'd be a good parent."

Her pain snagged his heart. She was standing beside him, close and yet distinctly separate. Alone as always, untouchable, daring the world to lay a finger on her, waiting to be blindsided and betrayed. He moved closer, took her face in his hands and tilted her chin. She felt fragile, so fragile. "Don't compare yourself to Alex, Madelaine. Alex was cruel and bitter and unfeeling."

"Lina thinks *I* don't feel anything. She thinks I'm cold and perfect and detached."

"She's not that stupid, Maddy. She's a garden-variety teenager, mixed up and running on hormones."

"No, it's not like that. She's like . . . *him*. You know she is."

Francis wished he could lie, but Madelaine was right; Lina was just like her father. Rebellious, wild, free-spirited. The kind of person who lived life recklessly—and sometimes hit brick walls. The kind of person who could walk away from everything at seventeen and never look back.

"No. She's smarter than him," he said finally, wanting to believe his own words. "And she might be mad now, but she loves you. Otherwise, she wouldn't try so hard to get your attention." He stared down into her huge, pain-darkened eyes and felt as if he were drowning in the need to hold her. God, he wished this were his moment, his daughter, his wife, his life. Without thinking, he leaned down and pulled her toward him, kissing her softly, slowly, on the forehead. Sensations swirled through him, made the blood pound in his head, and he knew he'd gone too far, kissed her too long. . . .

She drew back. "Francis? What was—"

"She loves you, Madelaine," he whispered against her skin, "like I do." The words slipped out, words he'd never had the courage to say before, but now seemed the most natural thing in the world.

She drew back and stared up at him.

He leaned forward, wanting to kiss her again, waiting breathlessly for her to speak.

Suddenly she smiled. "Oh, Francis, I love you, too. I don't know what I'd do without your friendship."

The words plunged into his gut. He stroked her silky hair and held her. Tears stung his eyes. He was such a coward—a man whose two loves couldn't possibly coexist, and between which he could never choose. A priest in love with a woman; a man in love with God.

But never before had his love for Madelaine compromised his vows—he'd loved her with a purity that didn't taint his priesthood. Or at least, those were the pretty lies he told himself as he lay in his lonely bed, thinking of her.

Until now. Now he'd kissed her—and not as her priest or as her friend, but as the man who loved her. He'd let the words slip out into the harsh light of day, and God help him, he'd waited breathlessly for her answer.

And that wasn't even his greatest sin. He'd told her—begged her—to keep the truth from Lina.

Lina, the daughter who was and wasn't his, whom he loved more than his own life. He'd furthered the lie that would break her heart.


Angel was back in Seattle. He stared out the cheesy little window in his hospital room and watched the rain drizzling down the glass. Of all the places to be, a hospital room in Seattle— *Seattle*—was the worst. Last night they'd flown him in by helicopter, under cover of night, strapped like a slab of meat on a gurney, his face masked, his name hidden.

He was a nobody in that helicopter, just another dying man being flown to a high-tech hospital. He'd been transferred under the strictest security to conceal his identity. *Mark Jones*—that's what they called him. A high-risk patient sent to a private wing in ICU. It was the way he'd wanted it, but still it angered him to be so anonymous. For years he'd been wined and dined and photographed wherever he went; for years he'd been *somebody*. And now he was just plain old Mark Jones, a nobody with a failing heart.

There was a knock at the door, a quietly spoken "Mr. Jones?"

He tried to sit up, but the needles in his veins resisted, sending spikes of pain shooting up his arm. Muttering a curse, he ignored the pinching and kept at it. By the time he was upright, he was winded and he thought for a humiliating second that he might puke. The room swam before his eyes. His heart pecked and stuck like a stutterer's words.

His chest didn't hurt, but he knew that was a false sense of security. He was shot full of drugs, and when they wore off, he was going to hurt like a son of a bitch. "Come in," he said in a wheezing, breathless voice.

The door opened and a tall, gray-haired man in a white coat sauntered in. The door squeaked shut behind him.

The new visitor sat down and scooted close to the bed, flipping through Angel's paperwork. "I'm Chris Allenford, head of the transplant team here at Saint Joseph's."

Angel concentrated on keeping his heart rate even—not easy with fear pulsing through his blood. He wanted to look casual and at ease right now, wanted to look *healthy*.

This was the man he'd been waiting for, the man he'd tried to believe in ever since this nightmare began. The man who could take the horror of the last few days and make it all vanish.

Angel used all of his acting skills and dredged up a cocky smile. "Hey, Doc."

"I've spoken with your doctors Kennedy and Gerlaine, and they tell me you've been briefed on your condition. I've also consulted with Dr. Jonson at Loma Linda, and we all agree on your prognosis."

"Gerlaine told me that corrective surgery was impossible. In LaGrangeville it probably is, but here . . ." He let the sentence trail off, afraid to actually ask the question.

Allenford frowned.

*I'm not ready*, Angel thought suddenly. *Not ready to talk about this.* Not ready for a frown.

Allenford laid the chart on the bedside table. "I could ramble on about how weakened and enlarged your heart is, but you've heard all this before. As a young man you contracted a primary viral myocarditis, which damaged your heart. You were advised to change your lifestyle. Advice which, apparently, you ignored." He shook his head. "The technical term for your present condition is end-stage cardiomyopathy. What that means is that your heart is shot. Used up. If you don't have the operation, you'll die. Soon."

Fury flashed through Angel, so hard and fast, he felt dizzy with it. "An operation. Christ, you doctors, you're all the same. You say 'you need an operation' like it's no different than telling me I need a wisdom tooth pulled." He struggled to sit up straighter and couldn't. The failure increased his anger. "Well, Doc, you let 'em cut your fucking heart out and then tell me how it was. If you still endorse the *operation,* I'll think about it."

Allenford never broke eye contact, but the wrinkles in his cheeks seemed to deepen. "I don't know . . . I've never been a very brave man."

The words were quietly stated and honest. Angel lost his hold on anger. Fear slipped in to replace it, twisting his insides. "My heart," he whispered, wanting to sound cocky and sure of himself, and knowing that again he'd failed.

Allenford stared down at him. "I can't pretend to know how you feel, Mr. DeMarco, but I can tell you a little bit about the surgery. Demystify it somewhat. Years ago, heart transplants were very risky ventures, very uncertain, and most patients died. But we've made great strides in the last decade. Anti-rejection drugs, tissue-typing, and immunosuppressants—they've all played a tremendous part in making this type of operation successful. And you're one of the lucky ones—only your heart has been damaged; your other organs are fuctioning amazingly well, given the life you've led. This gives you a jump on long-term post-op prognosis. Approximately ninety percent of all patients live a relatively normal life afterward."

"Relatively normal," Angel said, feeling sick at the thought.

"Yes, relatively. You'll take medications for the rest of your life, you'll have to watch your diet and exercise. No drugs, no smoking, no booze." He leaned forward, smiling gently. "That's the downside. The upside is that you'll be alive."

"Sounds like a great life. I can hardly wait."

Allenford's hawkish gray brows pulled together slowly. "I've got a seventy-year-old indigent apple picker down the hall who won't even be considered for a new heart. . . . Then there's the six-year-old girl who has been in constant arrest for the past week—all she wants is to live long enough to see seven candles on her birthday cake. Either of them would take your condition in a second."

Angel felt like shit. "Look, I'm sorry, I just . . ."

Allenford wouldn't let it go so easily. "I know you're a celebrity, but believe me, that doesn't mean anything in here. I won't put up with your tantrums and your selfishness. In here you're just another patient waiting for a new heart. The hard truth is, Mr. DeMarco, you're going to die. Without the surgery, you'll get weaker and weaker. You won't be able to move around much, and drawing a decent breath will seem like a gift from God. I know it's difficult, but you've got to understand what I'm telling you. Life as you know it is over."

Angel knew he should shut up now and pretend to be a team player. But he was scared and angry, and his fame had given him license to misbehave for so long, he didn't know any other way. "I could get up, walk out of here, and take my chances."

"Of course you could. And you could get hit by a bus before you die of heart failure."

"I could die screwing some woman's brains out."

"Yes, you could."

"Maybe that's what I want to do."

"Maybe it is."

Angel stared at the man. He'd never felt such a confusing jumble of emotions. His head was spinning with thoughts, possibilities, fears. Mostly fears. "If I did decide to have the surgery—"

"Let me tell you right now, Mr. DeMarco, it's not completely your decision."

"What do you mean?"

"We're talking about a heart transplant here, not capping a tooth. There are only so many hearts available. Unfortunately, most families choose not to donate a loved one's organs. Thousands of patients die every year waiting for a new heart."

"Are you telling me I could die *waiting* for a heart?"

"Yes."

"Jesus Christ, what a mess."

"Your condition is critical. If UNOS—that's the United Network for Organ Sharing—agrees that you're an acceptable candidate, they will put you on the top of their transplant list. The first heart that matches would be yours. But I couldn't guarantee anything."

The words hit him like a sucker punch. "Whoa. Now you're telling me I might not even be put on the list?"

"A psychological profile is required. We all need to believe that you'll change your life and take care of the heart."

The truth crept over Angel. He realized the significance of the doctor's words. For once, Angel couldn't storm or charm or buy his way out. All he could do was play ball—pretend to be worthy of this chance. And he didn't have a hope in hell that he was that good an actor. "Oh, this is just perfect. I'm going to die because I've got a shitty personality." He gave a bitter laugh. "My mother was right."

"Assuming you get on the list—and that will be up to your psychiatrist and your cardiologist—your chances of getting a new heart . . . in time, are running at about fifty-fifty."

He wanted to say, *Thanks for the morbid stats, Doc. I'll be sure to set my heart on the surgery*, but he bit back the sarcasm. Instead he asked, "How are you going to guarantee my anonymity while I'm here?"

"We've put a lid on everything—you're just Mark Jones, in for a heart transplant. Only my oldest and most trusted team members will know who you really are." He sighed. "To be honest, I don't know how long it will last, but we'll do our level best to protect your privacy. If a leak occurs, I'll report simply that you're here for cardiac surgery."

Angel knew from experience that sooner or later, the news would get out. He hoped to hell it was later. "Okay. I'll be a good boy, I'll change my life and cut out the booze and drugs. Where do I go to wait?"

"You're not going anywhere, Mr. DeMarco. You're far too sick to leave the hospital. I'll set up a meeting with your team cardiologist for early tomorrow morning—after we've run all the matching tests. She'll fill you in on the rest of the details."

"Oh, no," he said. "No women doctors."

Allenford laughed at him. "You're not famous in here, Mr. DeMarco. *I* pick the players for your team."

"Team." Angel said the word with disgust. "No *team* is gonna get their heart cut out, is it, Doc? Just little ole me on life support."

Dr. Allenford closed the chart and set it aside. "No, Mr. DeMarco, we're not going to face the knife . . . or the extensive recovery." He leaned forward. "But we will be the ones that find the heart, remove it, bring it here, and place it inside you. I, in particular, am the one who *wields* the knife." A smile slowly crossed his face. "So I'd think about an attitude adjustment if I were you."

They stared long and hard at each other, and Angel knew that neither one of them was used to losing. Finally he said, "Consider it adjusted."

Allenford grinned. "Good. I'll let the social worker fill you in on all the details. I'll speak with Dr. Hillyard tomorrow, and check on the results of your tests. After that, we'll make all the necessary decisions."

Angel got a queasy feeling in the pit of his stomach. He tried to ignore it, couldn't. He was in Seattle, scene of the old crime, and Madelaine's old man had always wanted her to be a doctor. "Dr. Hillyard?"

"Madelaine Hillyard is the best cardiologist on the team— and she doesn't mind difficult patients."

His ragged heart skipped a beat, maybe even stopped. It was the first time he'd heard her name spoken aloud in years, and it brought a sudden tide of memories. Fleeting images, remembered moments. Madelaine, her long brown hair tangled and dripping wet, her knees drawn up to her chest, her fingers plowing through the sand for hidden treasures, laughing, always laughing; the starlit night they'd huddled beneath a huge, old oak tree, burying bits and pieces of carnival glass amidst a shower of grown-up words. *I'll always love you, Angel . . . always.*

Madelaine, his first love, had become a cardiologist.

Bitterness drew a thin smile from his lips. Just what her daddy wanted.

He stared at Dr. Allenford, who was standing up, getting ready to leave. Angel wanted to say something, but his throat had seized up and nothing would come. At the doorway Allenford nodded, then left the room, closing the door behind him.

Angel lay motionless, breathing hard, feeling the catch and release of his stuttering heart, listening to the *blip-blip-blip* of the monitor. He'd run out of second chances, out of second opinions. His life came down to this moment, this instant in time when he was broken and alone.

What was he supposed to do now? Lie in this single metal-barred bed and wait for some poor sucker to die? Lie here and let them cut his chest open, rip his heart out, and throw it in the trash like so much garbage?

*Heart transplant.* The words were knives, tearing his guts open.

What they wanted to do to him was an abomination, an obscenity. And Madelaine would be the one to do it.

No way.

He threw the covers off his body and plucked the needles from his arms. He tossed his legs over the side of the bed and stood up. He was getting the hell out of this place. They weren't gonna cut his heart out and sew in someone else's. He couldn't— wouldn't—live that way. He'd die the way he'd always lived. Full tilt, taking no prisoners.

He took a single step, just that, and pain exploded in his chest. With a cry, he crashed to the floor. His arm flung out, caught a table and sent it sprawling. Water splashed the floor. Plastic cups and pitchers banged on the linoleum.

He lay there, unable to breathe, gasping for air like a mackerel. And hurting. Christ, even with the drugs, he was hurting like he'd never hurt before.

Suddenly he understood. He was *dying.* Maybe not today, maybe not tomorrow, but soon. Soon. It didn't matter whether he wanted the surgery, didn't matter that he'd be a freak when it was over. He had no choice.

He twisted around and crawled back to the bed. Grabbing the metal bed frame, he hauled himself upright and collapsed on the mattress.

He slid back under the covers and closed his eyes. It hurt so badly, he wanted to cry.

If only he had someone to talk to, someone real, who cared about him. Someone who was the kind of friend Francis and Madelaine had once been.

*Madelaine.*

How many nights had he lain awake in the dark, wondering how his brother was doing, what Madelaine had become? How many times had he picked up the phone to call them both, only to hang up before anyone answered?

He sighed heavily. *Madelaine.* Even now he could bring her face to mind, the thick brown hair that fell in waves to the middle of her back, the slashing eyebrows and Gypsy-tilted eyes, the rounded curves of her body. Most of all he could remember her laugh, throaty and soft.

Back then, she had laughed all the time.

Back then. Before he'd walked out on her.

The last time he'd seen Madelaine, she sat hunched on the end of the tattered sofa, looking so out of place in his family's trailer, her cashmere sweater drooping sadly across one shoulder, her cheeks stained with tears.

He allowed himself to remember it all again, and with remembrance came the burning shame. The lies he'd told her, the words that fell like poison from his lips, the feel of the blood money in his hand, the lingering memory of her perfume—baby powder and Ivory soap.

And now the ultimate revenge was hers.

His *life* depended on the woman he'd betrayed.

# chapter five

Madelaine sat on the edge of Lina's bed. Here and there she could see patches of the pale blue Laura Ashley striped wallpaper she'd put up so many years ago, but most of the walls were covered with posters of rock groups Madelaine had never heard of. Thousands of tiny tack holes in the expensive paper, each one an imprint of Lina's emerging personality.

Madelaine lay back on the bed and closed her eyes, thinking of her daughter. For a second all she could bring forth in her mind were long-gone images—puffy baby cheeks and laughing blue eyes, a pair of fat legs waddling across the dining room floor. A toothless first-grade grin.

Did all mothers feel this way? Did all mothers keep a portrait of their babies inside their hearts, expecting grown girls to still smell like talcum powder and baby shampoo?

Ah, she'd made so many mistakes. She should have told Lina the truth about her father years and years ago. Even last year, when she'd seen Lina sliding downward, she should have guessed at the cause and come clean. But she'd been so damn afraid of Lina not loving her anymore. So afraid of her baby leaving home . . .

It had been wonderful when it was just the two of them, the baby and the mother in the quiet house, making cookies and reading bedtime stories.

Long-forgotten memories crept into her mind of the days when she'd been a teenager going to college and raising a baby alone. Images of that horrible apartment of theirs on University Avenue, with the windows that didn't open and the radiator that never worked . . . the rickety steps to the purple front door . . . the car that stalled on the corner of Fifteenth and University every morning . . . the nights when they both ate Raisin Bran for dinner and she hoped the milk was still fresh. Yet, even in the worst of times—during the eighteen-hour workdays and night-time study sessions—Madelaine had always had Lina right there with her. A curious-minded toddler slung on an exhausted resident's hip. Back then, it was just the two of them against everyone. . . .

But the world had intruded, had come forth with its sticky fingers and demanded Lina's presence. That was beginning of the end—when Lina had begun to grow up and ask questions and see Madelaine's faults. Maybe if Madelaine had attended public schools, had grown up with girlfriends around her, she would have known how to handle the daily traumas. But her father would never have allowed such a thing. Would never have allowed Madelaine to mix with what he called the riffraff. Every day of her childhood had been spent alone, dreaming about friends who would never visit and excursions that would never take place. She didn't know anything about proms or mixers, and less about rebellion.

She didn't know anything about teenagers who were scared and belligerent and confused.

All Madelaine knew about was hiding, pretending, smiling when the ache was so strong and deep that sometimes you couldn't breathe. And she didn't want her baby to learn that skill.

Sighing, she got to her feet and stood there, uncertain. What was she going to do when Lina finally came home?

*If she came home.*

Madelaine shivered. She wouldn't think that way, wouldn't keep listening for the phone or the doorbell, waiting for the worst to happen. Wouldn't keep worrying that Lina would do what Madelaine had done so many years ago.

She moved toward the tape player that sat on Lina's desk and thumbed idly through the tapes and compact disks stacked beside it. At the bottom of the pile was the old Helen Reddy tape they used to listen to.

She picked it up, dusted off the clear plastic cover, and snapped it open. Then she put it on the machine and hit Play.

The music slid through the room on a tide of bittersweet memories.

"No fair, Mom," said a shaky voice.

Madelaine spun toward the door. Lina looked incredibly young and vulnerable, a child in grown-up clothes, her makeup smeared down her pale cheeks. She was so petite, her bones as fine as a baby bird's, her face small and heart-shaped. The jet black of her unruly hair contrasted sharply with the pale, pale cream of her skin. Skin that offset her electric, cornflower-blue eyes.

Madelaine gave her a tentative smile. "Hi, ba . . . Lina. I've been waiting for you."

Lina shoved a hand through her spiky black hair. "Yeah, right. Wanted to say happy birthday again, huh?"

Madelaine moved slowly toward her daughter, but halfway there, she stopped and instead sat on the bed, gazing up at her sixteen-year-old daughter.

"I have some explaining to do," she said at last.

"Yeah." Lina yanked a chair from beside her desk and sat down. Hunching forward, she rested her elbows on her knees and drilled her mother with an angry look. Four silver earrings sparkled in a ladderlike curl up her left ear. "So explain. Tell me about my dad."

*Dad.* The word was the nick of a razor. Madelaine flinched. He wasn't a dad; a dad stuck around, protected his family and helped when the baby had a fever or a nightmare. A dad didn't walk out on everyone.

Lina sighed dramatically. "Look, Jett is waiting for me outside—"

"You're dating a boy named Jet?"

"Are you gonna talk or not? Otherwise—"

"I met your . . . father when I was about your age." Madelaine tried to smile. "It's a story you've heard a million times before. I got pregnant and he . . . he couldn't leave town fast enough."

Lina's blue eyes narrowed. "Did you ever hear from him again?"

Madelaine tried not to remember how long she'd waited for a phone call, a letter, anything. Tried to forget how she'd cried every Christmas for years afterward. "No."

"What's his name?"

Madelaine knew this was the question that would ruin it all. No matter how she answered, it would be wrong. If she lied, Lina would hate her, and if she answered truthfully, Lina would contact her father. Only he wasn't the kind of man who'd welcome a midnight "Hi, I'm your daughter" call—if he'd wanted to know his child, he wouldn't have left in the first place.

If Lina found him, he'd break her heart. A word, a gesture, a little laugh—anything that meant he didn't care—would kill Lina.

"Well?" Lina demanded.

Madelaine knew she had no choice; this was something she should have done a long, long time ago. But she couldn't just throw his name out there. Madelaine had to speak to him before Lina did. The thought of it—just the thought of picking up the phone and calling him after all these years—terrified her. It would change everything. *God help us all.* "I can't tell you his name right now, but—"

"Don't." Lina jerked to her feet and kicked the chair away.

"Let me finish. I can't tell you his name *right now*. But I'll . . ." It took everything she had inside to form her next words. "I'll contact him and tell him about you."

Lina's eyes widened. A tiny smile plucked at her mouth. "You mean he doesn't know about me?"

Madelaine thought of all the ways she could answer that question—some angry, some bitter, some sad. In the end, she chose simple honesty. "As far as I know, he doesn't know you were ever born."

Lina bit down on her lower lip to stop a smile. Madelaine could see the excitement on her daughter's face, shining in the bright blue eyes. Lina wanted so desperately to believe that her father was a good man, a loving father who'd been robbed of his chance to parent. "I knew it."

Madelaine stared at her. Lina hadn't considered what the words really meant, and Madelaine was glad.

"You promise you'll tell him?"

"I've never lied to you, Lina."

"Only by omission."

Madelaine winced. "I'll tell him."

"He'll want to see me," Lina said, and Madelaine could hear the desire in her daughter's voice, the need.

Madelaine got to her feet, moved cautiously toward her. When she was close enough to touch her, she stopped, and though she wanted to stroke her baby's hacked-up hair, she didn't move, didn't lift a finger. "He might disappoint you, sweetheart."

"He won't," Lina whispered.

Madelaine couldn't help herself. She reached out. "Baby, you have to understand—"

"I'm not your baby! It's you he doesn't want. *You.* He won't disappoint me. You'll see."

Lina turned and ran from the room, slamming the door behind her. Madelaine heard her footsteps thundering through the house, then the faraway click of the front door closing.

And she was left, all alone in the room, listening to Helen Reddy. *You and me against the world.*


Hillhaven Nursing Home lay stretched across the narrow suburban street like a half-toppled pile of children's building blocks. On a low hill above the tree-lined road, it gazed serenely down on the quiet cul-de-sac. Cropped grass, burnished to an autumn brown by last night's cold snap, rolled alongside the cement driveway. Behind the six-foot ironwork fence, a few elderly men and women wandered through the dying gardens, talking softly among themselves.

Francis eased his tired Volkswagen up to the curb and parked at an awkward angle. Leaning over to the passenger seat, he plucked up his Bible and black leather bag, then climbed out of the car. Cool, rain-sweetened air ruffled his hair and sent a wayward lock into his eyes. He stood there for a moment, watching the goings-on in the yard. He could hear the familiar *thump-scrape* of metal walkers being pushed along the sidewalks and the distant, motorized whine of a mechanical wheelchair. Orderlies in crisp white uniforms milled casually among the patients, stopping here and there to offer assistance.

He walked up to the entrance and went into the yard. The gate closed behind him with a clang that cut through the conversations. A dozen heads turned to him, and he saw expectation light up every pair of eyes—all of them hoping, hoping, it would be a family member visiting.

"Father Francis!" Old Mrs. Bertolucci squealed, clapping her gnarled, arthritic hands.

He smiled at her. She looked so pretty right now, the sunlight tangled in her white hair, joy in her rheumy eyes. The left half of her face was paralyzed, but it didn't detract from her beauty. He'd known her for fifteen years—like so many of the people who resided here, she'd lived and worked in Francis's old neighborhood. He'd taken Communion alongside her for years, and now he was here to give it.

One by one, they shuffled toward him. He smiled. This was what he lived for.

And in that instant he felt at peace, blanketed once again by the comforting heat of his faith. He was meant to be here, had always been meant to be here. It was now, doing the work of the Lord, that he felt whole and content.

He knew that tonight, when he lay alone in bed, listening to the wind through the eaves and the rattling of the windowpanes, he would be vulnerable again. The doubt would creep through the ragged curtains and nibble at his soul, and he would wonder and worry. . . . He would think of Madelaine and Lina and all the choices he had made in his life; he would think of how he'd encouraged Madelaine to keep the truth from Lina, and the shame would suffocate him. And most of all, loneliness would close in on him like the walls of a fortress. But for now he was happy. It was why he'd hurried over to the home, an hour early. Here and now, with the white collar taut around his throat and a Bible tucked under his arm, he felt safe.

He knelt on the hard carpet of grass, and they gathered around him, all talking at once.

Fred Tubbs hacked out a cough, then pulled a worn pack of cards from his breast pocket—the same pack he'd been brandishing for years. "Time for a quick game of cards, Father?"

Francis grinned. "You cleaned me out last week, Freddy."

The old man winked. "I love to play cards with a man who has taken a vow of poverty."

"Well, maybe just one hand . . ." Francis said, knowing he'd spend hours in the recreation room, playing cards, looking at the same family photographs he'd seen a million times. rereading Christmas cards and letters from loved ones who never had the time to visit.

And they knew it, too—he could see the joy in their faces, the pleasure of simply being remembered on this sunny autumn afternoon.

He got to his feet and took hold of Mrs. Bertolucci's wheelchair. They were still talking to him, one at a time now, in their crackly, paper-thin voices as they moved toward the front door. He started up the ramp, then paused, looking around. "Where's Selma?"

Silence. And he knew. The usual sadness welled up in his chest.

"Yesterday," Sally MacMahon said, shaking her dyed head of jet-black hair. "Her daughter was with her."

There was a murmur of relief that Selma hadn't been alone.

"We thought maybe you could say a special Mass for her, Father," Fred said. "Miss Brine said it would be fine—in the rec room at four o'clock."

Francis reached out for the man and squeezed his rail-thin shoulder. He glanced at the faces around him, one by one, at the wrinkled, age-spotted skin and thinning hair, at the thick glasses and hearing aids and strands of Kmart pearls, and knew what they needed from him now.

Faith. Hope. Strength.

And he had it to give. The smile he gave them was slow and came from the depths of his heart. "She is beyond her pain now," he said softly, believing the words that he'd repeated many times before. "She is with God and the angels and her husband. It is we who feel the pain at her passing."

Mrs. Costanza laid her purplish, big-knuckled hand on Francis's arm and looked up at him through watery eyes. "Thank you for coming, Father," she said in her rickety voice. "We needed you."

He smiled at her lovely, time-ravaged face and remembered suddenly that she used to give him flowers from her corner shop on Cleveland Street. It was a hundred years ago . . . and it was yesterday. "And I need you all," he answered simply.

Carefully holding her cup of morning coffee, Madelaine waved at the nurses as she made her way down the wide, linoleum-floored hallway. She turned in to her office, a small, box-shaped cubicle, decorated in the English country style. Bold floral drapes in shades of burgundy and green parenthesized the small window. Heavy mahogany bookcases, filled to overflowing with hardback and paperback books and mementos from grateful patients, lined one wall. Plants huddled on the windowsill, and photographs of Francis and Lina hung in beribboned groupings on the green-striped wallpaper. A nineteenth-century dining room table served as Madelaine's desk, its glossy surface dotted with photos of Francis and Lina.

She sat at her desk and began thumbing through the stack of papers there. Before she got halfway through it, someone knocked at the door.

She didn't look up. "Come in."

Dr. Allenford, the transplant team's cardiovascular surgeon, pushed through the door and strode into her small office. "I don't suppose you have another cup of coffee?" he asked as he sat down in the floral visitor's chair.

She shook her head. "Sorry."

He shoved a hand through his steel-gray hair and sighed. "Ah well, Rita's been after me to quit drinking so much."

Madelaine chuckled and waited for Allenford to get to business.

"We've got a new transplant patient."

Madelaine never tired of hearing those words. Suddenly she wasn't exhausted or depressed at all, she was itching to hear more. "Really?"

"Don't look so excited. He's a bad risk. Former drug user, world-class partier and woman chaser—if the media is to be believed—and he definitely has a bad attitude."

"Oh." Madelaine edged back in her seat and studied the man who had taught her most of what she currently knew about heart transplants. Allenford was one of the top doctors in his field, driven, ambitious, and gifted. If Chris said the patient was a bad risk, he knew what he was talking about.

"The situation is critical."

"Stats?"

"Thirty-four-year-old male. HIV-negative and cancer-free. End-stage cardiomyopathy. I ran routine bloods yesterday and everything looks good." Chris leaned forward, slid the thin manila folder across the desk. "But as I've said, he's got a bad attitude. One of those rich, famous Hollywood types who thinks the world owes him something."

Madelaine had had this discussion with Chris before. As always, Chris looked to the success rate of the hospital and the long-term viability of a candidate's chances before allocating the very precious resource of a heart. Madelaine didn't envy Chris the enormous responsibility of his job. Every time he chose someone to receive a heart, there were other patients who would most likely die because of that choice. One lived, one died; it was as simple as that. They couldn't afford to put a new heart in someone who wouldn't take care of it.

"I'll talk to him, Chris," she said.

He looked up at her, and in a single glance, they communicated perfectly. They both knew that she had just stepped in, shouldered some of his burden. *I'll tell you if he should have this chance.*

It was a choice no human being should ever have to make about another person, yet they did it every day.

"We're protecting his anonymity at all costs. Got him checked in under an alias. So tell your staff—I'll have their jobs if his identity or prognosis is leaked to the press."

"Understood."

"I'll contact the team and get them up to speed. Hilda will need to run the rest of the tests and get him educated quickly." He gave her a swift, meaningful look. "If this one doesn't get a heart in record time, he's in big trouble."

She nodded in understanding. "You want to meet for coffee this afternoon to discuss the particulars?"

"Sure. Four o'clock unless something blows up."

"Good." Smiling at him, Madelaine flipped open the folder on her desk and looked at her patient's name. *Angelo Dominick DeMarco*.

She slapped the folder closed, but not quickly enough. Memories surged to the front of her mind, so powerful, it was as if he were standing in front of her. She remembered Angel's loud, cackling laugh and the slight swagger of his walk, the way he drove his hand through his long, brownish-black hair. But most of all she remembered his eyes, malachite green, sunk beneath dark, slashing black brows that made him look dangerous. Until he smiled.

Even all these years later, she remembered the power of that smile. It was like the cliché—sunlight bursting through the clouds.

*Francis*. She thought of him suddenly, and knew that this would break his heart. His baby brother was sick . . . maybe dying . . . God, how would she tell him?

"Madelaine?" Chris's voice broke in.

She looked across the desk at him, trying to find the words, but all she had were memories, images, and a stark, sudden fear. "I can't take this patient, Chris."

"What?"

"Angel is Father Francis's brother."

"Ah. Your priest. Do you know Angelo?"

It took Madelaine a second to collect herself. "Yes. No. Not really." She shrugged. "I knew him a long time ago. When we were kids."

Chris's eyes narrowed. "When you were kids, huh? Have you kept in contact with him?"

"No."

"Hate him?"

Madelaine swallowed hard, thinking. "No," she said at last. "I don't hate him."

He smiled. "Love him?"

The question caught her off guard. In her mind she saw a dozen pictures of Angel as he'd once been, the laughing, dark-haired boy with the big dreams, the boy who'd stolen her heart and kissed her for the very first time. Then came the darker images, the memories that hurt. "No. I don't love him."

"Good." He pushed to his feet and rested his hands on her desk, giving her a meaningful look. "He needs you, Madelaine."

"Don't do this to me, Chris. Give him to someone else."

"No one else is as good as you, damn it, and you know it. This young man is going to die, Madelaine. You're his best hope. At least meet with him."

She stared at Allenford, knowing that she had no choice. She couldn't just let Angel die. "Okay, Chris."

He smiled. "Great." He turned, heading for the door. Just as he opened it, he turned back around. "I'll need your report today. If he's going to get a new heart, he needs to be placed on the UNOS list immediately. And remember, we have to handle his celebrity status with kid gloves. I won't have this hospital's reputation compromised."

"Right."

Allenford left her office, closed the door behind him.

Madelaine sat, still stunned, her glassy eyes trained on the door.

Angel DeMarco was back.

# chapter six

                    ❧

She stood outside Angel's door so long, it became noticeable. Finally footsteps came up behind her, a warm, bony hand pressed against her shoulder.

"You okay, Madelaine?"

She stiffened, forced her chin up, and drew her gaze away from the name on the door. "I'm fine, Hilda," she said, turning slowly to face the small, no-nonsense nurse who ran the transplant team like a drill sergeant.

Hilda beamed up at her, her birdlike head tilting suddenly to the right. "I was going to see our Mr. Jones. Shall I wait until you're done?"

"Yes. I'd like some time alone with him."

Hilda gave her a quick wink. "If the staff knew who he was, you'd be stampeded. Only Sarah, Karen, and I will be allowed in here. We'll handle the security."

Madelaine tried to dredge up a smile, she really tried. "Good."

"Hollywood types," Hilda said disapprovingly. "According to the *Enquirer*—and God knows they're reputable on such things—he drinks like a fish and screws anything with tits bigger'n his." With another pat on the shoulder, Hilda turned and scurried down the hallway, vanishing into her office.

Madelaine took a deep, steadying breath and marched into the lion's den.

He was sleeping. *Thank God.*

Quietly she closed the door shut behind her. Weak autumn sunlight shone through the small window, giving the room a respite from the cold impersonality of fluorescent lighting. The narrow, metal-framed bed cut the room in half.

He lay as motionless as death, the washed-out gray sheeting tucked haphazardly across his chest. Dark brown hair lay in a tangled heap against the white cotton of the pillow. His chiseled face looked sunken and too thin; his lips were pale. A stubbly growth of black beard shadowed his triangular jaw and darkened his upper lip.

Even so, he was so handsome he took her breath away.

She sank unsteadily to the chair. For a second she couldn't think about his illness or what was at stake here. All she could think about was the past and how much she'd loved this man.

He had swept her, laughing, into a whole new world. A world of lights and possibility and hope, a place where rules and responsibility didn't exist. She'd clung to him, giggling, believing, following wherever he led, so proud that hers was the hand he wanted to hold. She'd fallen in love with him in the wild, abandoned way that only teenagers could. Making excuses during the day to be together, sneaking from her father's austere house in the middle of the night. It was the first time she'd ever disobeyed her father, and it had made her feel recklessly confident.

With the distance of so many years, she knew that she'd never really fallen in love with him, not in the way that lasts. She'd been consumed by his brushfire passion, transformed by him.

There had been that night, under the old oak tree at Carrington Park. . . .

They'd been lying in the grass, staring up at the night sky, wishing on stars, sharing their dreams, holding each other. But she'd known it was time to go home. Her father would be getting back from his business trip.

She pulled away from him, staring down the long, darkened street. The thought of leaving him, returning to that cold house and her even colder father, made her feel almost sick with desperation. "I don't want to go back. . . ." She realized instantly that she'd said too much. She held her breath, waiting for Angel to call her silly or stupid or childish—all the words her father hurled at her with such regularity.

But he didn't. He touched her cheek, gently turned her face to his. "Don't. Stay with me. We could run away . . . raise a family . . . *be* a family . . ."

Madelaine had never known what it could feel like to love someone until that moment. The emotion swept through her, filling her soul with heat until, suddenly, she was laughing, and then she was crying. "I love you, Angel."

Ah . . . it had been so painfully sweet. . . .

He pulled her into his arms, held her so tightly, she couldn't breathe. Together they dropped to their knees in the spongy grass. She felt his hands on her, stroking her hair, her back, her hips. And then he was kissing her, tasting her tears, claiming her so completely with his mouth that she felt dizzy.

At last he drew back and stared down at her. There was an intensity in his eyes that stole her breath, made her heart beat wildly. "I love you, Madelaine. I don't . . . I mean, I've never . . ." Tears squeezed past his eyelashes and he started to wipe them away.

She stopped his hand. "Don't be afraid," she whispered.

He gave her a trembling smile. In that instant she understood so much about him, about the way he was. He went about swaggering and blustering and acting like the rebel, but on the inside he was just like her. Scared and confused and lonely. He didn't believe in himself, didn't think he was good, but he was—she believed in him enough for both of them. And he loved her like no one had ever loved her before. . . .

Such powerful, powerful words: *I love you. . . .*

After that, she'd told him everything, opened her heart and soul to him and let him become a part of her. Without him, she hadn't thought she could live.

What if he could do that to her again?

She forced herself to remember the other things, the other moments, letting the pain wash through her in a cold, cleansing sweep.

She'd thought she'd forgiven him for what he'd done to her—for leaving her without so much as a good-bye. Honestly, truly, she thought she had. Time and again she'd replayed the sequence of events in her head. She told herself she didn't blame Angel for running out on her. She told herself that seventeen was young, so young, and with each advancing year of her life, it felt younger still. She told herself it had been for the best, that they never would have made it, that they would have ruined each other's lives.

Yes, she'd told herself a lot of things, but now, in this second, staring down at him, she recognized the truth at last. They were lies, all of them lies. Pretty foil paper on a dark, ugly gift.

She hadn't forgiven him. How could she?

He'd killed a part of her that summer, a part he'd created and nurtured and claimed to love. A part she'd never gotten back.

Angel came awake slowly. For a single blissful second he didn't know where he was or what had happened to him. Then the muted sucking sound of machines drifted to his ears, the murmur of the heart monitor.

After his futile jailbreak attempt, Hilda the bird-woman and a marine-sized nurse had hooked his useless heart back up. The machine kept its clicking record, spitting out reams of paper.

He felt like hell. His chest ached, his head pounded, and the needles in his arms burned like spots of fire. He couldn't move without hurting somewhere. He could feel the telltale whirring of drugs in his bloodstream; he'd used narcotics too often in his life to be fooled.

He groaned, letting his head loll to the side. The smell of old cotton, green Jell-O, and boiled turkey filled his nostrils.

Lunchtime in cardiac hell.

He winced as the sunlight stabbed deep in his head. Blinking, he tried to wet his parched lips, and reached shakily for the Wedgwood-blue plastic pitcher labeled 264-W.

"I'll get that for you."

The voice washed over him. At first all he noticed was the soothing huskiness of it, the Debra Winger throatiness. It reminded him of something, some distant night in his past when he'd picked up a waitress in Tulsa, taken her home, and fu—

*Oh, Jesus.* That wasn't the right memory at all.

His idiotic heart lurched, rammed into his rib cage, and started to knock like an old engine on bad gas. The monitor beside him spat a sudden Gatling-gun clatter into the room. He couldn't breathe.

*Breathe deeply, you asshole. Calm down.* Slowly he tilted his chin. And saw her beside him.

God, after all these years . . .

She sat perfectly erect, her upper body camouflaged by a lab coat, with only the barest hint of a forest-green sweater visible beneath the wide white lapels. Her face was magnificently emotionless, her wide, silver-green eyes utterly blank. No smile lurked at the edges of her full, unpainted lips.

For a second, an image flashed through his mind of a heart-broken sixteen-year-old girl standing at a barred window, her pale, slim hand pressed to the glass, her cheeks streaked with tears, mouthing his name.

He'd fallen in love with a candy striper with long brown hair and laughing, mist-green eyes, but there was no remnant of that girl in the woman sitting beside him. She was regal in her bearing, in the well-styled precision of her short, honey-brown hair, in the classical perfection of her face. The perfect physician in complete control.

Strangely, it pissed him off that she'd done so well for herself. He ought to have been happy—hell, he ought to have been proud of her—but all he felt was cheated and angry. As if all his memories of her were an invention. This woman couldn't have been broken by his betrayal, couldn't have cared for long. And obviously Daddy's money had financed the best possible education.

"Angel," she said in that barmaid's voice he'd never quite been able to forget. "How . . . interesting to see you again."

"You've done all right for yourself, Mad," he said bitterly. More bitterly than he intended.

"Don't call me Mad." She gave him a completely professional smile and flipped open his charts. "They tell me you need a new heart."

"It shouldn't surprise you."

"It doesn't."

He could feel the judgment radiating from her. That was all he needed—another pair of accusing eyes, another person judging him by some invisible standard and finding him lacking. "Look, Mad, I think we'd both agree, I should have another doc."

"Yes, I do. Unfortunately, Allenford wants you to have the best."

"So do I, but—"

"I'm the best there is, Angel. You're lucky to have me." She brightened. "But if you don't want me, I'll have you transferred to someone else."

He felt a twinge of irritation. "You don't want me as your patient?"

"Not particularly."

"Then I want you," he said sharply, regretting it the minute he said it. But he'd wanted to rattle her cage, shake up this woman he ought to know intimately and yet didn't know at all.

She studied his chart. "Lucky me."

The harsh tone of her voice seemed absurdly out of character for the polished, picture-perfect woman beside him. He couldn't help himself, he laughed. "I guess little Mad has grown up."

She looked at him, hard. "Med school will do that to a girl." She turned her gaze from his face and studied the pile of charts on her lap. "You appear not to have changed at all, Angel."

"That's not true. I have to shave every day now."

She didn't crack a smile. "Your blood work looks good. Despite obvious alcohol abuse, all of your organs are functioning well. Now it's a waiting game. Hopefully we'll find a suitable donor in time. As you have probably been told, fewer than one percent of all accidental deaths make suitable donors. Brain death is extremely rare."

"So it's a waiting game," he said, feeling the anger rising. He told himself that she was his cardiologist—the person who held his life in her hands. But he couldn't seem to stop the anger. She was the last person on earth who would give him a fair shake.

"If you improve substantially, you may be able to live outside the hospital—of course, you're too sick to do that now."

He couldn't believe it. She sat there, talking to him as if he were a child, looking at him as if he were an insect. So damned doctorlike. As if she'd never known him before, never cared about him. He knew it was irrational to suddenly be furious, but he'd never been a real rational guy and he saw no reason to start. "No."

That surprised her. She actually looked up from the paperwork and turned to him. "No? No, what?"

"No, *Doctor* Hillyard, I'm not going to lie here like a pincushion and wait for what you euphemistically call a 'donor.'"

Slowly she set the charts down again. "Angel—"

"And call me Mr. DeMarco. You don't know shit about me, lady. I'm not about to sit around *hoping* some perfectly nice guy gets broadsided by an eighteen-wheeler. That is what we're talking about here, isn't it? Somebody dies and I get a chance to live?"

She was slow to answer. "Yes. That's what we're talking about, Angel. Donor organs come from a body that has been declared brain-dead."

He shivered at the thought. Some guy lying on a slab of metal, doctors greedily harvesting his organs. "Well, no, thanks."

She stared at him for another full half minute, saying nothing. Then, finally, she shrugged. "Die, then."

It shocked him, that response. At first it made him angry, then fear crept in, leaving a sour taste in his mouth. "So compassionate, Dr. Hillyard."

"Look, Angel, I can't waste time feeling compassion for a person with a death wish. You smoke, you drink, and there were traces of marijuana in your urine. All of this after two heart attacks." She leaned toward him, drilled him with a steely look. "You're going to die—and pretty soon if you don't make some very hard choices."

"You think I deserve it."

She drew back. For a heartbeat, she looked at him through the eyes he remembered. "I'd say *you* think you deserve it, and I think . . ."

"What?"

"I have no right to say anything. I don't know you at all, do I?"

"You did once."

"No." She said the word softly, but it seemed to echo in the stillness of the room. "I only thought I did once . . . but the boy I fell in love with promised to be with me forever." She laughed—a hard, brittle sound that was nothing like the laughter he remembered. "Forever turned out to be about ten seconds."

"I guess that's my cue to apologize."

She frowned. "I don't want your apology, Angel. I stopped wanting anything from you a long time ago. Now I'm just your doctor, and as such, I want you to live, but make no mistake about it, I'm not going to waste something as valuable as a heart on a bad-boy loser who isn't going to change his life."

"You've learned to play hardball, Mad."

"This is a hardball game, Angel. No cut corners, no fly-by-the-seat-of-your-pants. You're going to have to decide how badly you want to live. Only you can answer that."

He was angry that she could talk about this so matter-of-factly, angry that she didn't seem to care what he did, and angriest of all that he felt so goddamn alone. He wished for a crazy, desperate minute that he'd never abandoned or betrayed her. She was the only person he ever had really been able to talk to, the one person he could cry in front of. And he needed that intimacy right now, needed a friend.

Angel swallowed the thick lump in his throat. It was too late to be friends with Madelaine, too late for a lot of things.

He needed strength and faith and hope. None of which he'd ever had. He looked at her, saw the momentary flash of pity in her eyes, and he lost it. "You'll make me into a freak."

"It may feel that way, Angel, but it's not true. With a few adjustments, you can live a full, rich life. I have a patient down the hall who fathered two children and ran in the Seattle marathon after a heart transplant."

"I don't want to run a goddamned marathon." Horrifyingly, his voice broke. "I want my life back."

"I don't know what to tell you. Living with a transplant isn't easy. It requires a real commitment, some follow-through."

She stared at him, and he knew what she was thinking—that

he was a flaky asshole who'd never committed to anything or anyone in his life. "You have no right to judge me."

"You're right; unfortunately, I have to." She leaned toward him, and for a second, just a second, he thought she was going to touch him. "A new heart is a gift, Angel. Please, please don't get in line for one if you don't really want to change your life. Out there, somewhere, is a father who is dying from heart failure—a man to whom a new heart would mean another chance to hold his daughter, or spend another night with the wife he's loved for years."

The truth of her words made him feel sick. He *was* a selfish prick who didn't deserve this kind of chance. "Another party at the Viper's Nest doesn't cut it?"

"Not in my book."

He gave her a weak smile. "We never did have the same book, did we, Mad?"

"No."

He thought for a second about how different their backgrounds were—her, growing up in that mansion behind the iron gates; him, living in a shitty little trailer park on the wrong side of the tracks. No, they'd never had the same book at all. "So how is the great Alexander Hillyard these days?"

She stiffened. "He died a long time ago."

He immediately felt like an idiot. "Oh. Sorry."

"I'm going to look over your paperwork and initiate some more testing." She got to her feet suddenly. "Please don't humiliate me by killing yourself before we can save your life."

And then she was gone.

# chapter seven

Angel tried not to think about Madelaine. God knew there were plenty of other things to think about, but she wouldn't leave his mind.

He squeezed his eyes shut, battling memories with everything inside him. The problem was, there was so damned little inside him. That had always been his problem. Deep, deep inside, in the place where poets and metaphysicians and priests thought there should be a soul, Angel had nothing. Ever since he was a kid, he'd known there was something vital missing in him, a true sense of honor, of right and wrong, of goodness. He was selfish in a cold, ruthless way. For years he'd tried to refashion that insight, telling himself he was simply a product of crappy parents, or the sleazy little house he'd grown up in, or the food that wasn't on the table.

But Francis had grown up in that trailer, too, hadn't he? Gone to the same schools, listened to the same drunken lectures from parents who didn't really care, and everyone knew that Francis had no puncture in his soul. Hell, Francis had more soul than the saint he was named for.

There had only been one time in Angel's life when he thought maybe he was wrong about himself. Thought maybe he had a chance.

*That summer*. The memories of that time were set apart in his mind, a brief and shining Camelot amidst the seedy taverns and dark holes he'd lived in since. And like Camelot, it was probably wrought more of myth than fact.

Still, he remembered what it had felt like to have hope, however transitory. When he'd looked into Madelaine's eyes, felt the warm comfort of her small hand tucked into his, clung to her body in the wet sand beneath the piers, he'd told himself he'd found a sliver of goodness at last, something worth fighting for, worth living for.

But then he'd gone into that silent, sparkling house on the hill, and faced the dark night of his own soul. He'd looked into Alexander Hillyard's fathomless eyes, and seen the debilitating truth. They were the same, he and Alex. Ruthless, selfish, ugly to the bone.

Francis had known it, of course. *Don't do it, man. Don't just run away. Whatever it is, we can talk about it. Figure out what to do.*

Ah, Angel thought, rubbing his temples, exhaling tiredly. Francis was right. Francis was *always* right. That was one of the things that stuck in Angel's craw, one of the things that kept him always running, harder, faster, going nowhere like a gerbil stuck in Habitrail hell. He was constantly trying to outrun the ghost of good old Francis.

He'd thought success would do it, that finally he would come out the winner, but no. He couldn't even do that right. He was a world-famous actor and richer than God. He was also a boozing, drugging, lying slut of a human being. And he *liked* being that way. He wasn't even a good enough person to feel regret at the way he'd wasted his life, and he knew that given the chance, he'd screw it up again.

And Francis loved him—*had* loved him anyway; he probably didn't anymore—through it all. Through all Angel's drunken harangues, the belligerent tauntings, the cruel jokes Angel made at his brother's expense. Francis had always known that he was the favored child in the family, their mother's sole ticket to Heaven, and he'd always been ashamed of her unequal affection, apologizing so often. But Angel had never wanted to listen. It hurt too much to be the screw-up, the one brought home by the police, the loser. He'd put up a brave, obnoxious front, hoping no one would notice his inner torment and pain, his sense of worthlessness, but Francis had noticed, of course, noticed and understood and forgiven. Angel had seen the forgiveness time and again, felt its soothing warmth. Still he couldn't cross the bridge back to brotherhood, could never reach out his hand and smile and say *my brother,* the way he wanted to. Could never control his temper long enough to apologize.

And so he was alone.

Someone knocked on his door, and before he could answer, it opened.

Madelaine strode into the room, wearing a taut, false smile that made her eyes crinkle in the corners. He realized for the first time that she had no laugh lines around her mouth or eyes, and he wondered why that was.

She stared down at him. "I lied and reported that you were a good psychological risk for the transplant."

"Great. I'll just lie here and hope someone gets hit by a bus. Hey, try to get me an athlete's ticker, will you? I like my sex rough-and-tumble."

He said it to see if he could get even a second's worth of human emotion from those eyes, the eyes that once had stared at him as if he'd hung the stars.

She looked at him with disappointment. God, he'd seen that look a thousand times in his life. It was not the emotion he'd wanted, and it pissed him off. "Don't look at me that way."

"You're going to be here awhile, Angel. Francis is going to want to visit you." She handed him a scrap of paper. "Here's the phone number."

"No." The word shot out, surprising him with its ferocity. He knew instantly that he'd erred. He'd thrown his vulnerability on the floor between them. "I mean, I don't want any visitors. I'm a celebrity," he said, realizing too late that he was yelling. "I don't want anyone to know I'm here."

"He's your brother, Angel. Not a reporter." She moved closer. "Don't do this to him, Angel. He's not like you. He hurts easily."

*Not like you, Angel.* Christ, she didn't know him at all. Otherwise, she'd know Angel DeMarco's dirty little truth that he was the most easily hurt human being alive. "No shit. What are you, married to him or something?"

She sighed. "Get some sleep, Angel."

It rattled him, that unexpected avoidance. She hadn't answered his question, and the silence sent doubt flooding into him. What if she *had* married Francis? Or lived with him, or was his great and true love?

Angel had never even considered it. All these years he'd imagined Francis as the perfect parish priest, and Madelaine pining away for her lost first love. But Mad wasn't pining—didn't look as if she'd ever pined. Maybe he was as wrong about Francis as he'd been about her. Maybe his brother had quit the seminary and moved to suburbia, maybe he sold Cadillacs at the corner dealership. . . .

Not once in all these years had it occurred to Angel that he'd left a door wide open, and that Francis—Francis the good and perfect—might have walked right through it.

He shouldn't care.

But he did. Suddenly, irrationally, he did. He didn't want Madelaine to be his brother's wife, his brother's love. He wanted her the way she'd always been. A brilliantly colored photograph in the sepia-toned memories of his life. His and his alone.

She stared at him for a long moment, looking disappointed, then, very quietly, she said, "You can get as famous as God, and it doesn't change the facts." She leaned close, so close he could smell her perfume. "You'll always be Francis DeMarco's kid brother."

"I forbid you to tell him I'm here."

"Oh, Angel."

At that moment, in that tone of voice, she made his name sound like a curse.

Madelaine moved woodenly toward her desk. She sat down, her back ramrod-straight, then, very slowly, she sagged forward, plopped her elbows on the desk, and closed her eyes.

It had taken considerable self-control to appear cold and disinterested. Of course, discipline was the one thing she had in spades. She'd practiced it since her hair was in pigtails—lying, pretending. In that big house on the hill, appearances had been everything.

*Yes, Father, of course, Father. Certainly I will.*

She was a master of such deception, but she'd never quite been able to overcome the unpleasant side effects—the dry mouth, the clattering heart, the sweaty palms. Any time she had to stand up for herself, she was a wreck afterward.

She'd expected Angel to have changed more. World-famous now, rich and good-looking and successful, he should have been surrounded by friends. But no flowers or cards or phone calls had come for him. There was no woman waiting in the hallway, no friend hovering about his bed. Now, when push came to shove, he was utterly alone.

What did he have now? she wondered. Where did his joy come from? Drug use, free sex, a brawl or two at some seedy tavern, an Oscar nomination? She wondered if all photographs she'd seen of him over the years were lies—brittle smiles for a flashing camera.

In the old days she'd known his soul—or thought she had. He'd always been all bluster and anger on the outside, but inside, he hurt as badly as she did. She'd known always that he had a hole inside him, a deep secret place from which he bled. She knew it because she had the same hole in her own soul. In her it had been born of loneliness and fed by the hard realization that her father despised her. Over the years she'd covered it with a sheer, thin wall of glass that made her feel fragile and easily bruised, but it was some protection at least.

With Angel, who knew?

The phone on her desk rang, interrupting her thoughts. She reached for it and heard Hilda's voice. "It's Tom, Madelaine. He's coding."

"Shit!" Madelaines threw the papers down on her desk and ran for the door. As she raced down the hallway, she heard the alarm blaring through the paging system. *Code blue, ICU . . . code blue, ICU.*

She skidded into the room. White- and blue-clad people clustered around the bed, yelling at one another, reaching for things. Hilda was already there, hunched over Tom, her hands clasped and pressing on his chest. She saw Madelaine and flashed her a panicked look. "We're losing him."

"Get me the cart," Madelaine barked, shoving through the crowd to the bedside. The cart skidded to a stop beside her. "Intubate him," she said.

"Lidocaine's started," the staff nurse answered.

Madelaine's gaze shot to the monitor. "Shit," she hissed again. It wasn't working. "*Shit.* Defib."

Someone handed her the defibrillator paddles, ready to go. Hilda wrenched Tom's gown open, and Madelaine pressed the paddles over the ugly red scar that bisected his chest. "Clear!"

Electricity slammed through Tom's battered body. His back

arched off the table, then collapsed back down. All eyes went to the monitor. Flat line.

"Again," Madelaine said.

Once more Tom jerked off the table in an inhuman spasm. Madelaine's breath caught; she stared at the black box. A tiny *blip-blip-blip* came from the monitor; a pink line humped and waved and skidded across.

"We've got a pulse. . . . BP's eighty over fifty and rising. . . ."

Madelaine sighed in relief—a sound she heard echoed by everyone in the room.

"Too close for government work," Hilda said with a tired smile as she extubated Tom.

Madelaine didn't answer. One by one the staff left the room, talking among the themselves. Already the emergency was over and it was back to life as usual.

Hilda remained behind. She put a hand on Madelaine's shoulder. "He's been doing well up to this point. Handling meds well. Biopsy came back negative."

Madelaine nodded. She tried to smile, but it took too much effort. "Thanks, Hilda. I'll stay with him a minute."

Hilda bustled out of the room and closed the door behind her.

Madelaine leaned down and whispered in Tom's ear. "Keep fighting, Tom. Keep working hard. You're going to be fine." She knew that most members of the medical community didn't agree, but Madelaine believed in the power of the mind and spirit to heal the body. At least, she wanted it to be true.

Tom's eyes fluttered open. "Hiya, Doc," he said in a scratchy voice. "It feels like someone drove a monster truck over my chest."

She smiled down at him. "Guilty as charged. I hit a good man when he was down."

"You women libbers . . . you're all the same."

She laughed quietly. "Women libbers. Now there's a phrase I haven't heard in a while. You're dating yourself, Tom."

"Believe me . . ." He coughed and rubbed his throat. "In my position you're *proud* of getting older." Then he touched her hand, so gently that for a second she didn't even recognize what he'd done. "Stay for a while."

She saw the fear in Tom's eyes, the emotion he was trying so hard to hide beneath a shield of jokes and easy comebacks. "When will Susan be here?"

"After work. Not too much longer."

Madelaine picked up the phone and dialed the rectory. The housekeeper got Francis on the line.

"Hi, Francis," she said softly. "Could you pick Lina up from school?"

"You bet. You want me to take her out for dinner?"

"That would be great," she answered. "I'll be home in a few hours."

She hung up the phone, then reached backward and pulled up a chair. Sitting down, she leaned close to the bed. "Last night you were telling me about your daughter's riding lessons. . . ."

Francis stood beneath the old oak tree on Pacific Street. Pale sunlight streamed through the yellowing leaves, creating a tangle of gold on the grass.

The bell rang. Within moments kids spilled from the brick building, loping down the wide cement steps. In the center area they split into lines and fanned out, walking toward the row of buses that were parked in the driveway.

As he'd expected, Lina was among the last to exit. She was walking with that hard-core group of hers—they looked like a bunch of refugees from a Red Cross emergency station.

He stepped away from the tree waved at her. "Lina! Over here."

He knew the instant she saw him—she smiled instinctively, then copped an attitude. Murmuring her good-byes to the crowd, she hitched up her oversized jeans and ambled toward him, her chopped hair bouncing with each step, her backpack hanging limply from her left hand. The canvas fabric grated along the cement sidewalk as she headed his way.

He smiled at her. "Still hanging out with the honor roll, I see."

"Tsk, tsk—that's not a very Christian comment." She gave him an arch look. "Besides, some of them are perfect Catholic candidates . . . They dig the missionary position."

Francis could feel the heat crawling up his cheeks. He saw Lina's wicked grin and knew she saw his blush. "I miss the days when I could wash your mouth out with soap."

"You never did that."

"No, I missed my chance, and now it's too late."

"I'll rinse with tequila, how's that?"

He stopped suddenly and turned to her. "That's not funny." He knew he should say more, but things were going well—she didn't seem to be angry at him for siding with Madelaine on her birthday. He didn't want to rock the boat. *Coward*, he thought, cringing inwardly, but still he didn't say more. "What do you say we get something to eat and rent a movie?"

Lina sighed. "Mom tied up in the paperwork of sainthood again?"

He put an arm around her shoulder and drew her close. "You're acting like a snot-nose teenager."

"I *am* a teenager."

"I know, I know, but allow me my little fantasies. I like to remember you as you were . . . when you didn't wear combat boots and your favorite four-letter word was *mama*." He was laughing and so was she as they made their way down the sidewalk.

Beside his car, Lina stopped and looked up at him. "What was I like . . . you know, when I was a kid? Was I so different from her then?"

Francis heard the pain in her voice, the uncertainty. He led her toward a wooden bench at the corner and they sat down.

She huddled close to him, and suddenly she didn't look nearly so cocky. She looked like a thin young girl in big, ugly clothes—a child eagerly wanting to find a way to womanhood.

He drew her close. Together they leaned back into the bench and stared up at the crisp autumn sky. "I remember your first day of school like it was yesterday. You and your mom lived in that gross apartment building in the U District. Those were the days when she was doing her residency at the UW hospital and she was working around the clock. You spent your days in the pediatric wing—hanging with the post-op kids in the recreational therapy room. Your mom never slept. She worked and studied, and every spare second she was with you, reading to you, playing with you, loving you like I'd never seen anyone loved before."

"Fairy tales," Lina murmured. "She used to read me fairy tales."

"Even back then, you were a fiery, independent little thing. On the first day of kindergarten, your mom took the day off from work. She dressed and re-dressed you until you looked like a doll with your shiny black shoes and pink hair ribbons and your Sesame Street lunch box. It was set up that parents could ride the bus in with the kids on the first day—and Maddy was so excited. She'd never ridden a school bus before, and she couldn't wait.

"But when you got to the bus stop, you turned to her and said you wanted to ride all by yourself."

Lina frowned. "I don't remember that."

"Well, I do. Your mom almost burst into tears, but she wouldn't let you see how hurt she was. Instead, she let go of your little hand and let you get on that big bus all by yourself. You didn't even wave good-bye, just marched to an empty seat and sat down. When the doors shut, Maddy raced home, jumped in that junker of a car she had, and followed the bus to school. Crying all the way there and back." He turned to her, touched her cheek. "She was so proud of you . . . and so scared."

"I know she loves me," Lina said, staring off into the distance. "And I love her. It's just . . . hard sometimes. I feel like I don't really belong with her. It's like some alien accidentally left me behind."

He tightened his hold. "That's part of growing up. None of us know where we belong. We spend a lifetime trying to find out."

"Easy for you to say. You love Mom and me, but you belong to God."

He found himself unable to answer her. But he wished—Lord, how he wished—that it seemed as simple to him. "Yes," he said slowly. "That pretty much sums up my life."

"Did you know Mom promised to contact my dad?"

For a second, Francis couldn't draw a decent breath. Finally he answered, "No, I didn't know that."

Lina flashed him a grin. "Yeah. I'm sorta nervous, but mostly I'm excited. Pretty soon I'll get to meet him."

Francis felt the fear returning, and on the heels of it came the shame. God forgive him, he didn't want Lina to know her father. "Well," he said at last. "What do you say we go get some pizza?"

"You're going to offer *pizza* to a cardiologist's kid?"

He laughed and it felt good, as if for a second everything in his world was normal. "I won't tell if you won't."

Long after she'd left him alone in his room, long after the nurses had finished poking and prodding him, long after Hilda had fired off her litany of rules for the soon-to-be-eviscerated, Angel still couldn't sleep. He'd asked for more drugs to help him sleep and been denied, so he lay there, wide awake.

Thinking was the last thing he wanted to do in this godforsaken place. But he couldn't force the images from his mind. *Francis and Madelaine humping wildly in a four-poster bed, twelve kids asleep in the bedroom next door. A white picket fence around a sparkling clean jungle gym.*

He closed his eyes and knew instantly that it was a mistake. The memory came to him, sharp and clear and in heartbreaking focus. . . .

It had been daylight, a sunny summer day, and Angel had been confined to a hospital bed. Francis was beside him, talking. But Angel was seventeen and too angry to listen—angry that he was sick, angry at the stupid doctors who told him he'd have to *change his life*, that he could *die* if he didn't take care of himself. He didn't know what the hell myocarditis was—and he didn't give a damn. All he knew was that he felt too good to be hospitalized. He didn't want to be trapped in a bed his mother wasted no time in telling him they couldn't afford.

The summer stretched out before him, long and boring, and the diagnosis—*viral infection affecting the heart*—battered him. The stupid doctors kept telling him he could die if he wasn't careful, that he had to quit smoking and drinking, but he felt perfectly healthy. There was nothing wrong with his heart.

The hospital door opened, but Angel didn't bother to move. He was too busy feeling sorry for himself. Francis leaned close, whispered an awestruck, "Jeez."

For a second Angel hadn't known what his brother was talking about. Then he turned his head and saw her. A thin wisp of a girl—candy striper volunteer—standing in the doorway, her eyes wide and unblinking, her teeth nipping ever so softly at her full bottom lip. She had pale ivory skin and dark eyebrows that looked like they'd been slashed on with a marking pen. She was clutching a pile of *Heartbeat* and *Tiger Beat* magazines to her chest.

Angel had thought she was pretty enough, in a bland, private schoolgirl sort of way, but then he'd seen her reflected in his brother's clear blue eyes, and suddenly she'd become more, so much more. The first girl Francis had ever looked at twice.

"Jeez Louise," Francis whispered again.

Angel made his move without even thinking about it. He flashed the quiet candy striper his trademark grin, the one he'd used mercilessly on the girls in his low-rent neighborhood. He knew he was good-looking—a tanned, dark-haired Italian-Irish kid with rebellion in his green eyes.

She smiled back, slowly at first, and then more broadly. The smile transformed her features, tilted the corners of her eyes, and made her look exotic and Gypsy-like. Waves of light brown hair, streaked in places to the color of sand, shimmered in the artificial light.

"I wouldn't mind some company," Angel said.

Her eyes widened, and he saw for the first time that they were a soft silver-green. "You wouldn't?"

Francis sighed—a deep, tired sound of defeat, then scooted back in his chair and got to his feet, a tall awkward blond kid, looking at her like a puppy dog, begging her silently to see him.

Angel felt a stab of regret, but it was too late to remedy what he'd done, and he didn't want to anyway. It was the first time in his life he'd gotten something Francis wanted, and it felt good.

The girl—he'd learned later that her name was Madelaine Hillyard—looked up at Francis as he left the room, gave him a pretty white smile, and whispered good-bye. She hadn't looked at Francis again, not then and not in the magical months that followed. Months that changed all their lives.

At first, Angel had wanted Madelaine because Francis wanted her; plain, unvarnished selfishness, made all the more ignoble and painful because of what was to follow.

Quite simply, Angel fell in love with her. Head, heart, body and soul, he fell in love for the first—perhaps the only—time in his life. The quite, unassuming teenager with the huge, haunting eyes had become his world for a brief, heart-wrenching summer. She saw something in him that no one had ever seen before—she *believed* in him—and when he held her in his arms he almost learned to believe in himself. But not enough; he hadn't believed in himself enough. . . .

And though he'd left her, he'd never been able to exorcise her from his soul. That was the tragedy in all of it. He'd abandoned her, broken all of their hearts, and for what? For a life spent drifting aimlessly from seedy bar to seedier hotel room, telling and retelling the same tired stories to dozens of overly made-up eyes, whispering the same worn lines against a hundred pairs of lips. But never the right lips, never the right words.

And here he was again, back in the hospital.

Only this time, maybe Francis had come out the winner, maybe it was Francis who slept with Madelaine now, Francis who sucked her pale, pink nipples and kissed her full lips.

He winced.

Jealousy sluiced through him, twisting his stomach, making him suddenly angry.

He didn't want Francis to have Madelaine.

"Christ," he whispered, wishing that it were a prayer and knowing that it was too late for that. It had always been too late.

# chapter eight

❧

Madelaine sat at the edge of the couch, her bare feet pressed together, her cold hands locked in her lap. It was Saturday morning, and she'd gotten up early to fix a good, healthy breakfast. She'd dressed carefully in baggy sweats and an oversized T-shirt. She looked as casual as she knew how.

But inside, she felt jittery and afraid.

*I promise I'll contact your father. . . .*

She heard the toilet flush down the hall and she jumped to her feet. Scrambling into the kitchen, she whisked out the cutting board and started busily cutting carrots.

It wasn't until she'd peeled and cut three of them that she realized she didn't need carrots for breakfast.

She pushed the vegetables aside and stared at the closed door. Her anxiety hitched up a notch. What if she couldn't pull it off—what if she couldn't lie well enough to protect her daughter?

The bathroom knob turned, the door swung open. Lina stood

in the doorway, wearing a tight-fitting ribbed sweater and a pair of pants that an NFL linebacker couldn't have filled out. The crotch hung between her knees, and the frayed, cut-off hem dragged on the floor.

"Hey, Mom," she said, slamming the door shut with an army-booted foot. Dragging a backpack, she headed down the hall toward the living room. "I'm going to the mall."

Madelaine's throat went dry. "Wait until you eat something."

Lina stopped dead. "You're *cooking*?"

"I-I am. Ham and cheese omelet and toast."

"Made with fake eggs and turkey ham? Yum, yum."

"You used to love turkey ham."

Lina rolled her eyes. "Get real, Mom. I was too young to know the difference."

"Well . . . you can eat the toast."

Lina tossed her backpack on the couch and shrugged. "Whatever." She started to head back into her bedroom.

Madelaine wanted to breathe a sigh of relief and let Lina go, but she refused to give in so easily. It was exactly that kind of cowardice that had broken their relationship—it would take a little bravery to bring it back.

*Rules. She reacts well to discipline.*

"I'd like you to set the table," she called out to her daughter's back.

Lina slowly turned around. "You want me to *what*?"

Madelaine wet her lips. "Set the table."

Lina eyed her. Ramming her hands in her baggy pockets, she crossed the room. "Mom?"

Madelaine forced herself to stand still for the scrutiny. "Yes?"

"Did we move to Stepford?"

Madelaine burst out laughing. "Go on, set the table."

Lina didn't move, just stood there, staring. Finally Madelaine couldn't help herself, she started to squirm. It was a mistake to try to pretend to be a family, to pretend that a little thing like

Saturday brunch could fix what was wrong between her and Lina.

"Did you call my dad yesterday?"

Madelaine flinched. There it was, the question she'd wanted to avoid, thrown down on the table like a gauntlet. *"Father,"* she snapped. She cleared her throat and tried to sound more rational. "He's your father. A dad is . . . different."

"Yeah, whatever. Did you call him?"

Madelaine's gaze fell. She stared down at the carrots, little bits of orange against the jade-green tile counter.

"Mom?"

Madelaine forced herself to meet her daughter's suspicious eyes. She tried to smile, tried and failed. A tiny headache pricked behind her eyes. "What?"

"Did you call him?"

"Did I *call* him?"

Lina bit nervously on her lower lip. "Don't do this to me, Mom." Her voice broke, and for a second Madelaine saw her daughter's stark, painful desperation.

It was more than *who is he*? It was *who am I*?

She set the knife down and walked around the edge of the counter. Looking steadily at Lina, she forced herself to reach out. Lina stared at her mother's hand, then her gaze lifted and their eyes locked.

Madelaine felt a rush of emotion in that single heartbeat. It had been so long since they'd looked at each other, really looked at each other. They'd spent months looking past, around, beyond.

Her eyes pleaded with Lina for a chance. She tried to answer, but found that she couldn't.

"You didn't contact him," Lina said dully. "Why?"

Madelaine maintained eye contact for as long as she could, until her guilt became a strangling hand around her throat. "I had such a busy day. This new patient is really—"

Lina lurched to her feet. She started laughing—or was it crying? Madelaine couldn't tell until Lina turned around, and she saw that her daughter was laughing through her tears. "Priceless, Mom. You were too *busy* to call my dad." She grabbed her backpack and slung it over her shoulder. Sniffing hard, she ran for the front door and wrenched it open. At the last second she stopped and turned back around, giving Madelaine a look that was drenched in hurt. "I don't know why I believed you."

Then she ran.

Francis leaned back in his chair and closed his eyes. Later, he had to go see Ilya Fiorelli, but he didn't want to think about that yet. And so he sat quietly, listening to *Phantom of the Opera*.

Music filled the rectory's common room, pulsed and pounded and then fell silent again. Slowly the next song started. "Music of the Night."

He sighed in anticipation. The music began leisurely, deftly, rolling in around him, drawing him into the world of the phantom. A lonely place, that world, filled with heartache and longing and unrequited love.

He remembered—as he always did—the first time he'd heard this music. He and Madelaine had gone to the theater together. Sitting beside her, feeling her presence, seeing the sparkle of the floodlights reflected in her eyes, he'd felt close to Heaven.

*Let your fantasies unwind in this darkness which you know you cannot fight. . . .*

Francis sang the words loudly, pretending for a second that he had talent. That he had a lot of things. The music built again, swirling, gathering power. High, pure notes as quivering and sweet as the song of a bird perched in the air, then they dove and tangled and became melancholy.

And the sadness came, as it always did, twisted in the midst of the glorious chords. Francis understood the pain in the phantom's song, the agony of living in the shadow of the woman you loved.

*Ah, Madelaine*, he thought with another sigh.

"Francis?"

He jerked upright, blinking at the sudden glare of sunlight that spilled through the rectory's open front door.

Lina stood in the doorway, backlit by the morning's golden glow. She looked impossibly young and fragile, dwarfed in her baggy pants and army jacket. But it was her eyes that drew his attention, made him frown in sudden concern.

He kicked down the La-Z-Boy's velour footrest and shot to his feet. "Lina, honey, what is it?"

She didn't answer.

"Lina?" He moved closer, and as he approached, he saw the little things the sunlight had blurred. The way she stood, hooked to one side, half in and half out of his doorway, the swollen redness of her eyes, the cheeks stained blue-black by mascara and tears.

And he knew. Lord help him, he knew why she was here, looking broken and lost. Madelaine had told her the truth.

*Oh, Lord* . . . He felt almost sick to his stomach at the thought. Unsteadily he flicked off the stereo and moved toward her.

And still she stood in the doorway, motionless. Pale, so pale, her bloodshot eyes filled with sadness. He remembered a hundred other visits. Times she'd come to him, laughing, bounding through his door, launching herself into his waiting arms.

"I didn't know where else to go," she said, biting her thumbnail, watching him through those sad, sad eyes.

He reached out for her and she seized his hand, squeezed hard. He saw glimmer of fresh tears glaze her eyes.

He shut the door and led her to the brown and gold sofa. Sitting beside her, he slipped an arm around her shoulders and drew her close. She pressed her cheek against his chest. He felt her shuddering, indrawn breaths. "Shh," he murmured.

He wanted to make everything better for her, the way he'd done a thousand times in her life.

She drew back suddenly, sucked in a rattling breath, and stared up at him. "Muh-Mom didn't call my father. She puh-promised, and then she didn't call him."

For a split second, all Francis felt was relief.

Tears squeezed past her lashes, fell one after another in a muddy smear down her pale cheeks. "I don't know why I believed she would."

"He walked out on you guys. Maybe it's best if you don't think about him."

"Tell me who he is," she asked quietly.

There would be no going back from this moment on; he knew it. Fear tightened in a band around his chest. Defeat rounded his shoulders, slipped from his mouth in a ragged sigh. He plucked a single tear from her cheek. "Oh, Lina-ballerina . . ."

"Don't do this to me, Francis, not you, too."

He felt shame welling up, spilling through him. "I can't tell you his name."

"Can't?" The word was a whisper of breath. "Or won't?"

"Lina—"

"Don't." She stared at him, and he saw, in that instant that felt like an eternity, he saw that she hated him. It hurt. Sweet Jesus above, it hurt.

"I used to watch *The Brady Bunch* reruns when I was a kid." She bit her lip and looked past him. It was a long, long time before she spoke again. "It used to make me cry. That silly, stupid sitcom used to make me cry."

Francis understood. Even as a child, she'd wanted that sense of family, of belonging. But he and Madelaine hadn't given it to her. They'd wanted to protect her with their silence, but it had only hurt her more. "I'm sorry, Lina."

She gave a bitter, trilling laugh. "Yeah, well, so am I." She got to her feet and snagged her backpack. Slinging it over her shoulder, she pushed past him and headed for the door.

He lurched to his feet. "Lina, wait—" He knew it wasn't the right thing to say, that there was no right thing left, and the words echoed in the room and fell into a frightening silence.

She gave him a hard, cold look. "What for?"

He moved toward her. She didn't move, just stood there, staring at him through those hurt blue eyes. Gently he took her face in his hands, brushed the tears away with his thumbs. "I love you, Lina. Always remember that."

"Yeah, sure you do." Her voice broke. "You and Mom both love me. But neither of you will tell me the truth."

Lina screeched to a stop in front of Savemore Drugs. The store stared silently back at her; its big, sprawling, well-lit face invited her in. She tossed her bike into the bushes.

Excitement pushed past the anger and heartbreak. She needed that excitement now, needed another emotion to sweep her up, embrace her. She swiped at her eyes, trying to erase the last of the useless tears. With the touch, she knew she had no mascara left on her eyelashes, knew it was all on her cheeks in a caked, blue-black smear. Probably all that was left of her "Oregon cherry" blusher was two streaks of war paint on either side of the blurred mascara.

Yeah, she had to look hot.

Sniffing, Lina jerked her chin up and narrowed her eyes. Just let someone say something. In fact, the way she was feeling, she wished they would.

*She didn't even care enough to call him. A lousy seven numbers, fifteen minutes out of her day . . .*

And Francis, the closest thing to a dad she'd ever known, betraying her. *I can't tell you his name.*

Lina felt the horrifying sting of fresh tears and she spun away from the store. Stumbling sideways, she slipped behind a holly tree and sat down on a pile of wooden pallets. Curling forward, she pressed her damp face into her knees and cried.

Her mother knew how important this was to her. She had to know. And yet, she was *too busy* to make a phone call.

Lina had always bent over backward to accommodate her mother's schedule. She was proud of her mother's job—it was way cooler than anyone else's mom. Lina had put up with all of the missed dates, the lonely nights, the rushed family meals. But enough was enough; she couldn't put up with any more.

She reached into her book bag and pulled out a Cover Girl compact. Flipping it open, she started at the small reflection of herself. Electric blue eyes, slashing black eyebrows, small, bow-shaped lips.

"Who are you?" she whispered to the girl in the glass. And who was he—this father who had left his mark on her face, her thoughts, her personality, and then moved on? He was the answer to it all. The loudness, the dissatisfaction, the anger—they were all personality traits that must have come from him, must be his living legacy.

She kept remembering her question. *Am I like him?*

And her mother's sad, reminiscing smile, the one that excluded Lina from her birthright, from the memories that should have belonged to her. *You're exactly like him.*

Her fantasies spun out again, capturing her in a silken web. They were *alike*, she and her daddy—her mom had said so. She was *like* her father. They would be more than just father/daughter. They would best friends. Her father wouldn't lie to her or discipline her. He wouldn't work all hours and come home tired or care if her homework wasn't done on time.

She didn't know how long she sat there, dreaming about him. Long enough for her tears to dry, for her bleeding sadness to harden into anger. Her mother had no right to keep this information from her. Not this.

Tired, depressed, she got to her feet and emerged from the bushes.

There was the store. She thought about turning away, just going home to think, but the store was so close.

She *needed* the jolt of adrenaline that came from outsmarting everyone. With a quick look in both directions, she repositioned her backpack over one shoulder and headed toward the store, down the wide, azalea-lined cement walkway.

Twin glass doors whooshed open in an electronic greeting. She slipped into the bright lights of the superdrugstore, feeling glaringly noticeable. A punk kid in ratty clothes in yuppie Heaven.

She grinned, knowing they were watching her, cataloging her, making a note of her for their detectives. She followed her own routine. First thing she did was buy a newspaper—it looked good to spend money right off the bat. She put two quarters in the slot and eased the front plate open, grabbing the newest edition of the small community newspaper. Tucking it under one arm, she strolled down the main aisle, then she turned off, glided down the makeup aisle. She touched everything that interested her, weighing it, feeling how it fit in her palm. Looking.

She touched a dozen things, putting each one back in its proper place.

Then she saw it, touched it, and her heart sped up. Excitement brought a quick, furtive smile.

A thin tube of Lash Intensifier in a clear plastic package.

Lina glanced around, saw no one. Her heart sped up even more, started thundering in her chest. A damp, itchy sweat broke out on her palms. The first, niggling sense of fear crept in, muttered that she couldn't do it, that she wasn't good enough.

Then came the other emotions—the cocky self-confidence she could only find in the overlit aisle of a drugstore, the pulse-pounding jolt of adrenaline.

*Can you do it, can you?*

She walked around for a while, just casually holding the mascara. Her fingers were so slick with sweat, she had to change hands three or four times. Once or twice she pretended to replace the mascara on the shelves—once with the deodorants, once with the aspirins.

In the toothpaste aisle she made her move.

She slipped the makeup in her pocket and yanked her hand back out.

It was done.

Breathing hard, heart pounding, she forced herself to keep moving casually down the store. She paused in front of the videos, flipped through a few horror books. The magazines captured her interest, so she stood there, leafing through the current issue of *Rolling Stone*.

Then, very calmly, she walked down the aisle, past the checkout counter toward the door. With a quick sideways glance, she saw that she was alone, and a grin broke across her face as the automatic doors whooshed open.

At the last second, a hand grabbed her shoulder and squeezed hard. A loud male voice said, "Just a minute, miss."

# chapter nine

❦

Francis walked slowly along the cracked stone path that led to the Fiorellis' modest white home. He couldn't help noticing the weeds and grass that furred the walkway and crept stubbornly through the autumn flowers.

Last summer this garden had been elegant and tended; now it ran wild, the rosebushes clinging to their dead and dying blossoms, the ground stained with multicolored petals, their edges curled and brown and split.

He reached the front door and paused. A small overhang blocked the midday sun from his eyes and cast him in the welcoming cool of shadow. In a niche on the right side of the door stood an old, weathered statue of Christ, His mildew-stained palms outstretched in greeting.

For a second, Francis was reluctant to go in. He felt the statue's painted eyes on him, silently condemning his cowardice. The Fiorellis had been friends for as long as he could remember.

Back when he and Angel were kids, they had played in this yard, thrown a thousand baseballs back and forth with the Fiorellis' grandsons.

But those days were gone, and he was back for another reason. He took a long, last breath of the rose-scented air and finally knocked.

There was a rustle of sound from within, and then the plain white door swung open, revealing a thin, stoop-shouldered old man in the entryway. His creased face split in a wide, toothy grin. "Hello, Father Francis. Come in, come in." The old man stepped aside.

Francis plunged into the cool, dark interior. The first thing he noticed was the smell—the vague, musty scent of a house in disrepair, a house in which the roof needed tending as badly as the rose garden. The tiny entry gave way immediately to a small, oval front room, defined on three sides by once-elegant plaster arches. Dozens of family pictures hung, cockeyed and dusty, from sagging nails, school photographs of children who now had children of their own. An old RCA television was tucked in the corner, its sound a dull, muted hush in the otherwise silent room.

Just last year, a beautiful Victorian settee and table had graced this room; they were gone now. In their place a hospital bed stood stark and threatening in the tiny space. A wheelchair huddled in the corner, waiting for use.

Ah, but even the time for that had passed.

Francis felt it again, the reluctance to intrude on their grief. "Hello." It was all he could say past the lump in his throat.

The old man looked up, his face pinched and pale. For a split second Francis remembered the man who'd once lived behind those dark eyes. He used to laugh all the time, even had difficulty keeping a smile off his face when he took Communion. And he'd always had a joke for Francis in the confessional, a "sin" that could be counted on to cause a young priest to grin behind the safety of the wooden shield. *Bless me, Father, for I put tuna in the chicken salad.*

"Can I get you something to drink, Father?" Mr. Fiorelli asked in a respectful voice. No smile now.

Francis shook his head, pressing a comforting hand on the man's shoulder, noticing how rail-thin he'd become. "No, thanks, Edward. How is she today?"

Edward looked up again, and in the pale light his face seemed to cave in on itself, collapse in a morass of folds. "Not good."

Francis came up to the side of the bed and sat down on the creaky wooden stool, scooting close. His knees hit the metal frame with a dull clang.

The woman in the bed, Ilya Fiorelli, blinked slowly awake. At the sight of him, she smiled. "Father Francis."

Edward moved to the other side of the bed and sat down, curling his age-spotted, big-knuckled hand around his wife's.

"I knew you would come today," she whispered, starting to say more, but then a rattling, phlegmy cough shuddered through her chest.

Francis stared down at the pale, withered old woman. Her white hair, brushed and combed to salon perfection, curled against the grayed pillow like wisps of goose down. He took hold of her other hand, so slim and fragile, and squeezed gently.

Dull, watery blue eyes blinked at him, the corners tucked into folds of wrinkled flesh. Even now, in the last, pain-riddled days of her life, she exuded a calm gentleness that touched his heart.

"Bless me, Father, for I have sinned."

She spoke so softly, he had to lean forward to hear the words.

"It has been two weeks since my last confession. I accuse myself of—"

Francis squeezed his eyes shut and swallowed the lump that lodged like old dust in his throat. *When was the last time you truly sinned, Ilya? When?*

How could a benevolent God heap such misery on a woman

like this? A loving, caring woman who'd never harmed a soul. All her life she'd helped people, and now here she lay, cancer eating through her bones, hopelessness spreading like a virus through her blood.

And what of Edward, her husband of fifty-seven years? What would he do after her death, how would he go on in this home that she had created for them?

"Edward," she said softly, "get Father Francis a cup of tea."

Edward let go of his wife's hand and left the bedside, disappearing into the kitchen.

She waited for the quiet click of the kitchen door before she spoke. "Father . . ." She paused, drew in a deep, shaking breath, her hand curling within his grasp into a tight fist. "I am afraid for him, Father. The look in his eyes lately . . . He isn't ready for me to die."

Francis touched her face, gently stroked the velvety wrinkles. "I'll help him, Ilya. I'll be here for him."

"I can't stay much longer. The pain . . ." Tears slid down her temples. She squeezed his hand. "Take care of him, Father. Please . . ."

Francis brushed the moist trail from her skin and tried to smile. "God will watch out for Edward, and He is infinitely more capable than I. God always has a—"

*Plan.*

He couldn't finish. He'd said the same thing a million times, but now he couldn't speak. He needed to say something that mattered, something that would ease this gentle woman's pain, and there was nothing. Nothing.

"Of course He has a plan," she whispered, making it painfully easy on him. "It's just . . . my Edward . . ."

Tears blurred Francis's vision. He tried to think of something meaningful to say, but in the end, he found nothing, so he lapsed into the ordinary, the rote, absolving her of her sins—although he knew there were none, not really—and blessing her soul for the thousandth time.

"Thank you, Father."

He stared into Ilya's blue eyes, seeing the sharpness of life in all its wondrous, pain-filled beauty reflected in her gaze. He saw all the things he'd denied himself, all the roads he hadn't taken. And suddenly he was thinking things he shouldn't. . . .

For thirty-five years Francis had slept alone, crawled into his narrow wooden bed on sheets that smelled of his own after-shave. Just once, he wanted to sleep on pillows that smelled of perfume.

It used to be enough to watch the world go by, loving other people's children, talking to other men's wives. But now, sitting here beside Mrs. Fiorelli, holding her withered hand, he knew how much he'd given up. He could baptize a million children, and not one of them would ever call him daddy.

He'd been a bystander to life. He still loved God, but some-times, in the middle of a cold, dark night, he positively *ached* for human contact. For Madelaine. A hundred times in the past few years, he'd hauled himself out of bed, kneeled on the hard floor, and prayed for guidance and strength.

Courage. That's what he needed, for Mrs. Fiorelli right now, and for himself. It was what he'd needed all his life and never really had. Angel had gotten all the courage in their family, and Francis had gotten all the faith.

If he'd had courage, just a little bit of it a long time ago, maybe he would have made different choices, taken a different turn.

But he'd taken the easy road many years ago. Back when Madelaine was pregnant and alone, Francis had offered to marry her. Only, he hadn't wanted to marry her, not really, and she'd known that, just as she'd always known everything about him. She knew that his love for God was the defining passion of his life and always would be.

*No, Francis,* she'd said quietly, crying. *Be my best friend, be my baby's best friend. Please . . .*

And they'd never spoken of it again.

There were so many things they'd never spoken of. . . .

He closed his eyes and prayed aloud, as much for himself as for Ilya. "I believe in God, the Father Almighty, Creator of heaven and earth; I believe in Jesus Christ, His only Son, our Lord." The words spilled through his mind like water from a bucket, one after another, soothing, cleansing, and he lost himself in them.

Ilya's voice joined his. "I believe in the Holy Spirit, the holy Catholic church, the communion of saints, the forgiveness of sins, the resurrection of the body, and life everlasting. Amen."

*The forgiveness of sins.*

The shame came back, left Francis no place to hide. He should have encouraged Madelaine to tell Lina the truth about her father, or *he* should have told Lina the truth.

He knew there could be no true forgiveness until he made things right.

"Father?" Mrs. Fiorelli's voice jerked him back to the present.

He shook the thoughts away and smiled down at the old woman. "I'm sorry, Mrs. Fiorelli."

"You looked sad for a second, Father," Ilya said. "What could a handsome young priest like yourself have to be sad about?"

He should lie to her, should don the mantle of distant perfection that was required of him, but he had no stomach for it. "Regrets, maybe," he answered quietly.

She reached out a withered, shaking hand and touched his chin in a flitting gesture of affection. "Take it from me, Father. Life is over quickly, and you only regret what you didn't do."

"Sometimes it's too late."

"Never," she breathed. "It's never too late."


Angel lay in his uncomfortable hospital bed, staring up at the acoustical tile ceiling.

God, he felt bad. Worse than bad. He hurt almost everywhere, and in the few places he didn't hurt, he was weak. Breathing had become a painful, unsatisfying chore. His fingers had started to turn cold. At first he'd thought it was nothing, then his toes had become blue.

*Diminishing blood circulation.*

Those were the words the nurses used, but Angel could hear past the words to the meaning. It was ending. His life was leaking away. Even yesterday he'd been ready to fight for it, but today he was too tired.

He wondered what he had to live for, and even as he had the thought it pissed him off. He'd lived a life that left no real mark, had no real meaning. He saw that now, saw it with a clarity he should have possessed all along.

Yesterday he'd been visited by the man in the room next door. Tom Grant.

"It's damned terrifying," Tom had said. Just like that, he'd thrown the fear and uncertainty on the bed between them, as if it were nothing to be ashamed of, as if a man didn't have to be strong.

Angel had been his asshole self at first. He hadn't wanted to see himself reflected in Tom Grant's eyes, hadn't wanted to admit he was as sick as Tom. "Ah," he'd said meanly, "so you're the heart transplant patient twice removed."

Tom had laughed, weakly.

It was the laughter that defused Angel's anger, and the honesty that pierced his armor.

"The worst part," Tom said, "is waiting for a donor. It makes you feel ghoulish and sick and perverted. And damned."

Angel had finally looked at the man, his puffy, medicated face, his flimsy hospital gown that covered a multitude of bloody, oozing, intubated atrocities, his tired, tired eyes, and felt as if he were looking into the future.

To his horror, Angel found himself starting to cry. He couldn't remember when he'd been so humiliated. "Christ," he muttered, wiping his face with his sleeve.

"I've cried more tears than a baby. Don't worry about it." Tom leaned close. "You gotta focus on how much better you're going to feel when it's over. I know it's scary to think about, but once it's over, it's like . . . a gift."

Angel sighed, wishing he could have such simple faith. "It isn't going to happen for me, man. God isn't going to give me another chance." He forced a cocky smile. "I can't even blame the Old Man. I've been pretty much of an asshole."

"Don't do that to yourself," Tom said. "Don't make this about morality or goodness or redemption. It's about medicine. Pure and simple. Good people are murdered as often as bad people. And everyone deserves a second chance."

Angel wanted to believe it, but it was too late in life to change that radically. He was selfish and reactionary. He had the devil's own temper and he always had. And becoming famous had made it even worse.

He'd accepted the truth about himself a long time ago—he sure as hell wasn't going to change now. What was the point?

He was dying. He understood that now, and after Tom left, Angel had lain there, waiting for his next breath, and the next, and the next, waiting for each feeble beat of his heart. A surge of loneliness had come over him then, settling deep and heavy in his ragged heart. He'd wanted someone—anyone—to sit with him, hold his hand, and tell him it was all right.

*He's not like you, Angel. He hurts easily.*

Her words had come back to him, stinging his conscience. He'd only ever loved two people in his life—Francis and Madelaine—and he'd hurt both of them.

The crazy part was, he'd never really meant to, never wanted to, at least. Suddenly he was thinking of the past, of the times his big brother—no more than eight years old himself—had hidden Angel from their drunken mother, the times Francis had tried futilely to turn her wrath on himself instead . . . times they'd sat in that old weedy lot beside the trailer park and spun their shaky dreams together.

How had he forgotten all that—how had he walked away from it?

Slowly he reached out and picked up the phone, dialing the number Madelaine had left him. An answering machine picked up on the third ring.

Angel left a message and hung up.

Angel was more than half asleep when he heard his door open. Quiet footsteps moved into the room.

Ah, he thought with relief, Attila the Nurse with his fix.

He opened his eyes and saw a tall man standing in the door. He had wheat-blond hair and pale skin and blue eyes, and he was wearing a gray UW sweatshirt and faded Levi's. For a second, Angel had no idea who it was, then he realized.

"Jesus Christ," he whispered. "Is that you, Franco?"

"Hi, Angel." It was the same voice after all these years.

Angel's first emotion was pure elation, a quick *Thank God* that someone cared, that someone had come. Then he thought of Madelaine, of Francis and Madelaine together, and jealousy started, sudden as a dart, piercing through the joy, ripping a little piece of it away. Then there was guilt, acrid and sour, the memories of Angel's betrayal and Francis's hurt. He forced a cocky grin. "It's good to see you, bro. Glad you had time to stop by."

Francis flinched. Angel immediately felt like a jerk. But wasn't that always the way of it? Why couldn't he ever do or say the right thing around Francis?

"How long have you been here?"

"Not long," Angel said at last. "I had another heart attack in Oregon and they flew me up here."

"Another one?"

He shrugged. "Technically it's an 'episode of heart failure,' but it sure as hell *feels* like an attack."

"Are you going to be okay?"

"I'm always okay—you should know that." He faked a smile. "They'll pump me full of drugs and send me home. Nothing to it."

Francis pulled out a chair and sat down. He looked older than his thirty-five years, and there was a sadness in his blue eyes that made Angel uncomfortable. Francis had always been such an optimist.

"How've you been, Franco?"

Francis didn't smile. "That's a hell of a question after all these years. What am I supposed to say, Angel? 'I've been fine. How about yourself?'"

Again Angel had said the wrong thing. He wanted to save this moment, make something of it, but he didn't know how. He and Franco had been fighting for all their lives—at least, Angel had been fighting with Francis, and Francis had taken it. He didn't know how to stop the cycle, how to break out of the mold and say, *Let's start over.*

"Have you seen her?" Francis asked.

No coyness there, not from Franco. No beating around the bush about who *she* was. Angel felt a sudden, undeniable friction settle into the room. "Yeah, I've seen her."

"And?"

Angel studied his brother, noticing that he was still blond and still had the lean body of a long-distance runner. Yeah, he was the same old Francis, nearly perfect in every way—good-looking and decent and moral. The kind of man a woman would feel safe with, loved by. The ideal guy to step in and mend a sixteen-year-old girl's broken heart.

The thought made Angel mad.

"Well?" Francis said.

"What do you want to know, Franco? Did I screw her? No, I didn't. It's a little tough hooked up to a heart monitor."

He saw the distaste in his brother's eyes, the disappointment. Francis sighed, ran a hand through his hair. "I know you didn't . . . sleep with her. That's not what I was asking."

Angel felt like an insect before his brother's penetrating gaze. And the worst of it was, Angel knew it was all in his own mind, knew that Francis felt none of this tension, none of this childish competition. But, as always, Francis brought out the worst in Angel.

"Are *you* screwing her?" Angel asked, sickened and shamed by his own question, but unable to hold it back.

Francis eyed him, saying nothing for a long time. Each second of silence felt like an hour. "I'm a priest," Francis said finally.

Angel felt a rush of relief, then a surprising pride. He remembered all the times he had sat on the front stoop with his big brother, listening to ten-year-old Francis's dreams of becoming a priest. "You did it, huh? Good for you."

"All in all, it's been good. It made Ma think God would overlook everything about her."

Angel found himself smiling. For a second, it felt as if they were kids again. "If she made it to Heaven, you've been screwed."

Francis laughed. "That's for sure."

"What's it like, being a priest?"

"Good. A little . . lonely sometimes."

Angel saw unhappiness in his brother's blue eyes, and a vague shadow of dissatisfaction. He knew suddenly, the way he used to just "know" things about Francis, that his brother was talking about Madelaine again. "You love her."

Francis flinched, then gave a feeble laugh. "You always could read my mind. Yeah, I do."

It hurt, that sad, quiet statement of fact. It irritated the hell out of him that it should hurt so much, after all these years. "And she loves you," Angel shot back. "Probably one of those sordid, heart-wrenching *Thorn Birds* kind of things. What do you do, lock eyes over the Communion wafer?"

"She's not a Catholic."

Angel frowned. It wasn't an answer at all. He felt the anger coming back, prickling him. *Now,* he thought. *Shut up now and you'll be okay*. But on the tide of the anger came the words, unstoppable, unchangeable. "What'd you do, help her through the rough times after I left?"

Francis's face turned surprisingly hard. "After you left, she was all alone. Alex cut her off and kicked her out of the house. She needed *somebody*."

"And there you were," Angel said in a bitter, sarcastic voice.

"And there you weren't."

Angel winced. "Touché, big brother."

Francis moved his chair closer. "What in God's name did you expect her to do?"

Angel squeezed his eyes shut. He refused to feel shame now, all these years later. It was a useless waste of time. She'd obviously done all right for herself.

"She believed in you, Angel," Francis said quietly. "We both did."

Shame tightened his stomach. "Yeah, well, life sucks. People let you down."

"They also change and apologize and seek redemption."

"Don't give me that saintly crap. It's too late for me to apologize or change, and redemption is way out of my reach. I think I'll just stumble along as I always have."

"You aren't going to see Madelaine anymore, then?"

"She's my doctor."

"That's not what I mean and you know it."

Angel's gaze snapped up. "Quit beating around the bush, Franco. You don't want me screwing her—that's what you're trying to say in that holier-than-thou way of yours, isn't it?"

"I don't want her hurt again. Madelaine is . . . fragile."

Angel thought of the ball-buster who'd read him the riot act about his heart and laughed out loud. "Yeah, a real magnolia petal."

"I mean it, Angel. It took her years to get over you last time. Don't break her heart again."

Angel laughed bitterly. "Don't worry, pal. If anyone's got a broken heart, it's me."

With a weary sigh, Francis pushed to his feet. "I've got a couples' retreat in Oregon for the rest of the month. I could cancel if—"

"If I'm gonna die tomorrow? Don't bother. I'll be fine."

"I'll come back and see you when I get home. Unless you're going to disappear again . . ."

Angel sighed. Already the anger was gone, faded back into insignificance next to the power of his love for his brother. Again he wished that he'd held back, that just once in his life, he'd had some self-control. "I'll be here, Franco."

"Good."

Angel forced a pathetic smile. "I'm sorry I yelled at you, man. Thanks for coming."

Francis looked down at him for a long, long time. Then, slowly, he smiled. "You're always sorry."

"Yeah," Angel said softly, stung by the truth of it.

# chapter ten

⮑

*Shoplifting.*

The phone slipped from Madelaine's hand and hit the floor with a clatter. She swayed and reached for the kitchen counter to steady herself. She took a deep breath, then another and another. Her shoulders inched back as years of discipline training kicked in. *Quit pouting, girl. All a Milquetoast ever gets is wet.*

She heard her father's booming voice as if he were in the room with her. *Buck up, act like a Hillyard and not some scared, stupid rabbit. Christ, you embarrass me, girl.*

Madelaine shivered at the memory and pushed it away.

"Get your purse, Madelaine." She spoke out loud to the too empty room. Woodenly she bent over and retrieved the phone, setting it down on the cradle with an exaggerated calm. Then she plucked her purse off the counter, slung it over her shoulder, and moved toward the front door.

Just as she reached for the knob, someone knocked. The door swung open as Madelaine stumbled to a stop.

Francis stood in the doorway. "Hi, Maddy."

She noticed that he wasn't smiling—odd, but she didn't have time to care, couldn't quite make herself care. "Hey, Francis," she responded automatically. She waited for him to move or say something, but he didn't. She blinked up at him, confused. "Did we have dinner plans?"

"No. I'm leaving for Portland tonight. I won't be back for a few weeks. There . . . there was something I wanted to talk to you about. . . . I saw An—"

"Oh, yeah. Portland. Have a nice trip." She gave him a distracted smile and waited for him to leave. When he didn't she said, "I've got to go to . . . town now."

"Maddy? I'm trying to tell you something important." He moved closer, gazed down at her with concern. "What is it, Maddy-girl?"

His gentleness made her want to cry. It saddened her that even now, even with Francis, she had so much difficulty speaking of her problems. "It's Lina. She's been . . ." Her voice fell to a whisper. "She's been arrested for shoplifting."

"Oh, my God. It's my fault."

"What?"

"Come on, I'll drive you to the police station." He slipped his arm around her waist and started to lead her from the house.

She slammed the door shut and let herself be carried away by him, helped along. But as they reached the garage, she knew it was wrong. She'd given away too many moments like this with Lina, let Francis shoulder too many of the painful times of her life. She had to stand up for herself and be as strong a parent as she was a doctor.

She stopped.

Francis turned to her. "Maddy?"

"I've got to do this alone, Francis. I'm her mother."

He took a quick step backward. "I left the number in Portland on your voice mail."

She moved toward him, gently tucked a lock of hair behind his ear. "I'll call you tonight and let you know how it went."

"Will you?" Still he didn't look at her, and there was a strange tension in his voice.

She touched his cheek, forcing him to look at her. When their gazes met, she saw the sheen of tears in his eyes, and it confused her. He looked hurt. "Francis?"

He stared at her for a heartbeat, then squeezed his eyes shut and shook his head. "Lina came to see me today. I let her down."

"Oh, Francis . . ." She tried to conjure a smile. "*I* let her down, Francis. Me."

"No. You're greedy as usual, my Maddy. But this time I'm taking some of the blame."

She hesitated. "Maybe you *should* come with me, Francis . . ."

"No, she's your daughter and you need to handle this. Besides, I've got to get on my way. Four married couples need the advice that only their celibate priest can offer." He smiled wanly and shook his head at the irony.

She wanted to say more, but she didn't know what it was he needed to hear, how she could make this moment what he wanted it to be. For the first time ever, he felt like a stranger to her. "Drive carefully," she said, not knowing what else to say.

"Don't I always?"

She shot a meaningful look at the dented side of his Bug.

He gave her a quick grin. "I'm leaving before you start in on my driving. 'Bye."

She watched as he folded into the dented old Volkswagen and drove away. The car sputtered down the narrow road, then turned the corner and disappeared. And she was alone again.

She stared down the empty street, sighing quietly. Francis, her Francis, who wore his heart on his sleeve and his soul in his eyes. Francis, who loved them all so much and only wanted to be a part of their lives. All he'd wanted was to help. She forgot sometimes how easily he could be hurt.

Regret sneaked up on her. Once again she'd made the wrong choice, said the wrong thing at the wrong time.

But she'd make up for it.

When Francis got home from this trip, she'd make up for hurting him today.


Juvenile Hall was a hive of activity. Harried-looking men and women crisscrossed the tile floor like ants, talking and gesturing among themselves. Brown vinyl chairs lined the walls, most empty, but some of them filled with adults who looked as nervous as Madelaine felt. In the center of it all, a white-haired woman sat at a huge desk, answering the phone and directing traffic with a nod of her head or a flick of her forefinger.

Madelaine felt acutely conspicuous as she crossed the busy lobby and walked up to the desk.

The heavily jowled woman peered up at her. "Hello."

She had to raise her voice to be heard above the din. "I'm here to pick up my daughter. Lina Hillyard."

The receptionist flipped through some paperwork. "Oh. Shoplifter. John Spencer is the social worker assigned to her case. You'll find him in room 108, down the hall, second door on the right."

Madelaine moved along the crowded hallway without making eye contact with anyone, her purse clutched tightly against her side. By the time she reached room 108, she had a terrible twisting ache in her stomach and she was afraid she was going to be sick.

She paused at the open door to room 108. Inside, a young African-American man sat at a hulking metal desk in a brown-walled office. Three cups of obviously cold coffee stood in a precise line along the upper right edge of the desk. At her entrance, he looked up. "Can I help you?"

"I'm Dr. Madelaine Hillyard. Lina's mother."

He nodded and flicked through the stack of files on his desk, gingerly pulling one out. Indicating a chair, he flipped the file open. "Please sit, Dr. Hillyard."

Madelaine crossed to the small, metal-framed black chair and perched nervously on its edge.

After a moment he looked up from the file and gave her a smile. "Your daughter's a real spitfire."

"Yes."

"The store detective at Savemore Drugs caught her shoplifting some makeup. Nailed her on the in-store video, too. Do you want to see it?"

Madelaine wished she needed to, but she knew Lina had done this—and she knew why. It was Lina's way of getting back at a mother who wouldn't make a phone call.

"No."

"Good. Some parents just can't believe their precious children would do anything wrong." He shoved back from the desk and stood up. "Here's the deal. It's a first offense and the store is willing to overlook what she's done."

Madelaine almost sagged with relief. But before she could revel in the feeling, Spencer went on, "Course, that won't do jack shit—pardon my French—for your daughter. She needs to face the consequences of her actions."

He looked right at Madelaine. "She's scared—they all are the first time—but from now on, it's up to you."

She wanted to ask what to do, to ask for help, but she didn't know how. The words tangled in her throat. She'd read dozens of books on parenting, and all of them told her to reason with Lina, to offer her daughter choices and teach her to make decisions. It was good advice, Madelaine knew it was, but it didn't work, not for her and Lina anyway. And the only other way she knew was her father's way.

"I've worked here a long time, Dr. Hillyard. Your daughter's on the brink of real trouble." Spencer moved closer and sat in the chair beside her. "This is a cry for attention. And the next cry might not be so easy to solve. The suicide rate among troubled teens—"

Madelaine gasped and broke eye contact, staring at the hands clasped in her lap. *Suicide.* A chill spread through her.

"Has she done this before?" That was the question she asked, the words she formed, but what she really wanted to know, needed to know, was *How many cries have I missed?*

"She had a definite routine. Looked to me like she'd done it before."

Madelaine squeezed her eyes shut. Of course Lina had done it before. If Lina were someone else's daughter, Madelaine would have noticed the warning signs long ago—dissatisfied teenager, angry and rebellious, looking for attention.

All of it fit Lina. All of it. The new interest in heavy metal music, the recent ear-piercing frenzy, the truancy, the wardrobe, the attitude. Lina was a teenager in trouble, and shoplifting—whether she knew it or not—was a cry for help. Madelaine had to be strong enough to answer the call.

"Dr. Hillyard?"

Slowly she lifted her chin and looked at the social worker. "I want to help her, Mr. Spencer, but . . ." The words seemed to drag her down, and it saddened her that she was afraid of this. How could a well-respected physician be so strong with strangers and so weak with her own child? She felt tears of shame and defeat sting her eyes.

"I've got a sixteen-year-old daughter myself, Dr. Hillyard. You can love them more than your own life, and give them everything you have. And . . ." He shrugged. "Shit happens."

"I . . . should have disciplined her better . . . been there more . . ."

"This isn't about whose fault it is, Dr. Hillyard. You're a parent, she's a teenager—believe me, there's plenty of blame to go around. Today, what you have to focus on is change."

She steeled herself. "How do I do it?"

"That's the sixty-four-thousand-dollar question. Me, I use honesty and consistency." He smiled, his eyes twinkled. "And when that doesn't work—take away the television, the learner's permit, *and* permission to use the phone."

Madeleine looked up, surprised. It wasn't the advice she'd expected. She flashed on her own childhood, on dark, frightening images of her father's "discipline," and felt nausea rise in her stomach. "That works? The books all say—"

He dismissed the experts with a wave of his hand. "The books are okay, I guess, but there comes a time when talking doesn't work anymore. A kid needs rules, pure and simple. Oh, and I'd make her apologize to the manager of the drugstore." He pushed to his feet. "So, Dr. Hillyard, why don't we get your daughter out of detention?"

Lina lay curled on the narrow, smelly cot, her knees drawn up to her chest. The tears she'd cried had long since dried on her cheeks.

Noises were everywhere in this shadowy place—the clang of iron-barred doors being opened and closed, the disgruntled voices and shrill-pitched shouts of teenaged gang members, the heavy thud of footsteps on the stone floor. Every sound made her curl tighter and tighter on the dirty bed.

*This place is gonna seem like a picnic, little lady, if they send you to the main ward.*

The social worker's words came back to Lina, frightening her all over again. She couldn't help thinking of her bed at home—big and fresh-smelling and covered in Laura Ashley sheets.

"I love ham-and-cheese omelets," she whispered, feeling the tears well again, clogging her throat and stinging her eyes.

What had made her act like such a bitch around her mother? Lina knew how hard her mother tried to please her—she'd noticed the baggy sweats, the lack of makeup, the too bright smile that tried to mask a sharp desperation in her mom's eyes.

Yeah, she knew her mom loved her, knew she only wanted to do the very best for Lina. So why couldn't Lina cut her some slack? Why did she wake up angry and stay angry all day? Sometimes she knew why she was mad, but more often than not, she couldn't place a cause. She just wasn't happy. Some mornings she felt fat, the next day she'd think she was skinny. Half the time she felt like crying for no reason at all.

She wanted everything to be like it used to be. She didn't want to feel so ugly and lost all the time. She wanted to fit in *somewhere*.

She knew she was a disappointment to her perfect mother— Madelaine, the child prodigy who'd earned her high school diploma before she turned fifteen. Saint Madelaine, who never had a hair out of place, who raised a daughter alone while she attended medical school, who never lost her temper or cried or asked for help from anyone.

"I'll never shoplift again, God," she whispered brokenly, squeezing her eyes shut against a fresh wave of tears.

Suddenly the door of her dormitory room rattled. Keys jangled in the lock, clicked hard, and the door screeched open.

"Hillyard, get up."

Lina rolled to face the door and lurched to her feet, her heart pounding with sudden anxiety. "Where am I going?"

The fat, polyester-clad woman gave her a deadpan look. "Do I look like a tour director?" She cocked her head down the corridor. "Get going."

Lina hugged herself tightly and eased past the woman. Moving slowly, she walked down the hallway, keeping her eyes down.

Finally they came to another locked door. The woman pushed the intercom and said, "Hillyard!" in a loud, booming voice.

The door swung open.

Lina hesitated for a second. The woman shoved her, and Lina stumbled forward. The first face she saw was John Spencer's. The second was her mother's.

She stared at her mom, saw the sadness in her mother's eyes, the disappointment that pursed her lips, and felt a wrenching guilt. She wanted to take a step forward, throw herself in her mom's arms and be swept up, comforted and held, but she couldn't seem to move.

"Lina," Mr. Spencer said, "your mother is prepared to take you home—*after* you make your apologies to the manager of Savemore Drugs." He dropped her backpack on the table beside him with a thunk.

Lina swallowed hard. "Okay." The word came out on a squeak.

Spencer closed the distance between them. His shadow fell across Lina's face. "You've spent an hour in detention, little girl. Believe me, you don't want to spend any more."

She was so scared, she could barely nod.

"I'm gonna keep in touch with your mom, and if you cause any more trouble . . ." He let the threat dangle between them. "You understand me?"

"Yes," she whispered.

"Yes, what?" he boomed.

"Y-yes, sir."

"Good." He turned to Madelaine. "I'll allow you to take the minor child home now, Dr. Hillyard. But I'll be calling once a week. I assume this is the last such incident I'll hear about."

Madelaine nodded. "Thank you, Mr. Spencer."

Then Spencer left the room, and Lina was alone with her mom. They stood there a minute, staring at each other.

Lina tried to think of what to say, how to say it. "I . . . I'm sorry, Mom."

It was an excruciating length of time before her mother answered. She looked confused, as frightened as Lina felt. "I'm sorry, too." She took a hesitant step forward, reached out one small hand.

It wasn't enough, just the offer of the hand. Lina wanted to be engulfed in her mother's arms, but she didn't know how to ask for such a thing, and she was afraid of making a fool of herself.

Madelaine stopped. Her hand fell slowly back to her side. "I guess we'd better go home and do some serious talking."

Lina stared at her mother, feeling further away than ever, more alone. Tears were so close, she had to turn her head. She stared at the floor through stinging eyes. "Yeah, sure. Whatever."

Madelaine knew that Lina was afraid, but for once, she had to be a parent, not a friend. She had to lay down the law and mean it, and if she failed—again—she would be hurting her daughter.

"Get your things," she said in a thick voice. "We've got to go home."

Side by side, in an almost unendurable silence, they walked out of the building. Late afternoon sunlight, weakened to chilly gold by the season, splashed their faces. Still quiet, they slipped into the Volvo and drove to the drugstore. Madelaine watched from a distance as Lina apologized to the manager for stealing the mascara, and when Lina finally turned away, Madelaine saw the tears swimming in her baby's eyes.

God, how it hurt to see her daughter's pain. Madelaine wanted to take Lina in her arms then and hold her and comfort her, but by sheer dint of will, she remained motionless and dry-eyed. Then, wordlessly, she led Lina back to the car and they drove home.

By the time they reached the house, Madelaine's nerves were stretched to the breaking point. It was one thing, she knew, to decide to become an enforcer of rules—it was another thing to look at her daughter, whom she loved more than her own life, and say no. *Mean* no.

Flicking the car engine off, she grabbed her purse. Lina bounded out of the car and ran up to the house, disappearing inside.

When Madelaine walked into the house, Lina was already on the telephone. Her daughter's voice was a loud, lively chatter, punctuated by ringing laughter.

"And *then* they locked me in this little room. . . . Yeah, it was way cool. Just like what happened to Brittany Levin . . ."

Madelaine stared at her daughter in disbelief. It was one of those crystallizing moments in life, tiny heartbeats of time that pass and leave you changed. Lina had gone through that terrible time in Juvenile Hall, she'd been terrified and apologetic, but the emotions were leaving her now, slipping away on the tide of the distance between her and the detention cell.

And she was counting on Madelaine to keep the memories away, counting on her mother to create some fantasy world in which the shoplifting had never happened.

Madelaine felt a stab of anger so swift and sudden, it surprised her. Lina was sure that Madelaine would want to sweep the whole messy incident under the rug, that the shoplifting could be yet another of the endless stream of things that Madelaine was afraid to talk about.

*Not this time.*

Madelaine forced her chin up and strode across the kitchen. Wordlessly she grabbed the phone from her daughter's hand and crashed the receiver down.

"Wh—huh?" Lina stammered, slamming her hands on her hips and glaring at her mother. "Nice, Mom. Now I'll have to call Jett back."

Madelaine stood her ground. "No, you won't," she said evenly. "You have no phone privileges anymore." She shoved her hand toward Lina, palm out. "Bike lock. *Now.*"

Lina stared at her mother in shocked amazement. "You must be kidding."

"Do I look like I'm kidding?"

Lina frowned suddenly. She took a step backward. "Hey, Mom, come on. . . ."

"Give me the lock and keys."

She fished them out of her book bag and tossed them to Madelaine. "Fine. Jett can drive me to school."

Madelaine shook her head. "I'll take you to school every morning and pick you up. You will go nowhere—*nowhere*—without permission from me."

Lina barked out a laugh. "Yeah, right. Mrs. Never-at-Home is gonna regulate my social life."

"I can make myself be at home, Lina. I can take a sabbatical from work and be home all the time. Is that what you want?"

"I *want* my father," she shouted back.

Madelaine should have known. It was only a matter of time before Lina used the incredible unknown father to wound her mother—but still it hurt. "Let's talk about him, Lina. That's what you want, right? You want to know about your father. Well, fine. Your father was a reckless, angry young man who didn't want a family."

"You're the one he didn't want."

Madelaine felt the anger rush out of her at the simple truth. "That's true," she said softly. "It was me he didn't want, me he didn't love. But he also didn't want . . ." Madelaine stared at her daughter, not knowing what to say, which truth to tell.

"Me?" Lina whispered.

"No." Madelaine's voice was quiet, barely a whisper. "He didn't want to grow up and make hard choices and sacrifices. He just wanted to have fun, and parenting at seventeen is definitely not fun."

Lina wrenched her gaze away and crossed her arms. "He's a grownup now," she said stubbornly. "He'll want me."

Madelaine stared at her daughter's profile, at the trembling mouth and pale skin, at the tears that streaked unchecked from her eyes. She moved closer, pressed her warm palm to Lina's cold cheek. "I want him to love you, Lina, I want him to want you, but . . ."

Lina turned to her. "But what?"

"I'm afraid, Lina. It's as simple as that."

She blinked. A tear rolled down her cheek. "Is he violent?"

"No, never that." Madelaine brushed Lina's tear away with her thumb. "He's . . . selfish. I'm afraid he'll break your heart."

Lina stared at her. "Don't you understand, Mom? He's breaking my heart now."

Madelaine sighed, thinking suddenly of all the promises she'd broken over the years—little things, a dinner missed here, a movie missed there—and how they'd added up, brought Lina and Madelaine to this moment. A mother and daughter who loved each other, and hurt each other, and didn't know how to change. "I know you don't believe me, baby," she whispered. "But I just want to do the right thing."

"I want to believe you, Mom," Lina said.

Madelaine heard the quietly spoken words, and they gave her a tiny, sparking ray of hope. She thought of a dozen responses, but in the end it all came down to empty words, promises made by a woman who'd broken too many.

Finally she said the only thing that really mattered. "I love you, Lina."

Lina's eyes filled with tears. "I know you do, Mom."

They weren't the words Madelaine wanted to hear. Not the right words at all.

# chapter eleven

❧

Tom Grant was sitting up in bed, laughing quietly at something his wife had said, when Madelaine walked into his room.

"Morning," she said, plucking his chart out of the sleeve and quickly reading the newest notations. "Everything looks good. We'll be taking you off the IV meds today, Tom. And those catheters—consider them gone. You're practically free."

He grinned at that. "When can I see my kids? Joe is home from college."

She went to the bedside and checked the two small wires that protruded from his chest. They were there to monitor the pace and electrical rhythm of the new heart. When she finished, she looked down at Tom. "I'm sorry, but that's not going to be possible today."

Tom's smile fell. "What's wrong?"

"Joe has a cold, and we don't want to risk it quite yet."

Susan released a heavy sigh. "Oh, God. I thought it was bad news."

Madelaine understood—the first few post-op days were always terrifying. "I'll talk to Joe myself. We'll monitor him closely for the next few days. Maybe by Monday . . ." She let the words trail off before they became a promise.

"He got straight A's this term," Tom said proudly, gazing up at his wife.

Madelaine almost said something inane—an ordinary response—then she caught herself. Instead she inched closer to the bed. "How did you guys do it . . . raise such healthy, happy kids?"

"Luck," Tom answered quickly.

"And no-shit weeks," Susan added with a laugh.

Madelaine turned to Susan. It was the first time she'd ever heard the woman swear, and it surprised her. "What do you mean?"

"Tom was gone—or sick—a lot of the time while the kids were growing up. Sometimes I used to tear my hair out. The kids were far apart in age, and they were each so different. It took me a long time to get the upper hand. But in the end, I started doing my 'no-shit' weeks. I would start on Monday, taking absolutely *no* crap from the kids. I didn't yell or scream; I just quietly, flatly let them know that I was the boss. Usually a week was all it took. After that, they were so tired of bucking the rules, they just toed the line." She grinned. "A good no-shit week would keep them on track for six months or so. Then it would start all over again."

"Really?" Madelaine said.

"Of course, I was often talking to a teenage boy with blue hair. But you've got to fight the big battles and let the little ones go."

Madelaine set the chart back in its sleeve and smiled at the two of them. "Well, I've got rounds to make. See you tomorrow."

Smiling to herself, she walked out of the room.

*No-shit weeks.* It had a certain appeal.

\*   \*   \*

Lina sat in the passenger seat of the cushy Volvo, her arms crossed, her jaw set mutinously. Things were *not* going well.

She cast a surreptitious glance at her mother. Madelaine sat as she always did, erect, chin up, eyes on the road, her hands at the invisible ten and two positions on the steering wheel.

Lina had tried every trick in her arsenal this morning to get to ride her bike to school—she'd screamed at her mother, begged her, stomped out of the kitchen, and slammed her bedroom door. She'd refused to eat breakfast and refused to pack a lunch. Heck, she'd even cried.

None of it had worked.

It was as if an alien had invaded her mother's body. Suddenly Madelaine was *Dr. Hillyard* all the time. Cold, detached, sure of herself. Not like her mother at all.

Lina didn't know what to make of it, how to act. It scared her, this turnaround on her mother's part. For years Lina had prided herself on running the household, on knowing how to wrap her wimpy mother around her finger with ease. All she'd ever had to do was cry—heck, just tear up—and Mom would give her the world. Lina had always been able to stay out too late, come home whenever she wanted, eat whatever she wanted. A tear here or there at the right moment, and Mom turned to jelly.

Until yesterday.

Madelaine eased the car up to the curb and shifted into park. The soft hum of the engine filled the interior. She turned. "I'll be here to pick you up at three-thirty."

Lina bristled at the order. This was getting ridiculous, and embarrassing. How was she gonna tell Jett that she couldn't go to the mall after school? That her mom had to pick her up like she was a baby or something?

"Mom, it's not like shoplifting's a felony. Lighten up. Jett'll bring me home after we go to the mall."

"I'll pick you up at three-thirty sharp. If you're not here, I'll call Mr. Spencer."

"And tell him what?" Lina snorted. "You've got a felony failure-to-pick-up-at-school situation?"

"I'll tell him you ran away."

Lina's jaw dropped. "They'd send me back to detention."

"Would they?"

Lina just stared at her mom, feeling as if she were suddenly falling and there was no one there to catch her. "You'd let them do that to me?"

"I have no choice, Lina. We've got some changes to make, you and I. You know we do."

"You want to make changes, Mom? Quit lying to me." With satisfaction, she saw her mother flinch.

"You're going to make everything about him, aren't you?" she said quietly.

"Everything *is* about him. It's your fault I shoplifted. I wouldn't have done that if you'd told me my father's name."

"I'll be here at three-thirty to pick you up."

Lina felt a rush of pure, blinding anger. How *dare* her mother be so calm and matter-of-fact and . . . and motherly? It made Lina feel off balance, confused. It wasn't supposed to be this way; she was supposed to get what she wanted by using the old tricks.

She yanked up her backpack and wrenched open the door. She lurched out of the car and spun around to stare at her mother. "I'll be home when I feel like it."

Madelaine stared at her, so cool and calm that Lina wanted to smack her perfect face. "Then give my regards to Mr. Spencer."

"I hate you," Lina hissed.

"That's too bad," her mother said quietly. "Because I love you." Then she leaned over and shut the door.

Lina stood there, so angry she was shaking. She wanted to yell or scream or cry. She wanted to kick something in. But all she could do was watch her mother drive away.

*     *     *

Madelaine ducked into one of the empty hospital rooms and peered into the bathroom mirror.

She looked like Sylvester Stallone at the end of the first *Rocky*.

She poked at the dark circles under her eyes and frowned. It was too bad Maybelline didn't make a combat fatigue face makeup. She looked like she hadn't slept all night—which she hadn't. This "no shit" parenting was harder than it looked.

She'd done the right thing with Lina. For once, she'd been a parent.

*And what if Lina ran away? What then, Miss Parent of the Year?* The voice was her father's, booming and authoritative, but the words were her own. It was that worry that had kept her up all night, trying to assuage her guilt in books about tough love and hard choices in parenting, but the experts' words were cold and dark against plain white pages. No comfort at all.

She left the bathroom and headed down the familiar white corridor toward Intensive Care. When she reached Angel's room, she knocked lightly and went inside.

She couldn't believe what she saw.

He was lying there, sucking on a cigarette, then blowing smoke into the air. An open bottle of tequila sat on the bedside table.

He didn't even have the common decency to look guilty. Instead he gave her a bleary, cockeyed grin. "Uh-oh, hall patrol." He reached for the bottle and hit it with his knuckles. It wobbled and crashed sideways, spraying golden liquid everywhere. The sickeningly sweet smell of tequila wafted upward. He stubbed out the cigarette on the bedside table.

A white-hot flash of anger swept through her. She grabbed the bottle and took it into the bathroom, pouring the remaining alcohol down the sink. The bottle hit the wastebasket with a satisfying thunk.

She spun around and surged back into the room. "You are the most selfish, self-centered son of a bitch I've ever known."

"Way to ruin a good party, Doc."

She could smell the cigarette smoke, hovering in the room, reminding her with every indrawn breath that Angel was too selfish to change, too weak to really make the decision to live. Even here, in the cold blankness of ICU, with machines hissing and spitting around him, holding his battered heart together with a dozen electric threads, even here he couldn't find the strength to change. Instead, he'd brought his partying, irresponsible life into the hospital.

"What in the hell were you trying to do?"

He laughed, a hacking, breathless sound, a pale shadow of the laugh she remembered. "Die of cancer."

Then, very slowly, he turned his head on the pillow and stared up at her through watery eyes. Suddenly he wasn't smiling anymore. He looked sick and weak and broken. His hair was greasy and uncombed. Two days' growth of beard stubbled his chin and darkened his upper lip. Even his eyes, those incredible green eyes, looked inestimably tired.

She'd seen this face before, a thousand times in her career. Sometimes the eyes were blue, sometimes brown, sometimes green, but they were always watery and sad and tired-looking.

He was dying.

The anger dissolved as suddenly as it had come. She walked over to the bed and pulled out a chair. "Oh, Angel," she said softly, shaking her head, releasing a heavy sigh.

"Don't do that to me," he said in a Demerol-slurred voice. "I . . . don't . . ."

The rattling wheeze of his breathing seemed to suck the words away. She had to scoot closer to hear him. "What is it?"

He stared at her, and the bleakness in his gaze was almost too much to bear. "I don't know what else to do."

Madelaine saw his fear, his uncertainty, and though she didn't want to be moved by it, she found herself being drawn to him. She touched his rough, unshaven jaw. "It's okay to be afraid."

"Who said I'm afraid?"

She smiled gently. "You don't fool me anymore."

He moved a little, immediately winced in pain. Grimacing, he dragged the bed's remote control onto his lap and pushed the button. *Click, grind,* the bed eased upward. Breathing hard, he stared at Madelaine. "What does that mean?"

She was surprised by the intimacy of the question. For a second she remembered so much about them, the little things, the tiny moments, the things they'd said to each other, promises they'd made in the dark of the night. *Until I met you, Mad, I wanted to die. . . .*

And her answer, so naive and afraid, *Don't say that, Angel, don't ever say that.*

"What do you mean?" he demanded.

She pushed the memories away and stared down at him. "When we were kids, you used to tell me that you wanted to die."

There was a long pause, and she didn't even realize she was waiting for his response until he answered. "That was a long time ago."

It struck her suddenly how different they both were, how, over time, the same words could take on such different meanings. As a young girl, his death wish had seemed wildly romantic, a gauntlet that she alone could pick up. But no more; now she saw the words for what they were—selfish and stupid. And a waste, such a waste. "You're a coward, Angel DeMarco, and you always were."

"Fuck you."

"Go ahead, swear at me. It doesn't change the truth that you're afraid to live."

Anger flashed in his eyes. The heart monitor beeped a warning. "Quit acting like you know me. You don't."

"I know who you were once, Angel, and frankly, I don't see much change. You never knew when to compromise, when to really try. What you knew how to do was run. Well, you've tried running and drinking and hiding. And you've ended up here, right where you began."

He stared at her a long, long time, until the anger faded from his eyes and was replaced by a worn resignation.

Finally he spoke, and when he did his voice was reed-thin. "I don't know how to change."

She felt something in that moment that surprised her, a sudden connection with this man, as if, for the single space of a breath, the past had never died, and she'd never watched him ride out of her life on a brand-new Harley-Davidson motorcycle. She remembered in that second the why and how of her love for him, the tiny chinks in his armor that had drawn her in, the bruised vulnerability she'd always seen in his eyes. She thought of how alike they'd once been. "I know how hard it is to really change. But you're home now, that must mean something. Francis is here, and I know how much he loves you, how ready he'd be to help you. You're home, Angel. Maybe if you look around, you'll find a reason to live."

He gave a weak smile. "I think it was Thomas Wolfe who said, 'You can never go home again.'"

"I don't know," she said slowly, meeting his gaze. "Home is part of us. It's in the scars we have on our knees and elbows, in the memories that surface when we sleep. I don't think you can ever really leave."

He started to respond, but before he could speak, Madelaine's beeper went off. It was a message from Allenford. She reached immediately for the bedside phone and punched in the four-digit extension.

Chris picked up on the first ring. "Allenford."

"Hi, Chris," Madelaine said. "What's going on?"

"DeMarco. I think we have a heart."

*    *    *

Angel had thought he understood fear. He'd known the sweaty palms, the knot in the pit of the stomach that tightened with every breath, the metallic taste on the tongue. Once he'd almost overdosed on drugs, and even that—waking up in the emergency room with a dozen faces peering over him—even that was nothing compared to this.

Fear was a living, breathing presence inside him, pushing at his skin, seeping from his pores in foul, salty beads of sweat.

He closed his eyes and knew immediately that it was a mistake. The images were there, waiting in the darkness like macabre specters—the accident that would bring him life, the "donor" who would never open his eyes again, never smile at his wife or hug his children. He saw blood—his, the donor's, the mingling of the two. . . .

He twisted slightly on the narrow bed, his hands curled talonlike around the warm metal rails. A groan slipped up his throat and released as a sigh. Slowly he opened his eyes and stared sightlessly ahead, until the white ceiling blurred into the silver fluorescent fixtures.

He wanted to pray, *needed* to pray, but it had been too long, and he knew that no one would listen. Oh, he knew he could seek absolution from a priest, from his own brother, in fact, but it was too easy, too pat. He couldn't believe in a God that was so forgiving. He knew that he deserved to suffer.

And he was suffering. Sweet Christ, he'd never been so afraid in his life.

"Angel?"

He heard Madelaine's throaty voice, and for a split second he remembered it all, every second they'd been together, every touch they'd shared. The memories brought an aching, bittersweet sense of loss. He wondered suddenly what it would have been like, that road not taken, the life he'd run away from.

Slowly, hurting, he turned his head to look at her.

She stood poised in the doorway, one slim, pale hand lingering tentatively on the jamb. As always, she stood perfectly erect, her chin upthrust just a little, her hair combed into a series of honey-brown curls around her face.

He wanted to smile at her, cockily, as if none of this mattered, and he tried. "Hiya, Doc."

"Hello, Angel. Are you ready?"

He was staring at her so intently that it took a second for her words to register. When they did, they hit with the force of a blow. "Ready?" he whispered, knowing how pathetic he sounded. He was lying there, shaved from chin to ankles, his skin discolored by antiseptic solution, his veins riddled with intravenous needles, his hair covered by a paper cap.

He was going to die, here and now, with his chest cut open and his heart taking its last feeble beats in another man's gloved hands.

Madelaine let the door shut behind her and moved quietly toward his bed, sitting down beside him. "Dr. Allenford is on his way to Tacoma to check out the donor heart."

*Donor heart.*

The words reverberated through his skull, echoing, echoing. *One heart cut out, another sewn in.*

"I don't know if I can do this, Mad," he said softly.

She leaned toward him, and her touch was cool and comforting on his damp cheek. "You never did have much faith in yourself," she said with a smile that came and went so fast, he wondered if he imagined it.

He gave a laugh that ended in a rattling cough. "When you're lying around waiting to die, you tend to think about what your life means."

Another smile, softer, longer-lasting. "Don't tell me you're getting philosophical."

He wanted to smile at her, but there was no smile inside him right now. There was only that yawning fear and the loneliness.

"Don't look so surprised. I almost qualified for *Jeopardy* in 1986. It was the morality category that screwed me."

"It would be."

He fell serious again. "My life doesn't mean much, Mad."

"Life is what you make it, Angel. Maybe . . . after the surgery you'll make a different one."

"Life is what you make it," he parroted, feeling a rush of unexpected bitterness toward her. The bitterness left him, and without it, he felt cold again. "Yeah, you're right," he conceded, staring at her, seeing for the first time the tiny lines that hung like commas at the corners of her mouth. Self-consciously she smoothed a nonexistent hair from her forehead, and he noticed that a button was missing from her sleeve.

It made her look so human, that little tangle of thread on her perfect silk blouse.

"I shouldn't have run out on you that way." He tossed the words out as if they meant nothing, but surprisingly, they did mean something. Even though the apology was pitiful and small and years too late, it felt good to admit to his mistake. He had spent a lifetime running from one bad decision, as if he could change it or outrun it. From a dozen dirty pay phones in towns he couldn't remember, he'd called Madelaine and Francis, dialed the numbers and listened to the intermittent ringing. But he'd always hung up before they answered.

What could he have said to them?

But still he'd tried, until the numbers he had for them had been disconnected.

"That was a long time ago, Angel."

"Sometimes it feels like aeons. And sometimes it feels like yesterday. Anyway, I know it doesn't matter, but I wanted you to know. I should have faced Alex with you."

She flinched. He watched as color fell from her cheeks, left her face an ashen white.

He saw the pain in her eyes, and it made him feel like an

ass. Of course, she didn't want to think about that. "Sorry," he whispered.

She didn't move, just sat there, staring at him.

Her beeper went off, blipping through the tense silence. Absently she reached for it, shut the noise off, and grabbed his phone. Punching in the numbers, she asked for Dr. Allenford. She spoke a few quiet words, then hung up.

He knew it was bad by the look on her face. "What is it?"

She covered her eyes with her hand, then slowly, slowly drew her hand away and looked at Angel. "It wasn't right. The heart wasn't in good enough shape. I'm sorry."

"No surgery?" He tried to draw a good breath, couldn't, heard himself wheezing. "I—" Before he could get the words out, he felt his heart seize up. Pain erupted in his chest. He tried to breathe, but he couldn't.

*I'm dying,* he thought suddenly, and he knew it was the truth. He reached out blindly.

Madelaine took hold of his hand, squeezed it hard. Dimly he heard her click a button, heard her yell, *Code blue Cardiac ICU 264 west. Stat. Get the cart.* Then he felt her hands at his chest, wrenching the cotton gown aside.

*Don't you die on me, Angel. God damn you, don't you die on me.*

He heard her voice through the fog in his mind, through the pain shoving through his chest, shredding his muscles. He wanted to answer, but he couldn't.

The pain twisted, turned into fire, and exploded in his heart.

# chapter twelve

❦

Rain drummed on the city streets, splashed on the asphalt roof of the building next door, and formed murky puddles in the loose gravel. Madelaine stood at the window, staring at the misty gray city two floors below her. Down there, it was such an ordinary October day. Nothing different, nothing new.

The Madison Street stoplight blipped from red to green to yellow. Multicolored umbrellas moved down the slick sidewalks, weaving in and out among one another. Cars started and stopped and turned down corners, disappearing beneath green canopies of the neighborhood trees.

Life went on.

But not for Madelaine. Even now, as she stood there, looking at the sights she'd seen a million times, she saw things she'd never seen before. She noticed how the pigeons that perched on the windowsill stuck together, cooing softly to one another; how the leaves that every so often blew from the trees and stuck to

the glass were steeped in color—red, gold, green, and brown—
how the sunlight could break through the clouds in a spear of
butter-yellow light that seemed to shoot from Heaven itself.

Slowly she turned away from the window and moved toward
the bed.

Angel lay as still as death, his skin ashen, his lips pale as
chalk. He was breathing—finally—without the help of a ventilator. Beside him, the cardiac monitor clicked away, spewing out a
second-by-second account of the heart that was failing.

*Failing. Had failed.*

She plucked up the seamless, narrow sheet of paper and studied the graphlike analysis of his heartbeat, then she leaned over
him, brushed the damp hair from his forehead. Her fingers lingered against his warm, sweaty skin. *Come on, Angel. Come on.*

His eyelids fluttered, but he didn't waken.

She pressed her hand to the side of his face and closed her
eyes. Quietly the memories tiptoed into her mind. She remembered the day she'd met Angel DeMarco. The mousy candy
striper and the hell-raiser.

That first day, she meant nothing to him; she'd known that,
of course. She could see the falseness in his smile—the way it
was just a fraction too calculated to be truly welcoming.

Yes, she saw from the beginning that it was a lie, but she
didn't care. Even a fake smile was so much more than she was
used to, and if she closed her eyes and listened only to his words,
it was all so painfully sweet. . . .

With the distance of time, she knew what had happened in
that moment when he'd first smiled at her. She'd been desperately lonely, and it had never occurred to her that someone
would smile at her with genuine affection. Her father had tram-
pled her fragile girl's self-esteem until she expected much too
little.

Angel had come to her when he was discharged, come to her
and held out his hand and whispered, "Come with me. . . ."

Even now, all these years later, the memory was a current of electricity. She'd been afraid to reach out, but more afraid not to, and so she'd stood there, paralyzed by her own inability to decide.

*Come with me....*

The second time he said it, it was like a gift. She felt herself go hot, then cold. Words bubbled in her throat and slipped out, unspoken, on a giggling laugh.

She knew he would turn away then in disgust and blow out of her life on the same wind that had brought him, and the panic of that realization made her heart hammer in her chest and her throat go dry. But he didn't move, he just stood there, his hand reaching toward her. He looked at her, really looked this time, and for a split second the false smile faded and a real one took its place. She knew then, in that instant, that she would do anything—anything—to see him smile at her like that again. . . .

Angel coughed, and the sound caught Madelaine's attention. She looked down at him.

He blinked, coughed again. She waited for him to waken, and when he didn't, she pulled up a chair and sat beside him, quietly reading aloud a passage from *The Hobbit,* which she'd begun an hour ago.

Halfway into the second chapter, he opened his eyes. She waited, not even realizing that she was holding her breath. She closed the book and set it on the bedside table.

"I'm gonna die, aren't I?" He gave her a quirky, fleeting smile, and for a second he was the old Angel again, and she was the girl who'd loved him with all her heart.

"I'm not going to stop believing in a miracle," she answered quietly, knowing it wasn't the answer he wanted, knowing, too, that there was nothing else to say.

"Tell me about this miracle," he said, "tell me about life with another man's heart. What will it be like?"

He said the words easily, as if he were asking for a bedtime story, but she saw the truth in his eyes, the fear he was asking her to assuage. He *did* want a bedtime story, something to cling to in the darkness of his pain, a reason to keep believing.

She moved closer to the bed. "I had this patient once, his name was Robert, and he came to us as broken as you are. He waited four months for a donor, and when finally one was found, he almost wouldn't go through with it. He probably wouldn't have, except that his wife insisted." She smiled softly. "Afterward, he moved back to his small Oregon town, and I didn't hear from him for two years. Then, one day, he came by to see me—and he brought his newborn baby girl with him. They'd named her Madelaine Allenford Hartfort."

It was a minute before Angel spoke, and when he did, his voice was ragged and hoarse. "How will it really be?"

The simple question hurt. He'd known that it was a fairy tale, that endings like that were for people who believed in them. "You'll be on medication for the rest of your life. You'll have to eat a heart-healthy diet and you'll have to exercise. Millions of Californians live that way by choice." She tried to smile, but found that she couldn't. She leaned closer, allowed herself to stroke the damp, sweaty hair from his eyes. "But you'll be *alive,* Angel. You can still act in movies, still throw temper tantrums, still be your larger-than-life self. Everything that matters in life will still be yours for the asking."

"What about children?"

It took her a second to respond. "Did you want children, Angel?"

He gave her a smile that didn't reach his eyes. "Please don't talk about me in the past tense. I'm particularly sensitive." He allowed a silence to slip between them before he finally answered. "Yeah, I wanted kids . . . once. I used to wonder sometimes . . . used to see myself playin' ball on an autumn evening with a blond-haired little boy. Course, now . . ."

Madelaine couldn't breathe. The silence stretched between

them, lengthening. Madelaine finally said, "Don't do that to yourself."

He turned his head slightly, stared at a place just to the left of her head. "Next time." His voice fell to a harsh whisper. "Next time don't save me. I don't want to . . ." He squeezed his eyes shut, but not before she saw the glistening of tears. "Not like this . . ."

And in that moment, so many things fell into place. She gazed down at him, remembering and forgetting everything in the space of a single breath. This man she once loved was hurting, and though he didn't know it, wouldn't admit it, he was reaching out to her just like she'd always secretly prayed he would. Some part of him was counting on the candy striper girl to care about him again.

He was the old Angel, the boy who'd taken her hand and showed her a whole new world, the boy who'd cried when he told her he loved her.

*This* man, with his secret dreams of a lost son and his quiet admission of defeat, this man maybe she could trust. . . .

She lurched to her feet and turned away from the bed. Chewing on her thumbnail, she walked over to the window and stared outside, watching the silver rain fall.

She was afraid of her own emotions right now, afraid she was *feeling* instead of thinking and every time she'd done that in her life, it had cost her dearly.

"You know, Mad . . ." His voice drifted softly toward her. Almost against her will, she turned back to face him.

He lay there, looking weak and broken. "You haunted me," he whispered, trying to give her a smile.

She saw the wrenching emotion in his eyes, the regret and the sorrow, and she realized that her own fear was nothing compared to his. He needed her now, needed her more than he'd ever needed that sixteen-year-old candy striper—and she needed to be strong. To face her fear of abandonment and do the right thing.

"You can't die, Angel," she said softly, so softly she wondered if he could even hear her. She swallowed thickly, feeling as if she were walking out on a narrow, shaky ledge, but there was no turning back. She couldn't let Angel die without giving him the one gift that might make him believe in the fairy tale.

He gave her a shadow of that famous grin. "Watch me."

She drew her hand back and gazed down at him. "If you died, your daughter would never forgive you."

It had to be the drugs. He couldn't have heard what he'd thought he heard.

*Your daughter.*

The words twisted deep. For a split second he felt a flash of pure, white-hot hope. "Sorry, Mad. I lost track of what we were talking about."

"I said you had a daughter."

"Is this a joke?" he whispered.

He thought he saw a sparkle of tears in her eyes, then they were gone. She shook her head slowly. "You think I'd be that cruel?"

"No. But . . ." He stopped, not knowing what to say or what to feel. "A daughter," he said slowly, trying to make it sink in.

A daughter. He squeezed his eyes shut.

Madelaine had kept her from him, hidden his child away as if he had no right to even know of her existence. She knew he'd thought she had an abortion, and she'd let him go on thinking that, let him live his life without ever *knowing* he was a father. "You bitch," he hissed. Anger was a black, bitter taste in his mouth, and he wanted to hurl curse words at her, wanted to make her feel as betrayed and hurt as he felt right now.

He was glad when she flinched. Then, wordlessly, she reached into her purse and pulled out a black leather wallet. Flipping it open, she withdrew a picture and handed it to him.

For a second his hands shook so hard, he couldn't focus on the picture. He closed his eyes and concentrated on his breathing, ignoring the stuttering misbeats of his ragged heart. Then, very slowly, he opened his eyes.

The girl who stared back at him was a mirror.

*His daughter.*

She looked young, with electric blue eyes and jet-black hair. The smile she wore was familiar—big and bright and mesmerizing. She was dressed in black, a man's tuxedo vest over a T-shirt, and several black loops hanging from each ear. There was a cocky defiance in her gaze that made Angel feel as if he knew her.

He couldn't release the picture. He held it, stroking the porous surface, as if by touching the photograph he could somehow get to know the girl. His daughter.

Slowly, the anger in him bled away, congealed into the cold hard rock of regret. Of course Madelaine had kept this secret from him—what else could she do? What choice had he given her?

"I'm sorry," he whispered. "I have no right . . ."

"No," she said in a steely voice, "you don't."

"I thought . . ." He found he couldn't say the words.

She nodded. "I know. You thought I had an abortion. My father couldn't wait to tell me of your reaction."

"Tell me what happened."

She looked away from him, covering her mouth with one hand for a long time. He knew how much this moment was hurting her. He wished he could touch her, tell her it was okay, that he understood, but he couldn't do it. He didn't understand a damned thing.

"It was a long time ago," Madelaine said at last. "After you left, Alex threw a fit." She gave a tired laugh. *"You will not have that greasy little wop's child, do you understand me?"* she said in a perfect imitation of Alex's blustering voice. "He locked me in my room for three days. I waited for you. . . ." She gave him a practiced smile. "When I saw the Harley, I knew what you'd done."

"Mad—"

She pushed a nonexistent lock of hair from her forehead and went on without looking at him. "Alex decreed that I would have an abortion and there would be *no more talk of this disgrace.*" She drew in a shaking breath. "I agreed. What else could I do, where else could I go?"

She swallowed hard and stared at her own hands. "I got in the limousine and let the driver take me to the doctor's office where Alex had set up the appointment. I was going to do what he asked, just let him decide what was best for me." She shook her head. "I didn't care about anything."

He watched as she slumped forward, saying nothing for a long time. Then slowly she straightened, her chin came up. He knew that she was waging a painful battle and she was fighting the only way she knew, the way Alex had taught her.

After a few more seconds, she went on and her voice was flat. "Everything changed when I got to the clinic." She shuddered, stared blankly at the gray wall. "That cold brick building . . . the yellow sofas filled with girls just like me. I remember when they called my name, I jumped. I followed the nurse to the examination room and took my clothes off. I put on that flimsy cotton hospital gown and climbed onto that paper-covered table."

She shuddered again. "I stared at those stirrups and thought about what they were going to do to me, to my baby . . . to our baby, and I couldn't do it."

Her pain knifed through him, hurt like hell. "Jesus, Mad . . ."

"I got dressed and sneaked outside. The limo was waiting at the curb, but I knew there was no going back. Alex had made that very clear. I could only please him—the great, unpleasable Alexander Hillyard—by having the abortion. So I called the only person I could think of."

Angel knew before she said it.

"Francis." She smiled when she said his name. "You remember what he was like back then. Eighteen. Shy, bookish. He had just started at the seminary and he was on his way to becoming a priest. But he came for me that day, and the next day and the next. He saved us both." She gave a breathy little laugh. "He didn't ask any questions, didn't say anything except *Hey, Maddy-girl, you're in the wrong part of town.* He set me up in a halfway house for pregnant teenagers, and I loved it. I'd never known other kids my age, never had any friends except you, and I learned a lot. I'd already gotten my high school diploma, so I started college at sixteen. Thank God my mother left me a trust fund to cover expenses. I busted my ass to get through med school in a hurry."

Angel closed his eyes. He could envision every moment of her life, the way Francis was always there to help out, a shelter from every storm. Not like Angel, who'd never stuck around for anything or anyone.

"Her name is Angelina Francesca Hillyard. I call her Lina."

*I call her Lina.* Suddenly she was a person, this girl in the picture who had his face. Not some imaginary word or image, but a real live person. A daughter who would want something from her father. Want a lot of things.

Panic sneaked up on him, twisted him into knots. "Does she know about me?"

"No."

He sighed in relief. "Thank God."

"You said you dreamed about a little boy. . . ."

"Dreams," he said dully, staring up at the ceiling. He could feel himself going down the wrong path, doing the wrong thing, but as always, he couldn't change it. Didn't really want to. He felt empty inside, eviscerated by her revelation and his own fear. "I said I'd wondered about a baby, but . . ." For a second he couldn't go on, his throat was so full. Finally he swallowed hard and looked at her. He could see the pain in her eyes, knew what he was doing to her right now, and though he regretted it, there wasn't a damn thing he could do to change it. "A dying man's talk, Mad. That's not a real dream. It's self-pity, regret. Pretend. It's like turning Catholic at the end just in case. It doesn't mean anything."

She was pale. "What are you saying?"

God, it hurt to let her down like this, to let himself down. But he wasn't worthy of being a father. He didn't deserve a gift like that. "Why did you tell me about her, Mad? Why?"

"I thought you needed a reason to live. I thought Lina might make a difference."

"No," he said, realizing midword that he was shouting. "What am I supposed to do, Mad, play daddy on a deathbed for some sixteen-year-old girl I've never met? Is that what you thought— that you could waltz some strange kid into my room and I'd hug and kiss her and die a happy man? That she could watch my last gasping breath and feel *better* for having known me?"

"No." The word was a croak of sound, broken. "I thought . . ." She shook her head. "I don't know what I thought."

"You were right not to contact me all those years." He sighed, knowing suddenly the truth about himself, hating it. "She wouldn't have made a difference, Mad. I would have walked from her just like I walked from you. It's what I do."

"But now—"

"I don't want to meet her, Mad."

She drew in a sharp breath. "Don't say that. She needs you."

"That's exactly why I don't want to meet her." His gaze pleaded with her for understanding. "You know me, Mad. Even if I live—which I won't—I have nothing to offer the kid. I'll be infatuated with her for a few days, maybe a month, and then the glow will wear off. My feet'll get itchy, I'll start drinking again, and I'll start resenting her for keeping me here." Bitterness tightened his voice. "And then one day I'll be gone."

"But—"

He reached out, touched her. She leaned into his hand, let his fingers curl around her chin. He gave her the only thing of value, the only truth he knew. "I'll break her heart, Mad. Whether I live or die, it doesn't matter—either way, I'll let her down. If you love her, protect her from me."

She looked at him, and in the depths of her eyes he saw the pain he'd caused, and something else, something he couldn't name. She kept staring at him, saying nothing, and as the clock ticked past the minutes, he began to feel uncomfortable. There was an expectancy in her gaze that nibbled at his self-confidence, confused him. "Don't look at me that way," he said.

"What way?"

"As if you know I'll change my mind."

"You will." Her voice trembled just a bit, belied the conviction of her words. Then, softer, "You have to."

Madelaine sat at her desk, staring at the photograph of Lina. The ornate crystal clock ticked past the minutes with a tiny *click . . . click . . . click.*

She closed her eyes and sighed. Even now, almost an hour after she'd seen Angel, she couldn't believe she'd told him the truth about Lina.

*Oh, Francis,* she thought, *where are you? I need you right now. . . .*

She swiveled around in her chair and stared at the window. The huddled row of plants smeared into a hazy green wash. It had surprised her so much, Angel's quietly spoken dream of a young son to play baseball with. Part of her had been terrified by the turn in the conversation, but another part—a hidden, secret part she hadn't known existed—was thrilled to hear that he'd thought of their baby, that maybe he'd even fantasized about her. And suddenly she'd *wanted* to tell him about Lina, wanted to rip the lid off the secret she'd kept for so long. She'd wanted to reach out for the young man she'd once loved and take his hand and walk with him . . . to laugh about the good times.

She found herself going over all of it in her mind, going back, back to the past she'd tried so hard to forget. . . .

It was on a sultry August night when she'd realized she was pregnant. At first she'd been happy. She and Angel had spun so many cotton-candy dreams together in the moonlight, dreams in which they married and had children, and neither one of them was ever lonely or lost or afraid again.

But telling him about the baby hadn't gone as she'd imagined. She remembered sitting in that horrible trailer, smelling his mother's cigarette smoke as she whispered her secret.

Oh, he'd said the right things, said he loved her and he'd stand by her, but she saw the look in his eyes, the wildness, the fear. He didn't want the baby, wasn't ready for it, and after that look, that second when she stared into his soul and saw the truth, she never believed the words again.

She didn't know what to do after that, and neither did he. She was sixteen, he was seventeen, and they'd thought they were immortal, thought their love could protect them from the ugliness of the world.

But the ugliness came anyway.

When Alexander Hillyard found out that his perfect daughter was pregnant, he went crazy. He locked her in her room and barred the windows with thick, black iron rails. No amount of tears or pleading words swayed him. He decreed that she would have an abortion, and they would never speak of her indiscretion again. He would not allow *this* to ruin her future.

She waited in that cold, impeccably decorated room for days, huddled alongside the window, staring out, waiting for Angel to come for her.

Finally she saw him, a slim shadow standing at the perimeter of the property. She launched herself at the window, clawing it with her fingers, crying out his name. But he didn't hear her.

She watched him walk up the brick walkway, then disappear into the house. She huddled at her locked door, listening desperately for footsteps.

Footsteps that never came.

Fifteen minutes later—the longest quarter of an hour of her life—he left the house. She scrambled back to the window and pressed her face to the glass. At the gate he turned around, his eyes searching the front of the house.

Their gazes met, and slowly, so slowly, he shook his head, then he turned and walked away. She thought she'd seen tears on his cheeks, but it could have been the rain, she'd never been sure.

Even after he left, she clung to a fraying thread of hope that he would be back. A thread that broke cleanly the next night.

She heard a rumbling sound outside and she raced to the window, shoving the Alençon lace curtains aside. He was at the side of the road, staring up at her window, sitting on a brand-new, chrome-plated Harley-Davidson motorcycle.

And that was when she knew: he'd taken money from her father.

This time she was certain that he was crying, but she didn't care. He gave her a wan, tired wave, and then he drove away.

It was the last time she'd seen Angel DeMarco—until he showed up in ICU, needing her to save his life.

She knew Angel had thought she'd had an abortion. Her father had wasted no time in telling the daddy-to-be that there would be no baby.

So what had made her risk it all now, opening the Pandora's box that had been shut for so long?

She didn't know the man lying in that bed down the hall, didn't honestly know a thing about him. But she knew his roots, knew where he came from and the kind of person he'd once been. The kind who roared away from responsibility on a brand-new Harley-Davidson.

People didn't change, not at their core. She had no doubt that the wild, hell-raising, rebellious seventeen-year-old boy was still alive and kicking in that broken thirty-four-year-old body.

One look. One smile. That's all he'd have to give Lina and she'd melt, just as Madelaine had done so many years ago.

She shuddered. Closing her eyes for a split second, she imagined Lina running away from the cold, perfect mother who never did anything right, running into the sunlight warmth of Angel's smile. Never looking back, never coming home.

But the time for such fear was past. Madelaine was tired of lying and hiding and pretending, tired of watching her precious daughter slide into an abyss. Madelaine knew—had always known—she had a rope, and she couldn't go on standing on the the sidelines, being a bystander to her own life. She was tired of being afraid.

Angel might break Lina's heart, might hurt her daughter irreparably, but maybe he wouldn't. That was the hope that had filled her awhile ago. *Maybe he wouldn't.*

Maybe the past wasn't what she'd always thought it to be, an immutable spreadsheet of facts and figures and moments found and lost. Maybe it was more amorphous, more forgiving. Maybe Lina and Angel could draw the best out of each other, save each other in this time when both of them were floundering and felt so alone.

She had to believe it.

He was running late—as usual.

Francis plunged his foot down on the accelerator, waiting several seconds for the action to kick in. The tired car stuttered and lurched forward, its engine humming loudly, rattling the cup of coffee wedged between his thighs.

The twisting gravel road arced to the left, then to the right and back to the left again, snaking through a forest of old-growth timber.

He drove up the mountain, twisting and turning, emerging every now and then onto the sweeping vista of the river valley below. Finally, at just over an hour late, he saw the resort's hand-carved sign. He turned in to the tree-lined drive and eased his pressure on the accelerator.

Multnomah Lodge sat like a wood-hewn tiara in a grove of towering evergreens. The sweeping circular drive curled into the front door, drawing guests in a friendly embrace toward the entrance. Lights glowed through mullioned windows cut into the log exterior. The last autumn flowers, chrysanthemums, hardy roses, Shasta daisies, lined the stone walkways.

He maneuvered his battered old Volkswagen up to the curb. The doorman rushed out and waited at attention.

Francis killed the engine, wincing as it sputtered and coughed. Yanking hard on the cold metal handle, he pushed the whining door open and got out. He retrieved his garment bag from the trunk and slung it over his shoulder, then gave the valet the keys and headed inside.

The interior of the resort was all wood and glass and stone. Northwest artifacts hung from the skinned log walls, and Native American baskets sat clustered on hammered copper tables. The chairs and sofas were overstuffed and upholstered in boldly patterned wool.

"Father Francis!" he heard a woman's voice shriek as he hurried across the stone foyer.

He stopped and looked around.

His group was seated in a small, glass-walled room that was kitty-corner to the main lobby. He knew immediately that they'd been there for over an hour, waiting for their priest who was always late.

He turned and headed toward the room. They were smiling at him as he walked, and he smiled back, looking at each one of them in turn. Old Joseph and Maria Santiago, who'd been married for thirty years and thought they wouldn't make thirty-one; Sarah and Levi Abramson, whose interfaith marriage was coming apart at the seams; Thomas and Hope Fitzgerald, who'd reached the crossroads in their marriage when Hope's biological clock began to tick louder—unfortunately, it was a sound only she could hear; and Ted and Janine Canfield, who were having trouble integrating stepchildren into a new family.

Such good people, all of them. People who loved each other and God and their families. People who were trying to hold fast to a commitment in an unraveling world that didn't seem to value the old words anymore.

And they were looking to Father Francis Xavier DeMarco to show them the way.

He felt like such a fraud. What did he, a man who'd experienced so little, have to offer as a torch in the darkness to couples who were afraid? He'd never been part of a loving family and he'd never held one together, he'd never made love to a woman or disciplined his own child or tried to find the money to put food on the table. He'd never worked a nine-to-five job and lived with those pressures.

*So many things he hadn't done.*

He sighed. Readjusting the garment bag's wide nylon strap over his shoulder, he crossed the few feet that separated the foyer from the meeting room. The four couples were seated comfortably on the overstuffed chairs and sofas in the room. Joe Santiago was playing chess with Janine Canfield at a table in the corner. Hope Fitzgerald was sitting on the hearth, her arms looped around her bent legs, her sad gaze fixed on her husband, who sat stiffly on the sofa alongside Sarah Abramson.

As Francis entered, they all smiled at him and said hello, but he heard so much more in the silence that came afterward than in the sound that accompanied his greeting. Emotions ran deep in this room—sadness, anger, grief, love.

He steepled his fingers, brushed the underside of his chin with his fingertips as he glanced from face to face, seeing their expectation, feeling the weight of it settling on his shoulders. He wanted to help these people.

The hell of it was, he knew that he couldn't. Maybe once, years and years ago, he could have come into this room on a tide of optimism, his thin white collar a protective shield. Back then, the collar never chafed his skin, never felt so tight that he couldn't breathe. It had been freeing, that scrap of starched white fabric, proof that he was a faithful servant of a Lord he loved. With each passing year, though, it had seemed to grow smaller and smaller, becoming at last a barrier between him and his fellow man.

And sometimes, like now, he ached to take it off, and ask instead of answer. He wanted to turn to Mrs. Santiago and beg her to tell him what it felt like to curl up in bed against the same body every night for thirty years, to wake to the same loving face. He wanted to ask if love was a safe harbor or a stormy sea.

He knew that he was experiencing a crisis of faith, knew, too, that it was no different from what thousands of priests had faced before him. But the knowledge didn't warm him. He missed the hot fire of his convictions—the love for God that had once driven his every waking moment. Without it, he felt confused . . . adrift.

He felt unfit to be a servant of the Lord. The memory of how he'd chosen to hurt Lina prickled on his conscience like a fresh burn.

"Father Francis?" Levi Abramson's scratchy voice cut into his thoughts.

Francis forced a smile. "Sorry, I'm just a bit tired tonight. How about if we begin this retreat by fashioning a list of goals we'd like to accomplish?"

There were nods and murmurs of agreement—as always. He saw the hope flash through their eyes, saw the tentative smiles that touched their faces. And Francis felt satisfied he could give them that, if nothing more concrete.

"Good," he said, giving them the first honest smile of the evening. "Let's start with a prayer."

# chapter thirteen

❧

Angel woke suddenly, a cold, crushing band of pain encircling his chest. Clammy sheets twisted around his legs, bunched in the hands that lay fisted at his sides. The pillows were damp, sweaty-smelling balls beneath his head.

The cardiac monitor blipped wildly. He waited in breathless silence for the computerized alarm to sound, but nothing happened. He released his breath slowly, evenly, focusing on nothing but each pain-riddled exhalation. *One, two, buckle my shoe . . . three, four, shut the door . . .* The childhood rhyme came back to him and he seized on it, trying to remember the words, trying to focus on anything except the pain.

His heart thumped and clattered dangerously. He reached tiredly for the button beside his bed and pressed the red dot.

The door to his room whooshed open and Sarah, the night nurse, waddled to his bedside. "You shouldn't be awake," she said reproachfully, checking the monitors that clustered around him, the bags of fluid that hung suspended above his head.

"I need more drugs," he said in a slurred voice.

"You get your next dose at six A.M." She lifted the thin white strand of paper from the cardiac monitor and studied it, her eyes narrowing. A quiet *tsk*ing sound pushed past her fleshy lips.

"How's your daughter?" he asked quietly.

She paused and looked down at him. Slowly she smiled. "She's doing better, thank you."

"I . . ." He winced. *God, it hurt to talk.* "I called my business manager. He's sending her an autographed picture."

Sarah beamed, then brushed a lock of sweaty hair from his forehead. "Thank you, Mr. DeMarco."

He whispered, "No problem."

She checked one last bag, then turned and bustled away. The door closed behind her and silence settled into the room again, punctuated only by the computerized *blip-blip-blip* of the monitor.

Angel sighed again, wishing that he could close his eyes and drift off to sleep. Knowing that he couldn't.

He turned slightly to look out the wall of glass beside his closed door. The Intensive Care Unit was silent and shadowy, the private rooms darkened for the night. Wraiths in white guarded the nurses' station, huddled together in pockets of glowing light.

He stared so long his vision blurred and the nurses and interns became shadows within shadows, talking among themselves, sipping coffee, laughing silently.

*I call her Lina.*

He squeezed his eyes shut. Regret was a raw, throbbing wound in his soul. He couldn't think of anything but the girl in the photograph. The look of her, so like him. The flame-blue eyes, the jet-black hair, the tiny little mole on the pale skin of her neck.

He wondered what she was like, this teenager who wore his smile on her heart-shaped face, but before he could even formulate a fantasy, it was gone.

He knew he couldn't be a father. Not when he was healthy and certainly not now, when he lay dying. It saddened him, that pathetic realization of his own inadequacy. No man should have to see himself so clearly, know his own bleak soul with such intimacy, but Angel had never been one to lie to himself—only to others. He'd always seen his own frayed edges and known that he couldn't change them. Change was too hard and the outcome too uncertain. Instead, he accepted himself, accepted and went on.

It was what he'd always done. Seen the truth and tucked his regrets so deeply in the pocket of his soul that after awhile, he'd forgotten they existed. Until a day like today when his shortcomings were exposed.

His thoughts spun out like a fisherman's line across the yawning darkness of the room. The years slid away from him, took him back, back.

It had been a breathtakingly beautiful summer evening—a week before he betrayed Madelaine. He remembered it clearly—a midnight sky lit with the bluish white of a full moon, the rustle of maple leaves overhead, and the faraway sounds of a carnival.

*Come on, Angel, take me on the Ferris wheel. I've never been on one. . . .*

He heard the softness of her words, whispered against his ear, remembered the gentle tugging of her hand as she pulled him down the midway.

It had been a Ferris wheel ride like no other. He felt the seat rock beneath him, sway and creak as it took them up, up, up, into the star-spangled sky.

When he looked down, he saw a whole new world. Gone was the tawdriness of the carnival, the dirt beneath the bright lights, and the crass cheapness of the prizes. Instead, he saw it as she saw it. Lights, action. *Magic.*

He held her close in that swaying seat, clinging to her, wanting her with all the pent-up desperation of a seventeen-year-old boy in love for the first time in his life. His hand had slid down her arm, feeling the softness of her skin and the sudden goose bumps his touch caused.

She turned to him then, and that instant was emblazoned on the ragged organ that was his heart—her hair ruffled by the wind, her eyes shining with love, her face backlit by a blanket of stars and moonlight. *I love you, Angel DeMarco.*

He gave her the same quiet declaration, feeling the humiliating sting of tears that he didn't bother to brush away. He felt safe with her in that second, safe enough to cry, and both of them knew it.

Afterward, they strolled hand in hand down the midway, and Angel was struck again by the magic of it all. He remembered how it had felt to be swept into that fantasyland; for a boy who'd grown up in a rickety trailer on the wrong side of town with an alcoholic mother, it was a dizzyingly heady time.

He spent his money at one booth after another, winning stuffed animals and a wineglass and a cheap bow-and-arrow set. But it was the last prize he remembered the most clearly.

*The earrings,* she whispered to him, pointing at a pair of garish red metal hoops. He knew instantly why she wanted them— they were so gaudy and cheap that Alex would be horrified to find them in her possession. She, with her pearls and diamonds and emeralds, the poor little rich girl who had never owned a carnival trinket.

It cost him eight dollars in quarters to place the earrings in her hand. But the look in her eyes was worth every cent.

After that, they walked to Carrington Park and stretched out beneath a hundred-year-old oak tree, wrapped in each other's arms as they stared up at the night sky. They talked forever, spilling secrets and making vows, dreaming aloud of their future.

He held her, kissed her, and vowed to always be there for her.

Dawn washed their night away in shades of pink and purple.

As they rose to leave, Madelaine pulled the hoops from her ears and stared down at them. "I can't bring them home. My father . . . he looks through my things."

He reached for them. "I'll keep them."

"Let's leave them here. That way a part of us will always exist under this old tree. When we're old, we can come back here with our grandchildren."

Ah, he could still remember it, the overwhelming love he'd felt for her in that moment.

They wrapped the cheap red earrings in one of Madelaine's expensive, monogrammed handkerchiefs and buried their treasure at the base of the tree.

Afterward, she looked at him, her eyes moist with tears. "I've got to get home now," she whispered.

The next time he saw her, she was sitting on his mother's ratty old couch, telling him about the baby.

He knew he said the wrong things then, but he didn't know what to say. He was so damned scared. For a week afterward, he called her house and hung up when her father answered. Finally he rode to her house and saw the iron bars that had been fixed across her bedroom window, and he knew what had happened. Alex had found out about the baby.

He wanted to turn tail and run and run and run. He almost did it, then he saw something—a shadow pass across the bright light in her bedroom—and he thought of that moment on the Ferris wheel. *I love you, Angel.*

The memory gave him the courage to park his bike. Flipping his collar up against the pouring rain, he walked up the pathway to the double front doors and knocked hard.

There was a rustling of feet, a click of metal on metal, then the door opened.

And God stood in the doorway, wearing a Brooks Brothers suit and holding a martini glass. Angel had never seen a man so big and overpowering, so intimidating; he had a voice that boomed into the darkness like a bullhorn. *So you're the little wop who screwed my daughter.*

The rest of the meeting melted as it always did into a blur of shame and regret. Instead of the actual sequence of events, he remembered bits and pieces of their conversation; words that drove through the heart and soul like razors.

*Who do you think you are to come to my house, to knock on my door as if you belong here? You're nothing. Nothing.*

With each word, delivered like a blow, Angel felt himself growing smaller and smaller, until, in the end, there was nothing left of him at all.

*What'll it take, kid, to get you the hell out of her life? One thousand dollars, five thousand, ten thousand? How about if I fire that drunk mother of yours? You didn't think I knew she worked in my mill, I see. The world's full of surprise, isn't it?*

It took a minute for the words to register, but finally Angel understood: Alex was offering him a way out.

*Ten thousand, kid. Think about it. . . .*

He didn't want to think about it, tried not to, but the offer seduced him.

*You're no hero, kid. Take the money.*

Angel closed his eyes, hearing, seeing, feeling it all over again, the moment that had forever defined him. He shouldn't have followed Alex into the house, but he had; he shouldn't have gone into that dark, shadowed office, but he had. He remembered it all suddenly—the sound of the desk drawer sliding open, the ripping hiss of the check as Alex eased it from his book.

Angel thought now of the moments, the seconds, he could have said no. Up until the last heartbeat, when he'd held the check in his hand and seen all those zeroes.

Alex had sensed Angel's uncertainty, smelled it, and gone in for the kill with a hunter's precision.

*What'll you give Madelaine? Life in some sleazy trailer, a beer with your TV dinner after work? And how about you—you*

*going to spend the rest of your life tossing toilet paper like your
mother? Or are you going to take what I'm offering and get the
hell out of this town?*

Angel thought of his parents—thirty years spent toiling on
the paper line, only to come home and get drunk and knock the
shit out of their son. His father, dead of alcohol poisoning before
his fortieth birthday.

Alex went on relentlessly, waving the check at Angel. *I've
seen a million guys like you in my life. You're nothing, going
nowhere. You're not good enough to lick her shit-covered shoes.*

Angel tried. God help him, he gathered his shredded courage
and tried. *I could be a good father.* But he knew, even as he said
it, he knew it was a lie, and Alex knew it, too.

The old man laughed. *To what? She's having an abortion
tomorrow. You didn't think she'd really have a child of yours,
did you? She's a* Hillyard, *for Christ's sake.*

Angel was relieved. Even now it sickened him to remember
how relieved he'd been by the words.

*Take the money, kid. It's all there is for you.*

And Angel did it. He turned and ran, the check clutched in
his sweaty fingers. All the way out, he told himself it didn't matter, that he could cash the check and spend the money and still
come back for Madelaine.

But by the time he reached his bike, he knew the truth, and it
ripped through him, twisting his insides until he thought he
might vomit in the street. He was leaving her because he *wanted*
to leave her, because he wasn't strong enough to stay and take a
job in some crummy factory and be a father to his unborn baby.

*There will be no baby.* He tried to take comfort from the
knowledge, but somehow it only hurt more.

He was scared. God, so scared. He didn't want to give up his
whole future, not yet.

Slowly he turned. He saw her up there, her pale oval face
trapped between the iron bars that blocked her window, captured in the rain-smeared glass.

Then he jumped on his brother's bike and rode away, the check as heavy as pieces of silver in his coat pocket.

Angel released his breath in a heavy sigh. Yeah, he'd ridden away, ridden hard and fast and long, and ended up right where he began.

*I call her Lina.*

The words slammed him back into the present.

And he felt the first threatening thud inside his chest.

He closed his eyes and lay still, taking shallow breaths. The sweat on his forehead turned cold, slid in streaks down the sides of his face.

He tried to reach for the nurses' button, but he was too weak. He couldn't lift his arm.

The cardiac monitor clattered and hummed, then screamed in alarm.

*Heart failure.*

Angel tried to keep breathing. His body seemed to encase him, bloating bigger and bigger, a seeping darkness that filled everything. And in the center of it all was the pain.

In some distant part of his brain, he heard the commotion— the door banging open, the light spilling in, the voices raised in alarm. He heard them calling his name, but he couldn't answer. There were layers and layers of darkness between him and the light, and he was tired, so tired. Hours seemed to pass.

Then he felt her touch, heard her voice through the screaming cacophony. "Angel?"

He tried to reach for her, but his body fought him, a limp dead thing without will or ability. He blinked hard, forced his eyes to open.

Madelaine was leaning over him, her hair transformed into a halo by the glaring overhead light. For a second he was back on the Ferris wheel, seeing her draped in starlight. "Mad," he croaked.

"Don't you die, Angel DeMarco. Don't you dare." She turned her head and gave orders in a composed, controlled voice that calmed him. Then she turned back to him, stroked his damp forehead again. "You're going to make it through this, Angel. We'll find you a heart. Just don't give up."

Her face kept going in and out of focus.

"Angel? Stay awake."

His eyelids felt heavy. He thought there was something he needed to say to her, then the thought was gone.

"Pulmonary edema," Madelaine said under her breath. Then louder, "Get the code cart. God *damn* it, people, let's move. . . ."

He knew the words should frighten him, but he couldn't feel anything anymore.

# chapter fourteen

The cool autumn evening sky had begun to soften, blurring at the edges in shades of pink and lavender and blue.

Francis sat Indian-style on the hardwood floor of the Quilcene Room, his gaze fixed on the night unfolding beyond the floor-to-ceiling window. Crows cawed to one another, swooping from their perches in the cedar trees, chasing smaller, weaker birds into hiding places along the eaves. He could hear the scraping of their clawed feet on the planks outside. It was just past twilight, the time of night when the horses and cows on nearby farms whickered and lowed for their nightly rations of hay, when deer warily crossed the country roads in search of the last sweet grass before winter.

Thick gray clouds drew cautiously together and sent a few spitting drops of rain downward. A breeze tapped the windows and kicked up a pile of browning leaves. Pine needles sprinkled to the ground, collecting here and there on the white-painted windowsills.

"Father Francis?"

Francis drew his gaze away from the window and glanced around the room at the men clustered near the fireplace. Shards of light leapt from the roaring fire, twisting across the serious faces that stared back at him.

It was their sixth night together, the last before a forty-eight-hour break when each of the couples would spend some romantic time together. Francis looked at the men and smiled.

As always, he'd refound his faith in both man and God by performing his priestly duties. Yes, he still felt a bit fraudulent, giving advice with so little experience to back it up, but over the days and nights he'd spent with these people, he'd seen the effects of his efforts . . . in the way Joe Santiago had begun to reach for his wife's hand as they walked to the dining room; in the fleeting smile Levi Abramson tossed to his bride when she spoke of their children; in the slowly developing sense of hope that had started as a nugget of promise and grown into something more.

It had strengthened Francis's faith again.

"Father?" It was Thomas Fitzgerald again, quietly bringing Francis back into the conversation.

Francis grinned. "Sorry, guys. I was just thinking."

"Any divine inspiration slide your way through the rain?" Levi asked with a laugh.

Francis started to respond, then stopped. Something—some wisp of knowledge—shivered in the air around him, collecting like tiny sparks of lightning on a thin metal rod. He could hear it, feel it, calling out to him in a quiet whispering voice.

*Could it be that simple?*

"You know, Levi," he said slowly, feeling his way like a blind man through the alley of his thoughts. "Maybe it did. Maybe divine inspiration isn't what we think it will be."

Thomas scooted closer. "What do you mean?"

Francis stared into the fire, feeling its heat, experiencing its dancing color, hearing the popping crack of a log. God felt close to him all at once, closer than He'd been in years. "Maybe it's divine intervention that brought us here in the first place. Maybe that's all God's supposed to do, point us on a road and wait. The road's there, it's always there, through the wind and the rain and the snow."

A silence slipped into the room, collected on the indrawn breaths of the men. Francis looked around, sensing their faith in him, in God, in themselves, and one another.

*Goodness. Hope. Faith.*

He saw it all in this room. "Like you, Joseph," he said quietly, looking at the older man. "You love Maria and she loves you, but somehow over the years, you've lost sight of that road. Yet still you're here, reaching for her hand, knowing it's her you want to walk with. Maybe what you have to do is stop searching so hard for the road beneath your feet. Just take her hand and begin to walk, and *believe* that the pavement is solid beneath you. God has given each of you the incredible gift of love."

"It can't be that easy," Thomas said. He exhaled a heavy sigh, and Francis could see the doubts that twisted the young man's face. "I love my wife with everything inside me, but she wants something I don't want."

"Are you so sure?" Francis asked.

Thomas closed his eyes for a second before answering. "I'm twenty-seven years old. I'm not ready to be a father."

"Have you told her that?" Levi asked.

Thomas sighed again. "Only a million times. I've told her I don't want a child."

Francis gave Thomas a small, encouraging smile. "That's not the same thing at all, Thomas."

Thomas looked surprised. "What do you mean?"

" 'I'm not ready' is not the same thing as 'I don't want a child.' "

"But I've told her I'm not ready a million times."

"Have you?" Francis said softly. "Or have those words been tangled up with other words, harsher words, maybe anger or resentment that she would ask?"

Thomas turned away, stared into the fire. "Maybe," he said at last. Then, softer, "Maybe."

"I remember when I was your age," Joseph said. "I was scared to death to be a father. We had no money, I had no job. Then, one day, Maria met me at the door with a glass of wine and told me we were having a baby. I laughed and hugged her and drank with her—and then went into the shower and cried." A fine mist covered his rheumy gray eyes and he gave a tiny, jerking smile. "And then came our Maggie. The first time I held her, I . . . changed. Sort of grew up. Now it feels like a second has passed, but my Maggie is a dentist in New Jersey. And sometimes I miss her so much, I ache."

"No man is ever ready to be a father," Ted Canfield agreed with a nod. "It's like that road Father is talking about. She gets pregnant and you take a step, praying like hell that something solid is beneath you."

Thomas looked at Francis. "How about you, Father? Did you ever want children?"

The question caught Francis off guard. He looked at the men around him, his gaze going from face to face. He knew he should change the course of the conversation—he was their priest, their counselor, and his problems were private—but he didn't want to. Just once, he wanted to be a man, only a man in a room of other men, talking about things that mattered. He began talking, slowly at first, uncomfortable with his honesty. "I always knew I wanted to be a priest. My mother said it was a calling, but I only knew that the church was safe. I entered the seminary when I was still wet behind the ears, and I loved it."

He stared down at his hands, clasped now in his lap, and thought of all the prayers he'd said, all the dreams he'd had. In the bleak days of his childhood, the church had been his escape, his sanctuary. No one drank or screamed or hit anyone there. It was quiet and peaceful, and he'd known—always—that it was where he belonged.

Even later, when he'd learned how difficult it was to become a priest, even when he'd learned all the things he would have to sacrifice for his God, still he'd wanted it fiercely. He knew now, with the distance of maturity and years, that when he'd asked Madelaine to marry him, it wasn't what he'd wanted. Not then. He'd been so filled with the fire of his faith. And she had known it.

"Did you ever regret it?" Joseph asked. "You know, all the things you gave up?"

*Regret.* Such a powerful word, steeped in sadness and pain. "No," Francis said quietly, realizing as he spoke that it was true. He'd never regretted becoming a priest. It had filled him up, his faith, given him a strength and a compassion and a mission. It wasn't until years later, years upon years, that he'd begun, not to regret, exactly . . .

*Want.* Yes, that was the word. He'd missed a lot, and sometimes, like Joseph, he'd gone into his darkened bedroom, alone, and cried for what he'd missed. The yearnings that couldn't be assuaged, all the moments that had never truly been his. Like when he'd first held the tiny, screaming Lina, and known that she wasn't his daughter, could never be his daughter. Or the times he'd looked into Madelaine's eyes and ached at the way she saw him, the chasteness of her love.

"Sometimes," he said at last, recognizing the truth of his words. "I guess I wanted it all—children, a wife, a family—but I wanted my faith too. We can't have everything we want. There are always sacrifices. . . ."

"I think we *can* get what we want in life," Levi said. "It's just that we have the devil of a time figuring out what that is."

"Yeah," Joseph added. "Sometimes you have to turn the world upside down to see it right side up."

"But Father is right," Thomas said. "Love is a gift from God—what we do with it is up to us."

Francis didn't want to think about that, about what he *could* have if he found the courage to change his life. Glancing at the clock, he saw that it was 7:00 P.M. "Okay, we have thirty minutes left, guys." He reached into his canvas pack and pulled out a stack of yellow legal pads and a handful of pens. "I want each of you to write a letter to your wife, telling her as much of your feelings, your fears, your hopes and dreams, as you can."

Thomas's black eyebrows quirked up. "And you pick yellow legal pads for our romantic letters?" He laughed. "Obviously you've never written a love letter, Father."

The men laughed as they reached for the pads and pens. Within moments, each of the men had retreated to a quiet corner and begun to write. Pens scratched quietly on paper.

*Did you ever want children, Father?*

*Wantwantwant.* The word repeated itself, ran together and stabbed deep. . . . Ah, he wanted so much, so many things he couldn't have. . . .

Visions of Madelaine and Lina came to him, whispering, insinuating their way into his heart, gathering in the air around him. He leaned forward, wanting to reach out, grab them, and draw them close.

She loved him; he knew that, had always known it.

*Love is a gift from God. . . .*

Francis's breath released in a quiet sigh of wonder. It was as if the words had somehow formed themselves just for him. The same words he'd said a million times in his life, but this time he understood them.

*Love is a gift from God.*

He knew the doctrine of his faith would call his love for Madelaine a sin, but Francis had never been able to believe that. Breaking vows, yes, that was a sin; but the simple, singular act of loving? He'd never believed that his precious God would deem it such. It was His gift to us, His ultimate blessing.

Madelaine wasn't his lover; he'd never truly thought of her

that way. She was his love. As was Lina—his precious, precious Lina—and Angel.

*Angel.* He thought of his brother, and as he did, a thousand remembered images sprang to his mind. At first they were the usual memories—the ones that had hurt at the time and kept on hurting, the ones that Francis could never quite get rid of. Their mother, getting nine-year-old Angel drunk and beating him up, locking him up in that dark closet until he promised to be as good as his brother. And the words, always the words, spoken to Angel in that gravelly, slurred voice, *I shoulda had an abortion.*

Francis had always tried to change what couldn't be changed. So many nights he'd held his bruised baby brother in his arms and cried to his God, his own trembling voice begging for help. Then, one day, Angel stopped reaching for his big brother, and that had been the most painful time of all. Francis had seen the dawning suspicion in Angel's eyes, the question that lurked there—*why?* those green eyes had asked. *Why am I so different?*

But Angel had never asked the question aloud, and Francis had never found an answer. So they went on, living side by side in that crappy little trailer, pretending to be brothers, when, with every passing day, they were becoming only strangers. And Angel—Angel had become what his mother had predicted he would become: a hell-raising, shit-kicking kid who didn't care about anything, especially himself.

There had only ever been two people who believed in Angel—Francis and Madelaine—and Francis had let him down. All those years he'd let their mother terrorize Angel, and he'd stood by, unable to do anything. He'd watched as the goodness was slowly, systematically ripped from his brother's soul.

And he'd done it again, just last week. He'd gone to the hospital, seen his baby brother lying in that narrow bed, and done nothing; he'd let the past swirl around them, just opened that damned door and let their mother's ugly spirit in. Francis wasn't a kid anymore and wasn't impotent. This time he could be the protector he should have been before. Maybe he could even give his little brother a reason to stay.

*Believe in the road.*

Angel coming back, now after all these years . . . Lina asking the question that had been unasked for so long . . . It had to mean something.

Francis could make it mean something. He could redeem himself in the eyes of God, and in his own eyes. He could rectify the mistakes he and Madelaine had made, and those that were his alone.

He rose to his feet and went to the window. He imagined himself standing in the midst of that rainy darkness, wanting to believe in the road beneath him. His heart was beating so quickly, he could hear it thudding in his ears. *Please God, show me the way.*

Suddenly he found it, the courage he'd been searching for his whole life. It was there in his heart, heating him like that last burning coal in the midst of a black, dead fire.

He knew where he belonged and what he had to do. For once in his life, he knew. How had he missed it? How had he not seen that for the first time in years, everything that mattered to him was at home—Madelaine, Lina, Angel? He could bring them together, and now, all these years later, they could be the family they should have been all along.

*Believe in the road. . . .*

With the thought, it came again, the sense of having been touched at last by the hand of the God he'd prayed to and believed in for all his life. The faith he'd thought he'd lost filled him to overflowing, warming the dark, cold corners of his soul with searing bright light.

Grinning, he glanced again at the clock. It was seven-thirty. He could be in Seattle by eleven-thirty and back here in time for the Monday morning breakfast.

Perfect.

*   *   *

He looked dead.

Madelaine's gaze shot to the cardiac monitor. The intermittent green line peaked and dipped in sharp, erratic beats across the blank screen, clicking along on its uneven rhythm. The pink line slid along beneath it.

She released a heavy sigh and shoved a hand through her hair again, leaning closer to the bed. Her chair screeched across the linoleum floor. Beside her, a tray of cold mashed potatoes and gravy sat congealing into the rolled white flaps of pressed turkey.

She knew it had been brought in by mistake, that sickening high-fat meal, but no one had come by to reclaim it yet. She guessed it was because no one thought there was any rush. Angel DeMarco, it was well known, hadn't noticed anything like a bad smell in almost a week.

He'd been in and out of consciousness briefly, here and there, bits of time when his eyes were open and his fingers trembled and she knew he wanted to speak. But by the time she got the tube from his throat, he was usually gone again, drifting, babbling, laughing, and crying.

As always, she stopped by and sat with him for an hour after her shift was over. She kept coming back, urging him to fight harder, to believe in a surgery she found she couldn't believe in much herself anymore.

She brushed the damp hair away from his warm forehead. "Lina and I watched one of your movies together last night. It was . . . interesting. Well, since you're unconscious, I guess I can be honest. It was dreadful, actually—too much blood and violence and sex. But Lina liked it, and your acting was incredible. She thought you were totally cool—not, of course, that she said this to me. She hasn't spoken to me in days."

Madelaine stroked his cheek absentmindedly, staring out the room's small window. The wind was driving against the glass in shuddering little spurts. Rain blurred the view into a wavering sheet of gray and black. It was the beginning of a powerhouse rainstorm, she could tell.

Madelaine went on talking to him, hoping against hope that somewhere inside all that feverish sleep, he could hear her. Maybe even that her voice could be a lifeline he could follow back to consciousness. "I don't know what to do about her, Angel. She's quiet one minute and furious the next. Nothing I do is right. She's in trouble. I . . . I need your help."

She realized suddenly that she was telling him the truth, not just some words made up to appease or communicate with him, but the truth. Her truth.

She jerked her hand back and stared down at it, seeing the tiny trembling in her fingers. *Oh, God . . .*

When had she done it, started to believe in him again?

She tried to think about it, to rationalize it all away, but sometime in the last week—she didn't know exactly when or how—she'd begun to think of Angel as Lina's father. Not in some abstract biological/genetic way that was clearly factual, but in a more insidious way. A dad. Someone to help out, be there, share the load. Someone who meant that Madelaine wouldn't always be alone in parenting.

It was ridiculous to expect that of him. Ridiculous and terrifying.

She couldn't count on Angel DeMarco—hadn't she learned that lesson well enough the first time?

"Maybe *I'm* the one in the coma," she said with a self-deprecating laugh.

Before she could say anything else, she heard her name paged over the hospital's intercom. She picked up the bedside phone and punched in the operator, who transferred a call to the room.

Madelaine answered on the first ring. "Hello?"

"Maddy?" The voice was broken by static, but she would have recognized it anywhere.

"Francis! Where are you?"

"I'm leaving Portland now. Can I meet you at your house?"

She glanced at the darkness outside, then at the wall clock. "It's seven forty-five. Why don't you wait—"

"Tonight."

"All right, Francis. I'll stay up. See you about what, eleven-thirty?"

"Maybe a little before. Okay?"

She laughed. "Francis, you've never been early in your life."

"You'll see."

She laughed again and felt her anxiety slip away. Tonight she'd make up to Francis for hurting his feelings the other day, and for a brief time—maybe just a night—things could be the way they'd always been. Francis, her Francis, would help her through this rough time and show her the right way. "Okay, Francis. 'Bye."

Then she hung up.

Thunder grumbled across the black night sky. Lightning snaked from the bloated clouds. Jet-black evergreen trees climbed up a steep granite slope to the right of the road. A ravine fell away from the left side, its edge marked by a silvery guardrail. The blacktop traversed the hillside, unfurled down, down, twisting and turning.

Francis leaned forward and wiped a hand across the foggy interior of the windshield, staring beyond the blurry streaks to the road in front of him. He had the driver's window partway down, and though it was freezing in the little car, it was the only way he could keep the windshield from getting completely fogged over by his breathing. The defroster was on the blink. Again.

Paul McCartney's voice crackled through the worn speakers in a mix of static and rhythm, breaking in and out as the serrated tree line grew and receded along the road.

Rain slashed at the car, ran in rivulets across the edge of the windshield, and splattered the side of his face from the half-open window. He couldn't risk taking a hand from the wheel to wipe the moisture away, so he let it slide down his neck and burrow beneath his sweater, collecting in a cold, itchy noose along his collar.

He hunched forward, peering through the cloudy glass, clutching the leather-wrapped steering wheel. The wiper blades stuttered across the wet glass in a metronomic *whick, whick, whick.*

He turned a corner and saw with relief that the road straightened. His headlights skipped along the intermittent yellow lane divider. A hint of gray light pushed through the thinning trees, a reminder that he was almost at the base of the hill. Soon he'd be on the interstate, and the storm wouldn't slow him down but a few miles an hour.

He glanced at the speedometer, saw that he was doing a leisurely thirty-five miles per hour, and tapped the accelerator. The red needle jerked a notch, then climbed up to forty, forty-five. The radio latched on to a solid signal and Patsy Cline's liquid voice oozed from the speakers. *Craaaazy . . . crazy for feelin' so blue . . .*

The road swept into a graceful arc to the right. The silvery guardrail glimmered in the headlight's glow, protecting the road from the steep bank beyond it.

He maneuvered around the turn, singing along with the radio.

He sensed the danger before he saw it. Instinctively Francis cut back on his speed, but it was too late.

In the dim glow of his headlights, he saw a flashing bud of red, heard the shrill whining of a siren. Flares throbbed through the darkness in scraps of color. He yanked his hand from the wheel and smeared his palm across the murky windshield.

It was a police car parked on the side of the road. Beside it, a yellow station wagon was angled across the two lanes. Shadows—

people, he realized with a dawning sense of horror—stood alongside the patrol car.

He tried to scream *oh, God, no,* but the cry lodged in his throat. His hands clamped around the wheel, gripping tight. His foot jumped from the accelerator and slammed onto the brake pedal.

He knew instantly that it was a mistake. The wheels locked hard, rubber screeched on the slick pavement. New tires, he thought irrationally, he needed new tires. These were old and bald and . . .

The back end of the car skidded around. Francis watched, horrified, as his headlights stabbed into the thicket of trees.

He took his foot off the brake and eased down on the accelerator, trying to regain control. But the car was on its own, pirouetting down the rain-wet asphalt in a horrifying dance that made him dizzy and sick to his stomach. The smell of burning rubber was everywhere.

The guardrail came flying at him. Behind it, a huge tree loomed in the darkness. He thought instantly of the seat belt he wasn't wearing.

*Oh, God,* he thought, *help me, help m—*

The car hit the guardrail and exploded in a shifting, grinding crunch of metal. Francis felt himself pitching forward, forward. *I believe in God, the Father—* Head smashing through something and the taste of blood. Shattering glass, glass everywhere . . .

And then quiet.

He heard the dull, whining drone of his car's horn, blaring through the darkness, and the pattering of rain on the curved metal roof of the Volkswagen. There were voices, coming at him from far, far away. *Jesus Christ, Sammy, call an ambulance.*

He crawled out of the wreckage, through the trail of broken glass. Strangely, he felt no pain, no pain at all, and the metallic taste of blood had vanished.

Slowly he straightened.

Rain slashed all around him, thumping on the road, running in rivulets in the concrete gully beside him. But he wasn't wet anymore.

It took him a minute to realize that. When he did, he felt a pinprick of fear.

He looked at the wreck, at the Volkswagen that was twisted and broken, one headlight shining into the sky like a single unseeing eye. The horn was still blaring; he could barely hear it above the shrieking of the wind and the hammering of the rain.

Then he saw his body, draped over the hood of the car, one arm bent at an awkward angle, the other flung to the right. Even from here he could see the blood that pooled beneath his stark, white profile and dripped down the hood. A fine dusting of glass sprinkled across his ripped, bloodied cardigan. His eyes were open.

People surged across the road, clustered around the remains of the car. One of the policeman picked up his limp wrist. *There's a pulse.*

Back in the patrol car, the other officer spoke urgently into a handheld radio, spitting out words that Francis couldn't quite make out.

Francis wanted to call, *I'm here, over here,* but he couldn't seem to speak. Or move. He just stood there, feeling warm and dry in the middle of the rainstorm, watching the strangers whirl around his body, poking, prodding.

An eerie pulling sensation started in the pit of his stomach and radiated outward. The world tilted slowly, slowly, and he felt himself being drawn away from the road. Or the road disappeared out from underneath him, he wasn't sure. He felt the darkness falling, closer, closer, the sky curling around him, soothing him.

His last thought was *Madelaine.*

And then there was nothing.

# chapter fifteen

⚜

At midnight Madelaine stretched her legs and rose from the couch. Credits rolled across a black screen on her television set, accompanied by sweeping, romantic music. She dabbed at her eyes, embarrassed even in the privacy of her own living room to be crying at such a bad movie. Not that she'd ever been able to help herself. It was the strangest thing—she hadn't cried when her mother died, nor at her father's funeral, but let her see a good Hallmark commercial and she wept like a baby.

She glanced at the clock on the mantel: 12:15.

Francis was late.

Nothing new in that, of course; he was always late. She reached down for her cup of decaf tea and downed the last luke-warm sugary sip. Crossing the room, she went to the front door and opened it, stepping onto the porch. She flicked the overhead fixture on and stood in the puddle of light.

The storm was still raging. Rain hammered the dead grass, forming itself into murky brown puddles in her flower bed, splashing on the walkway. Beside her, the porch swing creaked and rocked off kilter. A distant rumble of thunder echoed, followed by a flash of white lightning.

She frowned, staring through the gloom at the windswept street. Overhead, a heavy branch groaned, pinecones fell in swirls of blackened needles and bounced on the pavement below.

The streetlights flickered and went out.

Madelaine sighed. It was the third power outage this fall. Turning, she went back into the house and closed the door tightly. Feeling her way through the darkness, she went to the kitchen and eased the utility drawer open, searching through the mess until her fingers closed around a flashlight. She turned it on and pointed the powerful white beam of light toward the living room. Grabbing a box a matches, she set about lighting emergency candles and placing them on the coffee and end tables.

By the time she was finished, it was twelve forty-five.

She felt the first prickling of anxiety when she looked at her watch. Taking hold of a candle, she walked over to the window and stared out, searching through the jet-black night for a pair of twin headlights.

*Come on, Francis.*

By one-thirty the fear had grown big enough to take a bite. She thought of calling the lodge in Oregon, but knew it wouldn't do any good. All they'd tell her was that Francis had left around eight o'clock—the same thing he'd told her himself.

He should be here by now.

*Calm down.* She took a deep breath and went to the bookcase, pulling out her road atlas and flipping the heavy volume open to the side-by-side maps of Oregon and Washington. She found the tiny town at the base of Mount Hood and figured the lodge was around there. Then very methodically, she counted the red mile markers to Portland.

It was probably an hour and fifteen minutes. Maybe even an hour and a half.

And from Portland to Seattle, in this weather, it could take three and a half hours. Five hours, then.

She almost smiled. By her calculation, Francis should be pulling into the driveway any minute—assuming he'd left on time. Which, she knew well enough, he hadn't. As usual, he'd haphazardly figured how long the drive would take and thrown a number at her.

Feeling better, she crawled back onto the couch and drew the quilt around her, settling in. Her head hit the pillow and she closed her eyes.

She was awakened by the electricity coming back on. Noise blared from the television. Light stabbed her bleary eyes. She blinked heavily and sat up, staring blankly at the TV. A televangelist was asking for donations in a booming, authoritative voice. *God wants you to dig deep. . . .*

She reached for the remote control and meant to hit the Mute button. Instead she depressed Volume and the televangelist's voice screamed at her to *give, give to the Lord.* Wincing, she pressed another button and dropped the remote onto the couch. Then she glanced down at her watch.

Two forty-five.

"Francis," she whispered, lurching to her feet.

She raced to the front door and flung it open. The storm had given way to a gentle falling rain. Several cedar boughs lay tangled across her lawn. Falling leaves blew along her fence line. The driveway was empty.

"Mom?"

She spun around, her heart pumping so loudly, she could hear it in her ears, and saw Lina standing in the living room, a blanket wrapped around her shoulders. "Hi, honey," she said in a shaking voice, reluctantly closing the door. "Did the TV wake you? I'm sorry."

Lina shook her head.

For the first time Madelaine noticed how pale Lina was. She crossed the room toward her. "Baby, are you okay?"

"Don't call me that." Lina tightened the blanket around her body. "I had a nightmare. . . . I-Is Francis here yet?"

Madelaine hid her fear behind a quick, darting smile. "No, not yet, but you know Francis. . . ."

The phone rang.

As one, Madelaine and Lina looked at the phone, then at each other. They shared a single desperate thought: *Oh, God, not a phone call in the middle of the night.*

Lina took a step backward, shaking her head. "Don't answer it, Mom."

Madelaine stood there, unable to move, her stomach tightening. The phone jangled again, and she jumped toward it, yanking up the handset in shaking hands, lifting it to her ear. "H-Hello?"

"May I speak to Madelaine Hillyard?"

She recognized the voice instantly—it was cold, impersonal authority. "This is she."

"Ma'am, this is Officer Jim Braxton with the Oregon Highway Patrol."

She squeezed her eyes shut. "Yes." Her voice was a thin, trembling whisper.

"Do you know a Francis Xavier DeMarco?"

She drew in a sharp breath. "Yes."

"He had your name and phone number in his wallet. You're listed as the person to call in case of an emergency."

A memory of last Christmas flashed through her mind—when Francis had opened the wallet she'd given him and written her name on that cheesy little piece of paper that came tucked in the credit card slot. "Yes," was all she said. Her heart was beating so loudly, she could hardly hear.

"I'm sorry to inform you that there's been an accident."

She swayed and sank slowly to the couch. "Is he alive?"

"Oh, my God," Lina said.

"He's been taken to Claremont Hospital in Portland. I can give you that number."

She felt a quiver of hope. "They took him to the hospital? That means he's alive."

There was a pause on the other end of the phone. "He was alive when the ambulance arrived at the scene, ma'am. That's all I know."

She couldn't even say thank you. He gave her the number for the hospital, and she wrote it down in a fog. Then she punched in the number and asked for the emergency room.

Yes, they had a Francis DeMarco. Yes, he was still alive, listed in critical condition. There'd been an accident. . . . Was she a relative? No? Then there was no more information available. Mr. DeMarco was in surgery right now and could the doctor call her when he was finished?

Madelaine mumbled something about being right there and slammed the phone down on the receiver.

She turned to Lina, who was still standing in the same place, her face paler now, her eyes filled with tears. "He's dead," she said dully.

"No. He's alive. He's in surgery."

Lina started to cry. "Oh, Mom . . ."

Madelaine got to her feet and stood there, shaking. She took a deep, steadying breath. There was no time for this panic, this fear. Later she could fall apart, but now Francis needed her. Lina needed her.

She handled it the only way she knew how—with cold practicality. She donned the invisible white coat and became Dr. Hillyard, who dealt with these crises every day.

She went to Lina and pulled her daughter into her arms, holding her close. She felt Lina's arms curl around her at last, felt the shuddering of Lina's body against hers, felt the moisture of Lina's tears against her neck. "Shh," she whispered, stroking Lina's damp cheek.

"We've got to be strong for Francis now. There isn't time for what we're feeling. You go get dressed and pack us a bag. I'll call the airline."

Lina shook her head. "I can't."

Madelaine gripped her daughter by the shoulders. "You *can*. You have to." She softened a little bit, as much as she could allow herself. "He's in surgery, Lina. That means he's still alive. He needs us."

Lina looked up, her mouth trembling. "We need him, too, Mom."

The few small words hurt so badly that Madelaine felt her own tears rising, cresting. "Yes." She said the word in a whisper of her normal voice, but it boomed into the silence like a scream.

The drive to the airport and the flight to Portland seemed to take forever.

Madelaine stared out the airplane's small, oval window, seeing her own ashen features reflected in the fake glass. Her eyes looked like black holes burned into flesh-tone plastic; her mouth was a colorless crease.

Finally the plane started its ear-popping descent. Madelaine turned to Lina, saw the pallor of her daughter's cheek, the involuntary tremble of her lower lip.

She ached to say that Francis would be okay, but she couldn't make that kind of promise. The physician in her was too ingrained to trump the mother who wanted to offer unconditional hope.

"Don't stare at me, Mom." Lina didn't blink or turn, just gazed steadily at the burgundy-upholstered seat in front of her. A tear squeezed past her eyelashes and rolled down one colorless cheek, splashing on the nylon seat-belt strap.

Tentatively Madelaine reached out, covered Lina's cold hand with her own.

Quietly Lina said, "I think he's dead."

"No," Madelaine answered quickly. "He's in surgery. If he

were dead . . ." She couldn't go on, couldn't think about it. Her throat closed up. "If he were dead, I'd feel it."

Lina turned to her then, her eyes wide with hope. "What do you mean?"

Madelaine slipped her fingers through Lina's and held her hand until the flesh warmed again. Twisting slightly in her seat, she rested her head against it. "I was sixteen when I met Francis." She closed her eyes, remembering a dozen moments all at once. She saw him on that day when he'd come to the doctor's office to rescue her—the cavalry in the form of a bookish, starry-eyed eighteen-year-old with a heart as big as the whole outdoors. She'd been huddled alongside the public telephone, nervously jumping every time the door opened, certain Alex was going to come thundering through at any second. But it had only been Francis coming for her, reaching for her, taking her hand. *Maddy-girl, you're on the wrong side of town.*

*Help me*, she'd whispered, tears spilling down her cheeks. And his one-word answer, so easy, so fast. *Forever.*

Madelaine tried to find the words. "I'd *know* if he were dead. I'd feel . . ."

"What?" Lina pleaded.

"Nothing." She covered her heart with her hand, feeling the thudding pulse of her own life. "In here, I'd be empty." Her voice cracked as the images returned—Francis smiling, laughing, holding her hand, drying her tears, calling her his Maddy-girl. "I don't think I could breathe without him . . . and I'm breathing."

Madelaine fell silent, lost in the world of her memories. It took her a moment to notice that Lina was sitting too still, the tears rolling one after another down her cheeks.

Madelaine touched her daughter's chin. "Oh, baby . . ."

Lina swallowed hard, stared out the window behind Madelaine. "I yelled at him," she said in a quiet, anguished voice. "The last time I saw him . . ."

"Don't do that," Madelaine said in a rush.

Lina squeezed her eyes shut. "I hurt him."

"He told me he'd let *you* down. He wanted to come to Juvenile Hall to pick you up. . . ." Grief tightened around her chest until she could barely breathe. "He . . . he was afraid you wouldn't forgive *him*."

"I did," Lina whispered. "I did."

Madelaine pushed away the weight of her guilt and tried desperately to give her daughter a smile. "You tell him that when you see him."

Madelaine had been in hospital waiting rooms a thousand times in her career, and she'd never truly noticed what they were like. How the neutral walls closed in on you, how the Naugahyde chairs made your back ache. How magazines were useless. Insulting, even. What was she supposed to do now, read about some celebrity's valiant battle with cocaine?

She paced back and forth in front of the small window that overlooked the parking lot.

Lina sat stiffly in a chair by the pay phone. Neither one of them had spoken in the thirty minutes since they'd arrived. They'd been told that Francis was in surgery and that a Dr. Nusbaum would speak to them when the operation was over.

Madelaine had wanted to push her way into the OR, but she knew she wouldn't be of any use. The best help she could offer was to hold his hand when it was over.

She turned, glanced again at the big black schoolroom clock on the wall. Another sixty seconds of eternity clicked past.

Finally a tall, white-haired man in green surgical scrubs pushed into the tiny room, his mask hung loosely around his neck. Blood splattered his clothing in red-black splotches. She squeezed her eyes shut and tried not to think of Francis's blood.

The man shoved a hand through his thinning hair and sighed

heavily, glancing from Madelaine to Lina and back to Madelaine. "You're Mrs. DeMarco?"

It was strange how the question hurt. She shook her head, wringing her hands together and moving toward him, her gaze riveted on his face, searching for answers, pleading silently for hope. "No, I'm Dr. Madelaine Hillyard—cardiologist, St. Joe's," she added uselessly, wondering why she'd said it. "This is my daughter, Lina. We are Francis's . . . family."

"I'm sorry, Dr. Hillyard. . . ."

She didn't hear anything else. Blood roared in her ears, and she couldn't breathe. For a horrifying second she thought she was going to vomit, right there on the waiting room floor.

"The injury was too extensive. . . ."

She took a long, shaking breath and balled her hands into fists. She felt her nails digging into her flesh, tearing her skin as she fought for composure. She welcomed the pain—it gave her something to think about, however briefly. Finally, what emerged from the rubble of her mind were questions, objective, informed, practical questions that were like slipping on her protective white coat. "I need to see his charts. What happened?"

"Brain stem injury," he said gently, as if a softened voice could make a difference when the words were so cold and ugly. "He went through the windshield of his car and hit a tree with his head. Massive intracranial hemorrhage. We've got him on life support right now, but—"

"*What?*" Lina shouted. "You mean he's alive?" She looked at Madelaine in obvious confusion, then at the surgeon. "You said you were sorry—"

Nusbaum took a moment to choose his words. "Physically, he's functioning—with maximum intervention."

"Maximum intervention?" Lina said, her voice shrill. "What the hell is that?"

Nusbaum looked pointedly at Madelaine. "I've run three EEGs. They're completely flat. . . ." He let the sentence trail off, but Madelaine knew the procedure. Three flat EEGs and a patient was declared legally brain-dead.

"I'm sorry," he said again.

She stared at him blankly, thinking of all the times she'd said the same useless sentence to people—*I'm sorry, Mr. So-and-So. . . . best efforts . . . injuries were too extensive*. She'd never realized how stark and unforgiving the words were, how they twisted through your insides and pulled your guts out until you had no strength.

A terrifyingly familiar picture shot through her mind. She saw Francis, her Francis, lying in a bed somewhere in this cavernous building, his body hooked up to a dozen machines, his eyes—his warm, loving eyes—staring blankly at the ceiling. She felt a scream start deep inside her, building, gathering force until it choked her.

"What is he saying, Mom?" Lina asked.

Madelaine looked at her daughter and saw a six-year-old girl standing there, pigtails askew, tears staining her bright pink cheeks. For a split second her own grief faded, and all she could think about was her baby girl and what this news was doing to her, what it would do every moment for the rest of her life. She wanted to handle this just right, to explain the difference between a coma and brain death. To make Lina truly *understand* that the machines were keeping Francis's body alive, but his soul was gone, and soon the body would shut itself down with or without the machines. The body knew when its brain was gone. . . .

But she couldn't find the perfect words, or any words at all.

The sense of failure threaded through her pain and weighed her down. Slowly she crossed the room and slipped an arm around Lina's thin shoulders. "He's saying that Francis is gone, baby."

Lina jerked away from her and spun around, staring blankly out the window. Then, slowly, she sank onto the nearest chair and buried her face in her hands.

Tears scalded Madelaine's eyes. She wanted to give in to them as Lina had, allow herself the relief of crying, but she couldn't. She looked up at Dr. Nusbaum. "Can we see him?"

"Of course," he said softly. "Follow me."

The hospital hallway was eerily quiet. Nurses walked by on crepe-soled shoes, barely rippling the air with their presence. Room after room was dark, the curtains drawn. Empty chairs lined the white walls, magazines lay slumped on Formica tables.

Lina had grown up in hospitals. As a child, she'd played in corridors like this, waddling after smiling nurses, reading Dr. Seuss books on waiting-room chairs. She'd always thought of hospitals as her mother's workplace, no different from a lawyer's office or a beauty salon.

But now she saw them for what they were—shadowy warehouses where the dead and dying were housed in quiet, curtained rooms, where machines sucked and wheezed and held on to life through thick electrical cords.

She felt her mother beside her, heard her penny loafers click on the linoleum floor. She wanted to slip her hand through her mom's hand and squeeze, but she couldn't make herself do it. Her arms felt limp and heavy at her sides, her legs as rubbery as fresh Jell-O. Tears were a stinging, burning veil that turned everything into a smear of white.

Finally Dr. Nusbaum stopped at a room. The door was closed. Beside it, a large observation window revealed the room. A yellow curtain was drawn around the bed, shielding Francis from their eyes.

The doctor turned to them. "He looks . . ." He shot a quick glance at Lina, then spoke quietly to Madelaine. "The injury to the left side was extensive. He's bandaged, but . . ."

Lina thought instantly of Francis's smile, the big one that seemed to take over his face, crinkling his eyes, creating a dozen little folds across his cheeks.

She drew in a sharp breath.

"Thank you, Dr. Nusbaum," her mother said in a stiff, wooden voice. "I'll speak to you after I've seen him."

Lina stared at her mother in shock, wondering how she could be so matter-of-fact right now.

Dr. Nusbaum nodded and left them alone.

"I don't understand, Mom," she whispered, trying her best not to cry. "Maybe he's in a coma. . . . People come out of comas, don't they? Maybe if we talked to him—"

Mom swallowed hard. "It's not a coma, baby. Francis's brain is dead. The machines are keeping his body functioning, but everything that he is—he was—is gone."

"That man in Tennessee . . . he woke up. . . ."

Mom shook her head gently. "This is different, baby."

Lina wished she didn't understand, but she did. She was a doctor's kid, and she knew what brain death meant. In a coma, the brain functioned, and so there was hope. When the brain died, there was no hope. Francis, her Francis, was gone and he wasn't coming back.

For a long time—Lina could hear the quiet ticking of the clock above their heads—they stood there, staring past each other, saying nothing.

"I need to see him," her mother said finally.

Lina turned to the window, moving closer. She put her hands out, touched the pane, thinking—crazily—that it would be like touching Francis one last time. But all it felt was cold and flat.

Beyond the thin veil of the absurd yellow curtain, she could see the shadowy outline of a body in a bed, the rise and fall of a black cylinder beside it. She tried to see through it, to imagine just for a second what it would feel like to walk into that room, to see her Francis lying in a hospital bed, his checks white, his face slack, his eyes—oh, God, his blue, blue eyes . . .

"I can't do it, Mom," she whispered, shaking her head. The words stuck in her throat, felt so disloyal. But she couldn't do it, couldn't look at him and then sleep at night. Not if his eyes were blank, not if he couldn't smile at her and reach out his hand. "I can't look at him that way. . . ."

Her mother moved closer, swept a cold, reassuring hand along her cheek. Lina waited for her mom to look at her, but she never did, just kept staring at that curtained window.

"I saw my mother after she died," she said at last in a voice so twisted, Lina barely recognized it. "My father took me into her dark bedroom and told me to look at her, to touch her cheek. . . . It was so cold." She shivered slightly and drew her hand back, crossing her arms. "For years and years after that, when I thought of my mother, I thought of . . . the wrong picture, the wrong memory."

She turned to Lina at last. "I don't want that for you, baby. I want you to remember Francis the way he was." Her voice cracked.

*Was.*

"You should have told me, Mom."

Madelaine frowned slightly. "What do you mean?"

Lina stared at the window, at the shadowy outline of the man she'd taken for granted so many times. The man who'd dried her little girl's tears and held her hand when she was scared. She hadn't really realized until this very second how much of her world revolved around him. How much she loved him. "When I was throwing my tantrums and looking for my father . . ." She started to cry, hot, stinging tears that rolled one after another down her cheeks and splashed on her T-shirt. "You should have told me he was right there all along."

# chapter sixteen

Madelaine reached for the doorknob. She gave a last sidelong look at Lina, who wouldn't meet her gaze, then pushed the door open.

Sounds came at her, sounds she'd heard a million times in her life—the *whoosh-wheeze* of the ventilator, the steady electronic drone of the cardiac monitor. They should have meant nothing, those noises that were as familiar to her as the sound of her own breathing, but suddenly in the confines of this small, shadowy room, they were obscenely loud.

Taking a deep breath, she closed the door and went inside, circling around to the far side of the bed so that she wouldn't have to disturb the curtain.

He lay in the narrow, metal-railed bed, the covers tucked up to his slack chin, his arms pressed protectively to his sides. Clear plastic tubing invaded his mouth and nose, one going to his lungs to keep him breathing, the other providing a steady drip of fluids. Bottles and bags hung from metal poles beside the bed, sending a tangle of clear tubing into his wrists, throat, and chest. A huge, discolored layer of gauze hid half his face.

The room was dark except for a triangle of weak light from the streetlamp outside. He looked completely calm and serene, as if he couldn't have cared less that plastic tubing stormed his body and pumped air through his lungs.

She was so unsteady, she had to cling to the rails to keep from falling down. Finally she reached out, brushed a lock of hair from his eyes, tucking it beneath the white rim of the bandage. Beside her, the ventilator wheezed and dropped. His chest rose and fell, rose and fell.

She wanted to believe in a miracle right now, to believe that she could take his hand and lean close to his ear and help him find his way back to her, guide him back from the light so many patients spoke of.

But she'd been a doctor too long. His EEG was stone-flat. He'd had no reaction to the pain tests. Nothing. There was no life inside him anymore.

He would never smile at her, never call her his Maddy-girl.

At the thought, the grief she'd been holding at bay welled up inside her, spilling everywhere, streaking down her cheeks in hot, wet tears.

She remembered all the times they'd snuggled up on her couch to watch a movie together, all the times she'd held his hand in hers. She leaned over and pressed a kiss to his warm cheek.

And waited breathlessly for him to open his eyes and smile at her and say, *Maddy-girl, you didn't think it was real, did you?*

But he didn't answer, didn't move, just lay there breathing through a machine.

Without realizing what she was going to do, she lowered the bedrail and climbed into bed beside him, slipping an arm gently around his chest, staring at the side of his face that was un-harmed.

He looked peaceful from this angle, and she prayed that he was, needed to believe that he was. She clung to him, pressing her face against his throat, crying. She wanted to beg him not to leave her, not to be dead, but she was crying too hard to speak, too hard even to think.

She had no idea how long she lay there, tangled up with him, breathing the last subtle reminder of his aftershave—the one she'd given him for Christmas. Thinking of all the moments they'd never have again, all the times she'd reach instinctively for the phone to call him, only to realize he wasn't at home anymore.

She was roused at last by a knock on the door. She sniffed and wiped her eyes, intending to crawl out of the bed and stand by his side like the professional she'd always been. To *buck up and be strong*. But she couldn't move, couldn't leave him. So she lay there, holding him, and offered a harsh, raw "Come in."

The door opened and Dr. Nusbaum came up beside her. "I'm sorry—"

"Don't say it," she snapped. The moment the words left her mouth, she was horrified by her loss of control. She tried to force her trembling mouth into a smile and failed. "I'm sorry. It's just . . ." She couldn't go on. The tears came back, spilled helplessly down her cheeks. She balled her hands into fists and struggled to sit up. Without meeting Nusbaum's gaze, she climbed out of the bed.

"It's okay," he said in a quiet voice. After a long, silent moment, he added, "I've spoken to Dr. Allenford at St. Joseph's."

At first Madelaine was confused—what did Chris have to do with this?—then the explanation washed over her, rippling and icy cold. She sucked in a sharp, aching breath. Facts fell into place: Francis was brain-dead, but his organs were functioning. The organ procurement people had spoken with UNOS, who had referred them to Dr. Allenford.

"What did he say?" she asked quietly.

"He says he has a perfect match for your . . . friend's heart. A patient in Seattle."

Madelaine felt as if she were doing a free fall into a deep, dark hole. She couldn't reach out, couldn't catch her breath. Her own heart started hammering in her chest. She should have seen it instantly, *known* it. How had she missed the obvious?

Nusbaum looked a little uncomfortable. "I've never had this conversation with someone who knew more about transplants than I do. . . . Are you the patient's legal next of kin?"

"He's a priest, did you know that? A priest. He's never done a mean thing in his life. And now, now . . ." Words failed her.

Dr. Nusbaum gave her a gentle smile. "Would you like me to send the organ transplant coordinator in here? The bereavement counselor handles these things a hell of a lot better than I do."

"No. Yes. Let me think." She brushed the hair from Francis's face with a shaking hand.

He moved toward her, placed a hand on her shoulder. "It's not a coma, Dr. Hillyard, and I know you know the difference. Mr. DeMarco is legally brain-dead. Now his next of kin has to decide what to do. You know there isn't much time for the donation decision. Dr. Allenford said—"

She turned on him, balling the report in her fist. "Don't you think I know that?" Her voice cracked. "Leave us alone now."

"Certainly. Dr. Allenford said he could have the Lear down here in forty-five minutes."

"Yes," she said dully, stroking Francis's soft, soft cheek. "I know the procedure."

He left as quickly as he'd come, and when he was gone, she wished he hadn't left. It was too quiet in here; the electronic noises were so soulless, so inhuman.

"Oh, Francis," she whispered. Tears streamed down her cheeks.

She couldn't make a decision like this alone, and yet there was no one to take the burden from her shoulders. Angel was

Francis's only living relative, and God knew *he* couldn't help her. It would be inhuman to ask it of him.

The minutes ticked by, one after another, stitching into some endless quilt of time, minutes existing, then not existing, falling away.

It was so precious, time. Why was it you never realized that until it slipped through your fingers and lay forgotten at your feet?

"Why is that, Francis?" she asked, stroking his hair. She kept hoping against hope that he would hear her, blink his eyes, twitch one finger, something. But there was nothing except the droning hiss of the machines and the quiet strain of her own breathing.

"Oh, God," she whispered, feeling as if her soul were being slowly ripped in half.

She understood at last how so many of her patients' families had felt in this moment. She wanted to rail at the injustice of it all, but she'd learned long ago that life was unfair and unpredictable, that death stalked a family right up to the dinner table without once emitting a sound—she knew all this, had known it since she was six years old.

She knew, too, what Francis would have her do right now. He would want his death to mean something. And if he could save Angel's life, Francis would do it in a second, without hesitation. She knew that Francis's heart—his wonderful, loving heart—*could* save his brother's life.

But could she do it? Could she authorize the end of Francis's life support? Could she live with herself if she did? If she didn't?

Slowly she kneeled on the cold linoleum floor, and brought her hands together in prayer. "Please, God, help me make the right decision."

She waited, breath held, for a sign of some kind.

There was nothing but the click of the cardiac monitor and the *whoosh-thunk* of the respirator. She squeezed her eyes shut. "What do I do?" she whispered. "Help me, God, please. . . ."

*You know, Maddy-girl. You know.*

She lurched to her feet and stared down at him, studying everything about him, looking for . . . something that meant he'd spoken.

But of course, she knew he hadn't. His voice had been in her own mind. After a long minute, she straightened her shoulders and walked from the room.

Outside, Lina sat slumped on one of those uncomfortable chairs that hospitals set out for family members. At Madelaine's arrival, she jumped to her feet.

Her eyes were puffy and red, her cheeks streaked with dried tears.

Madelaine touched Lina's cheek in a gentle, intimate gesture that wasn't enough, wasn't nearly enough. "I need to talk to you about something. . . ."

Lina squeezed her eyes shut, shaking her head. "You think I don't know what it is, Mom? I've been sitting out here for almost an hour. I heard the diagnosis and the prognosis." She gave a laugh that was bitter. "I *am* a cardiologist's kid, you know."

Madelaine looked at her daughter in awe, and saw for the first time a hint of the woman that Lina would someday become—strong, focused, independent. "Yes," she said softly, wanting to say more but unable to find the words.

Lina bit down on her lower lip and stared at the curtained window. "You know what he would want."

"Yes." To her horror, she felt herself starting to cry, right there in front of her daughter, in front of the one person on earth she was supposed to always be strong in front of. But the tears came anyway, flooding, burning.

Lina took a hesitant step forward. "Don't cry, Mom. He . . . he wouldn't want you to cry."

Madelaine reached for her daughter, pulled her into a desperate hug. They stood that way for what felt like hours, holding each other, swaying in their grief, crying and stopping and crying again. Finally Madelaine drew back, gazed down at her daughter's beautiful, tear-filled eyes, and gave her a trembling smile. "I love you, baby, and I'm so, so proud of you right now. You're stronger than I ever was."

"So what happens now?"

Madelaine sighed, feeling old. "They've got a few more tests to run, and I've got to call Chris."

Madelaine went back into Francis's room and picked up the phone, dialing Chris's home number.

He picked up on the first ring. "Allenford here."

"Hi, Chris, it's Madelaine."

There was a moment's pause. "Madelaine?"

"I'm down at Claremont Hospital in Portland."

"Oh, Jesus, Madelaine . . . what happened?"

Her voice trembled. "It's Francis." She tried to say more, go on, but she couldn't.

"The donor is your priest? Angel's brother?"

"Yes," she whispered, trying desperately to keep her focus. "Third EEG was flat. No spontaneous activity off the ventilator, no response to pain tests. He's . . . he's gone. I'm the executor of his estate, Chris. I want to authorize the . . . donation."

"Okay, Madelaine," he said quietly. "I'll take it from here. Maybe you should come home, get some sleep."

"No," she said more sharply than she intended. "I'm not leaving him. I don't want anyone else near him." She realized how stupid and childish she sounded—she knew the teams that would descend on this hospital within the hour. Surgeons from all over the country, taking bits and pieces from Francis's body to save other lives. She tried to cling to that grain of hope— Francis's beautiful blue eyes still seeing the world, his kidneys saving a child's life, his bright living heart still beating. . . .

She squeezed her eyes shut, trying to remember that this was a miracle. And yet all she felt was dead and hollow and hurting. "I've got his durable power of attorney, Chris. I'll sign a waiver to donate Francis's eyes, heart, kidneys, pancreas, everything. It's what he'd want."

"NOPA and UNOS faxed me the stats—kidney and liver functions are good, dopamine level is acceptable, hydration okay. I knew he was a perfect match for Angel." His voice fell to a whisper. "Now I know why."

"Yes." It was all she could say.

"Madelaine." He said her name softly, and with an unusual intimacy. "He's going to save his brother's life."

She choked back a tiny sob. "I know."

"Will Angel accept—"

"I don't want Angel to know. What if . . ." She hesitated. "What if he thinks I did the wrong thing? What if—"

"The policy is confidentiality, Madelaine. I'll let you make the call. You can tell Angel or not—it's up to you."

The words were like tiny nicks from a razor blade, and she flinched at each one. "Thanks."

"Nusbaum knows how we want the body—" At her gasp, he cut himself off immediately. "He knows how we want Mr. DeMarco taken care of?"

"Francis," she corrected him softly. Then, "I'll make sure they do it right, Chris. How long until you can be down here?"

"I'm on my way. I'll contact UNOS and they can alert the rest of the teams across the country."

He didn't say good-bye, and neither did she. They both knew there were no words for a time like this, nothing but cold practicality and pain that would never go away.

Angel felt like he was in the middle of Safeway—the produce aisle with its glaring lights and gleaming silver metal bins and bland white ceiling. Here, in OR 9, the walls were colorless. Stainless steel tables were draped in surgical green fabric, their flat surfaces covered with precisely placed metal instruments. A television set hung from the ceiling, its screen a gaping black square. Computers and machines were everywhere, ticking, buzzing, whooshing. There were people all around him, none of whom he could see, of course, because they were masked and draped and gloved.

Not that any of them seemed to care about him—he was just *the patient.* Plain old Mark Jones. They didn't care that he was here, in this sterile room, stretched out on a steel table, naked, his body invaded by needles and tubes, his blood infected with medications. In the hour he'd lain here, no one had even spoken to him. Insead they talked around him, checking their gauges, monitoring his vital signs, looking at the clock. Every few minutes some new masked person would rush in with flight information, and some nurse would recheck the surgical instruments on the table beside him. All the while the big clock on the wall kept ticking.

He was shaved—again—from chin to foot and had been bathed in a stinging red-brown solution that made him look as if he'd been dipped in caramel sauce. More blue-green fabric draped his naked body.

*This is it. This is when they cut your heart out.*

He squeezed his eyes shut at the thought, fighting panic. He tried not to think about the surgeon's first cut, or his second, or the instruments that would crack his chest open, or the gloved hands that would take a few snip-snip-snips with the scissors and then reach deep, deep inside his chest.

His eyes snapped open and he lay there, breathing hard. "Oh, Christ," he whispered, wishing it were a prayer, wishing he knew what to say, what to beg for in this moment. But his whole life had been a headlong rush to death, and he had no hope, no real hope, that he would ever wake up again, that this stranger's heart would be his redemption.

A masked woman came over to him, peering down at him through eyes that were crinkled in the corners. It was pathetic how pleased he was to have her beside him, even if it was for a second, even if she didn't know or care who he was. At least he wasn't so alone.

"The heart has just landed at SeaTac, Mr. Jones," she said in a hushed voice. "We'll be ready to begin soon."

He pictured a huge, beating heart splatting on runway twelve, spraying blood everywhere. He winced, swallowed hard.

He reached out, grabbed the nurse's gloved hand. *Don't leave me.* The humiliating plea ached for release. Instead, he sucked in a sharp, shaking breath and whispered, "Where's Mad?"

Above the mask, he saw her frown. "You're mad?"

He shook her hand impatiently. "Dr. Hillyard, where is she?"

The frown faded. "She was on Lifeflight One with your new heart. Now they're on a helicopter. They should be here any second."

"Don't let them anesthetize me until she gets here, okay?"

She glanced at the clock. "It's not my decision, Mr. Jones."

He clung to her hand. "Please." He heard the pathetic shake in his voice, but he couldn't change it, didn't really care anymore. "Don't let anyone touch me until Madelaine gets here."

There was so much he needed to say to her before they did this abominable thing to his body. . . .

And to Francis.

*Francis.* Jesus, he had so many things to say to his big brother. So many things . . . and yet, only one. *I love you, bro.*

He winced at the memory of their last meeting, and closed his eyes. He'd make it up to Franco, if only God would give him a second chance. Just a second—a moment of consciousness before death, when Angel could say he was sorry. So damned sorry.

At exactly 3:15 a masked man came over to Angel, looked at the machines one by one, then finally said, "Hello, Mr. Jones. I'm Dr. Arche." He reached for one of the clear plastic bags hanging above Angel's head. "It's easy to remember—Dr. A. for anesthesia."

"Oh, good. Mnemonics." Angel sighed. "Just don't put me to sleep until Madelaine gets here."

"Don't worry, she'll be right beside you." Dr. Arche swept

past Angel in a blur of blue-green and settled with a whining squeak onto a stool. The wheels grated across the linoleum and took the anesthesiologist to his station.

Angel tried to lift his head off the hard table and couldn't. Instead, he turned, stared at the closed door. An image shimmered in front of bland steel.

*Francis,* he realized suddenly. It was his brother come to hold his hand.

*Heya, Angel.*

Angel started to say something and realized he didn't know what it was. Dizziness rolled through him. He blinked hard, and when he opened his eyes, Francis was gone.

Angel's cheek seemed to hit the table with a loud *thunk.*

They'd done it. The assholes had started the anesthesia.

He could feel the drugs oozing into his veins, crawling through his body in a swaying, intoxicating rhythm. He tried to concentrate . . . on the bag hanging above his head . . . the prick of the needle in his wrist. . . . It was dripping, dripping into his blood, seeping, seeping. . . .

He swallowed thickly; it felt as if cotton were wadded in his mouth and throat.

Dr. Arche wheeled back toward him. "Just relax, Mr. Jones. Go with the flow . . . the flow . . . the flow . . ."

Angel tried to lift his chin and couldn't. "Fu . . . fuck you . . . mother . . . fucker . . ."

Dr. Arche laughed quietly and wheeled back to his station.

Angel wanted to rip the IV needle from his arm, but he couldn't lift his hand. The lights overhead bled together and became the sun.

Panic pressed down on him, made his ragged heartbeat speed up.

"Whoa, Mr. Jones," Dr. Arche said in his ear, "calm down, fella, calm down. Go with the flow."

Angel's eyes fluttered shut. He forced them open again, tried to focus on the hot, hot sun.

Something was different. Noise, he realized groggily.

And then she was there, peering over him, filling his world like a Madonna. "Angel? Can you hear me?"

"Mad . . ." He sighed with relief, wanting—aching—to *feel* her hand in his; it wasn't enough to know she was touching him, he wanted to feel it. One last time. He wanted to rip that damned mask from her face and see her smile again. There was so much to say, so much, and the drugs were taking it all away from him. "Loved . . . you . . ."

She stroked his cheek, and it felt good, so good, he felt tears sting his eyes. He fought his way through the layers of fog that separated them.

She gave him a smile—he could see it above the mask, the way it crinkled her eyes. He remembered that smile, had always remembered it. Christ, so beautiful . . .

"Francis," he wheezed. "Sorry . . . tell him . . . loved him . . . too."

Suddenly he saw Francis standing beside her, smiling that cockeyed smile of his, whispering that it was okay, that it had always been okay. . . .

But Angel knew it wasn't real.

Tears glazed Madelaine's eyes, and he wanted to say, *Don't cry for me,* but he couldn't speak.

His eyelids fluttered again. He heard Dr. Arche's lilting voice, talking, talking, talking . . .

Then he was out.

Madelaine stood off to the side, watching the surgery.

Surgeons and residents and nurses were clustered around the table, working on Angel, poking, prodding, tubing, monitoring every breath he took, every pulse of blood through his heart and veins. He was intubated and catheterized and his body had been washed again with iodine, then he'd been redraped in sterile sheets. His hair was covered by a blue paper cap, and tiny strips of white adhesive tape kept his eyelids shut. The only part of his naked body that was exposed was a narrow strip of chest and upper abdomen, an orange belt of skin covered in taut, clear plastic and surrounded by blue-green sheets. A dehumanizing patch of color that seemed light-years away from Angel's ready smile or swaggering personality or towering temper.

*The patient.*

Madelaine tried to think of him that way, tried to be cold and distant and professional. But when Chris reached for the scalpel, touched its razor-sharp point to the skin at the base of Angel's throat, she flinched.

Instinctively she closed her eyes, and when she did, she found herself traveling back in time to another place. A Ferris wheel at a tawdry little carnival, a rocking ride with the boy of her dreams. She felt his arm slip around her, slide down the bare skin of her arm. *I love you, Mad.*

She heard the whining buzz of an electric saw and kept her eyes shut. She didn't want to see them cut open his chest, see his blood spill over the sterile little patch of green, splash on the linoleum floor.

"Chest spreader," Allenford barked.

Madelaine winced and tried to keep thinking about the carnival. That had been their last time together as lovers, and what a magical time it had been. Stars everywhere, the smell of popcorn, the faraway squeal of people on the midway. She remembered the earrings he'd won for her, the solemn way they'd buried the gaudy jewelry as a reminder of their love.

She thought of Francis, gentle, loving Francis, and the gift he was giving to his brother, the miracle that was unfolding just a few feet away.

"Get the bypass ready."

Madelaine opened her eyes. Reluctant to move and yet unable to remain where she was, she took a few steps toward the table. She saw instantly where they were in the operation—Angel's chest was a red, gaping hole in the surgical fabric. Cannulas had been inserted and sutured in the heart, and they were busily connecting Angel to the heart-lung bypass machine.

Everyone drew in a sharp breath as the bypass machine was started. The squat machine started whirring and pounding and pumping. A technician monitored the machine's function and said, "Everything looks good, Dr. Allenford."

"Okay," Chris said, reaching for his instruments, "let's go."

Madelaine moved toward the table, her gaze riveted on the surgery. She inched forward, mesmerized, watching Chris's bloody, gloved hands work. He removed Angel's damaged heart and handed it, still beating, to the pathologist, who put it in a metal bowl and disappeared.

Then Chris reached over and lifted Francis's heart in his capable hands. It looked so ordinary, she thought, a pale pink lump that had once held Francis's soul.

Chris studied the inert organ, then lowered it deep into Angel's chest.

It took almost an hour and a half to secure the new heart in place. Finally Chris looked over to the perfusionist monitoring the bypass machine. "Okay, let's warm him up."

Chris placed the final sutures in the pulmonary artery, and rich, warm blood began pouring into the heart, feeding it, warming it.

He glanced up suddenly, made eye contact with Madelaine. A single thought leapt between them: *This is it.*

Everyone in the room seemed to draw in a sudden, anticipatory breath. Madelaine stepped closer, until she was almost touching the table. She peered past the blue-green–clad bodies on either side of her, staring at the hole in Angel's chest, at the mass of pinkish tissue that lay there, motionless.

*Beat,* she pleaded silently. *Don't make it all for nothing. . . .*

The big old wall clock ticked past a minute, then another.

"Increase Isuprel," Allenford said evenly. "Go to four mics."

"Come on," Madelaine whispered, her hands curling into fists at her sides. *Come on, Francis.*

"You want the defibrillator?" someone said.

"Hush," Chris said.

The room fell utterly silent, all eyes trained on the new heart. After what felt like hours, it quivered.

Madelaine felt her own heart lurch in expectation.

"Come on," Chris urged the organ. "Come on."

Inside Angel's chest, Francis's heart jumped. Once, twice, three times, then it began a slow, steady thumping.

"Houston, we have a heartbeat," Chris said.

"Heart rate's going up," someone said. "Fifty-four. Sixty-three . . ."

A cheer went through the room. Madelaine tried to join in, but she couldn't move, couldn't speak, couldn't even smile. Her whole body was trembling and her eyes were stinging. She felt as if the spirit of God were inside her, filling her to overflowing, making her know—*know*—that what had just happened in this room was a miracle.

God had taken a life, and then He'd given one back.

She watched, mesmerized, as the healthy heart kept up its slow, rhythmic dance. Grinning, crying, she covered her masked mouth with her hands and looked up at the ceiling, as if, in that magical instant, she could *see* God.

*Love him, Maddy-girl.* She jumped at the sound and spun around, half expecting to see Francis standing beside her.

But there was no one there at all.

# chapter seventeen

Lina couldn't stand being in the house. Everywhere she looked, there were memories of Francis.

She stood on the porch, staring out at the first pink strands of drawn that crept along the shadowy street. Her lungs ached from the cigarettes she'd smoked, and her eyes stung from crying. She felt rubbery and hollow and sad. . . . Oh, God, how could there be such sadness?

She bit her lower lip and felt the burning glaze her eyes again. Turning, she saw the porch swing—the one he'd given them for Christmas last year—and suddenly she was crying again.

*Come back, Francis. I'm sorry. Oh, God, I'm so sorry. . . .*

In some dim part of her mind, she heard the whine of a car engine. Dully she looked up and saw her mother's car pull into the driveway. She walked to the edge of the railing and stood there.

Mom killed the engine and got out of the car. The *whack* of the Volvo's door shutting seemed obscenely loud in the predawn quiet. She was halfway up the walkway when she saw Lina standing on the shadowy porch.

Mom climbed the creaking steps and stopped, leaning against the wisteria-entwined white railing. Her gaze flicked over the ashtray on the floor, on the butts that were strewn everywhere. But when she looked at Lina, she didn't say a word.

Tears sprang to her mother's eyes, and she moved forward, opening her arms.

Woodenly Lina moved into the circle of her mother's embrace, felt the warm, loving arms enfold her, and suddenly she was a child again. Six years old, and she wanted to believe that her mother could make everything better.

She waited for her mother to say something, to give Lina some magical, miraculous words that would turn back the clock.

But her mother didn't speak, just held her.

And Lina knew. It would never be all right again.

He sits on the porch swing, trying to make it sway beneath him, but the wooden slats remain utterly motionless. The air is thick and heavy and smells of nothing. Before, he wouldn't have known what that was, nothingness, but now he does. He tries to remember the million smells that used to linger around her front porch. Roses and fresh-cut grass, the fecund humidity of muddy earth when the rains came, the smell of the wind itself as it blew leaves across the sidewalk. Even the dead brown wisteria vines that curl around her white railing used to have their own wintery smell.

Now there is nothing. The wind moves past him. He can see it touching the fallen leaves, swirling in minute whirlpools on the brown grass, but none of it touches him where he sits in the porch swing that can't be made to move.

He is waiting for something to happen, that's all he knows. There is a moment out there, hovering beyond his grasp; he feels it the way he used to feel rain on his cheeks or the wind at his back. He has something left to do.

He has learned that if he concentrates very, very hard, he can find himself inside her house, wandering among her things, reaching out for bits and pieces—mementos of a past he is rapidly forgetting. But it makes him tired, all that thinking, and it makes him feel things that hurt, and when he's done, he wishes he hadn't moved, had just sat here on this swing where he feels so at home.

Last night Lina was beside him, and when she first sat down, he felt the swing rustle and move beneath him. So much so, he could almost *feel* the movement of the wind, almost hear the creaking of the wooden slats. But he thinks, in the end, it was just a memory, that he couldn't hear those things at all.

She had cried, his precious baby, and in some pocket of his soul, he'd known that she was crying for him. He'd ached to touch her, comfort her, but he couldn't concentrate with the hacking sound of her sobs washing over him. So he'd done what he could, used the power that seemed to lie curled in the emptiness of his belly. He'd squeezed his eyes shut and spoken to her in his mind. Words, remnants of words he could barely remember.

*I'm here, Lina. I'm here. . . .*

He'd thought the words over and over and over, and still her tears had gone on, wrenching through him, making him ache.

Finally she'd gone into the house, and he'd followed her, drifting from room to room, wanting desperately to feel that he belonged in this place, the only real home he'd ever known. But with each passing bit of time, he'd felt himself getting weaker and weaker. Once, when he looked down, he couldn't see his feet, and in the next second, his legs were beginning to fade. Finally he'd curled up on the end of her bed like a cat and closed his eyes.

The next thing he knows, he's here again, stationed on the porch swing. Sunlight is all around him, streaming from billowy clouds perched high in a clear blue sky. A last yellow-green leaf rustles on the wisteria vine and floats to the lawn.

He looks down and his feet are still gone, his legs are inconstant shimmerings of shadow against the white paint of the porch floorboards. He wonders how long it will go on, this slow vanishing, and what will become of him when it is over.

And so he waits.

Angel was lying very still. Everything was dark. He could hear sounds, noises that were a confusing, frightening din. He blinked, tried to open his eyes. Failed.

"Angel?"

He heard her voice, coming at him from beyond the darkness. He needed her suddenly, needed her so much. . . . He tried again to open his eyes. His lashes flickered. It took so much energy. . . .

He heard her voice again, coaxing him, whispering his name. He fought to push aside the layers of cotton and fog that pressed around him. Finally one eye cracked open, and light stabbed him, sent him scurrying again for the comforting shadows.

"Come on, Angel, open your eyes."

Slowly, hesitantly, he tried again. And found her sitting beside him, her masked face inches from his. For a split second he was seventeen again, and she was his Madelaine, waiting for him.

He tried to remember where he was, why she was here.

Then he noticed his heartbeat, strong and even. *Ta-dum, ta-dum, ta-dum.*

He squeezed his eyes shut and all he could hear was his—someone else's—heart hammering away in his chest, thudding beneath his skin. He wanted to reach for the needles and tubes and rip them all out, but his hands were weak and shaking.

He'd never experienced such a devastating sense of violation, of loss. He felt invaded; the stranger's heart didn't belong in him. He felt it with every breath, thumping too loudly, aching in his damaged chest. Where was his own heart? Weak and useless as it was, it was *his,* and now it was gone. Lying in the trash somewhere . . .

His heart, the storehouse of his soul, his dreams, his ideas . . .

"Oh, Christ . . ." he whispered in a scratchy, broken voice that he didn't even recognize. Panic swooped in.

God, it wasn't even his voice anymore. There was nothing left of him, nothing. . . .

Then a word stopped his fall, left him breathless and shaking and more afraid than he'd ever been in his life. *DONOR.*

He forced his eyes open again and stared up at Madelaine. He knew he was crying, he could feel the tears coursing down his cheeks, and he didn't care. "Who?"

She flinched as if she'd been struck. "Angel," she said in a voice so calm that for a second, he was swayed. All he wanted to do was fall into that voice, that look in her eyes. "Don't think about those things now, just relax. The surgery went well. You're doing fine. Fine."

*The surgery.* He thought again of his heart, his own worthless heart, and the tears kept coming and coming. It felt as if he were grieving, but he didn't know for whom, for what. He just knew that this heart wasn't his and it was inside him, thumping too loudly, pumping too efficiently. His hands and feet were uncomfortably warm, and suddenly the cold numbness he'd had before was preferable to this . . . thing beating inside him.

The question came back to him, weighing on his thudding heart. *Whose heart is it?* He wanted to ask the question again, to demand an answer, but he couldn't do it, couldn't form the words or force them up his raw, burning throat. He wondered suddenly if he wanted to know. Sweet Jesus, did he want to know who was inside him, keeping him alive, warming his hands and toes?

Madelaine stroked the side of his face and it felt good, so good. He closed his eyes again and shook his head. He wanted to say something to her, but what? What?

The darkness came back for him, crooking its silent finger,

drawing him back to the black cocoon where he didn't remember, didn't care.

"Angel, you're going to be okay," came her voice again, soothing, calming. "You'll feel better when the anesthesia wears off completely. Trust me. You're experiencing disorientation, it's normal. To be expected. Don't worry."

He turned his head a little, felt the pillow sink beneath his cheek. Beside him, the cardiac monitor spat out reams of paper, showing its bright pink heart-line graph across the black screen. For a second he couldn't focus, couldn't make out what he was seeing. Then it struck him. There were two blurry pink lines running side by side on the computerized screen, where before there had only been one.

Fear welled up inside him, spilling through him in wave after wave. He started to shake, felt his insides knot up smaller and smaller.

Then he looked back at the monitor and it showed only one heartbeat. It should have calmed him, the realization that it had been a hallucination, but it didn't.

He could feel the drugs whirring through his bloodstream, dulling this moment, blurring his vision, but it didn't matter. The stranger's heart kept beating, beating, beating. . . .

"Oh, God," he whimpered. He'd never been so sick or afraid in his life. "You should have let me die."

"Just relax, Angel. Relax. We'll talk later."

He felt her squeeze his hand, felt her stroke his tear-soaked cheek, and he wanted to take comfort from her, ached to take comfort from her.

But he couldn't. It didn't matter what she said later, what she told him was normal or to be expected. He knew the truth, knew it with every beat of the stranger's heart.

Someone was living inside him.

*     *     *

It was cold along the shadowy streambed where Lina stood alone, waiting for her friends to drift down the loose embankment. They'd appear on the rise like they always did, one by one, their bodies silhouetted against the cool blue of an autumn sky, their hands jammed in their pockets, cigarettes hanging limply from their mouths. She'd hear them talking before they reached the crest of the ridge, their voices high and exuberant.

It always brought a swift stab of longing, that first sound of their laughing conversations. She'd rise to her feet, craning her neck to see the first familiar face, hear the first called-out "Hey, Lina! Hold that spot for me!"

Whenever they came careening down the ravine toward her, their tennis shoes skidding and sliding through the wet autumn leaves, their backpacks thumping against their bodies, she felt— for a few brief, shining moments—as if she belonged.

The crowd met here every morning before school, collecting like lost souls, drawn together to share cigarettes, booze, pot, and a sense of togetherness.

They were the "bad" kids, the problem ones. Everyone knew it, from the teachers to the counselors to the principal himself. Once a semester, one of the new teachers would come tearing down this crumbling bank, pointing an accusing finger and rousting them all. But by the end of the year, that teacher would be tired, and there would be more and more days when they stood here alone, talking among themselves, laughing at their own bravery, believing they were invincible.

But Lina didn't feel invincible anymore, and nothing as easily obtainable as a few cigarettes would ease the ache that pressed on her lungs until sometimes she didn't think she could breathe without starting to cry.

She jammed her hands in the baggy, linty confines of her jeans and sat down on a mossy rock. Two towering cedar trees stood stoically on either side of her, their graceful branches collapsing downward like an umbrella that had been left half-open after a rain.

"Hey, Lina!" It was Jett, standing at the crest of the hill, wearing all black, his buzz-cut hair dyed to match. He jumped over the edge like a skier, knees up, arms flung wide. His shoes hit the earth hard and skidded out from underneath him. With a whooping holler, he ran all the way down, leapt across the creek, and came to a breathless stop beside her.

She stared at him, this boy whom she'd had a crush on for almost two years, and felt suddenly as if she'd never seen him before. It made her feel a bit sick to her stomach, unsteady on her feet.

He grinned at her, flashing a set of white teeth. "Can I bum a smoke?"

It was always the first thing he said to her. "Sure," she mumbled, reaching into her leather pocket, pulling out a pack. She knew the second she touched it that it was empty. A frown darted across her face. When had she smoked them all?

Then she remembered the other night, when they'd landed back at SeaTac Airport. Mom had put Lina into a taxi and sent her home.

To that empty house with pictures of Francis everywhere. It felt as if every place she looked, she saw him, felt him, heard him. Finally she'd raced from her room and curled onto the porch swing—the one he'd bought them for Christmas last year—and cried and smoked until her mother came home.

"Sorry," she said, glancing up at Jett. "I guess I'm out."

His disappointment was obvious. "No prob."

They stood there a second longer, waiting for the other kids to arrive. Yesterday she would have tried to talk to him, would have pulled conversation from the chilly air around them and clung to each word he gave her, but today she was too tired to expend the effort.

She heard the magpie chatter of distant conversations and looked up just as five or six kids lurched over the crest of the

hill and skidded downward. Within seconds they were all standing alongside the stream, cigarettes going, talking loudly and
laughing.

Lina looked at them, from one face to another, and felt a
dawning sense of confusion. Why, when she was standing here
among her friends, did she feel so lonely that she wanted to cry?

It took her a second to realize that no one was talking to her,
a second more to realize she didn't care.

Jett pulled a thermos out of his backpack and twisted the lid
off. With a grin he said, "Kahlúa and Coke, anyone?"

Everyone cheered and reached for the thermos. But before
Jett could take the first swallow, another silhouette appeared on
the rise.

"You kids get back to school. The first bell rang five minutes
ago."

As one, they looked up and saw Vicki Owen, the new guidance counselor, standing above them. Beside her, Principal
Smithson looked ragged and tired, and Lina wasn't surprised by
his expression. Smithson had raided this ravine a couple of thousand times too often to believe it would make any difference.

The kids laughed at getting caught and tossed their still-
burning cigarettes into the stream. Lina watched the white butts
swirl together, mix with the fallen leaves, and float downstream.
It occurred to her that a bird could see that little white cylinder
and swoop down on it, swallowing the deadly man-made thing
before it realized what had happened.

"You, Lina Hillyard, I want to talk to you."

It was Miss Owen's voice. Lina looked up and realized that
she was the only one left at the stream. The other kids and Principal Smithson were gone; the only evidence that they'd been
there was a skidding trail of loose mud that cut through the
leaves and ferns.

With a sigh, Lina jumped over the stream and climbed up the
embankment. At the top she stopped alongside Miss Owen, and
saw her mother standing a few feet away.

Lina rolled her eyes. "Great."

Miss Owen stepped aside, then retreated wordlessly. Lina watched the counselor walk across the football field and disappear into the school.

Finally she turned and looked at her mother. She stood about ten feet away, her hair unbrushed and unkempt, her eyes puffy and red. It was the way they'd both looked in the two days since Francis's death. The walking wounded.

"Whaddaya want?" she said harshly, knowing what her mother wanted—knowing it was what they both wanted. Comfort, relief from the staggering grief. But there was no comfort. Lina had learned that the hard way. It just kept coming back, sneaking through your thoughts like a snake, pouncing at the most unexpected times. Every time the phone rang, Lina thought it was Francis—then *whap!* the snake bit.

There was a long pause before her mother spoke, a quiet in which Lina heard the squawking of the crows and the distant whine of a leaf blower. "Vicki Owen called me this morning, told me where you were. I thought . . . I thought we should talk."

Lina swallowed heavily. "Is that gonna bring him back, Mom?"

She shook her head. "Come on, baby. Walk with me."

She stared at her mother, watched as Madelaine turned and walked slowly toward the bleachers. Lina thought about not following, about just splitting and going somewhere—anywhere. But she didn't want to be alone, and her mother was the only person who really understood how Lina felt.

She followed her mother across the football field and up into the bleachers. They sat side by side, far enough apart that they weren't touching, but still somehow together in all the empty seats.

Lina glanced around, at the black scoreboard with the unlit entries for *home* and *guest*. A prowling black cat crawled across the wooden fencing, his tail wrapped through the sign that proudly proclaimed this place the home of the Panthers.

Lina had been here, of course, but never for a game. She'd never heard the crash of the helmets or the roar of the crowd, never met with a group of friends to watch their team battle another.

Years ago she'd wanted to, back when she was in seventh grade and Cara Milston was her best friend in the world. She'd tried to get her mother to take her to a game, but that was the beginning of Madelaine's "busy days." Days and nights and more days that blurred together in hospital shifts that never ended. There had only been a few home games that year, and Madelaine had been unable to go to every one of them. By the next year, Lina had collected a group of friends who wouldn't be caught dead at football game. Instead they'd spent their Friday nights down by the stream, sucking up whatever booze someone could get a hold of and chainsmoking.

Maybe if Lina had had a brother, or a boyfriend, it would have been different, or if she and Cara had stayed best friends. Or if her mom had gone to high school, maybe that would have made a difference, too.

"You never ask to go to football games anymore," Mom said quietly.

"Yeah, well, I got better things to do."

"Like smoking down by the creek?"

Lina shrugged and glanced around the bleachers, noticing the film of wrappers and old popcorn and spilled Coke that lay in sticky heaps on the metal flooring. "I thought you wanted to talk."

There was a long pause, then slowly, quietly, her mother began to speak. "I was six years old when my mom died. One night I kissed her good night and went off to bed. . . . When I woke up, she was gone. No one wanted to tell me how sick she was—my dad thought it didn't matter, I guess, preparing a little girl to lose her mother. But there were so many things I never got to say." There was a surprising bitterness in her mother's voice, a hardness she'd never heard before. She frowned a little. "After that, I saw the world differently. I knew it wasn't a safe place."

Lina felt the tears come back, stinging, burning. She thought about wiping them away, but didn't bother. "H-He was always there for me."

"He still is, baby."

Lina snorted and smeared a hand across her eyes. "Don't get into that God stuff. It doesn't help."

"You can call it God or Jesus or Allah or mumbo jumbo; it doesn't matter. What matters is looking inside yourself and discovering what *you* believe. If you don't, you'll have nothing to cling to, nothing to believe in, and everything will start falling apart. Trust me, I know."

"I don't want to think about that stuff now," Lina said in a tiny, broken voice. "If I do, all I end up thinking about is how gone he is, how he's never coming back, and how much I miss him."

"If Francis were right here, right now, what would he say to you?"

For a split second she could almost *feel* him beside her, whispering in her ear. A sad little smile plucked at her lips. "He'd tell me to ditch that loser bunch of friends and go home."

"You see? He's there, inside you. He always will be."

Lina wanted to smile, wanted it badly, but she couldn't. "He hated my friends. He thought they weren't going anywhere."

Madelaine didn't respond, but her silence seemed to say it all.

"I know he's right," Lina said shakily, "but I don't know what to do about it. I never did."

"The biggest journeys start with a single step. Maybe you could go to the Christmas dance. You'll see a whole different crowd of people there. A girl as pretty as you could get a date in a second."

Lina rolled her eyes. "As *if,* Mom. Jett Rodham wouldn't be caught dead at something as dopey as a school dance."

"What about you, Lina? Would *you* like to go?"

It was exactly the sort of idea Francis would have come up with. Lina thought about it, and wished immediately that she hadn't. The idea of attending a school dance was oh, so seductive. She thought about dressing up, fixing her hair, coming down the stairs and getting her picture taken with a boy who smiled shyly for the camera. She thought about her mother, grinning from ear to ear, slipping her arm around Francis's waist—

No. Francis wouldn't be there. He'd never be there again. . . .

Lina jerked to her feet. "Don't *talk* to me about these things," she hissed. It hurt so badly, missing him; she hadn't thought anything could hurt this bad. "I don't have that kind of life, damn it. It's too late for me to become some idiotic homecoming queen. Just leave well enough alone."

"Oh, baby . . ." Madelaine said on a sigh, reaching for her.

Lina could *feel* her mother's love—a heat that was inches beyond her grasp. But she couldn't get rid of the picture of her going to the prom, of Francis and her mother waiting up for her.

The thought of him twisted her insides into a tight, throbbing knot. Wordlessly she spun away from her mom's sad face and ran across the football field. She didn't know where she was going. It didn't matter.

She just knew she had to run.

# chapter eighteen

Madelaine slipped on her mask and paper slippers and headed for Angel's room in isolation. As she glanced through the glass observation doors, she saw the nurse standing alongside his bed, monitoring his every heartbeat.

She stepped quickly through the doors and stood beside the nurse. He lay completely still, his face pale and slightly gray, his body hooked up to a dozen machines and intravenous solutions. Two huge chest tubes lay alongside his new heart, sticking out from wounds at the base of his rib cage. Blood bubbled through the clear plastic and collected in a huge canister at the foot of the bed.

He looked peaceful now, but she knew it was an illusion. Every thirty minutes the special-care nurses turned his weakened body from side to side, pounding on his back to keep his lungs and swollen, hacked-up chest clear. They forced him to breathe into a tube to work his lungs. The massive doses of immunosuppressant drugs that he'd been given in the first twenty-four hours had been diminished somewhat on this, the second day after surgery, but the antibiotic dosage had been increased.

She reached for his charts and studied them, looking for anything that might be problematic. "How's our patient doing?"

The masked nurse gave her a wry look. "He's not very happy about all this. Physically his new heart is a winner. His body is reacting as well as can be expected to the meds."

"I'll sit with him for a while. Go ahead and take a break."

When the nurse was gone, Madelaine pulled up a chair and sat beside his bed. Reaching out, she gently took hold of his hand. "So, Angel, you're not playing well with others."

He lay there, unresponsive, his breathing slow and steady and unaided by machine.

She couldn't help but think of the other day, when he'd gone ballistic after surgery. She'd seen the fear in his eyes, the dawning horror as he felt the rhythmic beating of the new heart. The realization that someone had died to give him the chance at life.

Not someone, she thought. *Francis.*

What would Angel say if he knew the truth?

She frowned. She hadn't known Angel in years—maybe she never really had—but she knew him well enough to know that he would throw the mother of all tantrums if he knew what she had done. What she had authorized.

He wouldn't know how to grieve for something like this. In fairness, she knew that no one would. He would be plagued with regret and self-loathing. He would wonder if Francis was really dead before the surgery, or if Madelaine and her team had done the unforgivable.

She knew she could make the argument to anyone that Angel shouldn't know the truth—that it would hinder his recovery, that donor confidentiality could only be breached after massive discussion with the bereavement counselor, that it was best all the way around to keep Angel in the dark. It was standard policy to keep the donor's identity confidential.

But there was so much more here than just standard hospital procedure.

She was afraid to tell him the truth, afraid of the look that would cross his eyes, afraid of the words he would say to her. Words that, once said, could never be unsaid.

Because she also knew another truth. She didn't know when it had come to her, when it had become a part of her, but sometime in the last few weeks, Angel had crept under her skin again. It was his spirit—that great, larger-than-life spirit that dared the world to take him on. She'd fallen in love with it as a young girl, and she found that even as an adult, there was something almost magical about his strength of personality, his defiant will to forge his own path.

So unlike her own watered-down, Milquetoast will.

When she looked at him, even now, when he lay at death's door, she saw a shooting star of a man.

Behind her, the door opened. She turned just as Chris walked into the room. His eyes squinted in a smile above the mask. "How's our patient?"

Madelaine smiled. "Better than most. He's reacting well to the meds."

Chris pulled up a chair and sat down. He took a second to flip through the charts, then dropped them back into the sleeve at the foot of the bed. He looked up at Madelaine. "What are you going to do?"

She didn't pretend to misunderstand. "I'm going to remove myself as his cardiologist. After the . . . decision to donate, I don't have much choice."

"You could bring it up before the ethics committee—it's kind of a gray area."

She shook her head. "I'll bring Marcus Sarandon in. He'll do a great job."

Chris looked at Angel. "What will you tell him?"

She sighed. "I don't know."

Like all funerals, it was unbearable.

The funeral home was a palatial white brick building, complete with pillars and manicured lawns and young trees that would someday age into hundred-year-old oaks and give the new construction an air of old-fashioned elegance. It was, like so many of its kind, an edifice carefully contrived to evoke a common American fiction—the perfect family home, a sprawling southern mansion that harkened back to another time, when one generation turned into another and then another, when the circle of life was accepted and understood. You could almost imagine a small, well-tended family graveyard out back, its perimeter hemmed by white picket fence lines.

But of course, that was the greatest fiction of all. Behind the building lay acres and acres of green lawn, lawn that dipped and swelled and evened out in places like a golf course. Maple and alder trees dotted the various hillsides, spilling their multicolored leaves across the grassy quilt.

Madelaine and Lina stood side by side among the throng of grieving strangers. One by one the cars arrived, parking in an endless row along the driveway and down on the side of the road. People dressed in somber black clothing spilled from the cars, gathering together, murmuring among themselves. Women dabbed at their eyes and told stories of Father Francis. Men shook their heads and stared at the ground, patting their wives' and mothers' shoulders.

The mourners walked in a steady black line up the walkway toward the grave-site portion of the service. She recognized several faces—friends of Francis's from the nursing home.

She watched them file past her, seeing her own grief reflected in many eyes. Each face reminded her of Francis, made her realize how many lives he had touched, how much difference he had made in this world. He'd been gone for two days, and already it felt like a lifetime.

She looked at the sky above her, clutching the slim white memorial album in her cold hands. *Did you know that, Francis, did we tell you?*

"I don't want to go up there," Lina said quietly beside her.

Madelaine looked at her daughter, noticed the pallor of her cheeks, the haunted darkness in her blue eyes. She wondered suddenly what to say to this girl who wasn't a girl and wasn't a woman, either. She didn't know whether to force a bright smile and pretend that everything would be okay, or to be honest and show her own pain. She didn't know what would help Lina right now. If anything could.

Tentatively she reached out and caressed her daughter's moist cheek. "There's this place I go sometimes. . . ."

Lina sniffed hard and looked up at her. "Yeah?"

"Maybe we could go there and sort of . . . say good-bye to Francis in our own way."

Lina's lower lip started to quiver. Tears filled her eyes. "That's just it," she said softly. "I don't want to say good-bye."

Madelaine didn't know what to say to that, so instead of speaking, she slipped her hand around her daughter's waist and drew her close. Lina resisted for a heartbeat, maybe not even that long, then slid in close to Madelaine's side. Together, silently, they walked down the long black driveway, ignoring the cars that prowled past them in clouds of carbon-scented smoke and the headlights that shone in their eyes.

They climbed into the Volvo and slammed the doors shut, and for a split second Madelaine felt as if they were shutting the funeral away. But on the long drive out to her old neighborhood, she felt it coming back, flashing across her mind in bits and pieces—the sniffling sound that filled the church, the smell of hothouse lilies and smoke from a thousand votive candles. The archbishop's low, droning voice talking about a man Madelaine barely knew—Father Francis. Pious, serious, always ready to lend a hand, the archbishop said.

The whole time, all she could think about was that eighteen-year-old boy who'd come to her rescue. Who'd heard her small, pathetic *Help me*, and answered softly, *Forever, Maddy-girl. Forever.*

Shutting off the engine, she sat there for a minute, watching the first splashing raindrops hit the windshield. Through the blurred glass she saw her father's house, sitting there against the gray clouds, amidst the bare trees, its windows as dark as they'd been in the long years since his death. The lawn was too long and brown and covered with dying leaves.

Finally she sighed. "Let's go."

Madelaine led the way past her father's empty house—now her house, though she could never think of it that way. Her father had disinherited her in life and left her everything in death. The last grasping move of a sick man—leaving her saddled with the house and money that represented everything she despised about her childhood.

She strode up the brick steps, down the walkway, around the dead rose garden that once had been her mother's pride and joy, and onto the brown carpet of the backyard.

The lawn led to a low-banked waterfront, where the sea spit across the gray rocks in gentle spurts. Madelaine's high heels sank into the dead grass as she walked to the end of the creaking old dock and sat down.

Lina sat beside her, letting her bare legs swing over the edge.

They stayed that way for an eternity, both staring out at the clouds collecting above the tree line on the opposite shore. The rain picked up, splattered on the surface of the water.

"This is where my dad took me after my mom passed away," Madelaine said at last.

"That's your house, isn't it, the one where you grew up?"

Madelaine shivered and drew her coat more tightly around her body. "Yes, it is."

"There are bars on the upstairs window."

The urge came swiftly to lie, to cover up. She forced it away and nodded. "That was my bedroom."

"He locked you in?"

Madelaine gave a small laugh. "See? You don't have the worst parent in the history of the world."

Lina fell silent and turned to stare out at the sound. After a while she said quietly, "I keep . . . reaching for the phone to call him and then I have to stop myself."

Madelaine slipped an arm around Lina's shoulder and pulled her close. Rain fell all around them, slashed across their faces and pattered their clothing. "I talk to him every day, just like he was still beside me. Sometimes I think he's going to answer. . . ."

Lina nodded. "I want it to mean something, but . . ." She shrugged. "I don't know. I just miss him so much."

Madelaine stared at her daughter's profile, so pale and fragile-looking. She ached for Lina, and wanted to help her through the pain, to give her something to believe in that would make it all a little easier to bear.

*Angel.*

The word came to her so suddenly, she straightened and looked around. She thought, crazily, she'd heard Francis's voice. Then she realized it was only her own subconscious and she slumped again, staring down at the sea foaming beneath them.

The thought came again, *Give her a father.* That was what Francis would have said.

She turned to Lina, stared at her so long and so hard that Lina finally turned.

"What, Mom?"

Madelaine wet her lips and tasted rainwater. She felt a fluttering in her chest and knew it was fear. The easy thing to do right now was to turn away, laugh, and say it was nothing. But since Francis's death, she'd seen how fragile life was, how the wrong choices were sometimes permanent. How all you regretted was the words you didn't say . . .

It was time for her to stop being the doormat her father had raised her to be. She needed to stand up for herself, for Lina, for all of them. Maybe Lina would run away with Angel, maybe Angel would break her daughter's heart. . . . The possibilities were endless and everything could go wrong.

But for years she'd done nothing, and things had gone wrong anyway.

She tried to think of how best to say it, but in the end there was no softness, no blurring, no lead-in for something like this. There was only the truth, and she knew it would hit Lina like a blow. "I spoke with your father."

"Yeah, right."

Madelaine swallowed hard. "I did."

Very slowly Lina lifted her head and looked dully at her mother.

Madelaine waited for Lina to say something, but the silence between them lengthened. Finally Madelaine said, "He's very sick right now, and he can't see you, but soon—"

"You mean he *won't* see me." Lina lurched backward and shot to her feet. "Yeah, I'll bet he's sick as a dog to find out he's got a daughter. I can't believe you," she hissed, shaking her head.

Madelaine scrambled to get to her feet and reached for her daughter. "Lina—"

Lina smacked her hand away. "Don't touch me. I can't believe you, Mom. I'm sitting out here in the rain, after Francis's funeral, and you tell me—finally—that you've talked to my father. . . ." She laughed, and it was a shrill, hysterical sound. "So today— *today*—I get to find out that I have a father, but he doesn't care about me and doesn't want to see me. Perfect timing, Mom."

"Baby, please—"

Lina's eyes filled with tears. "I can't believe you thought this would make me feel *better*."

"Lina, please . . ."

"Just do me a favor, Mom. Don't try to cheer me up anymore, okay?" She gave Madelaine one last hurting look and spun away, running down the planked dock.

Madelaine stood there, watching helplessly. Defeated, she bent down and picked up her purse, then walked slowly down the dock, up the hillside, and to the car.

When she got inside, she looked at Lina, who sat pressed against the window, her arms crossed mutinously, her eyes slammed shut. She thought of a dozen things she could say right now, but they all sounded trite and stupid in light of her obvious error in judgment. Finally she said the only thing that made sense. "I'm sorry, Lina. I guess I shouldn't have told you. I wasn't thinking clearly. . . ." Her words faded into the silence and went unanswered. She couldn't think of anything to add, so she started the car's engine.

In silence they drove home.

*I'm sorry,* she'd said.

She should have known after this weekend how meaningless those little words were, how they dropped into an ocean of pain and didn't even leave a ripple behind.

Angel came awake slowly, listening to the sound of her voice. It took him a second to focus. She was reading to him—Anne Rice's *Tale of the Body Thief,* if he wasn't mistaken.

He forced his eyes open. "A rather macabre choice," he said, grinning weakly. "I hope it's not your way of telling me I need to drink blood from now on."

He could tell that beneath the mask, she was smiling. "Sorry, it's my personal reading. I thought you might like to hear . . ." She shrugged, gave a sharp little laugh. "I didn't think about the subject. Fairly sick, you're right. I just thought maybe you'd feel less alone if you heard someone's voice."

"You're babbling, Mad."

She laughed again and shut the book. "I am."

"You don't usually babble unless you're nervous. What happened—did the amazing dead person's heart quit while I was sleeping?"

"No," she said quietly, and he could see that all the humor had gone from her eyes. She looked at him now with a dawning sadness. "It's your heart now, Angel."

He felt a surge of bitterness. He thought of his heart, the *donor's* heart, and he felt it beating in there, in his chest, beating and beating and beating. He wondered sickly if it would keep beating after his body died. He flashed on a sick image of himself in a coffin, his body stone-dead and paper-white, and that heart just thumping away. The *thing* had been inside him for three days now, and it felt more alien every second. "Yeah, tell that to the dead guy. He thought it was his."

He lifted his head from the pillow, and it took an incredible, sickening amount of effort to do. "How could you let them do this to me, Mad?"

"We saved your life," she said softly.

"Don't look at me that way," he hissed, hating her in that moment, hating everything and everyone from God on down. "You didn't save my life, you prolonged my death. Look at me, for Christ's sake. I look like a fucking pumpkin head on a stick body—or didn't you notice that I've lost ten pounds and my head is the size of a watermelon? And what about the poor sucker who *donated* his heart to me? Donated." He laughed acidly at the irony. "You make it sound like he gave a can of soup to the hungry. But it was his heart, damn it, his *heart*. You think he liked having your grimy hands inside his chest, hacking away, yanking out his heart like you yanked out mine?"

She sat very still, as if she were controlling her own anger with a great force of will. "You have a second chance at life. That's what you should be focusing on right now."

"What if I don't want it?"

"How dare you? Someone *died* to give you this chance. If you throw it away, Angel DeMarco, I swear to God—" She shut up suddenly, as if she'd said too much. Breathing heavily, she wrenched her gaze from his face and stared at the wall.

Suddenly he felt tired, so tired. All the fight bled out of his body and collected in that damned canister at the foot of the bed. He reached up to push the hair from his eyes and felt the puffiness of his cheeks again. He was glad as hell he didn't have a mirror. "Jesus, you've turned me into the Pillsbury Dough Boy."

"It's the prednisone. The swelling will go down."

He looked at her. "I'm sorry, Mad." He tried to think of something else to say. "I had a dream about Francis last night."

She sank slowly back onto the seat. He noticed that her hands were shaking before she drew them into her lap. "Really?" she whispered. "What happened?"

"In the dream?" He tried to remember. "I dreamt I was cold. It was one of those dreams where you think you're awake. I thought I woke up and found the blankets all bunched at my ankles. I reached down to pull them up, and when I had them drawn back up, I glanced at the observation doors, and there was Franco, just standing there, smiling."

"What did he look like?"

"That was the weird part. He was soaking wet, like he'd been standing in a rainstorm. He touched the glass, as if he maybe wanted to go through but couldn't. I heard his voice inside my head. 'Heya, Angel,' he said. Then he smiled—you know the one I mean, where his whole face crinkles and his eyes almost disappear into slits." He shrugged. "Then he was gone."

Madelaine's eyes filled with tears.

"What is it, Mad?"

She stared at her own hands, clasped tightly in her lap. She looked incredibly fragile, pale. "Francis went to Portland last week."

"Yeah, I know."

Her head snapped up. "You do?"

"He came by here before he left."

Madelaine gave him an odd look. "He didn't tell me he saw you." She paused, and he thought she was frowning beneath the mask.

"I'm sure he doesn't tell you everything."

She swallowed hard. "I didn't want to tell you this quite yet because of your heart. . . ." Her eyes filled with tears again. "Your precious heart."

He got a cold, sick feeling in his gut. "What is it?"

"Francis was in a car accident outside of Portland."

The chill moved, spread through him. "Yeah?"

She met his gaze, and he saw the answer in her eyes. "I'm sorry, Angel. He didn't make it. He wasn't wearing a seat belt." She looked as if she wanted to say more, but she didn't. She just sat there, staring at him, slow tears spilling down her cheeks, collecting on the pale green of her mask.

*No.*

Francis couldn't be dead, not Francis, with the laughing eyes and the awesome faith, who'd never hurt anyone in his life.

"You're lying," he hissed, shaking his head. "It's not true."

But he saw in her eyes that it was true.

"Oh, Christ," he whispered, waiting for his secondhand heart to stop beating. The grief was a great, crunching pain on his chest, filling his throat, stinging his eyes. "God damn it, who doesn't wear a seat belt in the nineties?" He latched on to anger instead of the grief that grew with each indrawn breath. "And what the hell was he doing in Portland, anyway? He's a priest, not a traveling salesman. He never could drive for shit. I remember when we were kids—"

*No,* he thought desperately, *don't think about that now. Oh, Jesus, don't think about anything.* But he couldn't help himself. He remembered it all in sudden clarity, the day Francis had taught him to drive. How they'd driven around and around the school parking lot, that old Impala of their mom's jerking and spitting and dying every time one of them tried to switch gears . . . how they'd laughed and cursed and then laughed again. . . .

"Not Franco," he whispered, looking to Mad. "It should have been me instead."

The sadness in her eyes made his own tears fall. "I wish I could change it, Angel."

"Did . . . did he suffer?" He hated the question the minute he asked it—it was so ordinary and useless—but he needed an answer.

Her gaze skittered away from his. "The doctors on the scene said he was killed instantly. There was nothing they could do."

They sat there, crying side by side for what felt like hours. Angel cried for so many things—all the times he hadn't called Francis, all the Christmas cards he'd never sent. What had he thought, that they would all live forever?

"Jesus, Mad," he said brokenly, "I didn't say . . ." His words trailed off. There was so much he didn't say. So many mistakes and lost chances and selfishness. Christ, so much selfishness.

"He knew you loved him, Angel. He always knew that."

The knowledge sank through him, weighing him down. He wanted it to help—wished it helped—but it didn't. It only made it hurt more, knowing that Francis had always loved him. "He died on the way to Portland." He tried to make sense of it. "That must have been hours after I saw him. Jesus, how could I not have *known* that he was gone all this time?"

Madelaine looked away again, stared at the clock on the wall, then slowly met his gaze. "On the *way* to Portland," she said slowly. "Yes. Yes."

"Why did you wait all this time to tell me?"

"You heart was too fragile."

He wanted to say something mean and bitter to that, something about the dead man's heart in his chest, but he couldn't. "God, he's been dead over a week and I didn't know. Did you have a funeral without telling me, too?"

"His parishioners wanted a big Catholic funeral. I didn't tell you because you couldn't get out of isolation, and they couldn't wait any longer. We can do a quiet family memorial service when you feel better."

He closed his eyes, imagining some church filled with flowers, and a long wooden aisle that led up to the glossy coffin on the altar. Just like Pop's funeral, only this time it wouldn't be a old man's body lying on all that puffy white satin. It would be Francis—Francis lying dead in a wooden box. . . .

Draped in flowers—they always draped the coffins in flowers, as if the prettiness on the outside could change what lay within. The place would reek with the sickly sweet scent of the lilies, and they'd play that god-awful music, designed to make you cry.

"No," he said, feeling the tears creep back into his throat. "I don't want to remember Francis that way. I'll say good-bye to him in my own way when I get out of this place."

They fell silent again, staring at each other. Angel tried not to think about Francis, but he couldn't stop. "It's funny, Mad. . . ." He surprised himself by speaking aloud; he hadn't meant to. But she was the only person in the world whom he could talk to, the only person who knew Angel and Francis and the old days. "Even all those years I was gone, I always knew Francis was out there. Every time I got my picture on the cover of a magazine or a movie poster, I thought of Francis. I knew he'd pick it up and smile and shake his head. I knew he was waiting for my call, and I kept picking up the phone, but somehow I never dialed. And when he came to see me the other day, there were so many things I meant to say, but we fell into that old routine of Saint Francis and Angel the Screw-Up, and the words never got said." He looked at her, wishing she could grant him absolution for his sins. But it was his brother he should have asked for that, and now it was too late. "I guess I thought we were both immortal."

The smile that reached her eyes was sad. "I know what you mean. I . . . hurt Francis's feelings just before he left. I did it so easily, so thoughtlessly, and when I realized what I'd done, I thought I could make up for it with the same ease. . . ."

He saw her pain and it gave him an unexpected strength. "He loved you, Mad. From the first moment he saw you in the hospital room, he loved you."

"You remember that day?"

He didn't answer, didn't know what to say. She had every reason to believe he'd forgotten. Once, he thought he had, but now he knew the memories of her were still inside him, protected and cared for through all these years. He gazed at her so long, he felt his tears return. He wanted to open his arms to her, to draw her close so they could take from and give to each other, so that neither of them felt alone.

But he was afraid that if he touched her right now, if he curled his arms around her and felt her tears spill on his throat, he'd be lost.

"What are we going to do, Mad?" he whispered.

She crossed her arms and stared at him, her cheeks glossy with tears. "We're going to try to live without him."

Madelaine stood in front of the rectory, carrying a huge, empty box. To the left the big brick church sparkled with reflected light, but the small, nut-brown house was dark and deserted-looking. Bright orange and gold Thanksgiving decorations—made by the Sunday school class, no doubt—dotted the windows. Pilgrims and cornucopias and turkeys.

She thought of the dozens of children who'd hunched over tiny desks, cutting and pasting and coloring. Francis had been so proud to tape their creations on his bedroom window. . . .

Grief rippled through her, one wave after another after another, leaving her shaken and cold. She couldn't seem to make herself move. She just stood there, seeing a hundred moments pass before her eyes, a dozen times she'd loped up this path, her arms full of pizza or flowers or champagne. Like the time she'd passed her first biochemistry exam . . . or the day Francis had heard his first confession . . . Lina's baptism . . . Madelaine's last birthday . . .

She shuddered and forced herself to think about other things—Lina and Angel and the days that lay ahead.

Madelaine couldn't go on as she had been. It had been a week since Francis's death, and she'd been stumbling in a fog ever since, speaking only when spoken to, and not always even then. She knew that Lina needed her, needed her desperately, but Madelaine felt as if she had nothing inside her, just a gaping hole where Francis had once been. He'd been her rock, her lifeline, for more than half of her life. Without him, she felt lost.

She took a deep breath and tilted her chin up. She knew there was no point in putting this off, in pretending she didn't need to walk up this path, open that door, and pack up his things. His housekeeper had taken care of the household goods, but Madelaine had asked to pack up his personal possessions. She would have put it off forever, but a new priest would be moving in soon.

She went to the door and opened it wide, letting a swath of sunlight cut through the gloom. Gripping the empty box, she moved woodenly through the common room toward his bedroom.

When she opened his door and flicked on the light switch, memories hit her so hard that she staggered backward. The cardboard box slid from her fingers and hit the floor with a thud.

Tears blinded her. With a small, gulping sound of grief, she moved numbly around the tiny bedroom, touching things—photographs, books, the favorite baseball cap he wore on Saturdays. The rosary wound neatly on his Bible.

She saw a picture on the dresser and picked it up, letting her fingers trace the cool surface of the glass. It was her and Francis on the day they'd brought Lina home from the hospital. They were smiling, but there was such worry in their eyes, such grown-up fears on those adolescent faces. . . .

*Heya, Maddy-girl, you're on the wrong side of town.*

"Oh, Francis . . ." She pulled his pillow from the bed and

smoothed her hands over its rumpled cotton. The *Star Wars* sheets she'd given him as a joke last Christmas.

She'd told Angel that they had to learn to live without Francis—but how could she do that? How could you learn to live without the sunshine on your face?

The tears came again, stinging and hot, and she gave in to them. She sank slowly to her knees, sobbing into the pillow that smelled of her best friend in the world.

# chapter nineteen

༄

Lina stared out at the glassy surface of Lake Union. A huge black shadow slithered across the flat water. It reminded her of the monster that had lived behind the louvered doors of her closet when she was a little girl. Francis and her mom had told her that the monster existed in her imagination, and mostly she had believed them. But some nights when it was especially dark outside and rain fell like salt in the circle of the streetlamp outside her bedroom window, she'd known that the monster wasn't only in her mind. She'd heard it moving, scraping, rustling her metal clothes hangers.

By the time she was twelve, she'd begun to understand that whatever lived in the closet was part of her. She felt it inside her, moving every now and then, rearing its ugly head with a sort of formless, wordless dissatisfaction that colored her perceptions, her dreams, her nightmares. It was a loneliness that no amount of family Monopoly games or Disneyland vacations could fill.

It had started as a few bad nights in her thirteenth year and graduated to bad weeks by the time she was fifteen. She remembered the beginning so well—it had coincided with her first period, and no matter how many books her mother had showed her, no matter how many photographs of uteruses and ovaries Lina had seen, she knew the truth. The goodness was bleeding out of her, leaving its brownish stain on her underwear. After she'd started bleeding, the sleepless nights had begun. She'd found herself alternately crying over nothing and throwing temper tantrums that left her shaken by their sudden violence. In her black moods, everything upset her. Especially her mother.

But it had never been this bad before. The dissatisfaction and unhappiness had always come and gone, moments that set her on a path and then left her standing somewhere she didn't really want to be.

Now it wouldn't leave her. The blackness sat on her chest and filled her mouth with a bitter taste. It wrapped itself around words she'd never had a chance to say—*good-bye, I love you, I'm sorry.*

Without Francis, Lina felt lost and alone. So alone that sometimes she woke in the middle of the night unable to breathe, unable even to cry. She would turn her bike toward the rectory, then remember he wasn't there.

She was falling apart. Nothing satisfied her or made her happy, and she couldn't seem to concentrate on the simplest thing. All she felt was guilt and more guilt for how she'd treated Francis. She wanted to talk to her mother about it, but she couldn't find the words. And what was the point, anyway? Mom was as much the walking wounded as Lina was. They drifted side by side in that big old house that didn't feel like home, saying nothing, never smiling.

And now, into all that pain, her mother had produced *the father.*

Lina winced and drew her legs into her chest, staring sightlessly at the flat silver surface of Lake Union. The big, rusted pipes that gave Gasworks Park its name were a huge hulking shadow to her left.

A light rain started to fall, pattering the lake, pinging off the metal structure.

Just thinking about the day of the funeral made her blood boil. She couldn't believe her mom had picked that moment to give her the big news about her mysterious father.

She curled into a tight little ball and rolled onto her side. Tiny shoots of dead grass poked her cheek and rain splattered the sides of her face, falling in icy streaks down her collar.

She wanted to hate her mother for bringing it up, and a part of her did, but there was so much more inside her right now. Hate and anger and, worst of all, that niggling hope that wouldn't grow and yet couldn't quite die.

She lay there until her clothes were soaked and her hair was plastered to her face. She needed Francis to make everything all right.

But Francis was gone and he wasn't coming back.

Who would help her now that he was gone? Who would be her rock to lean on when the black moods came, who would throw his door open and grin and say, *Come on in, Lina-ballerina . . . ?*

*Daddy.*

She thought of the phantom that was her father, the man she'd dreamed of for years, waited for, prayed to, and believed in. She needed him now more than she'd ever needed him.

*I want him to love you, Lina. I want him to want you, but I'm afraid. . . . I'm afraid he'll break your heart.*

When she'd heard the words, Lina had known it was the truth. Her mother *was* afraid he'd break her heart. And maybe he would. It was impossible to keep hold of all her little-girl fantasies of a perfect father anymore. Since Francis's death, she understood how dark and frightening the world could be.

Lina sniffed and wiped a flannel-sleeved arm across her dripping nose. This man who was her father could hurt her. She understood that now and knew her mother's fear was real.

But maybe he could save her, too.

She wanted that to be true, wanted it so badly, she felt bruised by her need. She was so achingly lonely, and her mother's love didn't seem to help. She needed her father to open his arms to her and take her into his house, to ask about her life and listen. Oh, God, just listen . . .

She'd lost Francis, and all she had left was her daddy.

She would *make* him love her. She wouldn't take him for granted, as she'd done with Francis. With her daddy, she'd be perfect and witty and lovable. So lovable he'd cry for the years he'd lost.

It had to be possible.

Because if it wasn't—if he truly didn't want her—she didn't think she could survive.

Angel dreamed he was walking in the meadow again. It was winter this time. A thick blanket of sparkling white snow covered everything, and the sky was a brillaint shade of blue.

Like Francis's eyes . . .

And suddenly he was in an empty church. He blinked and looked around. Sunlight streamed through a huge stained-glass window, sending shards of multicolored light across the hardwood floor. A huge statue of the Virgin Mary, carved of white marble, stared down at him, her arms folded protectively around a swaddled bundle.

Angel turned slowly and saw a group of children huddled at the open doorway. When he turned back around, the church was full of people—parents poised with cameras, craning their necks to see the kids.

One by one the children walked into the church. They were dressed alike—girls in ruffly white dresses, boys in creased black pants and pressed white shirts, their hair slicked back in unnatural stiffness. Angel felt a smile start. It was a day he remembered so clearly. . . .

Francis appeared first, a gangly nine-year-old with overly starched black pants that made a tiny *whick-whick* sound when he walked. Angel followed his big brother so closely that when Francis stopped suddenly, Angel rammed into him. Angel heard his laughter trill through the quiet church before he could stop it.

"Shh," Francis hissed, turning around.

Angel gave his brother a wide grin. "Sorry," he whispered, trying to straighten up. He tugged on the worn white shirt and retucked it into his small black pants.

Then the line was moving again. They marched past the pews and took their stations alongside the organ. There was a moment of hushed silence before the song began. Parents grinned and leaned forward; cameras came up.

Angel inched toward his brother. Francis stood in the center of the row—the tallest boy in the CCD class—with his back stiff and his eyes straight ahead. He sang the song in the clear, pure voice of a true believer.

Angel reached slowly into his pocket. His fingers curled around the baby tree frog, feeling the slick, rounded surface of his back. Inch by inch he eased the frog out of his pocket and then set it, gently, gently, on Francis's shoulder.

In the middle of Francis's solo, the frog let out a loud *ribbit* and jumped onto Mary Ann McCallister's head. After that, all hell broke loose.

Girls screamed and clapped and ran away from each other. The boys pounced and dove after the frog. And Father just stared at Angel, shaking his head.

Angel laughed until tears ran down his cheeks. After a long minute, Francis joined in, and the two of them stood there, laughing amidst the pandemonium. And finally Francis wiped the tears from his face and handed Angel his first Communion rosary. "Here, Angel," he said, grinning. "You're definitely going to need two."

Francis's words echoed as the vision of the church shifted and began to disappear.

Suddenly Angel found himself in the meadow again, standing knee-deep in a freezing snow. The sky overhead was as black as a crow's wing, and snow fell in a blinding fury, landing on his cheeks in tiny spots of fire. He stood there alone, not knowing what to say, his heart hammering in his chest.

Then Francis was coming toward him, floating, reaching out.

Angel took his brother's hand and clung to it. "I'm sorry, Franco," he whispered, feeling himself start to cry. "I'm sorry. Jesus Christ, I'm sorry. . . ."

"Shh," Francis said with a smile, a slow, easy smile that crinkled his eyes into slits. "I know." He squeezed Angel's hand. "Just hang on, brother. I'm with you."

And Angel woke up crying.

Madelaine stood in the open doorway of OR 8, wondering what she was going to do about Angel. Allenford and his surgical nurse were huddled around the bed, preparing Angel for his first post-op biopsy. Even from here, Madelaine heard Angel's angry voice.

His mood swings were uncontrollable. One minute he was compliant and charming, and the next—*wham!* He threw the kind of temper tantrums that became legend almost before they were over. Nurses had started drawing straws to see who would have to check his vitals and adjust his meds. He'd become the six-hundred-pound gorilla in Intensive Care.

Physically, things were going well. He'd been weaned off all intravenous drugs, including dopamine and Isuprel. He was progressing in leaps and bounds, and had been able to leave isolation earlier than most patients. The physical therapist had already visited him twice and reported that he was up and walking at least forty minutes a day. The blood cultures were negative.

Yes, physically he was doing great. Mentally he was a mess. He seemed unable to come to terms with the new lifestyle. Every pill or shot or blood test drove him crazy. He couldn't stand the swelling in his cheeks or the weight he'd lost while he was sick.

In short, most of the time he was a pain in the ass.

But he wouldn't be one for long.

Soon Angel would be discharged from the hospital and he'd be on his own. No one to take care of him but him.

And if something didn't change quickly, she was afraid he wouldn't take it seriously enough. Hadn't that always been Angel's problem—that he took nothing seriously?

His meds schedule wasn't something he could ignore. He *had* to follow the rules, for once in his life. If he didn't . . .

She pushed the thought away, refusing to dwell on it. Angel had Francis's heart—all that was left of her laughing, blue-eyed priest—and she'd be damned if she'd let him throw the miracle away.

He was lost right now. She could see it in his eyes, feel it in the fleeting softness of his touch. And whenever Angel got scared, he got angry; she knew that, had always known it.

The question was, what was she going to do about it?

She walked over to his bedside, taking his hand in hers.

"Hey, Mad," he said in a drowsy voice, "guess you wanted to see old Allenford stick it to me again."

Chris dipped some cotton in the iodine solution and swabbed a spot at Angel's throat.

Angel flinched at the touch and squeezed his eyes shut.

Madelaine could see how afraid he was, and she tightened her grip on his hand. She wanted to tell him that everything would be okay, but she was a doctor, and she knew—as he did— that this procedure was too important to sluff off on generalities. It would alert them if his body was rejecting Francis's heart.

"I need more Valium," he muttered, opening his eyes to look at her.

She tried to smile. "We've already given you more than your fair share."

Half his mouth lifted in a sloppy grin. "I never was good at sharing my drugs. I have a high tolerance—I need more."

She heard the raw edge to his voice and wished she could calm him.

He lay there, his head twisted sharply to the side. The portion of his neck that was painted orange throbbed with a thick blue vein. Allenford injected a local anesthetic just below Angel's Adam's apple. When the anesthesia took effect, he inserted a needle into the jugular vein and eased the bioptome down, down, down toward Angel's heart.

All four heads turned toward the television monitor at the foot of the bed. Angel's heart appeared on the screen as a pumping, writhing shadow. Allenford nicked off a tiny piece of heart muscle—no bigger than a pinhead—and removed the bioptome.

"That's all, folks," he said, smiling as he placed the specimens in a container and bandaged the small incision. He peeled off the white rubber gloves and tossed them in the garbage, then stood up. "We should have the results in a few hours."

The surgical nurse wrapped everything up and left the room.

Allenford picked up his charts and began studying the notations. "Anything on your mind, Angel?"

Angel turned to stare up at the surgeon. "Yeah, since you asked. Mad here won't tell me anything about my *donor*." He said the last word as if it tasted bitter on his tongue.

Chris's gaze darted to her face for a second, and Madelaine felt her cheeks grow hot. Then he looked back at Angel. "There's strict protocol for these things, Angel. We have found in our years of practice that the transition proceeds much better if confidentiality is maintained."

Angel rolled his eyes and struggled to sit up. The polka-dotted hospital gown gaped across his bandaged chest. The orange iodine looked like an angry burn against his pale throat. "You asshole doctors, you think you're God, but you're not. You're just people with a few more years of college than a dental assistant. You have no right to play with my life."

Allenford looked sympathetic. "It's the grief and the meds that are making you act this way, Angel. Don't worry about it, it's completely normal. Of course you want to know about your donor—all recipients do—but the truth is, it's not a good idea to cross those wires. The donor family is as entitled to privacy as you are." He leaned down toward the bed, draped his arms atop the bedrail, and stared at Angel. "So don't think about what you can't change. Keep in mind that soon it will all be up to you. You can keep railing at the injustice of it all, or you can get on with what's left of your life."

"Yeah, so what if I die—it's just a black mark on your surgical history. *You'll* get over it."

Allenford frowned. His voice fell to a whisper. "Do you believe that, Angel?"

Angel seemed to shrink before their eyes. He sank into the pillow and sighed heavily. "That's the problem, Doc. I don't seem to believe anything. You want me to stop 'railing at the injustice of it all' and get on with my life. How in the Christ am I supposed to do that? If the biopsy comes back bad, I could have ten minutes left. It's pretty damned hard to plan for a life like that."

"That's not necessarily true, Angel, and you know it. You could live a long time. There's a man in California who's going on eighteen years—"

"Don't give me the stats again, or Nurse Ratchet will have to mop my puke off the floor. Believe me, nothing fills my *heart* like the knowledge that I can live a long, full life if I drink carrot juice and exercise." He laughed bitterly. "I get a second chance at life—yee-haw. All I have to do is act like Richard Simmons."

Allenford laughed quietly and straightened. "Richard Simmons is a new one. I'll get back to you with the biopsy results. Think positive."

Angel snorted. "Cross my heart and hope to die."

Allenford gave Madelaine a pointed glance, then left the operating room. Angel opened his mouth to say something to

Madeleine, but before he could speak, Dr. Marcus Sarandon came striding into the room.

Angel rolled his eyes. "Oh, good, another doctor. And this one looks like Malibu Ken."

Marcus laughed out loud. His gaze cut to Madeleine, got her quick nod, then turned back to Angel. "Well, I suppose if there's anyone who ought to recognize plastic, it would be a movie star."

Angel gave the man a grudging smile. "Touché, Doc."

Marcus held out his hand. "I'm Marcus Sarandon. I'm going to be . . . helping out Madeleine with your case."

Angel frowned. "No way."

Madeleine moved quickly toward the bed. "I'll explain later. For now, just listen to Marcus. He's a good guy."

"So's Clint Eastwood. That doesn't mean I want him for my doctor."

Marcus pulled a blue notebook out from beneath his arm. "This is your daily calendar—medicine dosages and times. Look it over and we'll talk tomorrow."

"I don't want to talk tomorrow."

Marcus grinned. "The perfect patient. Good. I'll talk and you listen." He gave Angel another quick, flashing smile, then left the room.

Angel picked up the meds calendar and threw it across the room. It hit the blank wall and slid to the floor.

With a sigh, Madeleine retrieved it and placed it carefully on the foot of the bed. Then she pulled up a chair. "You're acting like a spoiled child."

"Shut up."

She smiled. "Good comeback, Angel. What's next—you going to stick your tongue out at me?"

"Don't rule it out."

"You're making life hell for everyone on this floor."

He gave her a bleak look. "What do you think it's like for me? I lie here every day, getting poked and prodded and checked like I was a side of beef on a conveyor belt. And I keep dreaming. . . ." His voice faded and he turned away from her. "Go away, Mad."

She scooted closer. "What is it, Angel?"

He waited a few moments to answer. "I keep dreaming about Francis. The dreams all start differently, but end the same. We talk for a little while, and then he reaches over to me. I can feel my heart beating inside my chest like a bird trapped against a window. He whispers something—I can never remember what it is—then he takes hold of my hand and he disappears. And that's not all. It's like . . . he's inside me. Yesterday I asked that fat charge nurse, Betty Boop or whatever her name is, to change the radio station. I *asked* her to put on something by the Beatles." He sighed. "The *Beatles*, for Christ's sake. Before the surgery, I didn't listen to anything but hard rock—you know, the kind of music that makes you want to take your clothes off and snort busloads of cocaine. Now I want to listen to 'Yesterday.'" He gazed up at her, and those eyes that always seemed so full of life looked dull and colorless. "I feel like I'm losing my frigging mind, Mad."

She sat very still. Her own heartbeat fluttered in her chest. It was common for transplant patients to think they'd been invaded by the donor's personality, but Angel didn't know he had Francis's heart. He shouldn't be feeling these things; it wasn't medically possible. "We have a wonderful psychiatrist on staff, Angel. She knows what you're going through—it's very normal—and she'd be happy to talk to you."

"That's what I need, another doctor. Oh, and you haven't heard the best part. Last night I asked for a glass of *milk*."

She couldn't think of what to say. "Nonfat milk is good for you."

"If you're going to spout physician-babble like some sort of medical communist, you can get the hell out. I'm trying to talk to you, Mad. I'm tryin' to tell you . . . ." He released a heavy sigh and shoved a hand through his tangled hair. "Never mind."

She scooted closer. "What?"

He looked up at her, and the sadness in his eyes almost broke her heart. "You doctors keep offering me 'life' as if it were a plum role in a Spielberg flick, but it's not *my* life, Mad. This heart's like a shoe that doesn't fit right. It never lets me forget that I wasn't born with it. Maybe if Francis were alive, or I had someone to talk to, someone who could take my hand and help lead me somewhere . . . I don't know. I feel like a freak."

She reached out and took his hand, squeezing gently. "I'm here for you, Angel."

He tried to smile. "No offense, Mad, but you're like a mirage I can see but can't touch. Sometimes I think I dreamed our time together. That crazy, head-over-heels boy couldn't have been me. Now, the kid that roared out of town on a brand-new Harley, *that* kid was me."

She stared down at him, seeing the pain and loneliness that haunted his green eyes. She cared for him so much in that moment that the feeling was almost an ache in her chest. He was hurting now, for himself and for the brother he lost. She knew how it felt to lose someone suddenly. All you had left was faith, and if you didn't have that, the emptiness could swallow you whole.

And Angel had never truly believed in anything, least of all himself.

"A dream, you forget over time." She leaned toward him. "Have you forgotten me, Angel?"

The second she asked the loaded question, she saw the answer in his eyes, the flash of longing, the fear of responding. "No," he answered quietly.

"I know I'm not Francis. I know I'm not family, but I'm here for you, and I'm not going anywhere."

"Promise?" he asked in a harsh voice.

Madelaine nodded. "That's why I can't be your cardiologist anymore. I'm going to let Marcus Sarandon take over from here.

He's an excellent physician. I'll still be around for you whenever you want . . . as your friend."

He frowned. "I don't understand. . . ."

"I'm too emotionally involved." She swallowed hard and said quietly, "I care about you too much."

He was silent for a long minute, studying her, then he said, "I don't deserve you, Mad."

She gave him a quick, teasing smile. "You never did."

"Yeah, just ask Fr—"

"Francis," she finished, and her smile faded. Silence settled heavily between them.

"He loved you," Angel told her, watching her steadily as he spoke.

For a moment the grief was so strong, she couldn't speak. Finally she nodded. "He loved you, too."

"I miss him. It's strange . . . after all those years apart, I always knew he was just a phone call away. I hardly ever thought about him, and when I did, I laughed and had another drink and told myself I'd call in the morning. Course, I never did. And now he's gone, and sometimes I miss him so much. . . ."

Madelaine couldn't help herself. She went to him then. Placing her hands on his cheeks, she stared down at his handsome face, staring deep, deep into his eyes.

*Francis*, she thought. *Are you there? You'd better be there. . . .*

She had to take a chance on him—on all of them. It was time.

"He's not your only family, you know," she said quietly.

Angel frowned up at her. She knew the moment he understood what she was saying—his frown lifted and a cold, stark fear widened his eyes. He shook his head. "Don't you do it, Mad," he said, still shaking his head. "Don't put that on me."

Madelaine didn't look away. For the first time in her life, she felt strong and in control, and God, it felt good. She gave him a slow, steady smile. "Her name is Lina."

# chapter twenty

❧

Angel shifted uncomfortably and punched his pillow into a little ball, then shoved it behind his head. Above him, the television spewed commercial jingles.

He reached for the remote control and flipped through the channels. One of those tabloid pseudo-news programs splashed his picture across the screen. The picture switched immediately to Angel's cleaning lady from Las Vegas—wearing more makeup than Robin Williams in *Mrs. Doubtfire*. She was babbling about how Angel never dusted behind his bed and sometimes forgot to leave a check for her services. Then the bleach-blond reporter returned to the scene, offering a plastic smile as she said, "It is believed that Angel DeMarco is currently in a hospital somewhere in the Pacific Northwest. There's been no confirmation of his illness but the word *AIDS* has been whispered at more than one Hollywood party in recent days. Sources close to the bad-boy star say—"

In a burst of irritation, he jabbed the Off button and threw the remote control across the room. It hit the wall with a satisfying clatter and crashed to the linoleum floor.

He crossed his arms and sighed heavily.

He couldn't stop thinking about yesterday. No matter how hard he tried to push Madelaine's words away, they kept coming back, turning up again and again as he lay in this lonely room.

*Her name is Lina.*

Finally he gave up and lay back down. Wishboning his arms behind his head, he stared up at the white acoustical tile ceiling.

*A daughter.*

He tried to imagine what it would be like, having a kid. He'd never spent much time thinking about that sort of thing. In fact, the only time he ever thought about children was just before sex—it was the thing that made him reach for the rubbers in his pocket.

He wanted to push the whole discussion aside as irrelevant and ridiculous. And he was certain that before the surgery, he could have done just that. He could have met Madelaine at a concert or a movie premiere, heard about the amazingly wonderful child she'd given birth to sixteen years ago, and felt nothing. Less than nothing.

He would have offered her a straight shot of tequila and drunk a toast to the kid he'd fathered. But that would have been the extent of it. After he drank the tequila, he'd have exited stage right.

But he was beginning to understand that running didn't always get you anywhere, that sometimes you ended up right where you'd started.

He didn't think of himself as immortal anymore. How could he with the stranger's heart pulsing in his chest and the bright red Frankenstein scar in his flesh? Every time he got a shot or took a pill, he was reminded that he was alive by the grace of God—and the gift of a stranger. It was the sort of thing that made a man think about his life—even if he didn't want to.

Even before the surgery, he'd been tired of running and getting nowhere, tired of parties with women he couldn't remember and friends who disappeared when the cameras turned off. But he didn't know how to do anything else.

He'd never created a life for himself, not a real, honest-to-God *life*. He had an existence—a condominium in a high-rise tower in Las Vegas, friends who came and went as easily as film roles, cars that he drove for a year and then traded in, a job that kept him rolling in money and working less than four months a year.

What had he done the rest of the time? He could hardly remember now. When he thought back on his life, all he got were random images of parties and hangovers.

He wanted to remember the early days, when he'd been a serious actor who went on one grueling audition after another, playing Shakespeare in the Park. But that was the history he had devised—the fiction he'd given to the press as they created the persona of Angel DeMarco from snippets of reality and piles of fantasy.

The sad truth was, he didn't know anything about acting. He'd been hired for his looks on his first audition—an audition he'd attended on a dare. Val's mother had told a producer that her son was an agent, and voilà! Val was an agent. And when Val became an agent, it was only seconds until Angel became an actor.

Maybe getting that first job wouldn't have been so bad if he'd been a bit player and found a calling, but he was the star and the movie grossed over $150 million. After that, they would have let him play Othello if he'd wanted to. A *star* was born.

He frowned, wondering why he hadn't worked harder to learn his craft. Why hadn't he taken the spark of talent the critics saw and honed it into something special?

He couldn't remember the whys; even the whens and hows were beginning to blur for him. Everything about his life before the heart attack was beginning to feel like an ephemeral memory that belonged to someone else.

And yet he remembered things like the carnival in crystal clarity.

*A dream, you forget, Angel. Have you forgotten me?*

He had. Until he woke up in that damned hospital in Oregon, he had practically forgotten Madelaine; their time together had faded to a hazy memory of first love, tucked like all high school memories into the tattered scrapbook of the soul. But now it felt real, so real he could touch it. Maybe the only real thing in his life.

She wanted him to be a father to their daughter. It was the only thing she'd ever asked of him.

*She needs you,* Madelaine had said.

God help him, he didn't know what to do. In some small pocket of his soul, he wanted to reach out to this daughter who looked so much like him. He wanted to take hold of her and bring her into his life, and know he'd done something right in this world before he died.

But he was afraid. What kind of father could he be? He was an alcoholic who'd just stopped drinking and a drug addict who'd quit using. He could drop dead of another man's heart failure any second.

Hardly the best role model for a confused sixteen-year-old girl.

There was no doubt that he would let her down. No doubt at all.

Depressed by his own inadequacy, he reached toward the bedside table and flicked on the radio Madelaine had given him. Heavy-metal music blared out at him, and he winced. Without thinking, he spun the dial until the rich melody of *Phantom of the Opera* spilled through the tiny speakers.

He felt a shiver of peace move through him. The anger and fear that had tightened his stomach since yesterday began to go away. He lay back in the pillows, letting the music fill the room and calm his ragged heart.

*Be her friend, Angel.*

It was his brother's voice, threaded through the music.

Angel sat up wearily, wedging his elbows beneath him. Be her friend.

It was exactly what Francis would have said if he were still alive. Francis always knew the right thing to do in life, and he'd always done it. Quietly, without hoopla or soul-searching or questions.

Could Angel be like that? Could he even try?

In the old days—before the surgery—the answer would have come with blinding speed, crushing any inkling to be good. He would have known that he couldn't live up to a commitment like this. He would have laughed at the very idea of trying.

But now, lying here, listening to this music, he wondered. Maybe this heart of his had come from someone good. Maybe it had given him a chance his old heart wouldn't have allowed.

He ought to laugh at the absurdity of the idea. He knew that the heart was just an organ, not the storehouse of the soul or any of that nonsense. And yet, no matter how often he told himself that, he couldn't quite believe it. Since the surgery, he'd begun to *feel* different. He had different tastes in music, in food. One minute he'd be his angry self, and then something would happen—he'd hear a sad song or look out at the rain—and he'd know that there was something new inside him. A tiny thread of goodness that lay curled within the bad. It scared him, that feeling that he wasn't alone in his body anymore, but it also mesmerized him. With every beat of the stranger's heart, he felt a tiny surge of possibility, of goddamn near magic.

He wanted all of his pain and suffering to *mean* something. Madelaine and Chris and Hilda and Tom Grant had all told him that he'd been given a second chance at life. Maybe he could finally make a difference.

He wanted it suddenly, wanted it as much as he'd ever wanted anything.

It felt good to want something, to have a goal. Frankly, he hadn't had too many of those in his life. He'd never wanted much beyond the next movie role or the next woman or the next drink.

He felt, amazingly, as if he were growing up at last.

He was so deep in thought, it took him a second to realize that someone was knocking at his door. "Come in," he said.

Madelaine walked through the door. For a split second he almost didn't recognize her. She was wearing baggy Levi's and an oversized green cardigan that had seen better days. Her hair was limp around her face, and no makeup relieved the pallor of her cheeks.

"Heya, Angel," she said quietly, coming up beside the bed.

He looked up at her and felt a tightening in his chest. She looked sad and lost, not her usual self at all. In the old days he might not have noticed the ravages of grief, but his new heart knew things his old heart hadn't.

He gave her a big, fake smile. "Hey, Doc. How ya doin'?"

She pulled the chart from the foot of the bed and studied it quickly, then put it away. "I'm sure Sarandon told you that the biopsy showed no rejection at all. You're doing well."

"That's one of us."

A frown darted across her pale face. "What do you mean?"

"Have a seat."

She pulled up a chair and sat down beside the bed. When she noticed how he was staring at her, she pushed a hand through her hair. "It's my day off."

He wanted to cut to the chase and ask how she was feeling, but it made him feel awkward and uncertain, that kind of intimate honesty. So instead he cocked a head toward the television that hung on the wall. "I just saw my picture on some tabloid show. Seems I've got AIDS. You should have told me."

A quick smile quirked one side of her mouth. "I didn't want to depress you."

"What else are they saying, my beloved jackals of the media?"

"One of the supermarket tabloids reported a few days ago that you'd had a heart transplant—baboon, I believe, or maybe it was an alien. Another show is certain that a stripper in Boca Raton gave you AIDS." She looked at him. "It appears you had quite a sex life."

He couldn't help feeling a little wistful. "Yeah, it was," he said with a sigh.

"It can be again, you know. Some cardiologists recommend waiting six weeks to resume sexual relations, but I'm a little more lenient. Whenever you're up to it . . ." She realized the double entendre of her words, and a pretty pink blush crept up her throat. "I mean, whenever you feel good enough, sex is okay."

He gave her a direct look, then blasted her with his best bad-boy smile. "Is that a proposition?"

He thought he saw her shiver slightly. "I believe I'll let your new cardiologist have this discussion with you." She got to her feet. "Now I've got to run."

He reached for her hand and held it. "Don't go."

She stared down at him, long and hard, then quietly said, "Don't treat me like that, Angel. I'm not some Hollywood starlet who'd kill to spend a night in your bed."

He understood that he'd hurt her. "I'm sorry. Old life. Old lines." He shrugged but didn't let go of her hand. "You'll have to be patient with me. Changing overnight is a little tough."

Slowly she drew her hand back and sat down.

He waited for her to say something, and when she didn't he knew it was up to him. "I . . . I've been thinking about Franco a lot," he said, stumbling over the words like a fool.

She squeezed her eyes shut, and he could tell that she was battling for control.

"Is that his sweater?" Angel asked quietly.

She immediately touched her sleeve, her fingers stroking the worn wool. Wordlessly she nodded.

"When . . ." His voice fell to a raw whisper. "When does the healing start, when do we start feeling better?"

She swallowed thickly and looked up at him. "I don't know if there is healing. There's just . . . going on."

He looked at her, realizing in that instant how much he cared about her, how much he wanted her to care about him. "I guess that's what life is. Going on."

, She gave him a soft smile that for a second transformed her face. "I guess."

He'd given her that smile—with nothing more than a few honest words and a glimpse of his own heart. The realization swept through him, made him grin like an idiot. "This new heart of mine . . . it came from someone good."

She drew in a sharp breath. "Yes," she answered.

And for the first time, he *felt* like a new man.

Madelaine knew when the phone rang that it was something bad. Her stomach knotted up. Carefully she set down the novel she was reading and went into the kitchen, picking up the phone. When she heard Vicki Owen's voice slide through the lines, she closed her eyes and sighed tiredly. "Hello, Vicki."

"I'm sorry to bother you at home, Madelaine, but I wanted to let you know that Lina wasn't in school today."

Madelaine's gaze cut to her daughter's closed bedroom door. "I dropped her off at seven o'clock. She waved and went inside the building." She sighed, too tired suddenly to deal with this anymore. "I guess I should have walked her into the classroom."

"I saw you pick her up at three o'clock—that's why I called. I'm afraid she's headed toward real trouble if someone doesn't find a way reach her."

Madelaine almost denied it instinctively, but instead she dragged the phone into the living room and sat down on the overstuffed sofa. Since Francis's death, she didn't feel like herself anymore. She spent every moment realizing how fragile life was, how uncertain, and she didn't have the strength anymore to pretend she was perfect. She felt as if she were treading water in the deep end of the pool.

"I'm . . . confused, Vicki," she confided, and the moment the words left her mouth, she felt as if a weight had fallen from her shoulders. "Francis was more than a friend, he was part of the family. Whenever I try to talk about him, we both end up crying and neither one of us feels better. I know she's reaching out, but I don't have anything inside to give her, and even if I try, she won't wait long enough for me to stumble through the words."

"I know how you're feeling. My brother and his wife died last year, and I've been raising my nephew. For weeks afterward, we circled each other like wary lions. It's an impossible time."

"So what do I do?"

"Just keep trying, keep reaching out. And watch her for signs of real trouble. I'll try introducing her to my nephew, but it won't be easy." She laughed. "Your daughter's going to think he's a total nerd."

Madelaine smiled wearily. "I'd guess that means he's a great kid."

"He is . . . now. And see if you can find someone for Lina to talk to. I'll keep trying, but she doesn't want to listen to an authority figure."

"Yes," Madelaine answered. "I will. Thanks a lot, Vicki."

After she hung up, Madelaine got to her feet and walked down the hallway. She was at Lina's room before she'd even formulated a plan. But the minute she looked at the closed door, she knew what she was going to do.

*Someone to talk to.*

She knocked on the door.

No one answered.

Steeling herself, Madelaine opened the door anyway.

Lina was sitting on her bed, listening to music through big black headphones and smoking a cigarette. She was wearing a sweatshirt that read: *If you don't like my music, you're too frigging old.* There were tears streaming down her cheeks.

The sight of her baby sitting all alone in her room, rocking back and forth and crying, was almost more than Madelaine could bear. She walked over to the stereo and clicked it off.

"Damn it, Mom!" Lina wrenched the headphones off her head and tossed them onto the unmade bed. "You have no right to bust in here and shut off my music."

Worldlessly Madelaine took the cigarette from Lina's mouth and crushed it in the littered ashtray on the floor. Then she sat down beside her daughter.

For a second they just looked at each other, and the wary resentment in Lina's eyes hurt. Lord, how it hurt.

Madelaine reached out, brushed the ragged hair from her daughter's eyes.

Lina flinched and drew back, laughing shakily. "I'm not getting another haircut."

Madelaine sighed. So many misunderstandings. "I wasn't thinking you needed a haircut, baby. I was thinking you need a father."

Lina paled. "You said he doesn't want to see me."

"He thinks he doesn't, but sometimes a person can't see what's right in front of him." She gave her daughter a tentative smile. "Like you. I'm right here, I've always been right here, and yet you don't see me."

"Mom—"

"Don't interrupt me. I haven't been a good mother to you, Lina. I know that, don't you think I know that? But it's never been because I don't love you." She smiled softly. "I remember when you were born, and they set you on my stomach. You were so little, so perfect in every way, and I started to cry. Everyone thought I was crying because you were beautiful." She stroked Lina's damp check. "But I was crying because I was seventeen years old and afraid. I knew I'd never be good enough for you."

"Mom, don't . . ."

"Because I was afraid, I've been selfish. I've tried to keep you with me all the time, hoping that someday I'd get it right. But I haven't gotten it right. If I had, you wouldn't be skipping school and shoplifting and sitting alone in your room, crying. You need something I can't give you right now."

"I need Francis," she said in a small, shaking voice.

"We both do, baby. And we're going to keep on needing him every day for the rest of our lives. Maybe someday the pain will soften—everybody says it will—I pray it will. But for now, we have to go on with our lives, we have to grab for whatever happiness we can find. If there's one thing I learned from Francis's death, it's how fast it can all be gone. One phone call in the middle of the night and your life is changed."

"I want my old life back." Lina gave her a watery smile and shrugged. "I know, I know, I hated it when I had it."

Madelaine wanted to throw her arms around Lina in that moment and draw her close, but she was afraid it would end the conversation, and she still had a long way to go. Miles and miles. Instead, she cupped Lina's chin in her hand and smiled. "I want to change where I've gone wrong." She drew in a long breath and geared up for her next words. "I want to introduce you to your father."

Lina's eyes widened and she started to shake her head. "Not yet . . ."

"Yes. Now."

"What will he do?"

There was the question, the stinging little fear that niggled inside and couldn't be brushed aside. But the new honesty felt good, much better than all that hiding and pretending to be fearless and perfect. "I don't know."

"What if he doesn't want to see me?"

"Then we try again the next day and the next and the next."

Lina was quiet for a long time. Then she said, "I don't know if I can take that."

"You're stronger than you think."

"No."

Madelaine gazed at her daughter, loving her so much it hurt.

She knew that Lina was right to be frightened, but that the fear wasn't reason enough to stay away. If anyone knew that lesson, it was Madelaine. She'd been afraid her whole life, and what had it gotten her? A lonely bed and a daughter who felt unloved.

"If he hurts you, I'll be there, Lina."

"I'm scared."

"I know. I am, too."

Lina turned, stared at the huge poster of Johnny Depp that hung over her bed. Finally she sighed and looked back at Madelaine. "I have to try, don't I?"

Madelaine felt a surge of pride for her daughter. "We all do. It's all there is."

Angel dreamed he was in the field again.

He stood there, looking around, feeling peaceful and contented. Birds were circling overhead, cawing and chirping and swooping down to the sweet green grass. He could hear his heartbeat, thudding away, pulsing and pounding in his chest.

He knew Francis was coming before he arrived.

Angel turned in slow motion and saw his brother standing at the edge of the trees. Francis was wearing his severe black priest's clothes, and for a split second Angel almost didn't recognize him. Then Francis started to walk toward him, floating above the flower-bright grass.

He could hear his brother's laughter riding the breeze, joining with the crowing of the birds and the whispering of the leaves, and Angel found himself laughing, too.

Suddenly the world fell silent. The birds disappeared and the wind faded away. All he could hear was their two heartbeats, pounding out of beat in a rapid-fire rhythm.

Without thinking, he reached out. He felt Francis take his hand, felt the warm strength of his brother's grip, and he felt anchored and safe. Their heartbeats synchronized, became a single beat in the quiet field.

*I don't have long.*

Angel heard his brother's words, though Francis's lips hadn't moved.

"Stay," Angel whispered desperately. "I've got so much to say."

*The words don't matter.*

"They do, I know that now. Stay."

But Francis was already fading. His image shimmered and he pulled away.

He ran after Francis, reaching out, trying to take hold of the image, but it was moving faster than he was, disappearing into the dark shadows of the trees.

And Angel was alone. The sky overhead turned dark and ugly, throwing a shadowy pall across the field, burying the flowers and the grass.

"Angel?"

He lifted his face to the sky and stared at the gathering clouds. *Come back, Francis, come back. . . .*

"Angel?"

He woke with a start, and found Madelaine standing beside his bed. He stared up at her, his breath coming in great, wheezing pants. "H-Hi, Mad."

She pulled up a chair. "You okay?"

"No," he answered without thinking, throwing his vulnerability on the blankets between them. He almost yanked it back and said *Yes, hell yes,* then he looked into her gray-green eyes and realized that he was tired of lying, tired of covering up the truth. Yesterday he'd felt as if he'd seen a glimpse of the promised land, but today he felt lost again. Lonely and forgotten and sick. The dreams about Francis were killing him.

"No," he said again, quieter this time. "I'm not all right. I keep dreaming of Francis. It's not normal. It's like . . . like he's inside me. I feel him all the time, I hear him talking to me. Sometimes I even *think* like he used to."

"You couldn't have anyone better inside you, Angel."

"I know." He sighed. "Yesterday, in my dream, he said 'live for me.'" He swallowed hard. "How could *I* do that—live for a man like him? He was so much better than I'll ever be."

She scooted closer to the bed. "You've been given the second chance he never got, Angel. Only you can decide what to do with it."

"Oh, great, now pile a little guilt on me."

"Not guilt. Hope."

He grabbed the three-ring binder beside the bed. "How much hope can I have when this is my life?"

"Quit being so melodramatic. That notebook isn't your life—it's just your routine. The *schedule* of your new life. The medications you take—daily, I might add, if you want to see each new sunrise—and the foods you should eat. The exercises you'll have to begin. The dates of each checkup and test for the next six months. A plain old schedule. Ordinary people follow them all the time."

"Oh, I can't wait."

"It's too bad you're in such a foul mood today, because I have a surprise for you. Someone I want you to meet."

"If you put me in a room with that damn shrink again, I'm going to blow your recovery stats through the roof."

"No shrinks, no physical therapists, no nurses. Just a single sixteen-year-old girl."

Angel froze. He heard his heartbeat thudding in his ears, and the sound made him panic. Then came Francis's words, *Be her friend.*

He wanted to. Christ, he wanted to, but he was afraid. He was such a screw-up, and this was important. Not the sort of thing you could go into half-cocked and ready to run at the first sign of trouble. "I can't do it, Mad. I don't have it in me to be her father."

She started to say something, then, instead, she did the strangest thing. She reached out and placed her hand on his chest. He felt the warmth of her touch through the flimsy cotton of his hospital gown, through the layers of gauze that covered his scar. "Oh, Angel," she said, leaning close, so close he could see the silvery streaks in her green eyes, so close he could smell the subtle fragrance of her hair spray. "You have it in you, believe me."

He was mesmerized by her eyes. He thought, crazily, that he'd seen her look at him like this before, but that would have been years ago. He couldn't possibly remember . . .

"I'll screw up," he said, forcibly breaking the spell.

"Then I'll beat the shit out of you."

He knew she was serious this time, and he understood suddenly the risk she was taking here. She loved Lina, and she was scared that Angel would screw up and hurt their daughter. He knew, too, that if he did, there would never be a redemption for him. Never be a second chance.

"I don't want her to know about the transplant—she'll treat me like a freak."

"No, she won't. But it's your decision when—and if—to tell her about the surgery."

"How do I act? What do I do?"

"She loved Francis like a father, and she's grieving over his death. She needs someone to listen to her, to care about what she thinks and feels. That's a place to start. Be her friend."

He gave her a nervous smile. "That's what Franco . . . would have said."

"Yes," she said, her voice barely above a whisper. She gazed down at him expectantly, her eyes bright.

*Be her friend.*

## chapter twenty-one

Lina paced back and forth down the quiet corridor of the ICU. Every now and then a nurse or doc would say hello and she'd be forced to look up and mumble something in response, but other than that, she just kept moving.

Hilda scurried up the corridor and tapped her on the shoulder. "You're pacing like a caged cat, sweetie. What's wrong?"

Lina barely looked at her. It took all her self-control to stand still. Her foot tapped wildly. She'd known and loved Hilda for most of her life, but right now she was too nervous to make small talk. She remembered belatedly that Hilda had asked her a question, but she couldn't remember what it was.

Hilda peered up at Lina, giving her the same once-over she always did, then she clucked disapprovingly. "My daughter's a beautician, you know. She could do fabulous things with that hair of yours."

The transplant nurse had been dishing out beauty advice for

years. Every time she saw Lina, she came up, pinched her cheek, and shook her head, muttering something about how pretty Lina could be with a little less makeup. Ordinarily Lina laughed at Hilda's half-joking advice.

Not today.

Her *father* was going to see her in a few minutes. What if he thought she was ugly?

With a gasp, she shoved her hands in her pockets and spun around, leaving Hilda gape-mouthed behind her. She ran to her mom's office and sneaked inside, shutting the door. She hurried to the antique Victorian mirror beside the bookcase and peered into the glass.

The girl who stared back at her was pale and puffy-eyed from lack of sleep. Her hair stood out in a thousand uneven spikes. The black eye pencil she'd applied beneath her lower lashes made her look like she'd been punched in the face.

How come she'd never seen that before?

*Oh, God,* she thought in a sudden panic. Her daddy was going to think she was butt-ugly.

She rummaged through her mom's desk drawer and pulled out a comb, trying to rearrange her haircut, but it was no use.

When she went back to the mirror, she felt a sinking sense of fear. She still looked like one of those runaways you sometimes saw haunting the downtown streets after dark.

The door clicked open and Lina spun around again. She was so nervous, she dropped the comb. It hit the linoleum floor with a clatter.

Mom walked into the room, and Lina felt almost sick to her stomach. As always, her mother looked like she just stepped off the pages of a makeup advertisement—golden-brown hair swept off her face in carefully controlled curls, beautiful hazel eyes highlighted by just a little brown mascara. Wearing a cream-colored cashmere sweater and black pants, she was the picture of cool sophistication and class.

*That* was what her father thought was pretty.

Lina glanced at herself in the mirror again and winced. "I can't do it, Mom. I have to come back tomorrow. I think I got food poisoning from the cereal this morning."

"He's waiting for you," she answered quietly, closing the door behind her.

Lina felt her heartbeat speed up. "H-He said he'd see me?"

Mom frowned and moved toward her. "Are you okay?"

Lina nodded, then shook her head, then tried to nod again, but the tears came, flooding her eyes. "No," she whispered.

Mom stroked her cheek. "It's okay to be nervous."

"I'm ugly."

"You're gorgeous."

"I never should have let Jett cut my hair." She looked up at her mother quickly, waiting for the *I told you so,* but thankfully, it never came. Finally she said, "Do you think . . . maybe you could make me look like you?"

Mom studied her, a smile lurking at the corners of her mouth. "Oh, no . . . you're much prettier than I am."

"Yeah, right," she whined. "And Bosnia is a great vacation spot."

Mom took her hand and led her to the chair behind the desk. Lina sat down.

"Tilt your face up," Mom said. When Lina complied, her mother used some cream and a tissue to take off all Lina's makeup, then she reapplied just a little. Mascara, blush, and some pale pink lipstick. Then she combed Lina's hair back from her face and sprayed it with something.

Lina started to get up.

"Sit there," Mom commanded as she walked over to the antique armoire in the corner of her office. Easing the ornate doors open, she rummaged through the clothing and pulled out an ice-blue angora sweater. Turning back to the desk, she smiled. "This was supposed to be a Christmas present."

Lina stared at the soft sweater and felt ashamed. She knew that come Christmas, she would have glanced at something this feminine and tossed it away, thinking that her mom was a hopeless nerd. She turned her gaze to her mother. "It's way cool, Mom. Thanks."

Mom laughed. "Just what you would have said on Christmas morning."

Smiling, Lina pulled the Coors beer T-shirt over her head and threw it in the corner, then slid into the incredibly soft sweater. When her mother led her back to the mirror, Lina couldn't believe the change.

This time a beautiful young woman stared back at her. The sweater made her eyes look impossibly blue. For once, instead of looking ghostly white, she looked pale and sort of fragile, like those girls in the Calvin Klein ads. Impulsively she twirled around and threw her arms around her mom, holding her close.

Then she realized what she'd done and she drew back, embarrassed.

Mom smiled. "Your need to know that he's very sick, your father. He's just had heart surgery and he's got to take it easy. He'll be discharged in about an hour, but he's still going to be moving slowly. I've made arrangements—if things go well—to help him find a house today. All three of us."

"Sorta like a family," Lina said, surprised by the wistfulness in her voice.

Mom looked startled, then a little sad. "More like new friends."

Lina nodded. Taking a deep breath, she straightened her shoulders and tilted her chin up. "I'm ready, Mom."

"Good. He's in room 264-W."

"You're not coming with me?"

Mom shook her head. "I think you guys need some time alone."

Lina tamped down the flash of fear that came at her then. She thought about how pretty she looked, how the pale blue sweater made her eyes look as blue as Francis's, how her black hair looked sophisticated instead of ragged.

*I'll make him love me.* The vow came back to her and she grabbed hold of it, held it to her chest, and prayed she could make it come true. She looked up at her mom, and wanted to say something, but nothing seemed good enough. She could see the fear in her mother's eyes, and she knew that the fear was for both of them.

She gave her mom a quick smile and headed off. She hurried down the long hallway, past the nurses' station, past the family waiting room.

By the time she reached his room, her heart was beating wildly and there was a fine sheen of sweat on her palms.

She peered through the observation window and saw a man standing at the window on the opposite wall, his back to her. He was wearing a denim shirt and Levi's, and his hair was long and dark brown. A good sign, she thought—long hair.

She took a deep breath and knocked on the door. At his muffled "Come in," she pushed the door open and went inside.

"Hello, Lina," he said in a smooth, even voice that sent a shiver of recognition down her spine. It was a voice she knew but couldn't place.

She waited nervously for him to turn around.

Slowly he turned. Her breath caught as she recognized him. Her knees went weak. She would have reached out for something to hold onto, but there was nothing nearby.

It was Angel DeMarco.

"Oh, my God," she whispered, feeling disconnected and confused.

He flashed her the megawatt grin she'd seen a million times on-screen. "I see your mom didn't tell you who I was."

She tried to say no. The word came out as a high-pitched squeak.

"Come on over here."

She moved like an automaton, her mind whirling with

thoughts. Her father was Angel DeMarco. Her *father* was Angel DeMarco. Her father was *Angel DeMarco*. The kids weren't going to believe this. Brittany Levin was going to shit.

Then it hit her, so hard it wiped everything else from her mind. "DeMarco," she said.

He nodded, giving her a softer smile, more intimate than anything she'd seen on film. "I'm Francis's brother."

For a second she couldn't breathe right. "They never told me."

Something passed through his eyes at that, a darkness that made her think she'd hurt him.

"I never read that you were from Seattle, or that you had a brother. I . . . I thought I read somewhere that you were from the Midwest."

A smile crooked one corner of his mouth. "Tactical maneuvers to muddy the trail. I didn't want anyone to know where I'd grown up. Sorry." He came toward her, moving in the shuffling gait of all post-op patients. Instinctively she reached out for him, and he took both of her hands in his.

Lina looked up into his legendary green eyes, and for a heartbeat, she couldn't catch her breath. He had Francis's eyes—even though they were green instead of blue, they were Francis's beautiful eyes. And he had Francis's way of looking at you, really looking the way so few people did.

"You're more beautiful than I imagined," he said in a husky voice, his eyes filled with the same wonder she felt.

Tears stung her eyes and she didn't care. "Thank you."

"I . . . I don't know anything about being a father, you know."

"That's okay."

"Maybe we could start slow, just start out being friends."

*Friends.* The words caused a dizzying rush of excitement. It was what she'd always wanted—a father who was her best friend. She bit down on her lip to keep from laughing out loud again. He was going to be everything she ever wanted in a dad; she could tell. He was going to take all the pain and grief and fear in her life and make it go away. From now on, she'd always have a safe place to be.

He let go of her hand and touched her face, gazing deeply into her eyes. "Don't look at me that way, Angelina."

She drew in a sudden, surprised breath. For a disorienting second, she'd thought he was going to call her Angelina-ballerina. But he hadn't, of course he hadn't.

"What is it?" he said, eyeing her.

"Nothing . . . just that Francis used to call me Angelina . . . No one else does."

"It's your name," he said, then his voice fell to a whisper. "I mean it, Lina. Don't think I'm a god or something. I'll only let you down. . . ."

It was such a ridiculous thing to say, she ignored it. Instead she just kept staring up at him, memorizing everything about his face, about this moment, about how it felt when he held her hand. "Don't worry. I'll love—"

He pressed a finger to her lips suddenly, silencing her.

She blinked up at him in confusion. When he withdrew his hand, she said, "But—"

"Make me earn it," he said harshly, staring into her eyes with a seriousness that frightened her. Suddenly they weren't Francis's eyes at all. "It's the only chance we have."


Angel looked down at the piece of paper on the clipboard. All it required was his signature and he was as free as a bird.

He was strangely reluctant to sign it.

He glanced around at the cheesy little hospital room he'd inhabited for the last few weeks, and suddenly it felt like home. He recognized the birds that huddled along his windowsill, and the way the sun crept through his yellowed curtain at sunset. He'd started to like the smell of disinfectant and mashed potatoes and gravy. Even Sarah the Hun had become a friend.

"You okay?" Madelaine asked.

He didn't know what to say. He felt like an idiot, and yet he was suddenly afraid that he couldn't make it on the outside, that the heart that felt so strong and new in his chest would weaken out there, give out on him. Or that he'd fall into his old boozing, irresponsible lifestyle and be lost again.

"I don't know. I thought I was ready, but . . ."

"Lina and I will be here for you, Angel. You're not going to be alone out there."

"Thanks, Mad." He touched her face, a fleeting, tender caress that reassured him. "I don't know what I'd have done without you during all this."

She smiled. "You would have done fine."

He shrugged and looked around again. "I keep thinking I should have luggage . . . something to show for all the time I've been here."

She placed her hand on his chest, right over his heart. "You do."

Behind them, the door opened, and they both turned, expecting to see Sarandon and Allenford for the momentous good-bye.

A middle-aged woman stood in the room, wearing a ragged wool coat and mud-splattered rubber boots. "I'm looking for—" She saw Angel and her mouth dropped open. "Oh, my Lord, it's you. . . ." She looked at Madelaine. "It's Angel DeMarco."

Madelaine stood there for a second, then surged forward, gripping the woman's arm and guiding her outside, slamming the door shut behind her.

A minute later, Madelaine was back, looking grim and angry. "They let her walk past security. Her father's in 246-E."

"*Shit,*" Angel cursed. "We've got to get out of here. As soon as that woman gets to a phone, she's gonna think she's won the lottery. They'll pay her *and* give her her fifteen minutes of fame."

Madelaine looked at him. "I'm sorry."

"Don't be sorry—it had to happen." He grabbed a mask from the bedside table and tied it behind his neck. Before he lifted it to cover his face, he said, "Here's the story: I was here for an undisclosed amount of time and underwent successful cardiac surgery. I have been discharged and no one knows where I am. Anything beyond that is no comment. Have Allenford call a press conference as soon as possible. And let's get me out of here. Now."

Madelaine nodded. "Let's go."


Long before the first reporters showed up, Madelaine had Angel in her car, and they were speeding away from the hospital.

Lina and Angel had taken to each other like ducks to water. She glanced in the rearview mirror and watched them. They were sitting side by side, their heads cocked together, talking animatedly. Lina was saying it was *way cool* the way they'd hustled Angel out of the hospital. Angel was telling her about some time he'd hidden out in the back of a pickup while his fans stormed a soundstage.

Madelaine maneuvered the car down Magnolia Street and pulled up in front of the first house she'd chosen for him to view.

"What do you think of this one?" she asked, putting the car in park.

Lina and Angel looked out the window, then looked at each other and simultaneously shook their heads.

With a sigh, she shifted back into drive and headed off. It irritated Madelaine that they wouldn't even look at it, but more than that, it made her feel excluded. It wasn't as if she'd chosen the houses at random. She'd taken an inordinate amount of time. She'd spoken with several realtors about the best array of houses for rent within ten minutes of the hospital. Then she'd done a quick drive-by of the seven best, and made appointments to see them all today.

They were already on house number four, and Angel had yet to get out of the car. He'd hated the first three on sight.

Finally she pulled up in front of her favorite of the houses she'd chosen.

She killed the engine and cast a quick look at the house. She knew that Angel wouldn't like it, not Angel of the Las Vegas high-rise condo and the limousines, but she couldn't resist showing it to him. It was the kind of place that Francis would have loved.

It was a small log cabin with mullioned windows and a big wraparound porch. Built at the turn of the century, it had been a summer house for one of the city's founding fathers, and the subsequent generations had built other, more modern homes. So it sat on a sweeping Lake Washington waterfront lot, untended and vacant. Most people wouldn't pay the exorbitant rent the family wanted—for that money they could get first-class construction in Broadmoor.

Huge old maple trees lined the brick walkway that led from the winding asphalt road. Stubborn Shasta daisies grew in random clumps amid the grass.

"Next house," Madelaine said, waiting a split second for a two-voiced call to *move on*.

Silence.

She twisted around and looked in the backseat. Angel and Lina were both staring at the house.

"Francis would have loved this house," Lina said. Opening the door, she got out of the car and began walking up the path.

Madelaine looked at Angel.

"I've never imagined myself living in a log cabin," he said after a minute.

She smiled apologetically. "I know it's not your style."

He gave her a grin that was so quick and white, she felt stunned by it. "It didn't used to be, but neither were afternoons driving around in a Volvo." He shuddered dramatically.

She couldn't help laughing. "Let's go inside."

They got out of the car and came together at the end of the walkway. Angel stumbled. Without thinking, Madelaine curled an arm around his waist and let him lean against her.

She realized a split second later that she was holding him.

Her breath tangled in her throat and she turned slowly, meeting his questioning gaze. They stood that way for an eternity, neither one of them saying anything.

"I never told you thanks," he said finally.

She felt a fleeting disappointment, but didn't know why. "No need," she answered.

"Not true," he said, staring into her eyes so intently that she wondered what he saw. "I've learned there's always a need."

Impulsively she reached up and brushed a lock of hair from his eyes. She realized a split second later that she'd done it because he'd sounded so much like his brother. It was exactly the kind of thing Francis would have said in a moment like this. At the thought, she felt a pang of loneliness. "He would be proud of you right now."

There was no question of who *he* was. Angel grinned and looked down at her. "Because I'm holding his best girl?"

She saw a transformation in his eyes—this time there was no trace of Francis and his gentle, caring soul. This time there was only Angel, fiery-tempered and brutally honest, and he was looking at her as if she mattered. Her heartbeat sped up. Suddenly she felt as if she were sixteen again, standing in the arms of the boy who loved her.

She told herself not to care, not to want anything from this man who'd broken her heart, but she knew even as she had the thought it was too late, and the knowledge scared her to death. "No. Because you're changing, Angel. And we both know how hard that is to do."

He laughed and pulled away from her. Turning back to the log cabin, they started up the pathway together. Halfway there, Angel reached down and look Madelaine's hand in his.

The next morning, when she got to work, the parking lot was full of news vans. Reporters had descended on the hospital like a pack of ravenous hyenas, flashing photographs of anyone who walked up to the front door, barking questions at everyone they saw.

Madelaine was winded and irritated by the time she pushed through the crowd, muttering "No comment" a dozen times. When she got to her office, Sarandon and Allenford were waiting for her.

Madelaine sighed and tossed her suede coat over the back of her sofa. "Angel knew this was coming. He was seen yesterday just before we discharged him."

"Must be that lovely woman I saw on *Hard Copy,*" Sarandon said calmly, taking a sip of coffee.

"What does Angel want us to do?" Allenford asked.

"Confirm with the press that he had cardiac surgery. Say that the surgery was successful and he was discharged. Beyond that, he wants a no comment."

"That won't last long."

Madelaine heard the edge of eagerness in Chris's voice, and she supposed she understood it. The surgeon wanted the world to know about his great work. "No," she said. "It won't. But it'll buy him a little time."

"Okay." Chris pushed to his feet, and Sarandon popped up beside him. "Let's go . . . the three of us."

They strode out of the office and turned the corner, coming down the hallway of Intensive Care like the astronauts from *The Right Stuff.* Chris was in the middle, with Sarandon on his left and Madelaine on the right.

In step, they pushed through the front doors and marched down to the parking lot.

"I have a statement to make regarding Angel DeMarco," Chris said.

"Just a second," someone screamed.

Reporters and camera operators zoomed up to the three doctors, formed a tight circle around them. Microphones shot into Chris's face.

He looked calm and unruffled. "Mr. Angelo DeMarco was

recently a patient at this hospital. Following his much-publicized collapse in Oregon, he was transferred here for cardiac surgery. The surgery was completely successful, and Mr. DeMarco has been discharged."

"Does he have AIDS?" someone yelled.

"No, he does not."

"When was the surgery?" someone else wanted to know.

"I'm sorry, I don't have that date with me," Chris said calmly.

"Why are you hiding the date?"

Chris nodded briskly. "Thank you for your time."

Lights flashed, cameras clicked, questions rang out.

But the press conference was over.

It was quiet here in the early morning hour before school began. Thin yellow clouds spread across the treetops, and the first glimmering rays of the sun glanced off the metal bleachers. Lina could feel her feet sinking into the squishy, rain-soaked grass, and it made her feel strangely buoyant to leave a set of footprints across the football field. As if, for once, she was actually here.

She heard the kids talking long before she reached the lip of the ravine. Their chattering voices floated up from the dark copse of trees, accompanied by the sweet smell of marijuana.

She couldn't wait to join them. She jammed her hands in her pockets and raced to the edge of the ravine, staring down at the crowd she'd tried so desperately to belong to.

They were down there, clustered together, passing a thermos around in one direction, and a joint in the other. The few kids who weren't smoking pot were puffing away on their cigarettes.

Lina frowned, disappointed suddenly. Last night Angel—her *dad!*—had talked to her about drugs and booze and cigarettes.

She'd heard it all a million times before, but last night was different. First of all, Angel was her dad, and she wanted him to love her. But too, he seemed to understand her in a way no one ever had before. Last night, as they'd sat together on the porch swing, listening to the tinny clanks of her mom cooking inside, Lina had looked into her father's green eyes and felt as if she were looking into a mirror. He was the first adult she'd ever known who remembered what it felt like to be a kid.

When she told him that, he laughed and said it was because he'd never grown up. But then, in the middle of all their joking, he turned serious. When she pulled out a cigarette and started to light up, he grabbed her hand and stared at her so long, she became scared.

"First of all," he said, "you can't smoke around me because of my surgery. But more important, smoking is for idiots, and you seem like a smart kid to me."

His words made her feel small and stupid, and mumbling something, she put the cigarette away. After that, they lapsed into silence. Night fell slowly, drizzling across the untended yard, blurring the edges of the trees. A white moth came out of hiding and fluttered around the porch light.

Finally her dad spoke again, and this time she could tell that he was thinking long and hard before each word. "I'm an alcoholic, Angelina, and a drug abuser, and . . . worse. I know what sends a person out into the darkness, looking for a little bit of light—even if that light comes with a helluva price and only lasts for the length of an evening." He turned to her then, and she saw the disappointment in his eyes. "I've ruined my life—and drugs and booze were how I did it. Please, please don't be like me. It'd break my heart."

"Hey, Lina!" Jett's voice cut through her thoughts.

Distractedly Lina looked down the ravine and saw Jett standing in his usual spot, clutching the thermos in one hand and a joint in the other. "You bring anything to drink?"

Lina frowned. For the first time, it bothered her that Jett always asked for something from her. "Nope," she yelled down.

He looked away from her before the word was even finished.

"Bummer!" he yelled, and everyone laughed, then he went back to passing the joint around.

Lina stood there for another minute, waiting for someone else to call to her, or invite her down. But the kids seemed to have forgotten her existence. Shoving her hands in her pockets, she made her careful, picking way down the loose embankment, her tennis shoes crushing the muddy ivy and mushrooms in her path.

She moved into place beside Jett and said nothing. In the distance the second school bell rang and everyone laughed.

Someone handed Lina the joint. She stared at it, blinking at the smoke that stung her eyes. Then she passed it to the next person in line.

Jett frowned at her. "You don't wanna get high?"

She shrugged. "Don't feel like it."

"Why not?"

Everyone waited, breathless, for the answer.

"I met my dad last night." She felt a rush of adrenaline as she said the words.

Jett took a long drag and held it in, then exhaled the smoke at her face. "Oh, yeah?"

"Yeah," she said, grinning up at him. "He's Angel DeMarco."

There was a moment of stunned surprise, then everyone burst out laughing.

"Sure he is, Lina." Brittany laughed. "And my dad's Jack Nicholson."

Jett frowned at her. "So who is it really?"

Lina stared at them. All of a sudden she felt unwelcome here, and she wondered if she'd ever really belonged. "I told you, it's Angel DeMarco."

Jett stared at her, one black eyebrow rising slowly. "I read he had AIDS."

"No," she answered. "He just had bypass surgery. No big deal."

"Oh, right," Brittany said with a humph, "like *you* would know."

She spun to face the crowd. "I *do* know. I spent the whole weekend with him, and he told me he had bypass surgery."

"You're a liar," Jett said softly, and she knew the second he spoke that the group would follow him. Then he grinned at her. "Hey, give me a smoke, willya?"

"Buy your own," she snapped.

Jett spun to face her again. "What did you say?"

She stared up at him, seeing his drug-pale skin and bloodshot eyes and the too-black hair that fell across his forehead. She wondered what she'd ever seen in him. Disgusted, she shook her head. "My uncle Francis was right. You guys are a bunch of losers."

The look in Jett's eyes turned ugly. "Oh really?" he whispered.

She backed up. "Yeah, really."

Jett followed her. She tripped on a stone and thudded to a sit. He came up close, towering over her, grinning down at her. "Where do you think you're going?"

She squished her hands on the muddy earth and shot to her feet. "I'm getting the hell away from you guys."

He laughed, but it was a cold, angry sound that made her afraid—just like it was supposed to. "What're you gonna do, make friends with the cheerleaders? They wouldn't hang with a skank like you, Hillyard." He laughed again. "And no one's gonna believe a lame story about Angel DeMarco bein' your dad, either. Get real. We're the only friends you've got. Now, quit actin' like a bitch and give me a smoke."

Lina slapped his face. The smack reverberated in the dense, moist air. She realized a second too late what she'd done—she saw the anger dawn in his eyes, and she was off, scrambling up the bank and running across the football field. He reached for her, missed, and cursed, but by then she had a head start.

Lina didn't look back. She ran all the way to the school and skidded into the quiet hallways. Breathing hard, she raced to Vicki Owen's door and knocked hard. When the counselor said, "Come in," Lina burst through the door and slammed it shut behind her. Sinking onto the seat, she gulped in a few aching breaths, then looked up at Miss Owen. "I need help."

A half hour later, Lina sat in the school gym, alone, waiting for some guy she didn't know. Miss Owen's nephew or cousin or something.

Miss Owen had listened to Lina's story about Jett and the gang and said very simply, "You need new friends, Lina."

Lina had laughed. "Oh, yeah. I'll get some out of the Wheaties box tomorrow morning. All I need is a few proofs of purchase."

Miss Owen had just smiled and told Lina to go to the gym and wait. And so she was here, sitting on the cold wooden floor of the basketball court, her arms crossed. Waiting.

After about ten minutes, the door creaked open. A guy paused in the opening and then began slowly walking toward her. His footsteps left an echoing wake in the huge room.

Lina stared at him, making out more and more of his features with every step. He was tall—way taller than she was—and he had short blond hair. His skin was pale, with two ruddy spots of color on his cheeks. He wore a huge, baggy sweatshirt and oversized jeans.

She recognized him finally. He was the school's student vice president—Zach Owen. "Hi," he said, looking at her with a directness that made her uncomfortable.

She nodded but said nothing.

He flopped to a sit in front of her. "My aunt tells me you're in trouble."

"Nothing I can't handle." She raked him with her eyes. "Besides, what would you know about trouble?"

He laughed, and for a second he reminded her of Francis,

with his crinkly-faced smile. "It's an act," he said softly, as if he could read her mind. "Last year my parents died and I went off the deep end—drinking, drugging, you name it."

She eyed him suspiciously. "Yeah, right, and I'm Michael Jackson's love child."

He grinned at her. "You don't look like him."

"Very funny. Look, I gotta run—" She started to get to her feet and he grabbed her, held her in place.

"Don't run." It was all he said, just two simple words, but in his voice she could hear understanding. And suddenly the two words didn't seem simple at all. Slowly she bent back down to her knees and looked at him, really looked. "How'd you stop?"

"Aunt Vicki put me in detox. When I dried out, I transferred to this school. At first it was hard. . . . I didn't know anyone. But I ran for vice president to make friends, and I won." He grinned sheepishly. "Course, no one ran against me."

"I found out this weekend that Angel DeMarco is my dad." She hadn't meant to say it, somehow it just came blurting out. She waited, shoulders tensed, for him to respond. To make fun of her.

He studied her. "Yeah, you sorta look like him."

"I do?" She heard the completely dorky awe in her voice and she winced, embarrassed.

"You're way prettier, though."

The compliment fluttered through her. A quick smile jerked one side of her mouth. "Thanks."

She looked at him again, and saw for the first time that he sort of looked like a young Hugh Grant. Not really like a nerd at all.

# chapter twenty-two

❧

The doctors' lounge was uncustomarily quiet in the last few minutes before the close of the day shift. The tables were empty, their cheap brown surfaces cluttered with paper cups and plastic forks. A row of soda and candy machines stood waiting for the next shift of storm troopers to descend, quarters in hand.

Madelaine sat at the rickety table closest to the window, her fingers cupped around the comforting heat of a thick porcelain mug. The burnt scent of French roast coffee wafted upward.

At precisely 5:01 Allenford and Sarandon strode through the single doors, pulling down their surgical masks in unison. Both men nodded at her and headed for the coffee machine, plunking their money in one after another and waiting in silence for the paper cups to drop into the slot and fill with coffee. Then they carried their drinks to the table.

Chris had a pile of tabloids tucked under his arm, and he tossed them onto the table. Headlines jumped up at Madelaine.

*Angel DeMarco in St. Joseph's Hospital . . . AIDS . . . cancer . . . heart surgery . . . heart transplant.*

The two men sat down across from her. Chris reached instinctively for the cigarettes in his breast pocket. Pulling one from the pack, he stared down at it, caressing it absently.

Madelaine was used to his little ritual. He'd given up smoking three years ago—due to the sheer volume of staff and patient pressure—but he still held a cigarette when he'd had a hard day and he needed to think.

Finally he looked up at her. "The DeMarco situation is heating up."

Madelaine nodded. "I heard a photographer from one of the magazines caught him in physical therapy yesterday."

Sarandon gave a tired smile. "He wasn't happy—and he made sure everyone on the floor knew it."

Madelaine laughed softly. "I don't doubt it."

"The point is," Allenford said, "we can't hold out much longer. Our security is getting more sievelike every day. Obviously we've misled the press by implying he underwent simple cardiac surgery, but that won't last much longer."

Allenford took a long sip of coffee, eyeing Madelaine. "You know that security is not the only problem here."

Madelaine knew what he was going to say before he said it. She'd tried not to think about the repercussions of his celebrity, but they kept coming back, worming through her joy at Angel's progress. "You mean Francis," she said dully.

Allenford stared sympathetically at her. "Some reporter is going to discover the connection. The only reason they haven't discovered it yet is because there's been no official confirmation of the transplant—they're too busy trying to find the woman who supposedly gave him AIDS. The confusion has them more interested in his sex life than his heartbeat, but that won't last. Once they find out about the transplant, some smart reporter will track down the sequence of events . . . and find out about a patient in Oregon who donated his organs on the same night

Angel got his heart. When they hit that patient's name, it's going to rip through the headlines like a rocket. If he isn't prepared . . ." He said nothing more, let the implication hang in the air between them.

Madelaine's gaze dropped to the table. She studied the tiny black lines in the fake wood-grain veneer. She knew that Chris was right—she'd known it for days, she simply hadn't wanted to face it. "I'll tell him," she said quietly.

Sarandon got to his feet, leaving the half-empty coffee cup on the table. "Just let me know when you're going to do it." He grinned. "I'll advise the staff to grab their Kevlar vests." Then he shoved his chair out of the way and strode out of the room.

Madelaine watched him go, saying nothing. She tried to imagine what it would be like to tell Angel the truth, and the images caused a sick feeling. She didn't want to do it, didn't want to traipse in there and tell him what she'd done—what they'd all done. She was terrified of his response, and for more than the obvious reason.

The dreams bothered her.

She realized she'd been silent a long time. She felt Chris's gaze on her, and she met it. "What?"

He smiled. "You never were any good at games, Madelaine. Just say what's on your mind."

She knew it would be smart to say nothing, but she'd learned in the last few weeks that sometimes being smart left you feeling lonely and confused. "It's Angel," she said cautiously. "He's . . . changing."

"The good ones do."

"I think it's more . . . surprising than that. He's becoming . . ." She couldn't say it. The words caught in her throat.

Allenford stared at her a second. She saw the moment he understood what she wasn't saying. His eyes narrowed, and a frown tugged at his brows.

"He's listening to Francis's music, eating Francis's food. Before the surgery, he says, he was allergic to milk—now he loves it. He's . . . caring in a way I don't think he ever really was before."

"You said you hadn't seen him since you were kids. People change, Madelaine. Besides, they're brothers."

"Maybe." She leaned forward, crossed her arms on the table, and pinned a steady gaze on her old friend. "Could the heart have memory on a cellular level? Like a cell's instinctive ability to re-create itself or replicate or—"

"Stop it," Allenford said gently, touching her hand. "You're grieving, Madelaine. Let it go. Accept Angel for who he is and be thankful he's still around. Everything else . . . let it go."

"I've been trying to, but sometimes when he looks at me . . ."

"Don't you think you *want* to see Francis in Angel's eyes?"

She couldn't deny the truth of that. She missed Francis so much that she imagined him everywhere—sitting on her couch, swinging in her porch swing, driving up in that battered old car of his. Sometimes she'd turn around to talk to him, and realize instantly that he wasn't there, that she'd imagined his footsteps on the walk. "Yes," she whispered.

"What if you didn't know about the transplant—wouldn't you think that all these changes were ordinary recovery? Think about it. When a patient goes through this program, he tends to change his life. They're almost always more caring and more conservative. They've learned that each day, each moment of each day, is a miracle. That's bound to change a man's outlook."

The rationality of Chris's words soothed her. It was possible that she saw Francis in Angel because she wanted so desperately to believe that part of her best friend was still alive. "You're probably right."

He gave her a long look. "I don't believe in that stuff, but we've all seen anecdotal evidence for what you're talking about. Recipients who seem to know things about their donors that they can't possibly know. I'm not egotistical enough to believe that anything in this world is impossible." He touched her hand. "I met Francis—however briefly—and I know one thing."

"What's that?"

"If there is memory on a cellular level, your Angel couldn't have gotten a kinder heart."

Sighing tiredly, Angel went into the living room that Madelaine and Lina had created for him. He clicked on the television—and heard a reporter say, "Sources close to the superstar confirm that he has received a baboon's heart in a successful transplant operation. However, cardiologists at St. Joseph's will report only that—"

With a groan, he turned off the TV and flicked on the light switch.

It was cozy and comfortable, this living room that was and wasn't his. Big overstuffed denim sofas and Navajo-print chairs huddled around the huge river-rock fireplace that dominated the room. They'd even put a few framed pictures on the mantel—Lina's school picture, a shot of Francis and Lina snow-skiing, and an old, crackled photograph of Angel and Francis in front of their mom's Impala.

Pictures of everyone but Madelaine.

She'd given him the trappings of family life—comfortable furniture, photographs, milk (nonfat, of course) in the refrigerator—but it was too quiet to be real. There were no fingerprints on the glass of the pictures, no dust collecting beneath the furniture.

The only thing out of place in this perfect little cabin was him. The realization depressed him. Once again, he was just passing through life, observing as if through a window. For most of his life, that had been okay. Hell, it had been better than okay, it was what he'd wanted. He'd never wanted to be *real*, not like most men. He'd wanted to be Peter Pan, playing with the lost boys, gambling and boozing and ignoring the grownups' rules. That's why he'd sought out celebrity. It was life on Pleasure Island.

And if he didn't change, really truly change, he knew that soon he'd start to slip. He'd go back to the life he'd loved. He'd call the wrong friend or decide that a straight shot of tequila—just one—wouldn't hurt. But one would end up as two, then three, and he'd be back on the roller coaster.

He didn't belong there, didn't belong in his old life. But he didn't fit in this new world, either. He was like a ghost, moving shadowlike through some plane in which he could never really touch anything, never really be touched. He couldn't go back and he didn't know how the hell to go forward.

There was a knock at the door, and he felt a surge of relief. He stumbled across the tiny living room and flung the door open.

Val stood in the opening, smoking a cigarette, holding a bottle of tequila. "I can't believe you live in the *suburbs*." He shuddered. "What were you going to do next, mow the lawn or barbecue?"

Angel stared at the bottle, at the sloshing beads of gold that clung to the glass sides. The sweet, familiar smell of the smoke wafted to him, set off a longing deep inside.

*His old life.* It was here, standing in front of him, wearing designer jeans and long hair and a smile that held nothing but cynicism. And suddenly he wanted it again, wanted to be the same old shit-kicking hell-raiser he'd once been. He wanted that life that smelled of cigarette smoke and cheap perfume.

Grinning, he stepped aside. "Valentine. Where in the hell have you been?"

"Trying to find booze in a town that shuts down at twilight—*and* sells liquor only in state stores." He shuddered dramatically. "Christ, what an archaic custom."

Angel led the way into the darkened cabin, turning on a few lights as he went. Val followed, his boot heels clicking on the hardwood floor.

Val set the bottle down on the table with a clunk. "Cuervo Gold. Your favorite."

Angel looked longingly at the bottle. Could one drink really hurt?

The smoke tantalized him, swirled invisibly beneath his nose, leaving its stamp on the air.

Val collapsed on the overstuffed sofa, one arm flung out along the back. He tucked a long strand of hair behind an ear. "Nice furniture—what did you do, get a Ralph Lauren credit card?"

Angel thought of his high-rise in Vegas—the stark white walls and black leather furniture, the chrome and glass end tables, the bar that glittered in a dozen shades of gold when the lights came on. "Madelaine picked this stuff out."

One eyebrow shot upward. "Ah . . ."

Angel saw the cynicism in his friend's eyes, the inability to understand or appreciate a home like this, or a woman like Madelaine, and again he felt adrift and lost. A man who didn't belong anywhere. He thought suddenly of Lina, of the way she looked at him—as if he hung the moon—and the things she asked of him without even opening her mouth.

*Be my daddy . . . I love you . . . be there . . . be there . . . be there . . .*

He would only disappoint her if he tried to be a real father. What the hell did he know about being a father? And yet, he'd break her heart if he failed.

"Have a drink," Val said softly, moving the bottle toward him.

Angel took a step toward the table, his eyes trained on the tequila. Val's soft, metered voice echoed through him, and he knew it was what the devil's voice would be like, soft and soothing and reasonable. And it would say what you wanted to hear. . . .

He went so far as to reach out, to curl his fingers around the warm glass. He lifted the fifth, twisted it open, and smelled the pungent, sweet aroma of the liquor. He wanted to drink it all in one heady gulp, let the tequila flow down his throat and pool firelike in his gut, wanted to let this liquid take everything away—even if it only lasted for a night.

But he knew that if he had one drink—just one—he'd crawl into that bottle and find himself back where he'd begun.

He closed his eyes. Shaking, needing that drink so badly he felt queasy, he slammed the bottle back down on the table. "I can't do it, Val."

Val frowned. Something flashed through his friend's eyes— was it jealousy, or fear? Angel couldn't be sure. "You always do it. The other heart attacks—"

"It's not the same anymore. It can't be. I . . . I have a kid." He smiled. It was the first time he'd said the words out loud, and it made him feel surprisingly good. "Madelaine . . . you remember the girl I used to talk about?" At Val's quick nod, he went on. "Seems she—we—had a baby all those years ago. Her name is Lina and she's sixteen years old. I told her I'd quit partying if she would."

"Sounds like she's your daughter, all right."

Angel laughed uneasily. "She is."

Val released a sigh. A silence fell between them, and it was a long time before he spoke. "I'm proud of you, Angel. I always told you you were stronger than you thought. God knows you're stronger than I am."

"I'm not strong." He said the words quietly, wondering if Val even heard them.

"I was thinking of heading for New York—they're looking for someone to play the Green Hornet. I thought you might be interested, but . . . I guess not."

Angel stared at his friend and knew this was Val's way of saying a longer good-bye, of pulling back from a friendship that could never again be what it was. It hurt, knowing what was happening, but Angel understood.

"It's okay, Val." He said the easy words, the expected ones, though he knew that Val saw the truth in his eyes, the disappointment and the regret. "Keep in touch."

Slowly Val got to his feet. "You're gonna make it, Angel."

Angel nodded, though he wasn't so sure. "Yeah. Sure I will."

Angel woke up screaming his brother's name. He lay in the darkness, trying to control his ragged breathing. The heart ticked away in his chest, completely unaffected by the adrenaline pumping through his body. He felt as if Francis were close enough to touch.

He threw the covers back and stumbled into the kitchen. Wrenching the refrigerator open, he stood in the wedge of yellow-bright light, staring sightlessly at the jumble of jars that Madelaine and Lina had left for him. Without thinking, he reached for the pitcher of skim milk. As his fingers curled around the cold plastic, he snapped. He was about to drink *milk,* for God's sake. What was next—humming show tunes?

He flung his head back and stared up at the wood-beam ceiling. "Get out of my head, Franco." The words brought a wrenching sense of guilt. He slammed the refrigerator door and squeezed his eyes shut. "I've got to get on with my life. *My life . . .*"

But what was his life—and how did he find it?

He went into the living room and flopped into the Navajo-print chair. "What do I do, Franco? How do I change?"

He waited and waited, but no answer came to him. After a few minutes, he started to feel like an idiot. *I've gone off the deep end, bro. I'm asking for tips from the recently dead.*

His smile faded. It wasn't funny.

Restless and edgy, he got out of the chair and went to the back door, flinging it open. Outside, dawn was just beginning to break across the water, throwing pink spears across the rippling silver sea. Wind shivered through the trees, and for a weird moment, it sounded like Francis's laugh. "How do I change, Franco? How?"

*You already have.*

The words came to Angel from far away, threaded through the wind. At first he didn't understand, didn't remember his question. Then it fell into place.

He smiled. "Sure, Franco, go for the easy answer."

He laughed uneasily and closed the door, going back inside. Now he was talking to ghosts. Could channeling be far behind?

Angel knew he'd changed, but it didn't feel like anything that mattered much. Little changes—taste in music and food, a new need to be around people. It wasn't exactly earth-shattering. He hadn't *done* anything different, and he was a man who'd always judged himself by his actions, not his words or his feelings. Denying himself one drink and one cigarette wasn't enough. He had to *do* something.

He'd been in this cabin for almost a week, and he hadn't left once. Madelaine brought him food and left it on the porch, as if he were Quasimodo on a low-fat diet. There was a brand-new Mercedes in the driveway—the first time he'd ever owned a car with more than two seat belts and a metal roof—and a brand-new Harley-Davidson Sportster alongside it. He'd yet to drive either one.

He was hiding out here, protecting himself from what would happen when the world found out about his transplant. Now there was confusion about the diagnosis, but that wasn't going to last.

The world was going to find out, he knew that. Each day the rags offered more money for the inside story. Soon someone would talk.

*It should be you, Angel.*

He could almost hear his brother's voice. It was exactly the kind of thing Francis would have said.

Francis would tell Angel to come out of hiding and tell the truth about what he'd been through. Remind him that he could be a role model for someone else, some other poor schmuck who was lying in a lonely hospital bed, waiting for a heart.

He almost laughed out loud at the thought of him—*him!*—

being a role model to anyone. He was definitely on too many meds.

And yet he knew the truth when he heard it, knew what he should do.

Before he had time to think about it, he acted. He grabbed the phone and dialed information. He asked for the number for St. Joe's Hospital and punched it in. A practiced, polished voice answered and put him through to Allenford's voice mail. Angel left a message that was simple and to the point—please set up a press conference for ten o'clock Thursday morning.

When he'd done that, he felt better, but he knew it wasn't all he had to do. There was something more. . . .

He had no idea what.

*Something about the heart.*

For the first time, he thought about his donor's family, and what they must have gone through. Instead of caring about who his donor was or how he'd died, Angel wondered about the man's family (he could never think of his donor as a woman), the people who had chosen to give Angel a second chance at life.

All he'd cared about before was the donor's name. He'd thrown fit after fit trying to get Madelaine to break her blessed confidentiality. He fantasized about the mysterious man, wondered where he came from and how he died and what he believed in. But was that really the important part? Did it really matter whose heart he had, or did it simply matter that he made the best of the gift he'd been given? The miracle.

They deserved something from him.

*A thank-you.*

It came to him that easily, without bells or whistles or epiphanies. Just a simple realization that he owed someone his life. He reached forward and grabbed a pen and yellow legal pad off the heavy iron coffee table. He stared down at the thin blue lines and doodled a little heart in the corner.

Before he even realized what he was going to do, he started to write.

*Dear donor family:*

*This is perhaps the most difficult thing I have ever done, writing this letter to strangers who feel like family. There are no words to express my gratitude, or if there are, it would be left to greater minds than mine to find them.*

*I was in a coma and dying when your beloved family member was tragically killed. Until recently, I couldn't conceive of what that moment must have been like for you. Then I lost my brother in a sudden car accident. The grief was like nothing I'd known before—a wound that kept tearing itself open.*

*How is it possible that in a time like that, your family looked outward? Even in your incomparable grief, you looked to me and others like me across the country. You did this without knowing my name or my life or anything about me. The courage and compassion of your act makes me believe in the world, and in my fellow man, for the first time in years. And even more surprisingly, it has made me begin to believe in myself.*

*You have given me the most precious of gifts—the miracle of life itself—and though I will probably never meet you, I want you to know that I carry a piece of you and your whole family in my heart. I will do everything in my power to deserve the second chance you have given me.*

*May God bless you and your family.*

As he wrote the last sentence, Angel felt himself changing. It was as if sunlight, pure and hot and white, were flooding through his body, lighting places that had been cold and dark for years. For the first time in his life, he knew—irrevocably and completely—that he'd done the right thing.

\*    \*    \*

Madelaine reached into her closet for something to change into. Her fingertips brushed soft, well-worn flannel. Very slowly she pushed the silks and cottons aside and came to a blue and gray flannel shirt that had been Francis's.

She remembered the day he'd left that shirt here—a spring day that had started out cold and rainy and by noon turned almost summer-hot. He'd thrown off the old flannel shirt and put on one of those oversized T-shirts that the drug companies were always giving her.

For a moment the pain was almost unbearable. Blinded by stinging tears, she reached out for the shirt and pulled it from the hanger. She brought it to her nose and breathed deeply.

She could smell him. A trace of aftershave filled her senses, bringing a dozen treasured images to her mind. Francis unwrapping the small red and green plaid box, laughing as he always did when he saw the aftershave. *Oh, thank God, I was almost out.*

She realized in a rush that he wouldn't be here for Christmas this year, or Thanksgiving. She and Lina would have to make it through those days alone. How would they do it? Every one of their traditions had been forged as a threesome. Who would carve the turkey, who would hang the Christmas lights, who would eat the Christmas cookies they laid out for Santa Claus on the good Spode china?

She clutched the shirt to her face and breathed in deeply, as if she could somehow bring him back to life through the sheer force of her will.

God, how she wanted to turn around and find him there, her priest with the blue, blue eyes and the infectious laugh. She wanted to run into his waiting arms and hear him tell her he loved his Maddy-girl. She squeezed her eyes shut. *Just one more time, God . . . one more time.*

Solitude stretched taut around her. She heard the quiet ticking of her bedroom clock, the gentle tapping of the wind against the glass.

Standing in her own bedroom, in her own house, she'd never felt more alone.

Suddenly she couldn't endure it another second. She shoved her arms in Francis's shirt and buttoned it up, running headlong through the house. She wrenched the door open and felt the cold air hit her in the face.

When she opened her eyes, she saw Angel. He was leaning against the front end of his gray Mercedes—the one she'd bought for him with an American Express Platinum credit card. He was standing there, looking as if he didn't have a care in the world, in his snug blue Levi's jeans and faded Aerosmith T-shirt.

He pushed away from the car and strode up the walkway. Wind whipped a long strand of brown hair across his face.

Angel came to within a few feet of her and stopped. For once, he didn't smile. "I want to see Francis's grave."

She frowned. That wasn't what she'd expected him to say. "It's in Forest Lawn . . . in Magnolia Heights."

"I thought maybe you would come with me." He flashed the smile that had graced a hundred movie magazines, and she noticed for the first time that it was a little sad around the edges, and it didn't reach his eyes.

"What is it, Angel?"

His false smile faded and he looked up at her with an intensity that made her breath catch. "He's haunting me, Mad. It's because there were so many things I never said. I thought maybe . . . if I said them now, he'd let me get on with my life." He took a step toward her. "I'm starting to figure some things out, Mad, I can see a life ahead of me for the first time in years, but . . ."

She was drawn by the words he didn't say. It felt as if she were falling into the past, but she didn't care. All she knew was that she was lonely, had been lonely a very long time, and he was holding his hand out for her. She reached down and took it, felt his strong fingers close around hers, and her heartbeat sped up a notch. "I'll take you," she said softly, knowing that if she went with him to Francis's grave, she would tell him the truth about his heart and he might never offer his hand again. She squeezed tightly, clinging to him.

He led her down the path that cut between her faded flower beds to the sidewalk that guarded her house. The first hint of nightfall tinted the sky a deep, rich lavender blue. Wordlessly she climbed into the soft, sweet-smelling leather seat and directed him toward the freeway.

When they reached the cemetery, it was almost four o'clock. Pink and red fell in silken streaks across the twilight sky.

They walked up the granite path to the grassy knoll she'd chosen for Francis. The church had put up an exquisite white marble marker. Beside it was the wrought-iron bench that Madelaine had chosen.

She led Angel to the bench and sat down beside him. They stared at the marker for a long time, each lost in memories. Finally she drew the flannel shirt more tightly around her and stood up. "I'll give you a little time alone," she said, turning to leave.

He grabbed her hand. "Don't go."

She gazed down at him, seeing the pain in his eyes, the fear and the frustration and the loneliness, and it threw her back to another time, long ago, when he'd looked at her like that and said the very same words. Slowly, still holding his hand, she sat down.

Quietly he said, "I would change it all if I could."

She didn't know if he was speaking to her or Francis, but it didn't matter. The confession wrapped around her, connected them. "I know what you mean."

He laughed, but it was a hollow sound. "How could you? You've never run from anything in your life."

She sighed. "That only shows how little you know me, Angel. I've made a lot of mistakes with our daughter, and I think I took

Francis for granted. I thought he'd always be there for me." She tilted her chin and stared out at the endless acres of grass, watching tiny knife blades of night steal across the headstones. "I was afraid of Francis and Lina. They both loved so easily and so well. Unlike me. I could never seem to get it right, especially with Lina. I was always afraid I'd do the wrong thing, or say the wrong thing, and she'd leave me . . . just disappear one day and never come back."

He was silent for a minute, then he touched her chin, forced her to look at him. "Like I did."

She couldn't pretend his betrayal had meant nothing. "I kept waiting for you to come back."

"It wasn't you, Mad."

She tried to laugh. "I didn't see anyone else standing outside my bedroom window."

The smile he offered was sad. "It was *me*. I was scared of you and me and the baby. Scared of what I felt for you. How could I know . . ." His gaze held hers. She waited, breathless and a little afraid of what he would say next. He turned, stared out at the night sky, and when he finally spoke, his voice was raw. "How could I know I'd never feel that way again?"

The words were magical. She felt them wrap around her, squeeze her heart. Answers came to her, spiraling one after another, weaving themselves into a whole that terrified her. He was talking about the past, she knew that, and yet it felt like the future.

In the end she said nothing, and the quiet slipped between them.

"Say something, Mad."

She turned to him, knowing that her eyes were full of the emotion she was afraid to release. "What can I say, Angel? You want to know if I've ever felt that way again? The answer is no."

"Do you think you could?"

She knew that the answer, once given, could never be taken back. She'd be throwing her vulnerability at him again, giving him the power to break her heart. She thought about saying nothing, or lying, but she knew it was useless. Somehow, she'd already given him that power. "Yes," she whispered.

A quick smile tugged at one corner of his mouth and he turned quickly away, staring once again at the headstone. "I've got a long way to go, Mad. I'm not the man I was before . . . but I'm not anyone else yet. I can't make any promises."

Surprisingly, the words that should have hurt gave her hope. The old Angel would never have been so honest. "We're not kids anymore, Angel."

"What does that mean?"

"It means that everything doesn't have to happen overnight. It means that trust isn't given as easily or taken as casually. There's a lot of water under our bridge."

"Yeah." Angel fell silent again. Finally he pulled a piece of paper from his breast pocket. "I want you to read this," he said, handing it to her.

She frowned in confusion at the sudden turnaround. "What is it?"

"Just read it," he said.

She took the piece of paper and unfolded it, smoothing the wrinkles against her thighs. The first three words hit her hard. *Dear donor family.*

She looked up at him.

"It's a letter to my donor family. I worked on it for six hours, but it still isn't quite right. I thought you might want to help me. . . ."

Madelaine saw the uncertainty in his eyes, the need, and it touched her deeply. Forcing her gaze away, she read the letter, and when she was finished, she was crying. Very carefully she folded it back up and looked at him. She started to say that it was perfect, but she couldn't speak.

She knew that the time had come.

"They say the truth will set you free," she said quietly.

"The letter . . . is my way of trying to change, set my life right. I want to be a good father to Lina, but I don't know how. Sometimes I look at her and I wonder where all those years went and what my life would have been like if I'd walked her to kindergarten and seen her in the school Christmas pageants. I know I have a long way to go, but I've got to start somewhere—and the heart feels like the beginning."

Madelaine carefully set the letter on the bench and turned to look him full in the face. She realized in that instant that she'd never stopped loving him, and the knowledge made it difficult to breathe. "When I was talking about the truth setting you free, I didn't mean you. I was talking about me."

He flashed her a grin. "Another deep, dark secret you're keeping from me?" He saw her seriousness, and his smile faded. "Lina *is* my daughter?"

"Of course she is." Madelaine leaned closer. Almost against her will, she touched his chest, felt the heart beating, fluttering in perfect rhythm. She searched for the words, just the right ones.

"You're scaring me, Mad."

"I'm afraid you won't forgive me," she whispered. She wanted to heap explanations and apologies on him, to make him understand the miracle she'd given him, but he was watching her so closely, she couldn't think straight. "It made a miracle out of a tragedy, remember that. There was no time to decide, no time to talk to anyone. You were in a coma. You were dying and I had to save you."

"Madelaine." He touched her chin, tilted her face, and forced her to meet his gaze. "I know that. Why—"

"It was Francis's heart," she said, feeling her tears rise and fall in burning streaks down her face. "We gave you Francis's heart."

He froze, drew his hand back. He went so still, it was frightening.

"Say something," she pleaded.

He stared at her, his face pale. "You let them cut Franco's heart out?"

She flinched. "He was brain-dead, Angel. He wasn't going to get better. You have to understand—"

"Jesus Christ. *You let them cut his heart out?*"

"Angel—"

"You lied to me."

She shook her head. "Not a lie . . . I just let you believe . . ." She looked away from him, ashamed. "I lied," she admitted quietly. "I lied."

He lurched to his feet and strode away from her, stumbling and running across the dark cemetery.

She ran after him. "Angel, please—"

He spun around, slapping her with the coldness of his gaze. "Please what? Please understand that it was *right* to put Francis's heart in my body?"

She was crying so hard, she could barely see him. "It's what he would have wanted. . . ."

"And you think that *helps*?"

He ran from her, disappearing into the shadows.

She stood there forever, breathing hard. Then, woodenly, she turned and went back to the bench, collapsing on its metal seat. Curling forward, she buried her face in her hands and cried for all of them.

She didn't know how long she sat there, but when she looked up, it was dark. A few lights had come on around the cemetery, creating pockets of shimmery light.

Footsteps moved toward her slowly.

She straightened, tried to make out his shape among the shadows. "Angel?"

He stepped into a puddle of light about ten feet away. He was standing tall and straight, his hands plunged into his pants pockets. She couldn't see his face. "That's why I've been dreaming about him," he said in a dull, soft voice.

She didn't know how to answer. The physician in her wanted to deny it, wanted to tell him that the heart was just another organ, no different from the kidney or liver. But the woman in her, the woman who'd loved Francis and his brother, couldn't be so sure. "Maybe," she said. Then she realized it was a half answer, the kind of safety that had ruined her life, and she said, "Yes. I believe that's why you dream of him."

He moved toward her, his boots crunching on the cold grass. When he got closer, she could see the tear tracks on his cheeks, and it hurt to know how much she'd hurt him. She'd never wanted to do that, not even years ago. She wanted to tell him she was sorry, but the words were little and useless. So she sat there, staring at him, waiting.

He got to the bench and sat down beside her. "I want to hate you for this," he said at last.

"I know."

"But you're the person I wrote that letter to."

"Yes."

He wouldn't look at her. "It must have killed you."

She wanted to take his face in her hands and force him to look at her, but she didn't have the courage to touch him. "You know what got me through it?"

"Tell me."

She could hear the rawness in his voice, the need to understand. "It was Francis. He was a gentle, loving soul who would have given his life to save a stranger, let alone his own brother. He loved you, Angel, and there was no question about what he would have wanted."

"He was so damned good," he whispered. "Even when we were kids and I was such an asshole—he always believed the best of me."

"He didn't give up his life for you. It's important that you understand that. He died. Period. And what came afterward was a gift from the God he loved. Something good came out of his death, but it didn't cause it. *You* didn't cause his death."

"You don't understand, Mad. . . ."

This time she couldn't help touching him. The pain in his voice was like a knife. She leaned forward, touched his cheek in a gentle, fleeting caress. "Make me understand."

He stiffened, and she could tell that he was grasping for self-control. "I don't deserve his heart. I can't . . . be like him."

"Oh, Angel," she breathed. "It would hurt him to hear you say that. You know it would."

He drew back. "I can't live for him. I don't have it in me to be that noble."

She touched his chest, felt his heartbeat, and in that fluttering rhythm she found a dawning sense of hope. "You have Francis's heart and your soul, Angel. You have it in you to be anything."

Tears filled his eyes as he looked at her. She curled her arms around him and drew him to her. He buried his face in the crook of her neck. She stroked his hair and rocked him gently, telling him over and over again that it was okay.

Finally he drew back. "I'm scared, Maddy. . . ."

"I know."

"I don't know where to go from here, where Francis would want me to go."

"Just take it one day at a time."

He laughed. "You sound like my counselor at Betty Ford."

She smiled. "Where do you want to go from here, Angel? Why don't you start with that?"

He looked down at her, and she could have sworn there was love in his eyes. "Home," he said simply. "I want to go home."

# chapter twenty-three

He knows the night is growing colder. He can see evidence of the chill, even though he can't feel it. The sky has turned a dense black, the way it often does in the waning days of November. Trees huddle together alongside the roadway, and if he listens very carefully, he can hear them whispering among themselves, shivering at the cold. He wonders why he's never heard them talking before.

But now he hears so many different things—the percussive patter of raindrops when they hit the spiked top of the picket fence, the gentle thud of a fallen leaf. Even the starlight makes a sound, a low buzzing drone that reminds him of the bees that gather in her rose garden in the first full days of summer. Everything makes a sound, it seems, but the porch swing, which hangs heavy and still beneath him. And him. He is the quietest thing of all.

The neighborhood animals know he is here. On nights like this, when it is cold and dark, they creep past the house, their golden eyes trained on him, their hackles up. When he sees them, he thinks he feels something, a tingling in his fingertips that feels like memory, as if he could recall how soft they'd been, how comforting it had once been to pet a household cat. But the tingling is imaginary. He knows he has no real sense of touch anymore. He just remembers because it feels good to remember, and he has nothing else to do.

In the distance, a car turns toward the house, its headlights scouting ahead in shafts of yellow-bright light. When the light touches them, the trees go still. The car whips around and parks along the curb. The lights cut off.

He hears the sound of a door opening, then the easy rhythm of footsteps as Angel walks around to the other door, opening it. In the weak interior light, he sees Madelaine sitting in the passenger seat.

She climbs out of the car. The streetlamp casts a net of golden light around her, and the image reminds him of icons he has seen. She is smiling for the first time in days. He knows instinctively it is Angel who has given her back her smile.

It should hurt, seeing her look at another man with love in her eyes, and so he waits for the pain to hit, but it never comes, and the absence surprises him.

He knows he can still feel pain. He'd felt it earlier today when Madelaine had come out of the house. Her eyes had been puffy and red from crying, and he knew she'd been crying about him. The image of her standing there on the porch, wearing his old shirt, had made him hurt. Deep, deep inside him, in the place where his heart used to be.

But now she is smiling, and so radiantly beautiful that he finds it difficult to draw an even breath. She seems to float up the walkway toward him, her head cocked toward Angel, her beautiful face cast in golden light.

He realizes all at once that they look young and happy, both of them. It is the way they used to look at each other all the time, the way she never looked at him.

Strangely, the knowledge warms him, makes him feel light enough to float off the porch swing. A prickling sensation moves through him—this time he almost believes that it is real. It starts in his toes and works upward. It feels as if pure white-hot sunlight is slipping through his veins, illuminating him from the inside. He gets an almost giddy sense of weightlessness.

He expects to float away, and when he doesn't, he looks down, and finds that more of him is gone. From the waist down, he is nothing but shadow steeped in shadow.

It surprises and confuses him, the slow disappearing of his body, but it doesn't scare him. It feels . . . right.

When he looks back up, he sees that Madelaine is on the porch beside him. He can hear the hushed sound of her voice as she talks to his brother, though he can't make out her words. Angel's answer comes in a droning sound not unlike the whispering of the trees.

He wants to be near them, to wave his hand and say *I'm here, see me.*

She opens the door and flicks on the porch light, and there, in the golden glow, he sees a shadow standing alongside them.

He knows somehow that it is the shadow of the man he once was. Mesmerized, he watches himself slip into his brother's shadow and stand there, close enough to touch them.

It feels so right to be there in his brother's shadow, a part of Angel and yet separate. He can feel himself relaxing, easing back into the porch swing. A relieved sigh slips from his lips, and at the sound, a bird flaps its wings and soars from the apple tree in the front yard.

He knows at last what he has been waiting for, and the wait is almost over.

Lina looked up at the sky, and felt as if a whole new world had opened up for her. She didn't know why exactly. It was the same old night sky she'd been seeing since she was a kid, the same old stars. But tonight she noticed them in a way she never had before. The Milky Way was a smeary wash of gray-white light, dappled with twinkling stars. As she lay there, staring upward, a star shot across the heavens, leaving a glittering trail of light before it disappeared.

"Make a wish," Zach said.

Lina smiled. Jett wouldn't have been caught dead saying anything as corny as that. Yet even as she noticed the geekiness of the statement, something about it warmed her. The more she thought about it, the more whimsical and fun it became, almost a game.

She rolled onto her side and studied him. He lay stretched out beside her, his arms crossed behind his head. Sandy blond hair fell away from his face. She could see the starlight reflected in his eyes, and she thought dreamily that it was fitting—for it was he who'd shown her the magic in a night sky.

He turned to look at her and gave her a slow, sleepy smile. "Did you make a wish?"

She almost touched him then, but he'd never given her any indication that he wanted that. They'd spent the last two weeks together—eating lunch, hanging out at study hall, waiting for the bus. They talked about everything, about how it was lonely to be sixteen sometimes and about how parents had a hard time understanding. It was Zach who first made Lina question her feelings for her mother. He'd said it easily, on a night just like this one, when they'd sat on the bleachers at the twenty-yard line. She didn't think he meant to change her views, he was just talking, and she listened. . . .

"I remember when the hospital called," he'd said, leaning back into the bench seats behind them. "One minute my folks were there, flipping me shit about my hair and my clothes and my grades, and the next minute they were gone. Just *poof!* you're alone."

She'd leaned closer to him, not knowing what to say.

"I'd give up everything, Lina—everything—just to hear my mom bitch at me one more time."

Lina remembered the last hurtful things she'd said to Francis, and how she'd never gotten a chance to apologize, to tell him that he was the father she'd been searching for. She knew now that sometimes life didn't give you a second chance to apologize. Sometimes a terrible, tragic phone call ruined everything.

She loved her mother. It came to her in that instant, sweeping through her with a sudden, painful ferocity. If anything happened to her mother, Lina would want to curl up and die. And yet, she'd hurt her mother time and again, thrown stinging, hateful words at her as if she had forever to say she was sorry.

"You're so lucky," Zach had whispered into the darkness, his voice quiet.

She'd wanted to tell him that she felt lucky, but she felt bruised by her new maturity, ashamed by the awareness of her own self-ishness. But she felt something else, too. Hope. She'd spent the last year reacting to life—being a rebellious brat to rile her mother or a foul-mouthed smoker to please Jett. Now she just wanted to be herself—whoever that was. Suddenly the world felt as if it were opening up to her, glittering and full of possibilities.

And Zach had given that to her, with nothing more than a few honest words. She'd thought about taking his hand and holding it, squeezing it to let him know she understood, but she hadn't dared.

Now she moved just a little bit toward him, until she was close enough to see the tiny freckles on the bridge of his nose. She waited for him to look at her, but he didn't. He just kept staring up at that sky. She squeezed her eyes shut and thought *kiss me* as hard as she could.

He didn't move.

Finally she released an exasperated sigh. No wonder she was still a virgin. She couldn't even get a guy to kiss her. She'd spent two years trying to get Jett to look twice at her, and he never had. And now Zach treated her as if she were his kid sister's best friend.

"There's something wrong with me," she muttered, horrified to hear her words slip into the quiet between them.

He rolled toward her. Cocking one elbow up, he rested his cheek in his hand and smiled down at her.

She noticed how his blue eyes looked almost black at night, and how his nostrils flared just a little when he breathed. He had a face like her uncle Francis's—the kind that invited you in and made you feel like a friend. She wanted to ask him if he thought she was pretty or fat or what, but she didn't have the nerve, so she said nothing.

He smiled, and she got the uncomfortable feeling that he knew exactly what she was thinking. It humiliated her, the thought that her lack of self-esteem was so apparent. Nervously she tucked her hair behind her ear. "What is it?"

"You're the most beautiful girl I've ever seen," he said.

The words made her want to cry, and she wondered if that's what it felt like to fall in love. She wanted to know what to say—the right grown-up words—but she couldn't find them.

"You know, the winter prom is coming up. . . ." he said finally. "What . . . what do you say we go together?"

She felt a flash of fear; maybe he was making fun of her. "We'd look like Courtney Love and Mr. Rogers."

He laughed, and it was such a wonderful sound that she laughed right along with him. "So?"

She stared at him in awe. Her emotions were a confusing jumble, and her heart was clattering a crazy beat in her chest. "Okay."

He gave her one of those smiles of his, slow and steady, the kind that made her throat go dry. Then he kissed her.


Lina was still walking on air an hour later when Zach drove her home. In the driveway he stopped the minivan and cut the engine. Then he came around to her side and opened the door.

She took his hand and stumbled out of the car. She wished she had the nerve to ask for another kiss, but she didn't dare. She was afraid she'd melt into a little puddle right there alongside her mother's rose garden.

He moved closer, gazed down at her with an intensity that made it hard to breathe. "For the dance . . . wear something blue—like your eyes."

She couldn't even answer, just nodded.

Smiling, he led her up the path to her house. Halfway to the door, she realized that her dad was sitting on the porch steps. Just sitting there in the darkness, all by himself.

Lina and Zach stopped in front of him.

Angel got slowly to his feet, dusting off his jeans and extending a hand toward Zach. "I'm Angel," he said unnecessarily—as if he weren't a Hollywood superstar. "Angelina's father."

Zach shook his hand. "I'm Zachary Owen, Mr. DeMarco. I'll be taking Lina to the winter prom, if that's okay with you."

Angel laughed. "I'm not that kind of father. Any dating will have to be cleared through her mom."

The way he shook off the responsibility stung. Lina frowned.

Zach turned to her. "Night, Lina. See you tomorrow."

She nodded almost distractedly and watched him go, then she turned to Angel. "What are you doing out here?"

"Waiting for you."

A warm feeling spread through her. She grinned at him. "Cool."

"Maybe, maybe not. Come here." He led her to the top step and they sat down side by side. The darkened front yard stretched out in front of them.

"I have something to tell you," he said in a quiet, tentative voice that caused a flutter of apprehension in her stomach. "It might upset you."

She turned to him. "What is it?"

He looked away from her, as if he couldn't meet her gaze, and her anxiety arced into fear. *He's leaving, just like Mom said he would. He's going to tell me he doesn't want to be a dad anymore.*

"It's about my surgery," he said.

She felt a split second of relief, then another rush of anxiety. "Are you okay?"

He smiled gently. "I'm fine. Pretty good anyway, for . . ." His voice fell to a whisper, and he stared at her with an intensity that was unnerving. "Pretty good for a guy who had a heart transplant."

He looked so serious and scared that she almost laughed. "Is that your big 'I have something to tell you' thing? God, I thought you were dying."

"It doesn't gross you out?"

"Jeez, Dad, I'm a cardiologist's kid. I grew up in the ICU—I'll bet I know more heart recipients than you do."

He gave her a sudden smile, then slowly it disappeared. "That's not all of it."

She grinned. "I know, the tabloids were right. You have an alien's heart."

He laughed. "Is that the newest?"

They fell silent. Lina leaned back on her elbows and stared out at the spiky black rosebushes along the picket fence.

Angel stretched out beside her. "The thing is this, Lina. I have . . . I mean, I got . . ." He drew in a shaking breath and said nothing more.

Lina turned to him. Weak porchlight bathed his face, gave his pale skin a healthy golden glow. Dark brown hair, the color of coffee, spilled away from his face, curled on the light blue denim of his collar. He stared up at the starry November sky and sighed heavily.

Lina could tell that he was having trouble. It was funny, but even a week ago, she wouldn't have noticed something like that—an adult having trouble knowing what to say. She would have huffed impatiently and told him to spit it out, she didn't have all day.

But everything in the last few weeks had changed her perspective. And if there was one thing she understood, it was having trouble speaking your mind. So she waited patiently, saying nothing at all.

Finally he tried again. "I'm afraid to tell you this, Lina. I don't want to hurt you. . . ."

She didn't look at him. There was no need; she had his face burned into her memory. She wore it like a locket inside her heart. "Uncle Francis used to say, 'Love hurts, Angelina-ballerina, but it also heals.'" She sighed wistfully, remembering all the nights she'd sat in just this spot with Uncle Francis, talking about whatever was bothering her. She used to think he'd sit there forever if she asked him to.

"You loved Franco, didn't you?"

"Yes," she whispered. "I loved him."

"What if he were sort of . . . still around?"

"He is," she said quietly, "he's in my heart. And Mom's."

"And mine."

He said the words in a different tone of voice than she'd expected—almost flippant. It surprised her, the way he said it, made her wonder suddenly how Angel felt about his brother. They hadn't seen each other in years, and Francis had never once mentioned that his brother was the notorious Angel DeMarco. "You're making fun of me," she said accusingly.

"No. I'm just trying to find a way to tell you something, and I'm not having any luck."

"Just say it. I'm not a baby that has to be protected."

He turned to face her. Reaching out, he took hold of her hand and placed it against his chest. She could feel that thudding rhythm beneath the soft flannel of his shirt. "Feel my heartbeat," he said.

She nodded.

"That's from . . ." He swallowed hard, looked a little sick. "That's Francis's heartbeat."

It took the words a second to sink in. When they did, she yanked her hand back and blinked up at him. "A-Are you saying—"

"I have your uncle Francis's heart inside me."

She didn't know how to respond.

"Lina?"

She heard the fear in his voice, and it confused her. She turned to him. For a second she stared into his concerned eyes and felt as if she were falling through an endless darkness. She thought crazily, *I don't know this man at all. He's my father, and I don't know him at all. . . .*

Then she realized he was scared because he cared about her. He was afraid she'd think he'd done something bad. *He* was afraid of *her*. Another tiny piece of the puzzle fell into place—love meant always being a little afraid.

She smiled at him, feeling something in that moment that was so big, so breathtakingly cool, she wanted to scream out for the sheer joy of it. "You have Francis's heart," she said softly.

He went so still, he seemed not to breathe. "Yes."

She knew she held it all in the palm of her hand right then. Whatever she said next would define their relationship forever. Tears blurred her vision and she wiped them away. "I knew he wouldn't leave me," she whispered.

Relief flashed across his face. "You're really something, Lina."

Very slowly he opened his arms, and she moved into his embrace. It was the first time he'd ever hugged her, and she knew she'd never forget it, not ever. It felt like Francis . . . and it felt like Angel, as if they were both holding her, both of the men she loved so much.

She had no idea how long they sat there, twined together on the top step, talking about anything and everything that came to mind. But sometime around ten o'clock, about the time old Mrs. Hendicott opened her back door for the last time and tossed her tabby tomcat outside, it started to rain. Slow, plunking drops that came on a breath of unseasonably warm wind. Strangely, there wasn't a cloud in the sky.

Behind them, the porch swing squeaked and shot sideways, as if an unseen hand had given it a good shove. It made a whining, creaking noise. The wind picked up and whistled through the eaves, and it sounded—crazily—like Uncle Francis's laugh.

# chapter twenty-four

The media descended on St. Joe's like the circus coming to town. Reporters, technicians, camera operators, and anchorpeople from around the country poured from vans and rental cars, collecting in the hospital parking lot, buzzing back and forth as they checked and rechecked their equipment. They lugged their heavy black boxes and huge portable lights up the brick steps and down the main hallway.

The cafeteria had been closed for Angel's press conference, scheduled to begin at ten o'clock, and it was rapidly filling with people.

Black electrical cords slithered across the speckled linoleum floor in search of outlets. Clunky lights shone their bright beams on the podium Dr. Allenford had had set up beside the cash register. Dozens of reporters had broken off into little groups, each television station or magazine huddling in its own corner, testing its microphones. All except the newspaper reporters—they sat sprawled in uncomfortable chairs, notebooks in hand, looking disgustedly around at their competition.

Angel stood in the kitchen behind the cafeteria, watching the goings-on through a small round window in the door. He was next to a huge walk-in freezer, but he knew that wasn't what was making him feel so cold.

It was nerves.

Someone touched his shoulder and he jumped, spinning around. Madelaine and Chris and his new cardiologist, Sarandon, were all staring at him. Madelaine slowly drew her hand away from his shoulder.

Angel tried to grin. "I can't believe this . . . I'm nervous. Hell, I've done this a million times."

She gave him a wry look. "Sober?"

He thought about it. "Good point."

Allenford glanced at his watch. "It's ten o'clock."

Angel grabbed Madelaine's hand. "I don't know if I can do it."

"You can do anything, Angel DeMarco. When are you going to realize that?"

The way she said it was so calm, so matter-of-fact, as if it were a given truth that Angel could do anything, *be* anything. Her simple faith in him stunned him. He tried to smile back. "What would I do without you?"

She laughed, but it was an anxious, fluttery sound. "Are you ready?"

"Don't tell Lina I acted like this. She thinks I'm way cool."

Allenford squeezed Angel's shoulder and headed for the door. Sarandon followed him, the two physicians pushing through the swinging doors like Doc Holliday and Wyatt Earp striding into a saloon.

The minute the doctors came into the reporters' view, the lights started flashing, cameras clicked.

Allenford went to the podium, tapped his microphone to test it, and began to read his prepared statement.

Behind the doors, Angel heard bits and pieces of Allenford's statement.

". . . Angelo DeMarco was admitted to St. Joseph's Hospital, following his third and most severe heart attack. . . . Only a heart transplant could save his life. . . . Mr. DeMarco was placed on the UNOS—United Network for Organ Sharing—list as a potential recipient."

Someone asked a question that Angel couldn't quite hear.

"No," Allenford answered, his voice more strident than usual. "Mr. DeMarco did *not* receive special privileges because of his fame or financial status. He was put at the top of the transplant list because he was critically ill." Allenford folded up his prepared speech and shoved it in the pocket of his white lab coat. "He waited for a heart like anyone else. Longer than some, not as long as others. I performed the surgery, which went very well. Mr. DeMarco remained in the hospital for an undisclosed amount of time, and then was discharged. He is now beginning this new phase of his life. Thank you."

Questions came from the crowd like bullets. Reporters jumped up, hands waving in the air, microphones thrust forward. Angel couldn't hear the questions—they were just a droning buzz of static and confusion—but he knew they didn't matter. Allenford could say whatever he wanted; the feeding frenzy wouldn't end until Angel stepped forward.

Madelaine squeezed his hand. "You don't have to go out there, you know."

"It's a little intimidating," he admitted. "I can hear the *Jaws* theme song playing in my head. Either Francis is singing or I'm in danger."

She laughed. "You're a sick man, Angel DeMarco."

Beyond the cloudy glass, he saw Allenford step to the left of the podium—their signal for Angel to appear if he wanted to.

He turned to Madelaine. "Come with me."

"Of course."

He felt a sudden urge to kiss her. Instead, he smiled. Just

knowing that she would be beside him, urging him on, believing in him, gave him the power to do anything. It surprised him—how good it felt to have someone to lean on. In all the times he'd been afraid in his life, he'd been alone. He wondered now if he'd been afraid *because* he was alone. "You'd better go first. If they see us together, there will be hell to pay. Tomorrow the tabloids will be digging through your trash looking for my underwear. Some stripper in Deadwood will describe it."

He waited for her to laugh, but she didn't. She just stood there, staring at him. "You'll do great." She gave his hand a last squeeze, then left the kitchen in front of him. She slipped around the podium and took a seat in the back of the room.

*This is it*. He took a deep breath and prepared himself, exactly as he would have done for a role. With an ease born of practice, he slipped into the public persona of Angel DeMarco.

Smiling, he strolled out of the kitchen. He knew he looked like he didn't have a care in the world. He walked up to the podium and stopped.

*"It's him!"*

Cameras flashed like lightning through the crowd, popping and hissing. Questions erupted all at once, so many he couldn't draw a single one from the tangle.

Someone started to clap, then before he knew it, the questions had stopped and they were all clapping.

For the first time in two months, he was Angel DeMarco again—not anonymous Mark Jones, not the heart transplant in 264-W, not a screw-up younger brother, not an insta-father. He was Angel DeMarco, bad-boy actor of Hollywood, and he loved it.

The old feelings came back, filling him. The sound and fury of the applause pumped air into his ego until he thought he would burst from it. How had he forgotten this rush, this mesmerizing moment when he felt loved and adored by the world?

Grinning, he raised a hand. "Now, now, I didn't perform the surgery, I just lived through it."

Laughter rippled through the room. The applause died slowly away, and when it was gone, Angel noticed the sudden silence, the way they were watching him with unveiled curiosity.

It wasn't how they used to look at him. The long red scar that bisected his chest started to itch.

The air seeped from his ego, leaving him feeling hollow and ordinary. He wondered suddenly if he could survive this way, being just an average Joe.

He'd never thought so. In the old days he used to look at men with wives and families and nine-to-five jobs and laugh at them.

He'd always thought life was a party—either you were invited or you weren't. And if you weren't, you were part of the great cleanup crew that never had any fun.

But he was beginning to understand that fun was only part of what life could be. He thought of last night, the time he'd spent with Lina on the porch, the way she'd hugged him. And of Madelaine at Francis's grave, the tender words and smiles she'd given him to help him through the staggering grief. He'd felt more emotion in those few minutes with the two of them than he'd felt in the whole thirty-four years that came before.

"First of all," he said quietly, "I'd like to thank St. Joe's for their exceptional level of care. My doctors—Chris Allenford, Marcus Sarandon, and Madelaine Hillyard—fought to save my life even when I made it hard on them. And the nurses and therapists—"

"Angel—show us your scar!"

The jarring question wrenched Angel out of his thoughts and reminded him where he was. He knew instantly that he'd been quiet too long. Now they were really wondering what was wrong with him.

He laughed easily. "Come on, Jeff, you can do better than that. Do you really think my *scar* is what America wants to see?"

"How do you feel, Angel?"

"Great, thanks. St. Joe's did a topflight job on me."

Someone snickered. "They did a pretty good job on us, too. There was no scoop on you at all."

Angel nodded. "That was on my request. Hell, it took *me* a while to admit I was this sick. I wasn't ready to tell the world."

"And you are now?"

Angel knew a cue when he heard one. He reached into his pocket for the statement he'd prepared, but suddenly it felt too formal. He leaned his elbows over the podium and looked at the crowd. "Here's the thing. I'm still sick—I'm getting better and I'm gonna live a long time and all that, but I'm recovering from a hell of a cut. I need some time—and I'd really appreciate it if you guys'd give me that."

The room was quiet for a second, then someone said, "That doesn't sound like Angel DeMarco."

Angel glanced at the *People* magazine reporter who'd spoken—it was the woman who'd interviewed him last year. "It's me, Bobbie. But a person tends to change after something like this—I think you either change or die." He laughed. "Let's face it; I hit the brick wall at the end of the road, and I was damned lucky to hit it at St. Joe's. That should be your story, Bobbie. I'm one of the lucky ones. Upward of forty thousand people a year die *waiting* for organs."

"Who was your donor?" she asked in a sharp voice.

A hush of anticipation fell across the room.

Angel steeled himself. "That's confidential."

"Male or female?" someone asked from the corner.

Angel forced a smile. "Yep."

"When *exactly* did you have the surgery?" Bobbie asked, her pen poised to write down the date that would kick-start an investigation.

"That's no one's business but mine." Angel tossed them an easy smile to soften the words.

"What are you going to do now? We'd heard you were all set to shoot a new action picture."

It was strange how unimportant that sounded. A year ago

he'd sent Val after that role like a bird dog, with orders to do whatever it took to land the part. Now Angel couldn't have cared less. The thought of leaving Hollywood forever caused less than a tinge of regret. His old life had begun to have the shimmering, faded edges of a dream he could barely recall.

He thought about telling them his real goal—the Francis Xavier DeMarco Foundation for transplant research. But if he raised Francis's name, some yahoo would try to interview the mysterious brother, and when they found that he was dead—when they found how and when he'd died—it would all be over. Some eager-beaver reporter would dig until the story broke.

No, he'd tell them about Francis later, when the wound wasn't quite so fresh and raw. Someday, if and when he felt like it, he'd share the true nature of his miracle with the world.

Someday, but not today.

He flashed his trademark grin. "I'm going to try to settle down and have a regular life."

"*You?*" someone said, laughing.

Bobbie watched him intently. "That's what you said after that stint in Betty Ford."

Angel didn't blink. She was right, and they both knew it—he'd said it to her. "That's true, Bobbie," he said quietly. "The difference is, then I knew I was lying. I couldn't imagine my life as anything other than a movable feast." He couldn't help himself, he looked up at Madelaine. "Now I see a whole world of new possibilities."

"How long will you live?" someone asked.

He looked at the reporter. "How long will you?"

"Are you going to settle down and get married?"

Angel heard the derision in the question, and he knew he deserved it. Celebrities in trouble made this same speech all the time. *People* magazine had the wedding headlines—and the subsequent divorce headlines—to prove it. The media and the public had learned to disbelieve a celebrity who swore to change his or her life.

He had no way to convince them or himself. All he could do was try, and when he failed, try again.

"You didn't answer the question."

Angel looked at the reporter, who sat in the back row. The man looked rumpled and tired. There was no emotion in his face—just a bored look, as if to say, *Spit it out, DeMarco, I don't have all day.*

"Okay, boys and girls, here's your quote for the day. Angel DeMarco quits."

There was a general snickering from the crowd. They'd heard it all before and they didn't believe it. No one ever really walked away from fame.

"Hey, Angel," someone yelled from the back of the room. "Is all this a front for AIDS? That prostitute in Florida—"

Angel burst out laughing at the absurdity of the question. All of a sudden he felt young and carefree, almost buoyant. *I just walked away from it,* he thought. He hadn't meant to do that, to say that, but it had come out somehow, and now that he'd done it, he felt freer than he'd been in years. These people would continue watching him for a few days or weeks, but one day he'd wake up and they'd be gone; they wouldn't care anymore. He could live the way he wanted and not worry that every little rock in his wake would be turned over and examined under a microscope. He could be an average Joe—the idea was mesmerizing this time.

"I definitely don't have AIDS," he said. "The only infectious disease I ever had was fame." He felt himself starting to smile, a slow, natural grin that seemed to come up from the core of his new heart. "And now that's gone."

He waved briefly, and found himself hoping that he never had to face them again. "Good-bye."

Angel's smiling face appeared on the television screen. The bland walls of the cafeteria framed him, made him look incredibly vibrant and full of life. Even in the flawed color of the small portable TV, his eyes were an incredible, mesmerizing shade of green.

Madelaine grabbed the remote and flicked through the channels—he was on every one, saying the same words over and over again. *Okay, boys and girls, here's your quote for the day. Angel DeMarco quits . . . quits . . . quits . . .*

Even now, hours after the press conference, that statement surprised her. He'd never once indicated that he had any intention of quitting show business.

What would he do now?

She felt a flutter of fear. She didn't like to admit it, but she'd come to lean on Angel in the past few weeks. Since his surgery, he'd become the man she'd always expected him to be. She knew he thought it was because of Francis's heart, and maybe that was partially true, but not completely. In some ways, she thought she knew him better than he knew himself. It was because she looked past the quick temper and volatile nature. She believed in him—she always had, even when she hadn't wanted to. He'd always had a core of goodness in him, of compassion. All he had to do was believe in it and reach for it.

His face came on the screen again—CNN. Her heart gave a quick little jerk at the sight of him, so damned handsome. And yet, even as good as he looked on screen, he was more handsome in real life. Television didn't show any of the lines that creased the corners of his eyes when he grinned, didn't pick up the razor-thin scar that bisected his left eyebrow. The camera captured all of the perfection, but none of his soul.

That belonged to her and Lina.

The phone rang, interrupting her thoughts. She set down the remote and padded into the kitchen, picking up the phone on the second ring. "Hello?"

"Hi, Mom." Lina's enthusiastic voice came through the lines.

Madelaine couldn't help smiling. Lina sounded so happy lately—Angel and Zachary had given her that. Though she felt a little sting of jealousy, Madelaine was so pleased that Lina had begun to find her way that she didn't care who had brought the change about.

"I'm over at Vicki Owen's house. We're all playing Trivial Pursuit, then Zach asked me to go to the movies. Is that okay?"

Madelaine wanted to ask to speak to Vicki, but she knew Lina would be hurt by the obvious lack of trust. They were building a tenuous new relationship, and she wanted to do it right this time. "You'll be home by eleven?"

"Jeez, Mom. I'm not a baby."

Madelaine laughed at the familiar complaint. "You'll always be my baby."

"Yeah, yeah. Hey, Mom, did you see Dad's press conference?"

"Yes. I taped it for you."

There was a pause, then very quietly Lina said, "He didn't mention me."

Madelaine heard the disappointment in her daughter's voice, and she wondered what to do. She knew that Lina idolized her newfound father and that it was a dangerous way to feel about anyone. If Lina didn't grow up and see Angel as a man—flaws and all—she could be hurt. Every day Lina would see nicks in the armor of her perfect father, and each little dent would hurt, would feel like he'd let her down.

What would Lina do when she realized that her father wasn't Angel DeMarco the bad-boy actor, but plain old Angel—a man who was all too human?

She chose her words carefully. "Angel talked to me about that. He didn't want the press hounding you. But he's very proud of you."

"He mentioned you," she said.

"I'm one of his doctors."

There was a pause, then, "Did he really say he was proud of me?" The question sounded wistful.

"Yes, he did."

Lina laughed, a short, sharp sound that ended quickly. "Yeah, well, I've got my key. If you're asleep, I'll just let myself in and go to bed."

"Oh, right, Lina. Like I can sleep with you out. I'll be waiting up for you."

Lina laughed. "I can always hope. See you at eleven-thirty, Mom."

"Eleven. Be careful and have fun. Wear your seat belt."

"Mom . . ." She sighed dramatically. "Come on . . ."

Madelaine grinned at her own neuroses. "You're lucky I don't make you wear a crash helmet. Tell Vicki and Zach hello for me. And, Lina . . ."

"Yeah?"

"I love you."

There was another quiet pause, and Madelaine could hear her daughter breathing on the other end of the phone. "Yeah, Mom. I love you, too."

Madelaine hung up the phone and looked around. The house felt empty without Lina. It was amazing how much even a quiet, sullen teenager could enliven a room. She grabbed a mug and made herself a pot of Earl Grey tea, then took the cup into the living room, flicking on lights as she went.

She was just about to draw herself a bath when the doorbell rang. Setting her tea down on the pink marble rim of the bath-tub, she hurried to open the front door.

Angel stood there, looking for all the world like he belonged on her front porch. "Heya, Mad," he said, giving her a bright, boyish grin that made her heartbeat speed up. Then he whipped a bouquet of hothouse daisies out from behind his back.

She stared at them in shock, trying—idiotically—to remember the last time a man had given her flowers. "They're beauti-ful," she said—also idiotically, she thought. But she couldn't think straight. He looked so handsome standing there, backlit by a huge blanket of starry night sky.

He glanced down at the droopy bouquet, then up at her again.

"I was going to buy you a dozen red roses—even went into the flower shop—but it felt like my old life. The way I used to do things for women that didn't matter." He shrugged. "Anyway, I saw these daisies and thought about the ones that grow wild in front of my cabin . . . and I thought they were right for you."

The sentiment touched her so deeply that for a second she couldn't find her voice. She felt ridiculous and immature . . . and wonderful. She tried to think of something witty to say and came up empty. Nervously she hooked her thumb toward the kitchen. "I'll put them in water."

He grinned. "You do that."

She took the flowers and lifted them to her face, breathing deeply of the fresh, watery scent. Turning, she led him into the kitchen and pulled out a chipped porcelain vase—the only one she had. At his look, she shrugged. "I don't have flowers in the house very often."

He stared at her. "You should," he said in a feather-soft voice. "Now, put them in water so we can go."

She plopped them in the vase and wished fleetingly that she were gifted in floral arrangement. "Go?" she asked distractedly, moving one large blossom to the front of the vase. It snapped off in her fingers and she winced.

"I have big plans for us tonight."

She balanced the broken flower on the cracked golden rim. "I can't go out. . . . Lina—"

"Lina called me before I left the house. She told me she was going to the movies with Zach."

She turned to look at him. "Are you telling me we're going on a *date*?"

He laughed. "I see those fifteen years in college weren't a complete waste."

She couldn't help laughing. The idea of a date with Angel made her feel almost dizzy. "Where are we going?"

His smile faded, and for a second he looked so serious, she thought it must all be a lie, and then he smiled again.

"You'll see."

Before she could respond, he pulled a black bandana from his pants pocket and dangled it in front of her.

She eyed the black and white strip of cotton. "What's that?"

"I'm blindfolding you."

A surprised laugh slipped out. "So that stripper in Florida *was* telling the truth."

"Get your mind out of the gutter, Doc. I just have a little surprise for you."

"It doesn't involve handcuffs or dog collars, I hope."

He moved toward her. "Turn around."

She turned slowly away from him. He came up close behind her, so close she could feel the warmth of his breath stroking the back of her neck.

"Close your eyes."

She did as he asked. He tied the bandana behind her head, and in the complete darkness, her other senses sprang to life. She heard the quiet ticking of the mantel clock, the even rhythms of their tangled breathing, smelled the fresh scent of the daisies and the musky heat of his aftershave. His hands slid down her arms and gently twirled her to face him.

She could feel him; he was standing directly in front of her. The heat of his body touched her in a dozen places. She wanted to see his eyes, to know how he was looking at her right now.

Very gently his finger traced her upper lip, and she shivered in response. Then he took hold of her hand and led her across the room. She heard the front door creak open again, felt the blast of cold evening air on her face.

She reached up to touch the bandana. "This feels really weird."

"Trust me," he whispered.

She started to make a flip comment, but suddenly it felt important. She wanted to trust him, wanted it desperately. "Okay."

"Now, stand here. I'll go get you some walking shoes and turn off all the lights."

"My room is the first door on the left. The shoes are in my closet."

"Thank God you told me. I was going to look in the refrigerator."

She heard his footsteps disappear down the hallway. Cautiously she felt her way out the front door and stood on the porch.

The night was full of sounds. She could hear a door opening and closing somewhere on her street. An anemic breeze rustled the last leaf on her apple tree. Cool air shivered across her cheeks and tangled in her hair. Beside her, the porch swing creaked, the metal chains jangled. She thought she heard a sigh—but it had to be the wind—then she thought she smelled the tangy scent of Francis's cologne.

"Francis?" she whispered, feeling like a fool.

Angel shut the door behind her and led her to the porch swing, guiding her to take a seat. His knees creaked as he kneeled in front of her, gently took off her slippers, and eased her feet into shoes.

She felt like Cinderella.

Then he took her hand and led her down the steps, across the yard, and helped her climb into the passenger side of his Mercedes. In silence he started the car and pulled away from the curb.

Madelaine tried to keep track of where they were going, and she did pretty well for the first few blocks. Then all the twists and turns tangled in her mind and she leaned back, enjoying the drive.

Finally he came to a stop and killed the engine. She sat there, waiting for him to open her door. Anticipation was a sweet ache in her chest, a flutter in her breathing.

He helped her out of the car. She felt his hands on the bandana's knot. When it was untied, he held it in place and leaned closer to her, whispering in her ear, "Welcome to 1978."

He took off the blindfold and she couldn't believe her eyes.

They were in Carrington Park, but it had been transformed into a carnival, a garish, dramatic display of lights in the velvet darkness of the night. Stars were everywhere, drizzling down, getting captured in the flashing yellow and pink and red lights of the midway. A huge Ferris wheel sat in the center of it all like a mechanical king, turning slowly on its well-lighted track.

She could *feel* the magic of the carnival wrap around her, pulling her back into the past, until she was a young girl again, standing on the edge of forever with the boy of her dreams. It was so much like before. It smelled of popcorn and grease and possibility. The sounds of chattering barkers and mechanical-ride music floated on the still night air.

She turned to him, awestruck. "How did you know this would be here?"

He smiled, tucking a flyaway strand of hair behind her ear. "I *brought* it here. For you . . . for me."

She shook her head. "You mean you—"

"My former doctor is a tyrant. I knew she wouldn't let me go out in public, so I hired these guys. I promise I'll wear my mask around strangers and only take it off for you."

"You really don't need a mask anymore, you know. . . ."

"Are you going to stand here analyzing our date, or are you going to enjoy it?"

She looked out at the brightly colored midway. Closing her eyes, she drank in all of it. The past and the present came together in her mind until there was no then, no now, there was just her and Angel and the magic of the carnival. "I'm going to enjoy it."

"Thank God." He took her hand in his and pulled her down toward the lights. Laughing, she followed him, clinging to his hand as he led her back to the place where it all began.

## chapter twenty-five

❧

Madelaine and Angel walked hand in hand down the midway. The surreal smear of sound and color and light exploded around them. Barkers called out, laughing, urging Angel to try his hand at the ring toss, or buy a corn dog, or get his photograph taken with Heloise the fat woman in booth number six.

Madelaine was mesmerized by all of it. With each step she felt the years falling away. Angel's betrayal faded into insignificance, and the days and nights she'd waited for his return were forgotten. She couldn't carry that weight anymore, not now, when she felt lighter than air, and young . . . so young.

"Look!" Angel pointed at a booth on the midway and dragged her toward it. She stumbled after him, laughing, clinging to his hand.

At the booth he slipped on his mask and leaned over the wooden edge. The barker, a wrinkly-faced old man, grinned at him. "Win a bauble for your girl, mister?"

Madelaine saw what Angel was looking at, and her breath caught. It was a pair of gaudy, red plastic earrings, dangling from a coat hanger stapled to the wooden backboard.

She knew she shouldn't look at him right now. If she did, he'd see everything in her eyes. He'd know what this moment meant to her, what his remembering made her feel. But she couldn't look away.

When their gazes met, she felt a jolt of electricity. "The earrings," she whispered.

He smiled and tenderly touched her cheek.

"Okay, you lovebirds," the barker called out in a booming voice, jangling the change belt at his waist. "You gonna play or what?"

Angel grinned. "Or what."

Before Madelaine could ask what he meant, he'd grabbed her hand and was pulling her down the midway. Laughing, she clung to him, letting him sweep her away. It wasn't until they'd reached the edge of the carnival that she understood where he was taking her. She caught her breath and felt a tiny pinching pain in her heart.

He took her to the tree, their tree.

The memories came back in a rush, squeezing her chest until she could barely breathe.

He kneeled in the dying grass, dragging her down beside him. Wordlessly he let go of her hand and started clawing at the earth, digging until there was a pile of dirt at his knee. "Got 'em," he said at last, drawing the dirty red earrings from the damp black ground. He pulled the mask from his face, let it hang limply around his throat, then turned to look at her.

Madelaine stared down at the cheap plastic trinkets and remembered their last night together—when they'd lain under this old oak tree and promised to love each other forever.

It should hurt, remembering that; it always had in the past. But tonight, with the earrings in his hands and the smell of popcorn and magic in the air, nothing had the power to hurt her.

"You remembered," she whispered, biting down on her lower lip. When she looked at him, the tears came, cresting, slipping down her cheeks. She couldn't stop them, didn't want to.

He used one muddy finger to push a strand of hair from her eyes. "What did we say back then? Crazy teenaged words about our love never ending, about these earrings being a reminder of our love for always . . . "

She forced herself to laugh and wanted to say something glib or easy, but nothing came out except a croaking, quiet "Silly words."

No smile curved his lips. "Not silly. You said, 'Let's leave them here. That way a part of us will always exist under this old tree. When we're old, we can come back here with our grandchildren.'"

"Oh, my God," she whispered. "That's exactly what I said."

"I tried to forget, Mad. I ran and ran until there was nowhere left to go. A lot of the time I *did* forget, but the words were always back there, buried inside me." He took her hand in his and placed the cheap, filthy jewels in it. "I never forgot you. I know that doesn't make everything all right, but I never forgot. . . ."

She wanted to say *I love you* right then, wanted to say it so badly, the words burned in her throat. "I never forgot you, either."

It wasn't the right thing to say, but it was all the courage she had. This moment meant too much; she couldn't jeopardize it with words he wasn't ready to hear.

"Let's go on the Ferris wheel," he said.

She smiled at him and nodded. He pulled her to her feet and held her close. Together, clinging to each other like teenagers in love, they strolled down the midway. Halfway there, she bought a huge puff of cotton candy and pulled off a winding, sticky strip.

He stopped in front of the Ferris wheel, shaking his head at her. "I can't believe you're going to eat that stuff in front of a heart patient."

"You never did like it."

Surprise darted across his eyes, and then he smiled. "I forgot how well you knew me."

She pulled off another piece and popped it in her mouth.

He pulled out the bandana and wiped the sticky smear off of her nose. "You should have had stuff like that as a kid," he said.

She tried to laugh, but it wasn't funny and they both knew it.

"Come on." He took her hand and led her onto the Ferris wheel. The ride operator—a young girl with bleached hair and a pierced nostril—stared at Angel in obvious awe.

"M-Mr. DeMarco," she said, "are you the one who rented us for the night?"

He nodded. "Give us a long ride, willya, darlin'?" He dragged Madelaine onto the wide, black-vinyl-covered seat and clicked the safety bar in place. Then he gave the girl a thumbs-up. The ride began with a whining, mechanical groan, and they were pulled away from the ramp.

Madelaine leaned back and stared up at the night sky. The seat swayed and rocked and lifted them higher and higher into the darkness, until stars were all around them, close enough to touch, and the midway was a faraway haze of yellow and white light.

Angel draped an arm around her shoulders and drew her close to him. In the distance they could hear the rollicking calliope of the merry-go-round and the mechanical *whoosh* of the Round-up.

But up here, tangled in the blanket of stars and touched by the light of a half-moon, the carnival seemed a million miles away.

Angel twisted around to face her. "Mad . . ."

There was something in his tone of voice that frightened her—he sounded so serious. She was suddenly afraid that this was it, that he'd done all this just to say good-bye. Maybe he wanted to do it right this time. Now he had a daughter to think of—he didn't want to roar out of town on a Harley.

"Don't say anything," she whispered, gazing into his eyes, knowing in that instant that she'd never be able to forget him this time, never be able to get over him. If he was going to leave, she'd rather he just did it, just picked up his stuff and ran. She couldn't take a good-bye.

"I wanted to thank you for saving my life."

Her breath escaped in a rush of relief. She was so thankful for what he hadn't said that it took her a second to realize what he *had* said. "Thank you for saving your life?" She swallowed hard. "Is that what this is about, Angel? Thanking your cardiologist?" The words tasted bitter.

He smiled softly. "No. I don't mean thank you for saving my physical body—although I do appreciate it." He leaned toward her and touched her cheek, giving her a tender smile. "I mean, thank you for saving my *life*. Without you in these past few weeks, I couldn't have found the strength to go on. I think I would have drunk myself sick and run away. But you . . . and Lina, you gave me another way."

She didn't know what to say.

"That's my Mad," he said, laughing, tugging a strand of hair from her lip. "I'm going to kiss you now, Mad. If you've got a problem with that . . ." Smiling, he leaned toward her.

She stared at him, mesmerized by the yearning she saw in his eyes. The desire to kiss and be kissed by him was irresistible, and before she knew it, she was leaning toward him.

He took her face in his hands and tunneled his fingers through her tangled hair, tilting her face up. Slowly he kissed her.

His mouth fit hers perfectly, just as it had so many years ago. It started out soft and gentle, that first kiss after so many lost and lonely years. She clung to him, kissing him with everything in her, as if she could draw that essential spark of him into her very soul, as if she could have some piece of him to take away from this magical ride.

The kiss deepened, turned wrenching and dangerous. His tongue slipped into her mouth, tasting, exploring, memorizing, and still she clung to him, moaning her response, molding her body to his.

The Ferris wheel bucked and carried them back up into the stars, but Madelaine hardly noticed. All she felt was an overwhelming need to be touched and held and stroked by this man.

The ride came to a jerking stop.

"That long enough, Angel?"

Madelaine pulled out of his arms and stared at the young ride operator. The girl gave her a grin.

"I think we're done," Angel said, pulling his mask back into place. "Come on, Mad."

Madelaine felt light enough to float off the ride. He took her hand and led her, stumbling, down the midway.

They walked together for hours, talking, laughing, remembering the good times and letting go of the bad. Angel was his usual larger-than-life self, tossing dollar bills to the employees as he passed them, signing autographs, and standing patiently to have his photograph taken.

Finally they made their way back to the entrance. There he stopped to talk to an older gentleman in a ragged wool coat. "The first wave of kids will be here at ten o'clock tomorrow. Show them a good time and you'll see a hell of a tip."

Madelaine frowned at Angel as they walked away. "Who was that? What kids?"

He shrugged. "Tomorrow I've arranged for a bunch of kids from the Make-a-Wish Foundation to have the carnival to themselves. Them and the kids from Children's Orthopedic. No big deal."

Madelaine stared at him. "You really have changed."

He pulled the mask down and grinned at her. "You got off the Ferris wheel with your clothes on. Now, *that's* a change."

She didn't blink. "What makes you think I want them on?"

He swallowed hard. His smile fell. "Get in the car."

"Where are we—"

He unlocked her door and swung it open. "Let's go."

\*    \*    \*

Angel had never wanted to make love to a woman as desperately as he wanted to right now. Every time he looked at Madelaine, he felt the ache grow and swell. It had taken all of his self-control—and probably some of Francis's—to get off that Ferris wheel without ripping her clothes off.

It was all he'd thought about at the carnival, wanting her, needing her, and yet now that he had her close beside him, he was scared to death. He drove slowly through the deserted streets, his hands sweaty on the steering wheel. He tried not to think about having sex with her, but the thought kept coming back to torment him. He'd planned for it, fantasized about it, but—

*Could he do it?* That was the question that paralyzed him, made the sweat break out along his forehead. He didn't know if he could last the distance, or if he could even start the race. Before the surgery? No problem, but that was a hell of a before.

By the time they reached their destination, he was barely able to utter a coherent sentence. He eased the Mercedes up to the curb and killed the engine.

She gasped quietly and turned to him. He didn't need to hit the interior light to see the look on her face. Her eyes would be wide and unblinking, her teeth nipping nervously on her lower lip. "Why are we here?" she said softly.

He cracked his door open and let light splash across her face. "You'll see. Come on." He felt her reluctance and forced himself to ignore it. He'd given this thing a lot of thought, and it had to be done. Some demons could be swept under the rug, but some just had to be faced.

He reached under his seat for a flashlight, then got out of the car and waited patiently on the curb.

After a long minute, she hit the handle and opened her door. Climbing out, she slammed the door and stared up at the house he'd pulled up in front of. Her father's house.

344 K r i s t i n   H a n n a h

It stood on the hill like a castle, a peaked black silhouette against a starry sky. Moonlight glanced off the mullioned panes of glass and wound around the bars on her bedroom window. The white-pillared portico sheltered the front step from rain and cast the stoop in shadows. Four sculpted brick chimneys rose from the peaked roofline. A spike-tipped black iron gate guarded the hillside lot, kept the riffraff from wandering in.

It looked gloomy and angry, the darkened house she'd grown up in. Skeletal trees marched along the fence line, their limbs clinging to the last leaves of autumn.

"Only thing missing is a sign that says Bates Motel," Angel said wryly.

Madelaine didn't return his smile.

"Come on, Mad, " he said quietly, reaching out his hand for her.

She came toward him slowly, taking his hand, tucking her small, cold one in his. Wordlessly he led her to the front door, then scouted around for a rock. Finding one, he drew back, ready to fling it through the plate glass living room window.

She stopped his hand. "What are you doing?"

"Getting us inside."

She gave him a strange look. "Try the key. It's in the loose brick under the top step."

He cast a look downward, saw the brick sticking out. "It's not half as fun. . . ."

She didn't smile. "Use the key."

He found the key in the crumbling mortar of its hiding place and slipped it into the lock. The door opened with a whining creak. He flashed his flashlight into the gloom and walked into the shadowy foyer, her hand held tightly in his. Slamming the door shut behind them, he led her down the foyer, past the massive kitchen, into the dark room that had once been her father's office. Even now, all these years later, it still smelled of cigar smoke and power.

He fished a book of matches from his pocket and knelt before the huge white marble fireplace. Plucking firewood from the copper barrel on the hearth, he built a fire. Flames leapt and writhed on the long-dry wood. Heat pumped into the cold room.

And still she stood there, shivering, unmoving.

He went to her and took her hands in his. When their gazes met, he saw her anxiety, and the words he'd practiced stuck in his throat.

"Why are we here? You know how I feel about this place."

He heard the fear in her voice and he ached for her, just as he had so many times in the past. He didn't know the particulars of what had happened to her in this house, with that crazy, mean old man as her father, but he knew she'd been hurt. "This is where it happened, and it seemed right that this is where it ends . . . and maybe begins."

"I don't understand."

He looked around the room. It was exactly as he remembered it, except for the fine layer of dust that clung to the furniture now and the faint scent of mildew. Silver sconces, black with tarnish, still held thick white candles. Two huge burgundy leather chairs sat huddled in the corner, backed up to heavily paneled walls. Long, dirty windows parenthesized the fireplace, their panes half-covered by dusty drapes. The same bear rug covered most of the thick plank flooring. "This is where I sold my soul for ten thousand dollars."

"We don't have to talk about it," she said, and he could tell she meant it. But there was too much between them, too much at risk, to pretend he hadn't done what he'd done to her. If they were going to have any chance for a future, he had to atone for the past.

"I know we don't have to talk about it, but I need to apologize for what I did. I know an apology doesn't mean much—just a few words that are overused—but I'm sorry, Mad." His throat tightened. "If I'd known—"

She went so still, she seemed to have stopped breathing. A thin vein pulsed wildly at the base of her throat. She looked like a frightened deer, ready to bolt. "Known what?"

"I was seventeen years old. What did I know about life? You were the first girl I fell in love with, and you made it seem so damned easy—sort of like finding a killer toy in the Cracker Jack box." He touched her cheek, felt its velvety softness, and he smiled. "I didn't know I'd never feel that way again, or that you'd haunt me. I didn't know I'd spend the rest of my life dreaming about a girl I'd walked away from."

Her eyes met his, the look in them frank and unflinching—a long way from the teenage girl he'd fallen in love with. "I always understood what you did, you know. I even forgave you a little bit—or I thought I had until you showed up again. My father was a powerful man, hard to deny." She gave a throaty laugh. "I know that better than anyone."

She was offering an easy way out, and he wanted to take it. Before the surgery, he would have, but he couldn't do it this time. It was too important that he be honest—for both of their sakes. "It wasn't your father. I could have stood up to that asshole; it was *me*. I was afraid to swear I'd love you for the rest of my life." He shook his head. "Pregnant or not, you were for keeps, I knew that, and I knew if you vowed to love me forever, you'd keep your word. You *would* love me. . . ."

There were tears in her eyes. "Yes."

"It scared me, Mad. I couldn't handle your love—not at seventeen, hell, not even last year. I knew I'd start being the jerk, screwing around on you, drinking too much—all the things I always did." He moved closer and gently took her face in his hands. "I'm not that scared kid anymore. I know what I want now."

"Don't say anything else, Angel, please. . . ."

He knew what she was doing. She was afraid he'd say he loved her and then break her heart again. He wished he could blame her, but she had every reason to protect her heart from him. All he could do was try and keep on trying until one day she believed in him again.

He thought of all the things he could say to her right now, all the words he could use to tell her he loved her, but in the end, they were only words, and she'd heard them from him before. Instead, he leaned toward her, took her fragile, beautiful face in his hands, and kissed her, slowly and thoroughly, the way he hadn't even imagined back when they were kids. He hadn't known anything about love. He didn't know then how it twisted your insides and made you feel like you were made of glass. How sometimes—like now—you felt so brittle that a good wind could shatter your soul.

"Say something," he said softly.

She closed her fist around the earrings, then let them drop soundlessly to the floor. "I don't want to talk. I want . . ."

"What?" he asked. "What do you want? Just tell me and I'll move heaven and earth to get it for you."

"You, " she whispered. A slow, seductive smile spread across her face. She kicked one shoe off—it clanged against the spittoon in the corner. The other one hit the claw-foot desk leg. "I want you, Angel DeMarco."

His breath broke into wheezing little gasps. Had his heart been connected to his central nervous system, it would have been thumping out of control; instead, it kept up its steady, unflappable rhythm. He swallowed, noticing that his throat was dry.

She started to unbutton her sweater, and he grabbed her hand. The minute he did it, he felt like a fool. He tried to smile it off, but she'd seen the truth in his eyes. "I don't know if I can do it, Mad," he whispered, humiliation a cold stain in his stomach.

She didn't smile or pretend not to understand. "Your doctor advised you that you could resume sexual relations whenever you felt . . . up to it."

A smile quirked one corner of his mouth. "I have to admit, it turned me on when she said it."

"And how about now?" she asked softly, unbuttoning his shirt.

He shook his head. "I don't know. Maybe we should wait. . . ."

She smiled and undid another button. Her hand splayed across his chest, each finger as hot as a brand on his flesh. "Should we?"

He couldn't concentrate with her doing that. He felt her fingers, working nimbly on his shirt, her fingernails scraping the tender flesh of his chest. She peeled his shirt away, revealing the bright red scar.

He felt a moment's hesitation, an uncertainty. It meant so much, loving her, and he was afraid he couldn't do it. Afraid his secondhand heart would just give out.

She pressed onto her tiptoes and kissed the very top of his scar. Her lips were warm and pliant against the new flesh, and he shivered in response. He couldn't hold himself apart from her. He wanted to crush her to him, bury himself deep, deep inside her, so deep he couldn't tell where she began and he ended.

With a groan, he pulled her into his arms and kissed her with a passion he'd never felt before. He kissed her until he couldn't breathe for wanting her. Slowly he lowered himself to the bear rug, and she followed him, her fingers still working on the buttons. When they hit the rug, she pulled his shirt off and tossed it away.

He wrenched her soft green sweater off and threw it over his head, then he unhooked her bra and let it slide through his shaking fingers to the fur.

She knelt on the rug before him, her breasts glimmering and perfect in the firelight. She reached up to cover them.

"The baby—"

He pulled her hands away and studied the tiny, silvery lines she was trying to hide. He could tell by looking at her that she thought she was damaged somehow, that her woman's body couldn't compare to the girl's he'd loved before.

Very slowly he leaned forward and cupped her small, round breasts in his hands. "You're beautiful," he whispered, bending down to kiss the soft swell of one breast.

She shivered and released a tiny moan, then arched slightly toward him. He took a nipple in his mouth as he unbuttoned her jeans and pushed her down onto the rug.

He eased the pants off of her, then the underpants, until she lay there, glistening with firelight, her naked body stretched out before him, wearing nothing but a pair of fuzzy socks. He dug deep in his pocket for a condom and pulled it out, tossing the little foil packet on the floor. Drawing back, he yanked off the rest of his clothes and threw them toward the door, then he came down beside her, kissing her again, stroking her body until she arched toward him and pleaded in his ear. Quiet, breathy words that strained his self-control.

He drew back, breathing hard. His heart pumped in an irritatingly calm rhythm, reminded him that nothing about this was normal.

"I don't know, Mad," he whispered brokenly.

"Don't worry." She took the condom packet and ripped it open, letting the bits of foil fall to the floor. Smiling, she reached down. Her fingers closed around him, squeezing, stroking. "You seem okay so far."

Her hand was working magic. He moaned, closed his eyes.

"Should we keep going?" she breathed at his ear, licking the sensitive flesh of his lobe.

He felt drugged. It was all he could do to nod. His throat was too dry to form words. He felt her slip the condom in place and smooth it down, down the shaft.

With a groan deep in his throat, he rolled over and kissed her. Long, electrical kisses that sent him spiraling over the edge. He felt her take hold of him again, guiding him toward her, inside her.

He almost came right then, but he held himself back, biting down hard on his lower lip. She clung to him, whispering his name, her hips grinding, thrusting against his. They fell into a rhythm as old as time, but it felt new to Angel, so new. With incredible effort, he held his need in check, bringing her closer and closer to the brink. . . .

He felt the tiny pulse of her climax and he was lost. His own release was a shuddering explosion. Afterward, he thudded down on the rug beside her, his breath coming in hacking gasps.

"It was never like that when we were teenagers," he said.

She smiled, snuggling closer. "Not quite. It was more like 'Beat the Clock' back then."

They laughed together and lay there, wrapped in each other's arms, remembering so many things. He rested his cheek on the swell of her breast and studied her naked body in the writhing, golden firelight, tracing the flat surface of her belly with one finger. She was so beautiful. . . .

He didn't ever want to leave her. He wanted this moment, this intimacy, to go on and on, his soul cradled in the warmth of her touch, her smile.

But how did a man like him say that to a woman like her? What were the magic words that would make her believe that what they'd just done was special and that he'd finally grown up enough to realize it?

There were no words that he could think of, and so he used his body to tell her that he loved her, that he couldn't get enough of her. His hands, his lips, his tongue—he used them all to worship her body again, until she cried out with pleasure and then slumped against him.

They lay entwined forever. Then, with a trembling laugh, she tried to draw away. "We'd better get going. . . ."

"No way." He drew her closer, until their bodies were a sweaty, seamless whole. "It's probably not even midnight."

She rolled over and smiled down at him. Her hair spilled in a messy pile of honey brown, caressed by firelight, and her lips were puffy and swollen from his kisses. Her nipples caressed his bare chest. "Welcome to dating a single parent."

The words were like the tiny flick of a knife. He winced. "Is that what I'm doing, dating you?"

A frown darted across her face. Nervously she tucked a lock of hair behind her ear. "Well . . . what would you call it?"

He lifted a hand to her face, touched her cheek, traced the pink outline of her upper lip. He wondered suddenly how a man could survive, loving a woman this much; if she wanted to, she could rip his soul out and smash it beneath her foot. Just like he'd done to her.

For the first time, he understood—really understood—what he'd done to that beautiful, trusting sixteen-year-old girl, and the shame was almost overwhelming. And more than shame, there was regret, deep and aching and unquenchable.

He gazed up at her, loving her so much it hurt. "I'd call it falling in love."

# chapter twenty-six

❧

*I'd call it falling in love.*

For a second Madelaine couldn't move, couldn't even breathe. She lay beside him, still naked, the bear rug damp beneath her body. She bit her lip, afraid suddenly that she would say the words she shouldn't say, the words that, once spoken, couldn't be taken back, could never be unsaid.

She didn't want to think about the past now, but it came back to her, creeping into her mind on tiny, whispering feet. All the things they'd ever said to each other billowed up between them, hanging in the air above them. So many of her dreams had been tangled up with this man, and she was afraid—so afraid—to let him have the power over her again. And yet he did, already he did.

She twisted around to look at him. Her lips parted in a silent plea, an invitation.

He lifted himself from the floor and reached out for her. She knew he was moving slowly, as if he were scared she would turn away.

She remained motionless. His hand breezed down her bare arm, setting off a flurry of goose bumps. "Angel. . . ." His name fell from her lips on a breathless whisper of longing.

She stared into his green eyes, mesmerized by the possibilities she saw there. She knew then, as certainly as she'd ever known anything in her life, that he wasn't the boy he'd been at seventeen anymore. There was a depth of pain in his eyes that was new, a fear and a regret that she understood. He was, in his own way, as terrified in this moment as she. And seeing that, his fear and his insecurity, was like the brush of a warm, soothing wind on her own uncertainty.

He kissed her then, a light, breezing touch of lips that somehow stamped her soul more deeply than any of the lovemaking ever could. Her arms curled around him, held him close. One by one the years of loneliness and loss seemed to fall away from her. When he drew back, she saw the same dawning sense of wonder in his eyes that swelled in her own heart.

"Ah, Madelaine," he said. Just that and nothing more; yet it felt like everything.

At twelve-forty Lina clicked off the television and stood up. For the tenth time in as many minutes, she glanced at the clock on the mantel. The red and brown papier-mâché turkey she'd made in kindergarten huddled alongside it, a yearly reminder that Thanksgiving was just around the corner.

*Where in the hell is Mom?*

She crossed her arms and paced back and forth in the room. She had every light in the room on, but still it felt dark in here, a little lonely. It was the first time she'd ever been in her house this late alone. Whenever Mom had an emergency call at the hospital, Francis always came buzzing right over to keep Lina company.

The thought reminded her again of how much she missed

Francis, and she sighed heavily. She plopped into the big over-stuffed chair by the front door and sat there, waiting, her foot tapping impatiently on the hardwood floor.

Her mother had no right to be out this late—didn't she know that Lina would be worried sick? When Lina had spoken with Angel earlier, he'd said he had to talk to her mother tonight. *Talk*. So where were they?

She glanced at the phone and thought about calling the hospitals. She was just about to stand up when she reined herself in. It was ridiculous, worrying this way. Her mother was thirty-three years old; she could certainly stay out all night if she wanted to.

But it wasn't like her mom. Madelaine was way too responsible for something like this.

It was Angel's fault.

Suddenly she wondered about Angel. After all, what did they know about him, really? He'd come into their lives on a whirl-wind, all smiles and promises and fun. But he had a horrible reputation—what if he'd earned it, what if he slept with anyone and forgot their names in the morning, what if he was really a serial killer and the police looked the other way because he was Angel DeMarco, what if—

"Get a grip, Lina," she said aloud, trying to shake the worry from her mind. "Mom is fine. She's probably making him drive at twenty-five miles an hour and wear a crash helmet."

But she couldn't make herself believe it. Deep down she knew that something was wrong. She remembered the phone call they'd gotten in the middle of the night about Francis, and her heart started to race. She glanced nervously at the phone. A call like that could come at any time, could strike through your living room like lightning and leave you burning. . . .

She needed Zach right now, someone to talk to—

From the corner of her eye she saw headlights outside. "Thank God."

The Mercedes pulled up the driveway and stopped. The headlights flicked off.

She sat there, arms crossed, staring out the window, waiting for them to come inside. They didn't.

Finally they left the car and strode casually up the walkway. The lock clicked and the door swung open. Mom and Angel walked into the room, holding hands, gazing at each other with starry, faraway looks in their eyes.

Lina felt suddenly excluded. It was the way she wanted Angel to look at her, only *her*. She knew she was being stupid and selfish and childish, but it hurt. God, how it hurt. She'd wanted a daddy who was hers and hers alone. Her best friend in all the world. The way they looked at each other—as if they were in love—made Lina feel angry and empty inside. "Mom?" she whispered.

They looked startled—as if they hadn't even noticed she was in the room—and their disregard pissed her off even more. Mom blinked and pulled her hand away from Angel's. "Hi, baby," she said in a sleepy voice. "We thought you'd be in bed by now. You didn't have to wait up."

The words were like arrows, driving deep. They hadn't even thought about Lina, they'd forgotten her completely. She laughed bitterly. "Yeah, right. Like I could sleep with you out." She threw the words back at her mother, and felt a tiny thrill when she flinched.

Mom took a step toward her. The understanding in her eyes only made the hurt worse. "There's nothing for you to be scared of, baby. Nothing could change the way either of us feels about you."

Lina knew it was a lie. If her mother loved Angel, it changed everything, and suddenly she didn't want it changed. She wanted her old life back, wanted Francis out on that old porch swing and Mom puttering in the rose garden. She didn't want this dark-haired stranger to come between them.

She felt as if she were about to explode, but she didn't know why. It was as if all her little-girl dreams were crumbling around her. She stared at Angel. "You said you were *my* friend." Hurt plunged through her at the words, leaving her shaken and angry.

Suddenly she wanted to hurt him, hurt them both the way they were hurting her. "You're not my father," she said in a cold voice. "You have his heart, but you're not him." Her voice broke and it made her furious, that show of weakness. "You don't deserve his heart."

"Lina!" Mom said harshly.

"Shut up," Lina hissed.

Angel frowned suddenly, and the way it changed his face was frightening. He threw his coat toward the sofa and it caught a lampshade. The crystal lamp crashed to the floor. "Don't you dare talk to your mother that way, young lady."

It made her laugh, him trying suddenly to sound like her father. But he wasn't her father. *He* was up in Heaven right now, and he'd never looked at Lina that way, never made Lina feel like she was an outsider in her own house. "You're not my father."

"Lina," Mom said, "you don't mean that."

"You don't know what I mean. You don't know me. I hate you. . . . I *hate* you." She heard herself screaming at them and she knew it was a mistake, but she couldn't seem to stop. Anger and hurt twisted her up inside.

"Go to your room," Angel said in a voice so quiet and calm, it sent shivers up Lina's spine. "Get out of here. *Now.*"

Tears choked her, stung her eyes. She spun away from their Christmas-card love scene and stumbled blindly down the hallway, running into the refuge of her own room. But once she got there, it didn't even feel like her own room anymore. It felt alien and confining. She wrenched the window open and crawled outside.

Yanking her bike from the side of the porch, she jumped onto the hard plastic seat and sped down the driveway, over the curb, and onto the pavement. Anger spurred her on, made her punch the pedals until she was speeding away from the house.

By the time she reached the corner, it had started to rain. Infrequent, drizzling rain spat at her and fell in glistening drops on her handlebars. Wind whipped through her hair and stung her eyes.

With every mile she felt the dreams she'd concocted about her father slip further from her. She'd been an idiot to believe in him, to believe some stranger could come into her life and be her *daddy*. She should have known better. . . .

*I'm afraid he'll break your heart.*

She heard her mother's warning again, and it made her feel even more stupid and naive. Lina knew better—she knew that dreams didn't always come true. Hadn't she always known that? Why had she let herself be so stupid?

At Laurel Street she remembered the Saturday night parties that were an institution at Quilcene Park. She veered left and sped down the hill. Ten minutes later she turned the last corner and whizzed onto the driveway of the old park, her thin tires bumping over the ruts in the road, her fingers frozen around the rubber handles.

She ditched her bike at the edge of the asphalt parking lot and looked around. She waited breathlessly for someone to yell her name, to clap her on the back and welcome her to the party.

But no one came. Kids milled along the river and around the fire. She could hear the cackling of laughter and the quiet buzz of a dozen conversations. But the closer she got to the fire, the older the kids looked. She'd thought this was a party for high schoolers, but a bunch of the boys who were hanging out around the fire looked like they were in college—or should have been.

"Zach," she whispered, wanting him with her right now. But it was too late to call his house, and he wouldn't be at a party like this.

Plunging her hands deep in her pockets, she tried to look cool, like she fit in, as she strolled past one group of kids after another, looking for anyone to talk to.

Finally she reached the edge of the river and stood there, watching the swirling current. The anger she'd felt earlier slipped away, and without its heat, she felt cold. All around her, kids were laughing and talking and having a good time, but no one had spoken to her at all. It was as if she were a ghost, invisible and separate.

She heard a quiet, warbling laugh and it sounded familiar. She jerked her head up just as a girl and boy walked past her. Lina's eyes met the girl's—Cara Milston. There was a moment of stunned recognition on both their parts. A long time ago—first through seventh grades—they'd been best friends, but now they were worlds apart. Usually they didn't even make eye contact— the cheerleader and the bad girl.

Lina felt a sudden pang of loss for the girl she'd once been. She wondered what it would have been like if she hadn't changed friends in the eighth grade, if she hadn't started smoking down by the river before school, if she'd never taken that first burning sip of whiskey when she was fourteen.

She wanted it all back now, wanted Cara back. A best girl-friend to talk to.

Cara gave Lina a quick, jerking smile and walked past her.

Lina sighed heavily and sank slowly to her knees along the riverbank. She felt the cold, mushy mud squish all around her, chilling her to the bone, but she didn't care.

She couldn't remember when she'd felt so lonely. Everything about her life was a joke. No one was ever around when it really mattered. Even now, in the middle of the best school party of the year, she was alone. Forgotten.

Suddenly she wished things were different. She didn't want to be mad at her mother, didn't want to have the temper tantrums that seemed as natural to her as breathing. She wanted to be able to sit down with her mom and dad and tell them she loved them.

But she'd felt excluded when they came home, left out. And so, naturally, instead of talking to them like an adult, she'd thrown a tantrum and run away.

The dream of what she'd wanted—a *daddy*—seemed so far away, a little girl's nighttime wish. All she wanted now was to love him and be loved in return—loved for who she was. And that meant she had to love Angel for who he was.

He wasn't Francis and never would be. Francis had loved Lina in his quiet, gentle way; Angel's way would be different. He was like her—loud and reactionary and hot-tempered. Things with Angel would be unlike what she'd wanted . . . but had she really known what she wanted?

"No," she whispered into the night. She hadn't known until now, this very minute. She wanted them to be a family—all of them. And a family didn't happen overnight, a family didn't happen without tantrums and hurt feelings and apologies.

Hot tears squeezed past her eyelashes and streaked down her cheeks, mingling with the cold raindrops and splashing on her muddy pants. She was tired of running and being mad all the time, tired of feeling like she didn't belong anywhere. She thought of home—the Martha Stewart–perfect yard and her mother's rose garden, and the porch swing Francis had given them for Christmas—and longing squeezed her heart.

A family, she knew, meant going home.

Angel slammed the bedroom door shut. "She's not there."

He spun around, stared at Madelaine. His mouth fell open for words that wouldn't come.

She stood in the living room, unsmiling, unmoving, the color that had tinted her cheeks earlier replaced by a chalky pallor. She chewed on her lower lip and glanced worriedly at the front door.

"Did you hear me? She's not there. We've got to call the police or something." He could tell that he was yelling, but he couldn't control himself. Panic was an ice-cold tingling in his blood. He ran to the front door and flung it open.

All he saw out there was darkness. A gentle rain had begun to fall, studding the walkway, clattering on the roof over his head. She was out there somewhere, alone in the middle of all that blackness, alone and mad and hurt.

What the hell had happened? What had he done so wrong?

Madelaine came up beside him. He could hear the silent padding of her footsteps above the ragged harshness of his breathing. Gently she touched his arm, and he could feel that she was trying to comfort him, but he didn't want comfort.

"I didn't know," he whispered. Regret was a black, bitter taste in his mouth. He realized suddenly how lightly he'd taken everything, how cavalierly he'd accepted the burdens of fatherhood.

"What didn't you know?"

He heard the tenderness in her question, and it made him feel even worse. He turned to her, and for a second, when he looked in her worried eyes, he couldn't breathe. He couldn't be Lina's father or Madelaine's lover. . . . Most of all, he couldn't be what Francis had been to them.

*Francis.*

His brother would know what to do right now, what to say, how to make it all right. He threw his head back and closed his eyes in prayer. *What do I do now, Franco?*

The question gutted him. Slowly he turned back to Madelaine, and what he saw in her eyes shamed him to the depth of his soul. She cared about him, even now; he could see it, feel it, and though he wanted to take her in his arms and feel her warmth, he didn't deserve it. "I didn't know what it meant to be a father. I thought I could just hang out with her and be her friend. I thought she'd love me unconditionally and never ask for anything I couldn't give." Even as he said the words, he heard how hollow and selfish they were. He closed his eyes and shut up, disgusted with himself. "I didn't know it would be so *hard*. How did you do it alone all those years?"

She touched him, her warm hand molding to his cold, wet cheek. "I should have told you what parenthood was like."

His eyes flew open and anger came flooding back.

"It's not about you, Madelaine. Don't make it about you and what you should have done. I screwed up. *Me*. I shouldn't have said I'd be her daddy—I took on that commitment as if it were no more important than deciding what coat to wear. I didn't *think*."

She drew her hand back. "So what are you going to do about it? You spent your whole life running from things like this, Angel. Are you going to run away again—go nurse your fear with a bottle of tequila until you forget how much it hurts?"

The words hit him like blows. He flinched. "I don't know."

"That's not good enough. She'll be back—if she follows her usual routine, she'll be back in about an hour and she'll be mad as a hornet. What are you going to say to her? Hello or good-bye?"

He shook his head. "Don't put this on me, Mad. I'm not strong enough. . . ."

She gripped him by the shoulders and shook him, hard. "Don't you *dare* say that to me, not this time. Nobody's strong enough to be a parent. We just do it, blindly, going forward on faith and love and hope. That's all it is, Angel. Being afraid, being afraid in the marrow of your bones, and going on."

He stilled. A tiny shaft of hope flared in his heart. "You're afraid of her?"

She made a snorting sound that was almost a laugh. "I've been afraid since the moment they laid her in my arms. Every time she goes to school or to a friend's house or out on a date, I'm afraid. I'm afraid of what the world will do to my beautiful baby girl, afraid of what *I* will do to her. It never goes away, ever. You just live with it and love her and be there for her."

He let out his breath in a long, shaking sigh. "I don't know if I can do that."

She pulled away from him. "Only you can decide that, Angel. Only you."

## chapter twenty-seven

❧

Lina brought her bike to a stop at the end of the driveway. The lights were on at her house. She could see shadows moving across the living room window. A sinking feeling of shame tugged at her, but she pushed it away.

She walked her bike up the drive and leaned it against the wall. Slowly she climbed the creaking porch steps and paused at the front door. Steeling herself, she turned the knob and opened the door.

Her mother and father were at opposite ends of the room. As one, they spun to face the door and then froze.

Her mother smiled at her, a tender, understanding smile that made Lina want to start crying all over again. "Hi, baby."

Lina looked at her father—but he looked away quickly. The panic she'd held at bay sneaked up on her, hit hard. She'd ruined it, her stupid, little-girl temper tantrum had ruined it all. She raced for her bedroom and slammed the door shut behind her.

Yanking the stereo on, she turned the music to an earsplitting level.

She collapsed on her bed and tried to cry, but the tears that burned so badly wouldn't fall. Her shoulders rounded and she hung her head, staring at her feet.

"Oh, God," she whispered.

She thought of how her mother had looked earlier—her hair was messed up and her sweater was only half buttoned; her eyes were all misty and soft, and she had seemed unable to stop smiling.

*Happy*. Her mother looked happy.

And Lina had taken that away from her, she'd taken it away from them all.

Someone knocked on the door.

"Go away," she whispered, waiting for the sound of footsteps. Her mother always paused a few seconds, and then walked away. Tomorrow they'd both pretend this never happened.

But the knock came again, louder, more insistent. Lina ignored it, and the door swung open so hard, it cracked against her wall. A framed eight-by-ten of Brad Pitt crashed to the floor, spraying bits of glass across the blue carpet.

Angel stood in the doorway, filling it. His dark eyebrows were drawn together in a frown, and the ever-present smile was gone. He looked uncertain and ill at ease. With barely a glance her way, he stepped into the room and shut the door quietly behind him.

He crossed the room and clicked off the stereo, then slowly turned to face her.

"Go away," she said. The minute the words came out she willed them back. What she wanted to say was *don't go*, but she couldn't find her voice.

He stood there, his hands plunged in his Levi's pockets. "Look, I think I handled this thing badly. I don't know shit about being a father." He let out a little sigh and sat down beside her. The mattress squeaked in the silence. "But I know one thing—that woman in there loves you, and you hurt her feelings tonight. You know you did."

She felt a surge of regret and looked away, unable to meet his eyes.

He touched her chin and gently but firmly forced her to face him. "You acted like a selfish child out there, and I was ashamed of you. *You* should have been ashamed of you."

She knew he was telling the truth, and it stung. She felt the tears returning, and she tried to brush them away with her sleeve, but they kept coming back. "I . . . I know," she whispered.

She waited for him to soothe her, to tell her it wasn't her fault or it was okay to be a bitch sometimes or that he understood— all the things her mother would have said. But he just sat there, letting her feel the weight of her own shame.

Finally he smiled, smoothed a strand of hair from her face. "Growing up is hard—but at least you didn't have to get your heart cut out to do it."

It reminded her of what she'd said to him. "I . . . I'm sorry about what I said. . . . I didn't mean it . . . you know, about the heart."

He sighed quietly. "It scares me, too, Angelina. Francis was the best human being I've ever known, and I can't be him, I can't even try to be him. But . . ." He fell silent, looking at her.

She felt as if everything were hanging, suspended between them. She couldn't even draw a full breath. "But what?"

"I was wrong to want to be your friend. It was a kid's answer to a man's question. I know now what I really want."

"You do?"

"I want to be your dad. And if you'll let me try, I'll give it everything I have."

She felt the tears again, stinging and burning. "I want that, too," she said with a little hiccup.

"It's not going to be easy. I don't always do things right—like tonight, I should have told you I wanted to take your mother on a date. I should have told you that I love her, and that I want us to be a family. But no matter what happens between your mom and me, it won't change how I feel about you. You're my daughter, and I love you."

She launched herself at him, holding him tightly. "I love you, too, Daddy."

He stroked her hair, and his touch was soft and gentle, and made her feel safe for the first time in her life.

After a long time, he drew back. "Now, I think you have someone else to talk to, don't you?"

She stared into his green eyes and saw acceptance. It gave her strength, that look in his eyes. She nodded and slowly rose to her feet. At the door she paused and glanced back at him.

He smiled. "You can do it."

And she could; she knew that now. She turned away from him and left her room, walking down the long hallway toward the living room.

Her mother was standing alongside the fireplace. She was biting her lower lip—the way she always did when she was nervous—and Lina understood at last how much and how often she'd hurt her mother.

Her mother, who'd loved her and kept on loving her no matter what . . .

"I'm sorry, Mom," she said softly, wishing that she could take it all back. Everything, all the little slights and unkind words and cruelties.

Madelaine gave her a slow, understanding smile. "I love you, baby."

Lina threw herself in her mother's waiting arms and clung to her. "I love you, too, Mommy."

The sheer volume of knickknacks was astounding. Everywhere Angel looked, he saw turkeys and Pilgrims and cornucopias—candleholders, candy dishes, centerpieces. As he stood in front of the fireplace, feeling the warmth of the flames against his ankles, he stared at the row of decorations along the mantel. A rust-colored, half-painted papier-mâché turkey roosted in the middle of it all, Lina's illegibly scrawled name across one folded wing.

He moved from item to item, touching each one. He felt as if he were moving backward in time. The only store-bought decorations were candles—everything else, Lina had made in school. From kindergarten there was the turkey. First grade was represented by a Pilgrim's hat made from a shopping bag; second grade was a glazed clay thumb pot in the shape and color of a pumpkin.

He lingered over that one, his fingers gliding over the slick surface. With each year, he could see the progress in her writing and artistic skill. He tried to imagine her as a five-year-old with long black braids and a toothless smile, erupting through the front door with her newest treasure, but he couldn't quite picture it, and the inability made him sad. He'd missed so much of her life . . . so much . . . and there was no going back. No reclamation of lost years.

*Thanksgiving.*

He forced himself not to think about the past and instead to look to the future. True, he hadn't been there to hold her on her first day of life, or to take her hand on the first day of school, but he was here now, and he wasn't going anywhere. He would be there on her wedding day, and he would walk his first grandchild to school.

He turned back around, thinking that the painful swelling of emotion in his chest should somehow translate into the perfect words of love, but nothing came out.

Instead, he watched them, the women in his life. Madelaine was busy following a recipe for low-fat gravy—and by the scrunched-up expression on her face, it was not going well. Lina was setting the table.

He'd never seen such goings-on for a meal. Ma never worked

hard at Thanksgiving, that was for sure. He unearthed a sudden memory of the holiday from his childhood.

"Who wants white meat?" He could hear his mother's gravelly voice barking through the dingy darkness of the trailer. No one answered. A minute later, she stumbled from the kitchen, carrying two steaming Hungry Man turkey dinners, tossing them down on the brown Formica table. "Yours is on the counter, Angel. I couldn't carry three."

She hadn't made it through the entrée before the booze kicked in. Midsentence, she pitched face-first into the mashed potatoes and gravy. He and Francis had laughed until they cried, then carried their tin trays into the living room. Together they sat on the spongy sofa, eating, watching television, and talking.

*Brothers* . . .

"Dinner is ready." Madelaine's voice brought Angel back to the present. The misty memories of the past faded.

He blinked and looked at the table. Long and oval, it was covered in a white linen tablecloth. It was dotted with flickering candles and layered with platters of food. He moved away from the fireplace and headed toward the dining alcove.

Halfway there, he stopped. Splashes of color marred the perfect white of the tablecloth, and it took him a second to realize what he was seeing. There were three sets of multicolored handprints on the fabric. At one end of the table, on either side of the white and burgundy china place setting, were two navy-blue handprints—and painted carefully alongside was the name and date, *Madelaine, 1985.* To her left, a tiny red set that read *Lina*.

At the head of the table, stark and alone, a yellow set. *Francis.*

Across the table, Lina's gaze met his. "We . . . we did these a long time ago. I didn't think . . ."

Angel noticed his own place setting beside Madelaine's. There were no handprints, of course, just pristine white linen on either side of his plate. It made him feel ridiculously out of place.

Finally Madelaine emerged from the kitchen, and she was

carrying a jar of green paint. She caught his eye and stopped. He couldn't help noticing the pallor in her cheeks and the gentle tremble in her lower lip. "It's a family tradition," she said softly. She gave him a tender smile. "It's a little messy."

He took the paint and brush from her hands and wordlessly painted his palms, then, carefully, he pressed a hand on either side of his plate. When he was done, he stared down at his work, at the whole table, and felt as if he'd finally come home.

"I'll paint 1996 above your hands after dinner," Lina said.

Angel went to wash his hands, and when he came back, Madelaine and Lina were both seated. They were both staring at Francis's handprints at the head of the table, at his empty place.

It hadn't occurred to Angel how hard this would be for them—this first holiday without Francis. It should have, but it hadn't. Quietly he took his seat.

Silence settled in around them, leavened the mouthwatering aromas. "You both are lucky," he began softly. "You have so many memories of him, and you'll never lose those. Your tradition has brought him to this table with us, and he'll be here forever, his spirit in those crazy yellow fingerprints."

He heard Lina sniffle and saw her wipe her eyes.

"There are so many things I need to say to him and to you, but we'll have to do it one day at a time, one holiday at a time. For now, let's be thankful that we're here, together. It's what Francis would have wanted."

Madelaine looked up at him, smiling across the table, and reached for his hand. "I guess it's up to you to carve the turkey."

He felt the ghost of his brother leaning over him, breathing against his ear as he reached for the knife. A thousand things crowded in his mind, things he wanted to say, needed to say, but all that reached the surface was, "Come on, bro, show me how to cut up this bird."

He was just getting to his feet when a familiar voice burst inside his head: *Start at the breast, Angel. God knows, you should know how to do that.*

Angel felt himself starting to laugh. When he looked up, Madelaine and Lina were smiling at him, their tears gone.

And he started to carve the bird.

December settled on Seattle in a creaking, moaning layer of gray and white. Thick clouds hung low in the sky, obscuring all but the hardiest rays of the weak sun. Bare, shivering trees huddled along the roadsides, the wind a whimpering lament through their empty limbs. Evening had just begun to darken the horizon.

Angel felt a fluttering of nerves as he drove up to Madelaine's house. He'd been here a dozen nights and mornings since he'd first made love to her, but today the place looked different. Frost glazed the brick of the walkway, sparkled on the old brown shingles of the roof. The cold made everything seem glassy and fragile.

He left the engine running and got out of the car. Puffs of smoke rose from the exhaust pipes and disappeared in the chilly air.

He strode up to the front door and stopped, adjusting the fit of his dark blue suit, and then he knocked.

Lina answered the door. She was wearing a green velvet dress with a white lace collar and a big white sash. She looked so beautiful. He felt a swift surge of joy that, after all the missed years and missed moments, he was here, reaching out his hand for this lovely young woman who was his daughter.

"How's my best girl?" he said.

She smiled. "Fine. Is everything ready?"

He shrugged, feeling his nervousness return. "I hope so. I spoke with Father MacLaren about a million times yesterday. He said my choice in music was . . . unusual, but he let me do what I wanted."

This time her smile was a little shaky. "Good."

He took her hand, gazed into her eyes. "Are you up to this?"

She nodded. Before she could answer, Madelaine came into the living room behind them. Lina stepped back and Angel walked into the house.

He couldn't believe how breathtakingly gorgeous Madelaine looked. She was wearing an elegant navy-blue wool dress and a single strand of pearls. She smoothed the creaseless lines of her dress. "Why are you looking at me that way?"

"Nothing. Come on, let's go," he answered.

For a second she looked scared, and he understood. He reached out her hand and smiled when she took it. "Don't be afraid," he whispered.

The three of them left the house and climbed into the warm Mercedes. Wordlessly, each steeped in his or her own thoughts and memories, they drove to the church.

Angel pulled up at the curb and killed the engine. The huge brick church glinted in the last rays of the setting sun. Frost glittered on the mullioned windows and sparkled on the slanted roof.

Together, hand in hand, they walked up the walkway to the two huge open doors of the church. The first thing Angel noticed were the candles—they were everywhere, dozens and dozens of white candles standing in brass and silver candelabras, their dancing golden light sprayed against the walls. Boughs of evergreen were looped along the pews, held together by huge white bows. Noble firs lined the west wall, their green branches draped with glittering golden ribbon and tiny white lights.

And on the altar there was a huge heart-shaped wreath, made of white roses and evergreens held together by golden ribbons. In the center of the wreath was a picture of Francis, his face crinkled in a big smile, his hand lifted in a thumbs-up sign.

He looked so young and naive and full of life. . . .

"Ah, Jesus," Angel whispered as the grief hit.

"I haven't seen that picture in years," Madelaine said quietly beside him. "We took it up at Lake Crescent about three summers ago. . . ."

He heard the throaty catch in her voice and it almost undid him. It took all his willpower to keep the grief at bay. He turned to her, saw the sadness that had settled deep in her eyes, and he tried to smile. He wanted to tell her again how much she meant to him, but he couldn't seem to find his voice. Not here, not now, when Francis seemed so close and the pain of his death was so frighteningly real. . . .

She touched his cheek, and he started, realizing how long he'd been standing there, saying nothing, just staring into her eyes. "I don't know if I can do this." He glanced at the people congregated behind them.

The smile she gave him was steeped in confidence. "Of course you can. It's not a funeral—it's a mass to celebrate his life."

He nodded and closed his eyes for a second, trying to banish the sorrow that kept creeping into his throat. He wanted so badly for this to be a celebration of Francis's life, but sweet Jesus, it was hard. How could you celebrate when all you wanted to do was crawl into a hole and never come out again?

He followed Lina and Madelaine into the front pew, surprising himself when he genuflected. He thought instantly of Francis—how his big brother would have laughed to see Angel kneeling in the house of the Lord. . . .

Angel clung to that memory. *That* was the Francis he wanted to remember. Not the priest, but the big brother who'd tried to protect Angel . . . the man who'd taken care of Madelaine and Lina all those years, and never asked for anything from anyone except that he be allowed to love them. . . .

After what seemed like hours, Father MacLaren strode to the altar, his white robes radiant in the candlelight.

"We come together in this holiday season to remember one of our own. Father Francis Xavier DeMarco, who was one of the shining lights in this parish. You all remember him as a loving, caring, gentle man who was always there for you when you needed him, beside you with a ready smile and a willing heart. We have mourned his passing and will continue to, even as we

celebrate that he is now with the God he loved so keenly in life."
He turned, lifted a hand toward Angel. "We have with us Father
Francis's brother, who was unable to attend the funeral, and
wishes now to say a few words about his brother."

Madelaine gave his hand a squeeze.

Angel swallowed. It was the hardest thing he'd ever done,
just standing. Unsteady on his feet, he walked toward the altar
and took his place beside Father MacLaren.

He looked out at the crowd of oval faces and felt suddenly
out of place. All these people—strangers—knew Francis better
than he did; each one of them probably had better, truer words
to say.

The sadness that came was almost overwhelming. Angel
bowed his head. After what seemed like hours, he found his
voice. "You all know a different Francis than I did," he started
softly, finding his way through the darkness one word at a time.
"You speak of a caring, quiet priest, but that's not who I knew
at all. I knew a big brother who always waited to walk me home
after football practice, even though he had so many better things
to do; I knew a lanky kid with a crooked grin who always believed the best in me, even when I proved him wrong. I knew a
boy who stole cookies with me one day, and then made me eat
them all because wasting food was a bigger sin than stealing. I
knew a young man who held me when I cried and promised that
someday he would make things okay. . . .

"But I never gave him the chance. I used to think I was afraid
to believe in him; truth is, I was afraid to believe in myself. If I
had . . ." He sighed. "If I had, I wouldn't be standing here, talking to you about a man I loved but didn't know. . . ."

He turned and looked at the picture of Francis in the wreath,
and suddenly felt a deep longing for his brother. He couldn't
seem to latch on to his memories, couldn't find one that he could
talk about. He wanted to find something that would make them
all laugh, take this wrenching moment and make it something
different, something that didn't hurt so badly.

But he didn't know what to do or say or think, except *I miss you, Francis, I'm sorry. . . .*

He saw Madelaine rise to her feet amidst the crowd. She turned to the choir director and gave a quick nod. There was a momentary fumbling of cassettes, and then the music hit: "That Old Time Rock 'n' Roll," by Bob Seger and the Silver Bullet Band.

The lyrics came at him like an old friend. . . . *that kind of music just soothes your soul . . .*

Music swelled in the church, wildly inappropriate, and it took him back to his childhood, back to the crazy days when he and Francis were together all the time, when all they had was each other. They'd danced to songs like this one, and laughed to them and played them again and again on that old turntable in the living room.

He looked at Madelaine, and saw that she was laughing through her tears. He saw the glassy, faraway look in her eyes and knew that she was remembering Francis. Their Francis. Not the quiet, serious priest, but the gangly blond kid with the blue, blue eyes and the smile that seemed to light up a room and a heart as big as tomorrow.

In the space of a heartbeat, he remembered it all, the good times and the bad, the nights when they'd laughed and the mornings they'd cried.

And he couldn't imagine why he'd ever left all that, or why he'd never come home. At the thought, he felt tears sting his eyes, and within seconds, he couldn't focus. The glittering church swam before him until it was nothing but a smear of white flowers and flickering candlelight. He knew that he'd remember the smell of this church forever—that from now on, when he smelled evergreens and roses, he would think of his big brother.

*I'm home, Franco. . . .* He squeezed his eyes shut, unashamed of the tears that coursed down his cheeks. *I'm home again, big brother, and I'm not going anywhere this time.*

Thoughts crowded his head and he tried to sort them out,

tried to come up with the words he should offer to the man he loved so deeply, but in the end he realized it didn't matter. It wasn't about words or apologies or memories—it was about the simplicity of love.

Just that. Love. A brother's love, a father's love, a family's love. And love wasn't like bodies—it didn't go away, not ever. It stayed there inside of you, tangled in moments and memories.

He opened his eyes slowly, saw Madelaine and Lina through the burning glaze of his tears. *I'll see it through with them, Franco. I swear to God I will.*

The music came to a sudden, crashing halt and silence fell again, blanketing the church. Angel looked at the crowd, and realized that they weren't strangers at all. He saw old Mrs. Costanza from the corner flower shop, and Mr. Tubbs from the garage on Tenth Street, and Mr. Fiorelli, the pharmacist. . . .

He focused on Madelaine and Lina, gave them a trembling, heartfelt smile. "I can't thank you all enough. When I look around, I see my brother, see glimpses of the man he became. I can see the way he touched all your lives, and I know how much you all must have mattered to him. And most of all, I thank you for loving him, for caring for him, for letting him love you. The world will be a little dimmer place without him, but I know now that he'll never really be gone . . . because he's inside all of us."

# chapter twenty-eight

✥

Lina looked at herself in the mirror and she wanted to scream. Her hair looked awful. She glanced at the dress her mother had bought for her; it lay on her unmade bed, a glorious, sophisticated swath of midnight-blue velvet.

Longing tightened her chest. It didn't matter if she wore that beautiful dress—she was never going to fit in. All those snobby cheerleader types were going to laugh themselves silly when hell-raising Lina Hillyard walked through those gymnasium doors in a strapless dress. She could practically hear their snickers now. *Get a load of Owen's date. What grave did he dig her out of?*

She wouldn't go. Couldn't go.

A knock rattled her door. "Come in," Lina said, turning around.

Her mom stood in the doorway, carrying a big wicker basket.

She was wearing a pair of black wool pants that made her look about four inches across the hips and a fuzzy emerald sweater that highlighted her silvery-green eyes. Not a hair was out of place, and her makeup was flawless. She looked so beautiful that Lina wanted to throw up.

Mom gave her a tentative, fleeting smile. "I thought maybe I could help you do your hair."

Instinctively Lina bristled. She heard the subtle censure in her mother's voice, and she almost lashed out. Then she looked at her mom—really looked at her—and saw that there was no disapproval in her face, just an honest willingness to help out. And maybe a little fear that Lina would throw a fit and say no.

"Lina?" she said, moving forward, easing the door shut behind her. "Are you okay?"

At the question, so quietly spoken and full of concern, Lina almost crumpled. "I don't know, Mom. I was thinking of bagging the whole thing. Who cares about a stupid school dance anyway?"

Her mom set the basket down on the dresser and pulled up a chair. "I remember when I was almost your age—just a few months younger—I read about the local homecoming dance in the newspaper." A smile tugged at her mouth. "I wanted to go, but of course, it was out of the question. My father wouldn't have considered it—and I had no one to take me, anyway."

Lina stared at her mother in shock. She sounded so . . . human—not Miss Perfect and In-Control Cardiologist at all. Lina pushed the hem of the dress aside and sat down on the bed. "Keep going."

Mom flashed her a conspiratorial smile. "I told my father I needed to go to the UW medical library to research a paper for my tutor. He dropped me off and I waited at the window for him to leave. When I was sure he'd gone, I sneaked out of the library and walked sixteen blocks in the pouring rain to Ridgecrest High School."

Lina leaned forward. "What was it like?"

Mom sighed wistfully. "It was . . . magical. They'd taken the most ordinary things—glitter, tissue paper, foil—and turned that huge gymnasium into a snowy castle, like the one in *Dr. Zhivago*. The theme was *Nights in White Satin*." She laughed, apparently surprised that she remembered something so insignificant. "Anyway, I huddled at the doorway like a church mouse, watching all those Cinderellas dancing." Her smile faded and her voice dropped to a whisper. "That's when I realized how lonely I really was, how different from the other girls. My mom would have let me go—or at least, I like to believe she would have."

Lina was beginning to see her mother as a young girl, frightened and alone in that big house on the hill. She remembered the bars she'd seen on her mother's old bedroom window, and her words, *See? You don't have the worst parent in the world*. All at once she felt . . . connected to her mother. As if they had something in common after all, as if her mom could truly understand her. "But maybe you wouldn't have fit in—no one knew you. They might have made fun of you."

"Yes," Mom said, gazing steadily at Lina. "There are always times in life when you don't fit in. But you have to go forward and make a place for yourself. That's what growing up is all about. Being strong and believing in yourself—even when you're most afraid."

Lina bit her lip. "Zach's friends won't like me. I have a . . . bad reputation, and he's so squeaky clean."

Mom looked as if she really understood. "I wish I could give you a magic pill that would make it all okay, but I think I've screwed up with you in always pretending that life was easy. Sometimes it's hard and unfair, and sometimes people are cruel and selfish." She reached out, took Lina's hand in hers. "But I know this: You're a bright, beautiful girl and you have a wonderful young man who wants to spend an evening dancing with you. If you don't go because you're afraid, then you'll be heading down a long, lonely road. Believe me, I know how fear can get ahold of you, and once it gets inside, it ruins everything. Don't let that happen to you, baby."

Lina knew her mother was right. She had never let fear run her life before, and this was no time to start. She gave her mother a quick, darting smile. "Could you make me pretty again?"

Madelaine grinned. "Oh, baby, that's the easy part."

The doorbell rang at exactly 7:45. Madelaine jumped at the sound and dropped the teakettle on the burner. It hit with a clang and slid sideways, sloshing water across the black steel surface. She laughed at her own nervousness and wiped her hands on a dishrag. Reaching for her camera, she hurried to the door and wrenched it open, expecting to see Zachary in his rented tuxedo.

But it was Angel who stood on her porch. He was wearing a pair of baggy blue mechanic's coveralls that were zipped all the way to his throat.

She smiled at him. "Come to fix my bathroom pipes, have you?"

The grin he gave her was so sexy, it took her breath away. He whipped a huge bouquet of pink roses from behind his back.

She bit back a sudden smile. "For me?"

He shook his head. "You're not the only lady in my life, you know."

Madelaine loved him more in that moment than she would have thought possible. Smiling, she backed up to let him come inside.

He set the flowers on the table. "Is she ready?"

Madelaine saw the nervousness in his eyes as he glanced toward Lina's bedroom, and she had to stifle a smile. "Almost. Are you?"

He looked startled by the question, as if he thought he'd hidden his anxiety. Then he caught her gaze and he smiled. "I don't think so, Mad. Are you sure she's old enough to date?"

"I was her age when I met you, and we—"

"*Don't* remind me of that." He tried to smile again, but it looked weak and a little sick. He spun away from the table and paced the room. He kept glancing at Lina's room, then at the front door, and with each look, his lips tightened.

She sat on the sofa and patted the cushion beside her. "Come here."

He strode over and slumped to a sit beside her. Easing an arm around her shoulders, he drew her close. "Christ, I'm as nervous as a cat on a hot tin roof. I don't know about this fatherhood crap. I don't think I'll be any good at it."

She leaned against him, reveling in the comfort of his body, the feel of his arm around her. "Welcome to parenting. It's not a job, it's an adventure."

The fire in the fireplace crackled in the silence that fell between them. She snuggled closer. She still felt fluttery and nervous about the dance, but something about having Angel here with her, sharing her anxiety, made it all seem manageable, maybe even a little fun. "I guess this is how all parents feel when their daughter goes to her first school dance."

He turned to her then, and his face was serious. "This dad shit scares me."

She touched his face, gazing up at him. "It scares you because it's forever and you're a never kind of guy." Even as she said the words, and heard the truth in them, she felt the sadness spreading through her. "But you're doing a great job, really."

Before Angel could answer, the doorbell rang again.

Instinctively they snapped apart like a couple of teenagers getting caught by their parents. Then they looked at each other and burst out laughing.

With a sigh, Angel got to his feet and went to the door, ushering Zach inside.

"Zachary Owen," Angel said, studying the boy with narrowed, disapproving eyes.

"H-Hello again, Mr. DeMarco."

Angel didn't smile. He turned to Madelaine. "Give me that camera. I want to take a picture of him—for identification purposes."

"I-I-I—"

"Angel!" Madelaine said on a burst of laughter, rising to her feet.

Angel laughed uneasily and slapped Zach on the back. "Just a little parent humor."

Zach deflated and coughed up a wan smile. "Oh."

"You'll have her home by midnight?" Angel said sharply.

Zach nodded and showed them his watch. "I will."

"You have batteries in that? If not—" Angel started to take the Rolex watch off his wrist.

Madelaine grabbed Angel's arm, squeezing so hard he made a little sound. "Don't worry, Zach," she said, flashing Angel a pointed look. "We trust you."

Angel turned to her, and there wasn't one iota of trust on his face. His thick black eyebrows were drawn forbiddingly together and his lips were pressed into a thin line. When he opened his mouth to speak, she shook her head firmly.

His gaze cut to Zach, then back to Madelaine. "I'll go get Lina," he said.

Madelaine almost laughed out loud at the sullenness in his voice. "You do that."

Angel snagged the bouquet of roses and strolled down the hallway toward Lina's room. To his credit, he didn't look back once.

Madelaine smiled at Zach. "He's just learning how to be a father."

Zach pulled uncomfortably at his collar. "He's doing a good job."

Silence fell between them after that. Madelaine surreptitiously studied the young man. He looked rail-thin and awkwardly tall in his rented navy-blue tuxedo, his sandy hair a fresh-cut path across his brow. His cheeks looked like they'd been scrubbed with low-grade sandpaper.

Before she could ask how school was going, she heard Lina's door open and she glanced down the hallway in time to see her step from her bedroom.

Madelaine's breath caught. Lina stood in the hall, facing her father. The strapless blue velvet clung to her body in waves that looked electric blue in some places and black in others. Her jet-black hair was pulled back from her forehead and held in place by a glittery silver headband that matched her shoes and handbag.

She looked so grown-up. Madelaine felt a rush of emotion—regret, fear, pride. She realized suddenly that her little girl would be a woman soon, and then she'd be gone, and the realization brought a needling sting of tears to her eyes.

She dashed the tears away and stared at Lina and Angel, watching breathlessly as Angel gave his daughter the dozen roses. Even from this distance, Madelaine could see the tears that sprang to Lina's eyes.

*Oh, God*, Madelaine thought. She wanted to tuck this moment in her heart like a treasured photograph. When she was old and gray, she'd bring it out, stroke it, remembering. . . .

Instinctively she turned to look for Francis.

But he wasn't there.

Wiping the moisture from her eyes, she glanced up at the ceiling, trying to imagine the stars sparkling in the black heavens beyond. *I hope you're seeing this, Francis . . . her first dance. . . .*

Lina came around the corner and stood beside the fireplace.

Zach gasped at the sight of her. "Oh, my God."

Lina paled. Her hands flew to her hair, smoothing it back. "Is something wrong?"

"You look great," Zach said, grinning from ear to ear.

A smile swept across Lina's face, lighting her eyes until they looked like blue flames dancing between her thick black lashes. Pink tinged her cheeks. "Thanks."

Zach surged toward her, thrusting out a small plastic box. "It's a wrist corsage. The florist said they were the best kind."

"Jeez," Lina sighed, staring down at the delicate white blossom. "It's beautiful." She slipped the elasticized band on her wrist and lifted it for them all to see.

"Okay, guys," Madelaine said, reaching for her camera. "Get in front of the Christmas tree. I want to take some pictures."

Lina rolled her eyes. "Aw, Mom . . ."

Madelaine made a sweeping gesture with her hand, laughing. "Come on."

Lina and Zach came awkwardly together. He slipped his arm around her tiny waist, and she held the wrist corsage up for the photo. Behind them, the Christmas tree sparkled in a hundred multicolored lights.

Grinning, Madelaine snapped a few quick shots. "Okay, one with your dad now."

Zach faded to the left, and Angel took his place. He curled an arm around Lina and drew her close, smiling for the camera.

Madelaine saw them through the viewfinder and frowned, easing the camera from her face. "Don't give me that poster-boy smile, Angel. I want to see her *father*, not some Hollywood hotshot."

Angel looked nonplussed for a second, then a slow, admiring grin spread across his face. "God, she's a demanding woman," he said to no one in particular.

"Cardiologist," was Lina's laughing reply. "They're all like that."

Madelaine laughed, clicking away. God, how she loved this moment, this feeling. It was the antithesis of every memory of her childhood, the coming together of every dream she'd ever had.

She wondered how long it would last this time, how long a person could be allowed this happiness in life.

She wanted to go to him then, slip her arms around him and

know that he would always be there, standing in her living room as if he belonged, smiling down at her with that recklessness in his green eyes.

"Mrs. Hillyard," Zach said, interrupting her thoughts. "Let me get a picture of the whole family."

Whole family.

God, she wanted it so badly, she hurt.

She relinquished the camera and hurried to the fireplace. She saw the three stockings hung from the evergreen-laden mantel and couldn't help smiling. She slipped into place beside Angel and felt his hand settle possessively on her hip.

It felt so incredibly *right* to be standing here, the three of them, linked by so much more than the arms that bound them together. *If only it could last*. She knew the smile she gave the camera was sad and more than a little wistful.

"Smile, Dr. Hillyard," Zach ordered.

She forced her melancholy away and focused on the joy of the moment. At the tiny click of the camera and the blinding flash, Madelaine knew they'd captured the moment forever.

And she told herself that it was enough for now.


The high school sat on a big corner lot, its brick sides lit here and there by spotlights implanted in the winter-brown grass. A huge dark sign identified it as the home of the Panthers. When she saw it, Lina's nervousness jumped up a notch, her mouth went dry.

Zach maneuvered the car into the student lot and parked it. He rushed around to her side of the car and opened her door. She stepped out into the cool night air, clasping her hands together to keep them from shaking.

All around, kids were getting out of cars and congregating in giggling, chattering groups. The boys slapped each other's hands in high-fives, and the girls oohed and aahed over each other's dresses.

Lina recognized a dozen faces as she and Zach came up to a crowd of kids. There was a moment of stunned surprise as everyone turned to gape at her. But it was one face that held her attention, one pair of eyes she couldn't look away from.

Cara Milston stood in the center of the crowd. She was staring at Lina.

Zach slipped an arm around her and squeezed gently. "You all know Lina?"

Slowly Cara let go of her jock boyfriend's hand and moved toward Lina in a cloud of glittery white satin. "Killer dress, Lina." Her voice was quiet, a little uncertain.

Lina hadn't even realized she'd been holding her breath until it came whooshing out of her in a sigh. A tentative smile crooked one corner of her mouth. All at once she remembered a million things about her and Cara—times they'd shared lunch on the playground and spent the night at each other's house. She realized with a sudden ferocity that she wanted that again. "Thanks." She tried to think of what to say to Cara, but nothing came.

Cara smiled. "I missed you, Lina."

Lina realized then how simple it was. All she had to do was say what was in her heart and it was a beginning. "I've missed you, too, Cara." She smiled.

After that, the night took on a magical, larger-than-life quality. The sky looked bigger and darker, a velvet drapery beaded with stars. Fallen leaves lay scattered across the road up to the school, catching on the girls' high-heeled shoes and sticking to their shimmering hose.

They all went, talking and laughing, into the gymnasium. Lina was the only girl in the crowd who hadn't volunteered on the decorating committee, and when she saw what they'd done, she stopped dead. "God, it looks *great*."

Gauze hung draped in rippling folds against the vanilla-bland walls. White butcher paper was taped to the basketball court floor, its surface littered with gold and silver glitter. A huge Christmas tree dominated the room, its branches full of white

lights and tinfoil stars. In the corner, a winter-wonderland photographer's backdrop memorialized each couple's night. The
band hammered out raucous music on an octagonal stage at one
end of the gym.

Cara sidled up to her. "We could use some help on decorating
for the spring Sadie Hawkins dance."

Lina felt unsure of herself. "I-I don't have much talent."

Cara laughed, a high, clear sound like the tinkling of silver
bells. "Can you use masking tape?"

Lina immediately felt like a fool. A hot blush spread up her
cheeks and angry words popped onto her tongue. She bit them
back when she realized that Cara wasn't making fun of her—she
was inviting Lina in. And Lina—idiot that she was—was standing there with her mouth hanging open. "I can use masking tape."

Before Cara could respond, Zach took hold of Lina's hand
and dragged her onto the dance floor. A hackneyed version of a
Hootie and the Blowfish song was pulsing from the huge speakers in the corner.

Lina couldn't help laughing as he twirled her into the crowd
and started dancing.

It was the beginning of the best night of her life.


Madelaine paced back and forth across the living room, picking up knickknacks and moving them from table to table, studying the manufacturer's marks on her china candy dishes as if
she'd never seen them before. Each and every Christmas decora-
tion held her avid attention. For the fifteenth time in as many
minutes, she looked at the mantel clock. The Christmas tree
sparkled in the corner.

"Thirty minutes," she said, more to herself than to Angel.
"They should be dancing by now."

Angel turned away from the window, where he'd been standing motionless and silent for the same thirty minutes. "Okay,
enough is enough."

Madelaine stopped and looked at him. "What do you mean?"

"She's at the dance, she's having a great time. She hasn't been kidnapped by terrorists. I'm going to try and forget my negative fantasy—which is, by the way, that she gets in a car with that red-faced kid and keeps on going, stopping only long enough to get pregnant and rob a liquor store."

Madelaine laughed, and it felt good to make light of it all. "You're right. We have to relax."

He whipped the living room curtains shut and turned around, giving her a smoldering smile. "Now I have you all to myself."

She felt a shiver of anticipation. "So you do."

"Good, let's talk."

She knew she looked ridiculously disappointed, but she couldn't help it. "We're alone for once, and you want to *talk*?"

He grabbed her hand and led her to the sofa. They sat down side by side, and he turned to her. "You said earlier that I was a never kind of guy."

Her heart seemed to stall for a second, then pick up speed. She tried to make light of it. "Forget it, I didn't mean—"

"What *did* you mean?"

There was no laughter in his eyes, just an intensity that stole her breath. She knew it mattered to him, what she said, and she didn't know what was the right thing. She wanted to blurt out that she was afraid—afraid of so many things, loving him, not loving him, everything. "I meant that I know you, Angel. I understand the kind of man you are." She gazed up at him, trying to smile. "I'm not sixteen anymore, and you can't break my heart like you did before. We can just . . . be . . . this time. No promises, no guarantees. It's enough for me."

He looked at her sadly. "It's not enough for me, Mad."

"What do you mean?"

His gaze left her face, traveled around the room as if he were searching for something. After what seemed like hours, he took hold of her hand and held it to his chest. She felt the fluttering rhythm of his heart beneath the heavy cotton fabric of his coveralls. "I want so much for us, Mad. I want to be here for you, with you, forever. I want to bounce our children and our grandchildren on my knee. I want to go to bed with you every night and wake up with you every morning for the rest of my life . . . but I don't know how long that will be."

The words sank deep inside her, twisted around her heart, and brought tears to her eyes. "No one ever knows those things, Angel."

"I missed so much of Lina's life. . . ." He looked away again. "I wish I could have those years back. I threw them away so easily. . . . I'll never do that again. I love you, Madelaine Hillyard. And I know I've said that before, but you're just going to have to give me a second chance."

It was all there in the words he was offering, in the look in his eyes, everything she'd ever wanted. The love, the family, the commitment—everything. She wanted *him*, beside her on this couch and in her bed for as long as forever could be.

She wanted to answer, but the words tangled in the thickness in her throat and wouldn't come out. And then he was holding her, kissing her so passionately, the world began to spin. She clung to him, loving him so much that the emotion was a sharp pain in her chest.

He pulled slightly away. His breathing was ragged and shallow as he rested his lips against her cheek. "Say it, Mad, say it before I rip the house apart."

She drew back, laughing. It would always be this way with him, she realized. He would always be able to rattle her senses and confuse her, and he would always demand things in that arrogant, selfish way of his, as if the world owed him everything. And he would always be the one person in the world she wanted to sit on this sofa with. "I love you, Angel DeMarco. And if you take that lightly again, I'll—"

He covered her mouth with his, whispering, "Never."

He kissed her until she was breathless. Then, with a suddenness that should have surprised her, but didn't, he lurched to his feet and dragged her into the center of the living room.

"Stand there," he ordered.

She protested and he ignored her. Instead, he went around and flicked off all the lights, until the room was completely dark except for the glowing red of the firelight and the sparkling gold and white of the Christmas tree. "Close your eyes."

She couldn't help laughing. "It's a little pointless, don't you think? The room is dark."

"Doctors," he said with mock disgust. "Just close your eyes."

Grinning, she complied. "I'm getting the feeling you're not used to dating career women."

She heard him chuckle. "Most of my women had the IQ of field mice. Now, keep your eyes closed."

"And the bodies of Playboy bunnies," Madelaine muttered under her breath.

She stood there, eyes closed, arms crossed, trying to figure out what he was doing. She heard the front door open, then close. She listened and knew he was no longer in the house. She thought about peeking and decided it would be no fun.

In the distance she heard a car door open and close; a few seconds later, her front door shut again. He dragged something—a chair—across the hardwood floor. Wood creaked and groaned, and she thought he was climbing onto the chair. Then he pushed it back across the floor.

"Okay now, don't look." he said again, and she heard him walking toward her.

She felt him come up close, so close she could smell the musky tang of his aftershave and feel the moist heat of his breath on her forehead. He started to unbutton her sweater.

She kept her eyes shut by sheer force of will. He didn't say anything, didn't touch her anywhere except on the sweater, un-popping each button. Then he peeled the sweater off, his palms dragging sensually across her bare shoulders.

Cool air swept across her flesh, sent goose bumps scurrying down her arms.

She heard his bones creak as he knelt in front of her. He unhooked her leather belt and let it dangle, then he unbuttoned the waistband and slowly, slowly, lowered the zipper. She felt his fingertips brushing against her belly.

Her pants fell to the floor. His hands formed to her thighs, branding her with their heat, then moved up, up her legs, dipped in at her waist, and kept moving up toward her breasts. At the last second his touch moved to her back and he unhooked her bra, let it fall to the floor with the pants.

She tried to imagine herself as he saw her now, standing there in the middle of her living room, lit only by the soft gold of firelight, wearing nothing but white underwear and black knee socks. It was amazingly erotic, fantasizing about how she looked, about how he saw her.

She waited breathlessly for him to touch her. Her skin seemed to tighten in anticipation, her heartbeat sped up. But he didn't touch her; instead, he slipped something silky and slippery over her head. She knew it was a gown—maybe a nightgown—that hugged her every curve and fell all the way to the floor. The silk felt whispery and delicious against her bare skin.

He moved away from her, and she felt a flutter of frustration. "Angel," she said, wanting him back, aching for his touch.

There was an electronic click, and music came on. The slow, romantic voice of Dan Fogelberg drifted through the room. "Longer." She recognized the song instantly, and she smiled at the sheer romance of it.

"Open your eyes," Angel said, and she realized that he was right in front of her. Smiling, she opened her eyes.

He was wearing a gorgeous black tuxedo—and he looked stunningly handsome. He'd dressed her in an elegant black silk sheath dress that was so sexy and daring, she'd never have bought it for herslef. She started to reach for him, to throw her arms around him and kiss him, then she noticed everything else he'd done and her breath caught in her throat.

There was a huge, mirrored ball hanging from the chandelier above the dining room table. Each little square of glass caught the candlelight and threw beads of light across the walls, the ceiling, the floor.

He'd created a high school prom in her living room.

"Oh, my," was all she could think of to say. It was such a wild and crazy and romantic thing to do—so totally *Angel*.

He reached his hand out, and in his palm lay a black velvet box. "Open it," he said softly.

She looked up at him. Slowly, her hands shaking, she reached for the box and snapped it open. A brilliant diamond blinked up at her. "Oh, Angel . . ."

He eased the ring from the box and fit it onto her finger. "Marry me, Madelaine."

She stared down at the ring, laughing and crying at the same time. It was an absurdly big diamond—conspicuous and dazzling and flashy—just like the man who'd bought it. She knew suddenly that her life would be different with Angel, more different than she could imagine. He would never do things the way other men did—he was like a flame, hot and dancing and capable of great destruction. But she knew—God, she'd known since she was sixteen years old—that there was no one else for her. "It's so big. . . . You shouldn't have. . . . Oh, Angel . . ."

He grinned. "I'm from Hollywood—the land of big jewelry. I want the world to know you're mine." He moved closer, and his smile faded. He looked at her with a seriousness that made her heart feel achingly full. "You are mine, aren't you, Mad?"

"Always."

His grin came back, brighter than the diamond. "Good. Now, dance with me, Mrs. DeMarco."

The laughter rose through her and spilled out in a light, airy sound of pure joy. "Why, Mr. DeMarco, I thought you'd never ask."

# epilogue

He sits on the porch swing, trying to make it sway beneath him. He can hear the high, clear sound of Lina's laughter floating on the air. In the yard just in front of him, Madelaine and Lina and Angel are untangling a strand of Christmas lights. On the corner beyond, a young man stands in the shadow of a hundred-year-old oak tree, his hands jammed in his Levi's pockets. No one in the yard has seen the boy yet, but he knows that they will. Soon Lina will look up and see the boy and go running down the walkway toward him.

He feels himself start to smile. It feels good, that slow, easy curving of the lips, and he realizes halfway into it that he can *feel* himself smiling. He notices that the wind is brushing his cheek, rustling his hair, and that he can smell the thick, puffy snowflakes that blanket the winter grass. He notices, too, that the birds have come back, and he can hear their magpie chatter.

He looks down, and for the first time in forever, he can see himself again. He places his feet firmly on the ground and gives a little push. The porch swing begins, very slowly, to rock beneath him. He hears the quiet, creaking whine of its movement.

In the yard, Madelaine pauses, her arms full of dark lights, her eyes—her beautiful mist-green eyes—riveted on the porch swing. He feels the heat of her gaze on him, and the heat grows stronger and stronger until it is so hot, he feels as if he'll surely melt beneath it. The sunlight seems to come at him from all angles, sparkling on the new-fallen snow, glancing off the white fence posts, sifting down from a blue break in the clouds. It's as if he's standing in the path of the sun, and it warms him, oh, how it warms him.

"Look," Angel says quietly, slipping his arm around Madelaine's waist, drawing her close.

"The porch swing," Lina says, moving toward her parents.

Together they walk toward him. He can feel their eyes on him, and he wants to sing out in triumph. He concentrates very hard and rises to his feet, and keeps rising.

He feels the laughter welling up inside him, spilling everywhere as he hovers above the ground, weightless and free. He hears his laughter in a dozen sounds—the chatter of the birds, the creaking of the swing, the falling of the snow from overburdened branches. In the distance a snowblower whirs to life, and he hears his laughter in that, too.

And through it all he can hear his old heart beating in Angel's chest, beating and beating and beating like the steady hum of the wind as it pushes through the leaves.

For the first time in his life, he doesn't feel as if there's a hole inside him. Instead, he feels lighter than air, giddy with a sense of promise and discovery. He looks up at the sky, sees the distant blues and grays and whites whirl together in an impossible glow.

He looks at Madelaine, his Maddy-girl, and in a flash he sees her whole life, spinning out in front of him like the stuttering scenes of an old black-and-white movie. Her hair will never turn gray, it will instead turn a bright snow white, and she will live in this house, and sip lemonade on his porch swing, up until the day she dies. She will wear baggy sweats as an old woman and never need glasses, and she and Angel will name their son Francis, and they will call him Frank.

Because there's already been a Francis.

He knows that she will miss him, always, and for the rest of her life, just as he will miss her. But she will have Angel, an Angel he never really got to know but always believed in, and she will have Lina. His precious Lina.

And he knows suddenly what kept him on the porch swing, watching the days bleed into one another and turn into shadowy nights. He is still part of that family on the snow-covered lawn, his family, and he always will be. He had it all wrong, and he realizes that perhaps that's what life is, getting it wrong and going on, and still believing, always believing.

He feels himself going higher and higher, until they are three specks of darkness against a white, white world. After a few moments the porch swing settles again, and the family below goes back to setting up the Christmas lights.

He stares down at them, the three he loved so well, and knows that they will talk about this moment in the years to come.

They will talk of the afternoon that the porch swing creaked on its own and the winter sunlight seemed hot enough to cook eggs. They will offer to one another the comfort of belief, the promise of magic, and they will spend their lifetimes watching that old porch swing and thinking of a man they loved.

Francis smiles at the thought. And in the whisper of the wind, he hears their laughter for the very last time.

# home again

KRISTIN HANNAH

A Reader's Guide

# A Conversation with Kristin Hannah

**Random House Reader's Circle:** What inspired you to write *Home Again*?

**Kristin Hannah:** *Home Again* was inspired by a real-life event. I was watching television one day—a talk show—and the guest was a man who had recently had a heart transplant. This was remarkable enough, but as the interview went on, and the story unfolded, I listened in awe as this man related the story of his transplant. He had been on his deathbed and his daughter had been in a terrible motorcycle accident on the way to saying her final good-bye. He then had to make the wonderful/terrible decision to accept his daughter's heart. I don't think anyone could hear this extraordinary story and not be moved. I knew immediately that I had the inspiration for my next novel.

**RHRC:** *Home Again* is different from your other books in that there's a supernatural element to the story. Was this always something you planned to include in the plot or did it happen organically as you were writing?

**KH:** Actually, early on in my career I included supernatural elements into my novels on a fairly regular basis. I touched on reincarnation, "going into the light," and time travel. The supernatural element in this book arose very naturally from the subject matter. For me, heart transplantation led inexorably to questions of spirituality. Anyone who has read my body of work knows that I am endlessly fascinated with life-and-death issues, and this novel is really an extension of that interest.

**RHRC:** Madelaine's a cardiologist, Francis is a priest, and Angel is an actor. In all your novels, your characters have interesting and varied careers. How do you choose the careers of your characters? What is the process of creating a character like for you?

**KH:** One of the things I love most about writing is the research into people's lives. I love to learn about other careers and how people live. As far as choosing the careers of my characters, it's really a question of fitting all the pieces together. Each of the various components of a character's life—his or her backstory, career, education, hobbies, family relationships, and self-image—has to serve the issue or theme that I've set as the foundation of the story. That's really what it's all about for me: an exploration of a theme.

**RHRC:** You've written a few books that have a teenager's perspective; is there a particular reason why you chose to include a teen viewpoint in many of your works?

**KH:** I think it's because the teen years are so pivotal in our lives. In our youth, we are often faced with difficult, potentially life-altering decisions, yet we don't have the experience to handle it all with grace. We stumble and fall and learn to stand on our own. I am particularly drawn to the intense pressure that our teens are under these days.

**RHRC:** Do you ever draw from your own life for your stories or your characters?

**KH:** I don't write autobiographical pieces per se, but I am constantly drawing from my own life and my own experiences.

**RHRC:** What was the biggest challenge you faced while writing *Home Again*?

**KH:** There were several challenges in writing *Home Again*. First off, it was my first contemporary novel, so I had to nurture and develop a different voice. It was in finding that voice that I glimpsed the future of my career. Once I began writing about modern women, I was hooked. The other challenge of the novel was the research. It was really important to me that the novel be as accurate as I could make it about this important topic.

**RHRC:** At the core of your stories, there is always a message, often related to mothers and daughters, husbands and wives, sisters. What is the message that you'd like readers to take from this book?

**KH:** I never set out to impart a "message" in a novel. Really, I just intend to tell a powerful, emotional, universal story. That being said, I do find that my work as a whole contains definite thematic similarities. It's obvious that I believe in forgiveness, redemption, second chances, and the power of love to transform our lives. Each of those themes is definitely present in *Home Again*. I also really believe in the triumph of the human spirit to overcome adversity.

**RHRC:** Francis is a priest who is confronting regrets about the path he has taken in life. Why did you include this character in this story? Was it hard to get into the mind of a priest?

**KH:** No, it wasn't any more difficult to write a priest than to write any other character. It required the same combination of research and imagination that most characterizations require. I chose a priest because of the questions of spirituality raised by the issue of heart transplantation. Obviously, the heart is a physical part of our bodies, but culturally, it represents so much more. I needed a character whose spirituality was so profound that it could be nearly transcendent.

# Questions and Topics for Discussion

1. Seventeen-year-old Angel betrays Madelaine by taking money from her father in exchange for ending their relationship. Why do you think he chose to do this? Do you understand his decision? Do you believe that a thing like this can or should be forgiven? Do you think he would have made the same choice had he known that she was going to have the baby?

2. When Angel hears that he needs a heart transplant, he is both troubled and torn by the thought of having someone else's heart in his body. This is actually a common reaction. How do you think you would feel in that situation?

3. Do you think a person has a right to know about his or her organ donor, or is it better if confidentiality is maintained? Why or why not?

4. Should Madelaine have revealed Lina's father to her earlier? Is there an appropriate moment or age to have this kind of discussion with your child?

5. Francis and Angel were treated differently by their mother. How do you think this affected each man?

6. Madelaine tries so hard to be Lina's friend that she sometimes fails as a parent. In what instances do you believe Madelaine is a bad parent? When is she a good parent?

7. There is some scientific evidence that states that organs may hold memories on a cellular level. Do you believe that's possible? If so, do you believe that these memories can be transferred to the recipient? How does that possibility affect your opinion on organ donation?

8. Would Madelaine have told Angel about his donor if the media weren't involved? Do you think she should have kept it a secret?

9. Francis faces regrets about his life; do you believe that priesthood was truly his calling? How do you feel about his conflicted feelings between his love for his God and his faith and his longing for what could have been?

10. Lina is an angry and confused young girl who wants her mother's love yet rejects it. Why do you think it's so hard for children to express their feelings to their parents?

11. Madelaine grew up with a stern, rigid father, while Lina grew up with no father at all. How did this impact their lives and their characters?

12. Imagine these characters in five years. In ten. What do you think their lives will be like?

# ABOUT THE AUTHOR

KRISTIN HANNAH is the *New York Times* bestselling author of twenty novels. A lawyer turned writer, she is the mother of one son and lives with her husband in the Pacific Northwest and Hawaii.

www.KristinHannah.com

# Chat.
# Comment.
# Connect.

Visit our online book club community at
Facebook.com/RHReadersCircle

## Chat
Meet fellow book lovers and discuss what you're reading.

## Comment
Post reviews of books, ask—and answer—thought-provoking
questions, or give and receive book club ideas.

## Connect
Find an author on tour, visit our author blog, or invite one of
our 150 available authors to chat with your group on the phone.

## Explore
Also visit our site for discussion questions, excerpts, author
interviews, videos, free books, news on the latest releases,
and more.

**Books are better with buddies.**
Facebook.com/RHReadersCircle

THE RANDOM HOUSE PUBLISHING GROUP